The

QUEEN'S LOVER

FRANCINE DU PLESSIX GRAY

PENGUIN BOOKS

PENGUIN BOOKS
Published by the Penguin Group
Penguin Group (USA) Inc., 375 Hudson Street,
New York, New York 10014, USA

USA | Canada | UK | Australia | New Zealand | India | South Africa | China
Penguin Books Ltd, Registered Offices: 80 Strand, London WC2R 0RL, England
For more information about the Penguin Group visit penguin.com

First published in the United States of America by The Penguin Press,
a member of Penguin Group (USA) Inc. 2012
Published in Penguin Books 2013

Portrait of Hans Axel von Fersen by Peter Dreuillon, © Swedish Portrait
Archives / The National Museum of Fine Arts Stockholm.

THE LIBRARY OF CONGRESS HAS CATALOGED THE HARDCOVER EDITION AS FOLLOWS:
Gray, Francine du Plessix.
The queen's lover : a novel / Francine du Plessix Gray.
p.   cm.
ISBN 978-1-59420-337-4 (hc.)
ISBN 978-0-14-312356-9 (pbk.)
1. Fersen, Hans Axel von, greve, 1755–1810—Fiction.   2. Marie Antoinette, Queen,
consort of Louis XVI, King of France, 1755–1793—Fiction.   3. Statesmen—
Sweden—Fiction.   4. France—Court and courtiers—Fiction. I. Title.
PS3557.R294Q83 2012
813'.54—dc22
2012000418

Printed in the United States of America
1   3   5   7   9   10   8   6   4   2

Designed by Marysarah Quinn

Praise for *The Queen's Lover*

"Deeply intelligent . . . spellbinding . . . If you liked Antonia Fraser's *Marie Antoinette* or Hilary Mantel's *Wolf Hall*—if you admired Gabriel García Márquez's close lens in *The General in His Labyrinth*—you will be richly rewarded by du Plessix Gray's amalgam of history and drama. Read it for its insights on Versailles; read it for its eye-opening glimpses into an equally venal Stockholm. But read it, when all is said and done, for its heartbreakingly wistful romance."
                                                —Marie Arana, *The Washington Post*

"The voice of history rises up out of the pages of [this] persuasive new novel. [A] lively, incredibly readable, definitely R-rated version of the life and death of Marie Antoinette."   —Alan Cheuse, NPR

"Ms. Gray has created fully developed, flawed, and complex characters in a way that would probably not have been possible within the confines of biography. [She] conjures up a world she knows well, in riveting detail. [*The Queen's Lover* is] a feat of research and imagination."
                                                —Moira Hodgson, *The Wall Street Journal*

"Don't remember anything about the French Revolution from high school? This is one of those books where you'll learn—or relearn—history effortlessly, as du Plessix Gray spins the affair of Marie Antoinette and a Swedish count into riveting drama."   —*Entertainment Weekly*

"[A] triumph of scholarship and storytelling . . . a remarkable book."
                                                —*The Daily Beast*

"Well researched . . . bold and moving. Fans of history—both true and fictional—will revel in du Plessix Gray's vivid evocation of turbulent times."
                                                —*Publishers Weekly*

"Readers will pay closest attention to how and in what situations Fersen views the queen—but also, and not incidentally, to his reactions to the king. He sees through the former's reputation for emptiness and the latter's for dullness to give us a balanced view of what transpired within the mirrored halls of Versailles. By also making us privy to all his political escapades back in his native Sweden, and there were plenty, the story broadens into a wider picture of European monarchy in transition."   —*Booklist* (starred review)

"The author has expertly re-created the world of the French royal family, depicting them in print as they once existed in life: lighthearted, calculating, and complex. Gray's subtle treatment of her characters allows them to come alive in this creative account of the French royal family and the French Revolution." —*Library Journal*

"Set against the backdrop of royal opulence and revolution, du Plessix Gray's richly detailed chronicle of love and loss provides startling insight into the complex and tragic inner life of the iconic and controversial French queen Marie Antoinette." —Amanda Foreman, author of *A World on Fire: Britain's Crucial Role in the American Civil War*

"The story of the strange, then sad, then finally tragic life of Marie Antoinette has been told many times, but never with more humane feeling and historical point than Francine du Plessix Gray does in her new novel. Seen from the startling point of view of the queen's Swedish lover, Count Axel von Fersen, *The Queen's Lover* makes a familiar story newly poignant, and, without ever being pedantic, places that story in a broader context of European politics, too often missed." —Adam Gopnik, author of *Paris to the Moon*

"*The Queen's Lover* is a thrilling book. It has everything—suspense, intrigue, love, luxury, tragedy, and romantic and familial love. It tells a familiar story from a new point of view." —Edmund White, author of *Jack Holmes and His Friend*

"In *The Queen's Lover*, Francine du Plessix Gray brings her peerless narrative gifts to bear on one of history's all-time greatest love stories: the secret romance between Marie Antoinette and Count Axel von Fersen. Set against the backdrop of the French monarchy's cataclysmic fall, the affair between the doomed queen and the dashing Swede is at once an achingly tender tale of two lovers and a tragic story of unspeakably brutal, broad-based societal change. With a historian's eye for evocative contextual detail and a novelist's ear for the lyricism of 'le grand amour,' Gray weaves an unforgettable portrait of a couple whose lives were transfigured by love . . . and shattered by revolution." —Caroline Weber, author of *Queen of Fashion: What Marie Antoinette Wore to the Revolution*

PENGUIN BOOKS

THE QUEEN'S LOVER

Francine du Plessix Gray is the author of numerous books of fiction and nonfiction, including *Them: A Memoir of Parents*, and has been a regular contributor to the *New Yorker* and the *New York Review of Books*. She lives in Connecticut.

To the memory of
Gabrielle Van Zuylen,
muse, dearest friend

Axel von Fersen

CONTENTS

PREFACE

BY *Sophie von Fersen*, Countess Piper

MY LATE BROTHER, *Count Axel von Fersen, was a notorious seducer, known throughout Europe as "le beau Fersen," and in our Swedish homeland as "Långe Fersen," "tall Fersen." Part of his legendary handsomeness was his majestic stature and the elegance of his long, slender limbs. His auburn hair was thick and wavy; he had a high, oval forehead, a beautifully shaped mouth, and the gaze of his very large, dark brown eyes had a melancholy which women found entrancing. But it is important to note that most men as handsome as my brother have something of the coxcomb about them, a dash of presumption or arrogance. Axel's demeanor, at the contrary, veered if anything toward too much gravity, too much diffidence. "A heart of fire in a shell of ice" was the way many of his friends described him.*

My brother had an extraordinary life. He fought on the American side in the American War of Independence, serving as General de Rochambeau's chief aide-de-camp. He was the lover of the most glamorous, controversial Queen of eighteenth-century Europe, Marie Antoinette, who inspired his greatest acts of selflessness and courage. In his later years he served as the Grand Marshal of Sweden, one of the highest positions any citizen could aspire to in our country. In part because of his diffident, somewhat secretive personality, Axel was often misunderstood. His aloofness could often endow him with a hauteur that was perceived as presumption but that served, above all, as a way of retaining his full dignity and independence. He may have been haughty with his aristocratic peers, but was most affable to persons of lower rank. Let me add that notwithstanding his air of detachment he was of immense generosity. He provided all support, for instance, for an old aunt of ours who had been robbed by her domestic, and who would not have survived without him. He was a noted art collector, and a bon vivant of the highest order. He furnished his quarters magnificently, entertained lavishly, and hired some of the greatest chefs in Europe to run his kitchen.

A few years before his untimely demise at the age of fifty-four, my brother began to write his memoirs, and he continued to write them until the very evening before his death. Having taken on the task of editing and publishing these documents, I had scruples about including their more intimate passages, but decided to retain them in order to offer my brother's readers a more vivid sense of his generation's mores. I have also occasionally had to interject chapters that would have been too painful for him to compose, or that he was too modest to commit to paper himself. It is these writings—my remarkable brother's memoirs—that I wish to share with the world.

PART I

CHAPTER I

Axel von Fersen:

AT THE PARIS OPERA

HERE'S HOW IT BEGAN, the central passion of my life:

It all began some three decades ago, in 1774, at one of the weekly balls given at the Paris Opera during the winter months. I'd recently arrived in France from my native Sweden, Louis XV was still king, and this was the first time I was attending such an event. I stood in mid-room, dazed by the radiance of the women's diamonds, the glare of the chandeliers, the flouncing of courtiers' plumed hats, the twinkling of minuets, the courtiers' sibilant whisperings, the smart clicking of valets' heels as they passed ices and wines. I, Count Axel von Fersen, brought up in the relative frugality of Sweden's aristocracy, was then barely nineteen years old: I was dazzled, and felt a bit lost. Experiencing this Parisian assault on the senses was akin to traveling from my country's pristine pine forests to some opulent Oriental bazaar. . . . Yes, that's how Paris struck me, downright Oriental! Its lustrous affluence, its denseness, its stench.

I tried to allay my unease by pacing about the shuffling crowd, every member of which wore a mask, a protocol of Paris opera balls. Some masks, enormous and surreal, covering the wearer's entire face, were surmounted by the beaks of birds or the snouts of mammals; others, like mine, were simpler slips of black satin, allowing the sight of a smooth or wrinkled forehead, of a stubbly or dimpled chin. Because they'd already been pointed out to me at an earlier event, I recognized the leading nabobs of the French court. Over there, lightly masked, was Comte d'Artois, the Dauphin Louis-Auguste's dandyish youngest brother, slender and mincing, a disdainful, teasing smile ever playing about his malicious mouth; the court's fashion icon, he owned 365 pairs of shoes so that he might wear a new pair every day, and was so manically fastidious about his dress that four valets held him aloft so that his trousers could remain wrinkle-free as he slipped into them. I duly noted his wife, a red-faced, loutish Savoyarde princess who consoled herself for her husband's legendary philandering with numerous guardsmen. Strutting about a few dozen yards away was the dauphin's other brother, Comte de Provence, known officially as Monsieur, and less officially as *Gros Monsieur*, an obese hunk of a prince compared to whom his older sibling, the corpulent dauphin, looked downright svelte, and who always seemed to be eavesdropping on conversations, accumulating shards of information with which to fuel his intrigues. Whereas Artois was looked on as a relatively harmless carouser, too busy unbuttoning himself to every passing beauty to have time for plotting mischief, Provence, obsessively jealous of his older brother the dauphin, was mostly focused on consolidating his power and influence. He chased the girls too, however, and his wife, Comtesse d'Artois's equally ugly sister, took solace in persons of her own gender; she was always attended by her paramour, a wan little countess with a beak nose who sought refuge in Comtesse de Provence's arms because of her husband's predilection for sodomy (my informer on court matters, our Swedish ambassador, Count Creutz, relished such details). *Gode Gud*, what a crew! I said to myself as I continued to scrutinize the crowd. I'd been in Paris for three months, completing a grand tour; and I was already beginning to miss the more respectable aura of my little Stockholm—seventy thousand citizens versus Paris's half million!—and of its court, that of my beloved monarch Gustavus III.

Whom else did I recognize at that opera ball? Mercy d'Argenteau, Austria's ambassador to France, whose baptismal name—Florimond— was well suited to his mincing, tiny-footed gait; another elegant rascal, the Comte de Vaudreuil, baptized with an equally botanical name— Joseph Hyacinthe—who was spending his fortune in a manner as ostentatious as possible, having taken on as mistress Yolande de Polignac, a favorite of Dauphine Marie Antoinette; the dauphin's cousin Duc de Chartres, later to be Duc d'Orléans, a zealous real estate speculator who was currently restoring the Palais-Royal, a site renowned for having the greatest density of streetwalkers in Paris. These were only a few of the more eminent persons in this teeming crowd. The particular earmark of opera balls was that anyone properly masked could attend them for the modest fee of two livres; butchers and bakers' wives, merchants of all kinds, could mingle here with counts and duchesses, and this democratic blending—slumming without danger—seemed to offer many eminences something akin to an erotic thrill.

Another of my Swedish traits—a certain priggishness—flared up as I began noticing the outlandish hairdos sported by the more daring women. Although I jot down these recollections in my advanced age, recalling events of over thirty years ago, I still have a precise memory of those inane coiffures, some of them so high—two or three feet high— that they required their wearers to kneel in their carriages, or sit with their heads thrusting out of their coaches' windows: there were hairdos that replicated ships, complete with sails, anchors, tiny lifeboats; others that pretended to be garden bowers, depicting trees, little grottoes, and lakes simulated by sparkling mirrors; yet others, powered by clockwork mechanisms, that featured whirling windmills edged with jewels. Such atrocities, I'd heard, came from the diseased imagination of

one Monsieur Léonard, personal coiffeur to the Dauphine Marie Antoinette, considered so indispensable to Her Highness that she had given
him an apartment of his own at Versailles, a floor above hers, in order
that he might ever be on call.

Just as I was observing these vapid creations a tall, slender young
woman with dark golden hair, more heavily masked than others, came
to my side and stared at me with a warm, bemused gaze. "*Bonjour, Beau
Masque,*" she said caressingly, her words marked by a faint trace of for-
eignness I could not quite identify. I greeted the lady in reply, and had a
few moments to study her features before she spoke again. The first
thing that struck me was the extraordinary incandescence of her skin.
Pick a tea rose, and look deep into that innermost place of the flower
where the petal begins, a very pale pink at its most tender and delicate—
that's what her face was like, an oval expanse of the most luminous skin
I'd ever seen. But as soon as you'd finished being dazzled by that face's
surface you encountered the eyes, fringed by sumptuously thick lashes,
and were conquered anew by their singular dark-blueness, akin to that
deep blue the sky takes on in the predusk hours of a brilliant day. And
their expression, you will ask, what was their expression? That's harder
to describe, for her moods seemed to change at mercurial speed. One
second the eyes were merry, vivacious, mocking; the next moment they
were most melancholy, revealing a very great solitude and anxiety. The
young woman's moods seemed akin to a sky over which clouds are
blown by a very swift wind, creating different weather patterns in a
matter of minutes. . . . Yet I should admit that notwithstanding all the
attributes I've noted—the splendor of the eyes, that astonishing skin—
you couldn't have called her beautiful, because of the curious set of her
mouth, the slightly pendulous lower lip, which could emanate an aura of
disdain and hauteur. On the night I met her, however, all haughtiness
was absent as she addressed me again, in the same tone of warm
playfulness.

"Do you like forests?" she asked.

"Well, yes, I do," I answered, taken aback by the humdrum topic. "There are many splendid forests on my family's estates."

"And where is that country where your family has estates?"

"Sweden," I said, with a small bow. "I am Count Axel von Fersen, from Sweden."

"Ah, *la Suède*!" she exclaimed. "*La Suède*," she repeated, the foreign intonation sharpening the *d*. "I've never met anyone from there except for that very boring Monsieur Creutz, your ambassador!"

And she burst into laughter, a pealing, very girlish laughter, accompanied by a mocking flutter of her hands that revealed the wedding band gleaming on her ring finger. She laughed again. "Oh, surely you know your ambassador, Mr. Creutz, the most boring man to be found in any European court!"

"He is like a parent to me," I said stiffly. I'm aware of my tendency to be overly formal, if not starchy, but this time the stiffness was intended— Creutz was indeed a humorless old bugger, but he was my father's closest friend and was masterminding with extreme kindness my introductions to European courts.

"Oh, I'm sorry!" she exclaimed, putting her hand impulsively on my sleeve. "Please forgive my . . . my indiscretion! It's one of my greatest faults. You see, I'm surrounded by so many old people, I yearn, very much yearn, for friends of my age, and they can be hard to find at our court." And so the conversation went. She asked many questions, on matters totally unrelated, her mind darting here and there like a child skipping at varied angles down a street. Do you like horses? How many siblings do you have? Describe the lakes in your country. Do you like opera? Ah, you're fond of singing yourself? How lovely! Well, perhaps someday . . .

The young woman was so deliciously pretty and amiable, the conversation so delightfully erratic that it would have been my pleasure to

continue it indefinitely. But I suddenly realized that a circle of courtiers—a dozen or so—had gathered about her; that their attention was
centered on me, which made me sense that this was a young woman of
some importance, that scrutiny would inevitably focus on any person
upon whom she lavished such attention. My new friend also had grown
aware, quite suddenly, of the band that had gathered about her; and
without saying good-bye, as impulsively as she had begun our conversation, she wheeled around and swiftly walked away, briefly lifting the
gray velvet mask off her face with an exasperated gesture, as if it were
smothering her and she needed to inhale a deep breath of air. It was in
that split second that I realized who she was—that I recognized her as
Marie Antoinette, Archduchess of Austria-Hungary, beloved daughter of
the mighty Empress Maria Theresa, and now the wife of the notoriously
timid, reclusive Dauphin Louis-Auguste, who might at any moment
become the king of France.

And so I watched my new friend leave the room, surrounded by the
acolytes who had gathered about her. And as I observed her making her
exit I was captivated by yet other attributes—her carriage and her walk.
But wait, "walking" is a wrong word for her style of motion. When she
moved through a room she glided or floated rather than strode, reminding one of those music box figurines that waltz about a skating
rink, sliding silently, serenely across the make-believe ice. And her carriage! Erect like a little soldier—no, that's too stiff a term, erect like a
ballet dancer who's just made some wondrously perilous series of *tours
jetés* and walks toward the exit amid bursts of applause, head held tri-
umphantly high and slightly to one side, proud and regal yet not arrogant. . . . Her grandfather-in-law, Louis XV, who appreciated female
charms as did few rulers of his time and was particularly enchanted
with Marie Antoinette, was said to have described her as "a dainty little
morsel."

. . .

AT ABOUT THE time I met the dauphine at that opera ball I was enjoying a liaison with the Marquise de Blacas, a handsomely plump, lusty
matron who had been the first to introduce me to the joy of the senses.
High time, I was nineteen. I finally felt that I was reaching adulthood,
and was also getting to know Europe. Immediately upon my arrival in
France, Creutz had taken me to Versailles to present me to that old roué
Louis XV (my prim mother would have fainted if she'd known I'd
kissed the hand of his paramour, Madame du Barry, whom she referred
to as "that vulgar courtesan"). Creutz had also introduced me to the
Duc d'Aiguillon, whose esteem I seemed to have readily won, and who
invited me to the card parties held every Monday night at the Dauphine
Marie Antoinette's. But until that crucial night at the opera ball, the
Marquise de Blacas's sensual demands, and the additional social schedule she held me to—dinners, balls, supper parties—had kept me too
busy to attend the dauphine's events.

There was something fateful about the timing of my encounter with
Marie Antoinette, as if destiny was trying to keep us apart. Lent began a
fortnight after I met her, and all social occasions were discontinued
until after Easter. Shortly after that, family business forced me to go to
England, where I was to visit with my beloved younger sister, Sophie,
one of Stockholm's most beautiful young women, who was making her
first visit to a foreign country.

The day before I left for London, Louis XV died of the smallpox, a
few days after he had ordered his mistress of many years, Madame du
Barry, to leave Versailles, and shortly after he had made his first confession in thirty-eight years. The details of his passing had a singular fascination for me: As reported by those who witnessed it, the disease was
feared to be so contagious that the king's doctors refused to embalm the

corpse; the entire medical team fled the premises, leaving his devoted servants—lackeys, coachmen—to immerse the royal body in a lead coffin, which upon doctors' orders was filled with the strongest spirits available. In order to safeguard the royal lineage, the sixteen-year-old dauphine and the eighteen-year-old dauphin (who unlike his wife had not been inoculated, the Bourbons being the only royal family in Europe that had not taken this precaution) had been banned from the king's room. They stood in a hallway that faced, across a courtyard, his bed-chamber. A candle had been lit on the king's windowsill. The young-sters were told that they would learn of the king's death when the candle was snuffed out. They stood at the window, staring at the light in the patriarch's room. As a courtier extinguished it, they fell to their knees, a spontaneous impulse that much moved those who witnessed it. They were said to be both in tears. "Help us, dear God," the adolescent new king, Louis XVI, was heard to exclaim; "we are too young to rule!"

Hardly had he spoken those words than, according to the dauphine's first chambermaid, Madame Campan, a dreadful noise, "absolutely sim-ilar to that of thunder," was suddenly heard heading toward the pitiful young couple. First sounding like a distant rumble, it grew like a furi-ously approaching storm. . . . This turbulence, which swelled to a ter-rifying din, was caused by the stampede of courtiers running from the room of the deceased monarch to salute the new one. The giggling, merry girl who had approached me at the opera ball, and had seduced me upon first sight, had become the queen of France.

AFTER MY STAYS IN PARIS and London I went back to Sweden for a few years, to be deeply bored. When attending the court of Gustavus III I played second violin to my monarch's favorite, Baron Armfelt. As captain of the king's light-horse cavalry all I had to do was put my men through their paces every few months. I took care to gently elude the advances of the king's adorable sister-in-law, Charlotte, Duchess of Södermanland, who had conceived a passion for me in her adolescence. I spent much of my time in Löfstad, my family's estate south of Stockholm, where I kept my diary, practiced my singing, played backgammon with Sophie and my parents, and painted watercolors of the lakes and meadows surrounding our palace. I was longing for the military life, yearning to see action, but war was nowhere in sight. When I turned twenty-two the issue of marriage inevitably arose. My father wished me to marry the daughter of a wealthy British banker, a Miss Leyel, and I traveled to London to make her acquaintance. She was pretty and accomplished, and I managed to address her some ritual phrases of affection that might have led to a betrothal; but she feared leaving her family, to whom she was deeply attached, to live in Sweden. There was little to please me in Great Britain. Upon visiting the royal court I was amazed by its drabness: nothing about its inhabitants or its furnishings betokened the grandeur of monarchy. King George III was in the process of going mad, and mumbled unintelligibly to conceal the fact that he spoke the same phrase to everyone he met. He slept in an old bed of frayed red velvet, blackened by smoke and shiny with grease. Even the palace's chandeliers were made of wood. The queen was ugly and without elegance. London society was equally drab. I tried to make friends with some colleague officers but found them disdainful and small-spirited. In 1778, with what relief I returned to Paris, the city of my dreams!

It was my good fortune to be immediately reintroduced to the French court by Ambassador Creutz. Upon my first visit I was greeted most amiably by the new queen, who was then undergoing her first pregnancy, and who remembered more than clearly our meeting at the opera ball. "Ah, but it's an old acquaintance!" she exclaimed as she held her hand out to me. I then began to frequent the court assiduously and to think about you every hour of the day, Dearest Majesty, and I could not help but note some characteristics of yours that particularly struck me, and that in my view were clearly traceable to your childhood. At your mother's Schönbrunn Palace you'd been the kind of unruly, tomboyish child who is the despair of many parents, the kind who refuses to concentrate on her studies and prefers romping through the forest with her friends, who disrupts social gatherings by giggling behind her fan at the silliness of elders. You were also phenomenally uneducated, poor girl; your ignorance was in part traceable to the fact that you were extremely myopic, and for the rest of your life you preferred to be read to in order to acquire most book knowledge. But this was deceptive: when you truly fancied a literary treasure, such as Italian poetry, you were capable of productive studying, and even translated some verses of Dante's *Inferno*.

As for your guileless, forthright manner: as Maria Theresa's fifteenth child you'd been brought up at a court known for its dowdy simplicity, a warm, familial court where etiquette was minimal, where intrigues were ill-considered. Compare Schönbrunn to its French counterpart! One marvels at the nonchalance with which your mother launched you, naive, guileless waif, into Europe's wiliest, most scheming aristocracy. In May 1770, when you signed the register that sealed your marriage to Dauphin Louis-Auguste, you left a large blotch of ink on the page. You were so nearsighted and so awkward with your pen that you could barely sign your name.

But I intended to write history, not love letters; I must strive to be more objective. . . . What struck me first about the queen when I began to visit her regularly was her extreme gentleness and civility of manner, which she extended to the most humble of her attendants. "*Auriez vous la gentillesse,*" "Would you be kind enough," was the phrase that prefaced all of her demands. Brusqueness or impatience was seldom known to her. She spoke to the women who served her—chambermaids and dressmakers as well as highborn ladies-in-waiting—with a friendliness that bordered on complicity. It was my compatriot's wife, Germaine de

Staël, who might have had one of the last words about Marie Antoinette. Her manner, Staël wrote, "had a kind of affability which did not allow us to forget that she was a queen yet persuaded us that she'd forgotten all about it." A kindly streak had been part of her character since childhood. When she was eight, little Wolfgang Amadeus Mozart, who had come to play at Schönbrunn, slipped and fell to the floor upon rising from his piano stool. Marie Antoinette was the first to run over to him and allay his tears. Her amiability of voice, of demeanor, made even more pleasurable the graciousness which marked all that pertained to her—her furniture, her objets d'art.

I very soon noticed her preference for small, intimate, crowded spaces—a throwback, perhaps, to her childhood at Schönbrunn, and a reaction against the inane grandeur of Versailles, which she detested. In her warmly elegant private apartments one could, indeed, barely move, so brimming were they with little footstools, richly upholstered *poufs*, gilded lamps, flowery silk curtains, china braziers in which she burned flower essences to dispel the castle's reek, and the multitude of bibelots set upon the tables, desks, mantelpieces of her rooms. Further encumbrance was caused by the three or four little white dogs whom she adored, who followed her everywhere and constantly jumped upon any daybeds, chaise longues, armchairs they fancied; and by the retinue of young black boys assigned to carry her umbrellas when she went out, but whom she also beckoned to her quarters much of the time, especially in the early years when she was childless, since they satisfied her deep maternal feelings and she amused herself by fondling and teasing them, lifting them up in her arms, chasing them about the room. Upon my visits, to which I always brought my own beloved spaniel, Odin, all mayhem broke loose. As the kids dressed in gold-trimmed red suits pranced about, and Odin joined the queen's dogs in jumping upon and down from her sofas and daybeds, I stood protectively close to a table upon which her women always placed a glass of barley-sugar water and a dish of crème fraîche sprinkled with currants. The nourishment these sweets provided was important, for at meals the queen barely ate, the only fare that struck her fancy being small pieces of boneless chicken breast and quantities of water—unlike her husband, she hated wine. When dining she moved her gold fork and knife slowly about her plate, pushing her food around in small circular motions, seldom lifting anything beyond the tiniest morsel to her mouth as she amiably immersed herself in chatting with her guests. But one had to be careful about conversations: they began to displease her when they extended to anything with which she was not familiar—speculative notions such as Voltaire's concept of justice, say, or Rousseau's view of mercy; at the mere sound of such high-minded chat she started to vigorously agitate her fan, as if to chase away the mental smog created by such pointless banter. Yet how she brightened at the mention of music! We both had a passion for opera. Gluck had been her beloved music teacher in Vienna, and she remained loyal to him throughout his life, often beckoning him to her apartments, and ever urging musicians to perform his works. She played the clavichord beautifully and had a small but fairly true voice; many were the times when we sang *"J'ai perdu mon Eurydice"* as she accompanied us on her spinet, her little coloratura nicely enhancing my baritone.

But it may surprise those who did not know the queen well to learn that she was essentially of a melancholy nature; she was terrified of solitude, and prone to fits of great depression. And since I too was often plagued with bouts of melancholy, these mutual traits would only deepen our eventual friendship. How often did I come to her apartments and find her seated at a table, her head down, her hands wrapping her face as if in a gesture of mourning! As soon as she heard me enter she straightened up into her good little soldier posture and put on a shining smile, but I came to know the nuances of her expressions so well that I knew the smile was forced. This chaste, ingenuous girl was incapable

of deceit, and not that good an actress. She did, however, have a considerable instinct for self-preservation: the fetes, galas, balls, gambling
parties into which she threw herself so feverishly, and that did such
harm to her reputation, were palliatives—gambling in particular much
raised her spirits—with which she tried to keep her depressions at bay.
Early on in her reign, she started raising her morale by keeping company with the Comte and Comtesse de Polignac, a high-living, insolvent couple who milked her for every cent they could—she gave the
count the post of equerry, which made him a wealthy man. And she
immensely enjoyed the company of her fellow cardsharps. (One of her
favorite partners at the gaming table, Abbé Quelquechose, was so ad-
dicted that he kept playing until dawn, and went straight from the royal
gambling den to the altar of his church to say his first morning Mass.)

I'm the first to concede that the queen committed many imprudences.
For instance, she was given to riding in a gilded sled, made all the more
noticeable by the ringing of its one hundred little bells, without an escort or mounted guard or any other outward sign of ceremony. Citizens
were aghast at such a lack of decorum. I shall also admit that the queen
was truly vain, though if you wished to excuse her for even that weak-
ness you might see her passion for apparel as another way of keeping the
saturnine demons away. She had daily meetings with Mademoiselle
Rose Bertin, her dressmaker. Great swaths of satin, velvet, and silk were
brought into her rooms, and the two women hovered at length over
these materials, deciding which of them would be used for the next
design. The queen did not wish her costumes to be seen until the first
time she wore them; so any new outfits that arrived at the palace were
heavily veiled with white linen sheets and traveled throughout the public corridors of Versailles like great ghosts, their porters avoiding the
smaller, more private routes because of the queen's dread that the garments might be damaged. The only other person allowed to see her
dresses at their inception was her favorite friend, Princesse de Lamballe,

the widow of a noted rake, an adorably round-faced, dimpled little creature whose manner and tone of voice were as gracious as the queen's,
but far more self-effacing. She provided, at all moments, a kind of
sounding board for her sovereign's every whim and desire, never con-
tradicting or criticizing, smiling through every crisis. And during the
queen's childless years Lamballe was the only being with whom she
could satisfy her considerable need for physical affection: to come into
the queen's quarters and see the two women sitting on a sofa, tenderly
embracing, kissing each other's cheeks, shoulders, hands, was as sweet
and disturbing a sight as I had during my visits to the palace—it caused
her enemies to make inane accusations of sapphism, but led me to sense
the full weight of my friend's solitude and frustration, her poignant need
for friendship and intimacy.

YET AS THE MONTHS WORE ON, as my visits to the royal couple mul-
tiplied, it was upon the king, Louis XVI, that I began to focus my attention, quite as much as on Her adorable Majesty. For what a man, Louis
XVI, what a man! I'm only too aware of the extent to which he's been
disdained and ridiculed for his timid, awkward manner. But may I say
that immediately upon meeting him I felt we were soul brothers: both
diffident, studious, reclusive, not easily given to words, utterly incapable
of the vain swift chatter that passed at the court for conversation. Certainly he was even shier than I, because of his all too evident un-
gainliness: his large gauche body; his clumsy way of moving about a
room; his sloppy table manners—loving his food and wine, he ate
swiftly and greedily, crumbs and gravy spilling about his huge chest, a
glaring contrast to his wife's delicate frugality. Moreover, he had an
uncomely habit of keeping his mouth a tad open at all times, as if he
were aware that it could take him a painfully long time to prepare a sentence. The king, indeed, had little reason for self-assurance beyond the

pleasure he took in his legendary physical strength; he enjoyed demonstrating it by seating one of his adolescent pages on the end of a shovel, and lifting him off the ground to shoulder height. He could be rougher in displaying his vigor. Upon the first of the queen's confinements, on a warm July day, she fainted from lack of air after her doctor had ordered all windows closed. In a passion of good sense Louis thrust his arm violently through a pane of glass, and was joyful to see the burst of air return his wife to consciousness.

Louis's principal problem was that he had not wanted to be king. He had been brought up in the shadow of his older brother, a brilliant, charming, domineering child, much beloved by all, who had died at the age of ten. So Louis, as retiring and insecure as his brother had been self-confident, never got over the sense that destiny had unfairly snatched the monarchy from his more qualified, competent sibling, and that he, Louis, was no more fit for it than the workmen repairing the roofs of his palace. (Upon his coronation in Reims, when the archbishop daubed him with unguents held in the same vial that had been used 1,300 years earlier to anoint Clovis, the first king of France, and the emerald-and-ruby-studded crown of Charlemagne was set upon his head, he grumbled, "*Ca me gêne,*" "It bothers me.") As for his gaucheness, Louis often tried to remedy it by resorting to his childlike sense of humor, which many found highly disconcerting. He would often back one of his courtiers across the room, for instance, forcing the poor fellow to lean against a wall as he strove to say something witty, and then, the words not coming to him, he would burst into a brusque laugh, turn on his heels, and walk away. Or else, at his *coucher*, as whatever fop assigned the great privilege of proffering the king his nightshirt tried to hand him the vestment, the royal prankster tried to tickle the courtier and started running about the room in great circles, giggling like a child as he taunted the poor man and chased him all about the bedchamber.

Moreover, there was Louis's notorious indifference to his own ap-

pearance. Wigs were often slipping off his head; wig powder was ever ·
sprinkled about his shoulders; his shoes grew muddy as soon as he
stepped outside; he had a habit of toying with the edges of his jacket to
allay his social anxiety, and buttons were constantly popping off his
clothes. Our attitude to vestments—that may have been our principal
difference. Even taller than the king and very slender, I was aware that I
was referred to as "*le beau* Fersen," and I admit that I attempted to live
up to that designation by remaining as fastidiously dressed as the fanci-
est courtiers. How content I would have been to offer a touch of my
dandyism to the French monarch! But his sloppy mien and his childlike
pranks made me love him all the more. As soon as he spoke to me, in his
slightly high-pitched, well-modulated voice, I was entranced. Certainly
not by his words, which were of singular plainness, devoid of the flour-
ishes and embellishments of courtly talk, but by the kindness and the
warmth of his eyes, which looked at you with the most benign gaze
imaginable, and above all by his utter simplicity and common touch. It
is well known that Louis XVI was one of the most skilled horseback
riders of his day, that he loved hunting and other physical occupations
such as welding and blacksmithing, and specialized in the making of
keys. He went far further in his rustic pursuits. Whenever he glimpsed
workers repairing a roof or a wall at Versailles, for instance, he would
run toward them, cast off his jackets, pull up his sleeves, and join them
at their work. Overlooking appointments with ministers, counselors,
ambassadors, what have you, he would labor alongside them until they
left at day's end. While his courtiers denoted him, a tad disdainfully, as
"*Louis le Vertueux*," "Louis the Virtuous," because of his utter lack of
interest in womanizing, the simple citizens he so enjoyed working with
referred to him lovingly as "*le roi travailleur*," "the worker king," or "*le
bon papa*," "the good daddy." Never have I known of a ruler more at
ease with his humbler subjects, better able to make them feel equally at
ease in his presence. One should note that the queen was a bit miffed by

her husband's democratic predilections. As soon as he came back from his physical labors, grimy, disheveled, reeking of sweat, beaming with happiness, she would ring for his valets and cry out, *"Bon Dieu, nettoyez et habillez le roi! Nettoyez le!"*

Let me add that the king's egalitarianism was joined by a most gifted intellect. Louis XVI was a scholar, one of the best-read men of his day, and would have been quite as happy studying books around the clock as he was repairing roofs alongside his subjects. Writing about the king to my sister Sophie, a most intelligent woman, I could not emphasize enough that he was one of the most gifted Latinists of his time, that he was equally fluent in English. He knew reams of Milton by heart, and had even translated many of that poet's verses into French. He could also recite long passages of Racine's plays, sometimes enlivening the nightly *coucher* with surprisingly expressive recitations. European history was an open book to him, and he was a consummate geographer and cartographer. It came as no surprise to learn that this studious, reclusive man loathed crowds. The queen having once persuaded him to attend the opera ball, although he was masked and cloaked beyond recognition he fled after a half hour. How could this earnest fellow have enjoyed the persiflage that was at the heart of such events?

Another of the king's singular traits was his passion for numbers; he counted all the time; he went to the thermometer affixed to one of the palace's windows every few hours to record that day's temperature, and announced it to his entourage. The day would not end without his having noted in his journal, and also announced to his courtiers, how many partridges, pheasants, or other game he had killed at his daily hunt. He looked at the clock constantly in the after-supper hours, and went to bed at eleven o'clock sharp every night. The queen and her ladies, who along with the Comte d'Artois enjoyed sitting up at their whist and backgammon games until the predawn hours, often played a prank to make sure that the king went to bed even earlier: one of them would sneak up to the clock in the queen's drawing room just before the family gathered there after supper, and move the clock an hour forward. After amiably playing a few games of cards, the king unfailingly said good night at what he thought was 11 p.m. to retreat into his evening prayers and his deep, contented sleep, leaving the queen and d'Artois to gamble until long past midnight and make sly comments about the monarch's virtuous, drowsy nature. There was an edge of disdain about Toinette's attitude toward her husband, in fact, that I thought inappropriate and for which I'd have sternly reprimanded her had I been in the position to do so. ("Toinette": so I'd refer to her in my enamored musings long before I dared to thus address her.)

Before ending this brief portrait of the couple who would soon become central to my life, I should clarify the gossip about the royal couple's initial marital problems, which concerned the fact that they did not consummate their marriage for an entire SEVEN years. It was simply a case of juvenile ignorance. Imagine the fourteen-year-old girl and sixteen-year-old boy forced into bed without any marital instructions whatever beyond the minimal information that big sow of an empress, Maria Theresa, had offered her daughter. Having given birth to a whopping fifteen children, Maria Theresa was the kind of royal mother who trotted out her offspring two or three times a month, whenever truly important guests came to dine, leading them to believe that she was as accomplished and devoted a mother as she was a ruler. But this appearance of "loving attention" was another instance of her talent for public relations—in reality she totally abandoned her progeny to the whims of their numerous tutors and governesses. She was far too busy attempting to carve up Poland, or stopping Russia from invading Finland, to instruct even her favorite daughter on the techniques of bedding. She had been vigilant about only one aspect of her daughter's life—her marriageability, thus recording for posterity the precise moment of Toinette's first period—5:15 p.m. of Thursday, February 14th, 1770, two months before she was shipped off to France. Otherwise, "Be lavish with your affections!" is all she would intone as she wrote the dauphine throughout the terrible years during which the young couple could not consummate their marriage.

Let's be blunt about their problems: the dauphin had no trouble getting an erection, but experienced terrible pain as soon as he'd begun the coital act. After a few minutes he apologized, kissed his bride's cheek as he bade her good night, and retired to his own bedroom. This went on for seven dreadful years! The lack of significant stains on the princely sheets was a matter of public knowledge throughout Europe. In France anti-Austrian feelings already ran high, and courtiers enjoyed making lewd jokes about Viennese wenches having a saltpeter effect, giggle giggle, who could get it up properly with an Austrian? Within two years of the dauphine's marriage, fishwives started shouting at the poor girl as her carriage passed through the streets, "Are you a woman or not? Give us an heir!" This private debacle and public opprobrium did much to deepen Marie Antoinette's depressions. The d'Artois, who already had children, and the Provences, who had trouble conceiving, took equal delight in snickering behind the young royals' backs. "Be prodigal with your caresses, etc.," Maria Theresa continued to intone.

After seven years of this nonsense—by this time Louis XV had died and Marie Antoinette was queen—her oldest brother, Emperor Joseph II of Austria, who ruled in consort with his mother, decided to investigate a nuptial predicament that was threatening the very balance of power in Europe. Those Hapsburgs are blunt people, good at man-to-man talk. Joseph appeared at Versailles and, after scolding his little sister for her frivolous behavior and presciently warning her that "there will be a cruel revolution if you don't take steps to prevent it," asked Louis some brutally forthright questions. He then wrote the following report to his brother, Leopold, in Vienna: "[The king] has normal erections; he introduces his member, stays there without moving for about two minutes, then withdraws without ejaculating and, still erect, bids good night. This is incomprehensible because he sometimes has nocturnal emissions, but while inside and in the process, never. . . . Oh, if I could only have been present once, I would have taken care of him; he should be whipped so hard that he would discharge like a donkey. . . . Together they are total fumblers."

Fumblers indeed! The youngsters' ignorance was such, Joseph was astounded to learn, that they'd thought their little rubbings could induce pregnancy. Having summoned a doctor and listened to his diagnosis, Joseph convinced his brother-in-law that he suffered from a readily curable condition called phimosis: Louis's foreskin was abnormally tight, causing serious pain whenever he attempted coitus; but this could be perfectly remedied by a brief operation that caused a minimum of pain. So after some weeks of demurring Louis agreed, was given a big shot of brandy, and within some twenty minutes of the surgeon's ministrations, voilà! He came out of it with an absolutely normal peenie. The young couple set to work again. Within a few months the dauphine reported to her ladies-in-waiting that her period, which she referred to by the Austrian euphemism "General Krottendorf," was two or three weeks late; and then she felt the first little waves of nausea, and shortly thereafter the doctor came and confirmed it all. "Mama, mama," she wrote the empress, "I'm pregnant at last!" Provence brooded and withdrew into his billiards game. Artois stopped smirking for a few weeks. The kind young king exulted. Over the years, he had fallen passionately in love with his wife.

The irony is this: notwithstanding the affection that Marie Antoinette lavished on her, the royal couple's long-awaited first child, Marie-Thérèse, known as Madame Royale, would grow up adoring her father but disliking her mother. When she was six or so, she was playing next to her mother while Marie Antoinette was telling her confessor, Abbé

Vermond, about a very serious riding accident she'd just had. The abbé asked the child if she realized her mother had almost died. "I wouldn't care," said the little girl, who would later be noted for her haughtiness and aloofness. "I wouldn't see Mother anymore and I'd be very happy because I could do as I pleased." The queen wept over this incident for a long while.

WELL NOW, I'd like to interrupt my reflections on France's royal family and say a word about their home: I defy you to find anyone in Europe who detested Versailles more fervently than I did. How scathingly did I convey this loathing in my letters home to Sophie! I need not dwell on the presumptions and arrogance, the delusions of grandeur, that led XIV to commission such an elephantine habitation—Versailles Palace could accommodate five thousand persons! But even the site is a monstrosity, a large murky swamp that, however diligently the authorities dredged it, continued to emit a fetid stench and breed an infestation of insects—few were the court beauties whose white throats were not spotted with red pustules from their bites. What was indeed most striking was the discrepancy between the gleaming gilded grandeur of the palace's outer surface and the filthy, insalubrious conditions that prevailed inside it. Many courtiers as well as visitors (the French populace had full right of entry to the palace as long as they kept away from the royal apartments) had a habit of snacking as they ambled through Versailles—a lamb chop here, an apple or pastry there—and bits of food could be found scattered throughout hundreds of rooms: in the upholstery, under the edge of carpets, in the bottom folds of curtains. . . . Well, the rodents had a ball. No courtier ever loved a palace as much as rats loved Versailles. They mostly feasted at night, and every morning their droppings were serpentinely scattered throughout the *Schloss*, to be swept into closets or under the carpet by indolent domestics. All kinds of diseases were obviously spread by this negligence. Beyond the habitual ailments that yearly decimated hundreds of courtiers—typhoid, smallpox—various respiratory and digestive illnesses were spread by the nightly visitors. Versailles habitués were constantly wheezing, coughing, aggravating the dire conditions created by the vagrant barefoot children, prostitutes, and inebriated courtiers who pissed and defecated in corners of the grand galleries.

Versailles's rats were night creatures. Come daylight and the mice prepared for their *grand bal*, having caused court ladies, for over a century, to react with various degrees of hysteria. Mademoiselle de la Vallière, the gorgeous, ill-fated blond waif who had been among the first of Louis XIV's favorites, used to leap up on the top of her spinet in fear of the creatures, creating cacophonous sounds as her feet hit the keys. The XV's wife, Marie Leczinskaya, is said to have jumped up on chairs at the sight of the mice, emitting shrieks that her husband, in his first, enamored years, found adorable. On the other hand Marie-Thérèse, legal wife of the XIV, was so used to all forms of critters that she amiably swallowed whatever spiders floated on her hot chocolate.

But Versailles's filth did not repel me as much as a more vexing blight: its sheer stench. Coming from a nation in which cleanliness is looked on as being close to you-know-what-ness, in which even those not fortunate enough to own a bathing vessel take a daily plunge into the nearest pond, the first time I walked down the Galerie des Glaces amid its great crowd of unwashed nobles I came very close to fainting. I had the wits to head for a corner of the gallery; I collapsed right behind a large chair, rolled up like a child, my kerchief held close to my face, recalling that Toinette, brought up in the same principles of hygiene as I, was thought to be bizarre for insisting on a daily bath. So there I was behind my chair when a kindly woman, someone's chambermaid, came to my aid with a whiff of smelling salts—never did the scent of lavender seem more paradisiac than at that moment. Upon fully coming to I decided never to enter this space again without covering my face with a large handkerchief, as the queen was often seen doing. Suffocation if not asphyxiation, I decided, was the essence of Versailles. Think of it: the palace that the rulers of Europe's greatest capitals—Saint Petersburg, Vienna, Stockholm—most aspired to emulate was a vast compound reeking of filth and befouled with ordure.

No wonder many courtiers followed suit, and stank as powerfully as the site. Take one particular high-ranking noble, for instance, the Vicomte de Saint-Aignan, whose malodorousness reached legendary proportions. He was a tall, elegant, enormously amiable man, always fastidiously dressed, loving to show off his jewels and decorations, whose smell was detectable two or three rooms away. Writing to Sweden, I kept searching for similes to describe his stench: he smelled like several dozens of pigs who had just rolled in their excrement, like several dozens of overripe, foot-wide Camembert cheeses stored for months in a warm closet. It was said that even as a child he had refused as much as a monthly bath; and that in his late teens, the day of his presentation at court, when his attendants tried to force him into a tub he fought them off so hard that he broke one valet's arm and knocked out the other one's teeth. In his early youth Saint-Aignan's parents had destined him for the diplomatic corps, but by the time he was eighteen the notion was dropped, since his odorous presence at foreign courts might have led to severe diplomatic disasters.

Saint-Aignan was reported to have had his own singular reasons for choosing to remain malodorous: he believed that every time one washed, a bit of one's selfhood was lost. The day of his presentation at court, after he had roughed up his valets, a pair of felt boots were superimposed upon his shoes, in hopes that this, at least, would minimize the stink emanating from that part of his body. But upon the approach of the young lord, Louis XVI, ever attempting to be diplomatic, had taken a few steps back and, instead of offering his cheek for the traditional kiss, had put his hands over his face in a gesture that habitually signaled the onset of a migraine. A virtuoso of denial, Saint-Aignan did not take the hint. He believed that the king did have a genuine headache; and, following protocol, he courteously backed away from the monarch amid dozens of his handkerchief-clutching peers, his status as a high-ranking noble protecting him from being totally excluded from society. There came the moment when the king had to choose a government post for this exotic citizen. He had a brainstorm: he named him keeper of the Royal Zoo, hoping that this establishment's inmates might be the only ones of God's creatures who would not be repelled by the vicomte's stench.

Saint-Aignan was an extreme case—let's say his malodorousness was two, three times as powerful as that of the average courtier. But you can imagine the reek of several dozen odor-afflicted persons crowded into one salon. *Merci bien!* That asphyxiation which was at the heart of the detestable Versailles had an end-of-the-world quality, that of a world struck with pestilence; close your eyes and you could imagine you were in London in 1348 at the time of the Black Death. This was the impact wrought upon me by the world's most "brilliant" capital; this was the home of the most delicate, fragrant, refined princess in Europe, Marie Antoinette. How happy I was when she acquired the Petit Trianon! Here, at least, she could start afresh.

I KEEP REMEMBERING the sweet sight of her lying on a bed of dried moss that had been set up for her in a little cave a half mile from the Petit Trianon's "Hamlet," drinking a glass of milk from one of her own cows, a delicate white haze spread about her sweet and happy mouth. I can't forget the tinkle of her laughter as we played blind man's buff with the Princesse de Lamballe and the Comtesse de Polignac in the meadows surrounding the Petit Trianon. Forty years later I am still haunted by the memory of having her at my side as we rode together in the nearby forests. She had become an exceedingly skilled rider since coming to Versailles, and though I was noted as the best horseman at court, she enjoyed challenging me to a race, betting that she could beat me if I gave her a small handicap. When I slowed down my habitual pace, however, she pouted and chastised me: "I could beat you to the goal without your doing me such favors!" she'd exclaim. Back at the Petit Trianon, in her little blue-and-gold sitting room, we played backgammon, her favorite form of gambling, at which she was so skilled that she had to give *me* a handicap. "Six and one, my favorite throw!" she'd cry out delightedly after tossing the dice onto the board with a smart flick of her wrist. Every few evenings we sang together. Along with arias from Gluck's *Orpheus and Eurydice*, her favorite verses, which she performed with a sly teasing glance in my direction, were from Piccinni's *Didon*, "Ah I was well inspired / When I received you at my court."

Tongues wagged, of course, at the frequency with which we kept company. But you know what? On the whole the courtiers, and the king himself, might have far preferred a foreign cavalier for the queen, rather than a French one. A discreet, often distant admirer such as I, frequently absent in his native land, suited them far better than a native noble who'd have spent his time in intrigues, and in trying to gather all the favors he could for himself and his relatives. So they left us alone, to enjoy a relationship curiously medieval in tone: that of the *chevalier pur et sans reproche* who courts his lady from afar, without a trace of physicality ever tainting the purity of his admiring devotion (so, I'd resigned myself, our relations had to remain for the time being).

CHAPTER 2

Sophie:

OUR FAMILY, THE VON FERSENS

THERE WERE MANY similarities between my brother and our father, Frederick Axel von Fersen, who was the grand marshal of Sweden a few decades before his son rose to that post. "*Père*," as we called him, was descended from a Scottish clan, the Macphersons, which had settled in Sweden in the sixteenth century. He was our nation's most influential citizen and its greatest landowner, the proprietor of several superb estates spread throughout the country. He was also the leader of one of Sweden's two principal political factions, the pro-French Hat party, which represented the upper aristocracy—the other faction, the Caps, tended to be pro-Russian and were identified with the clergy, farmers, and the lower nobility. *Père* was as handsome and prodigal as Axel, like his son was possessed of a golden heart, and was equally revered by members of our four estates—the clergy, the aristocracy, the burgher class, the peasantry.

As for our mother, née de la Gardie, whose large dark eyes my siblings and I had inherited, during our youth she served as principal lady-in-waiting to the queen of Sweden. She was descended from a family of Gascon Calvinists who had sought refuge in Sweden during the Renaissance, and who had been all-powerful since Queen Christina's reign—her great-grandfather had been Christina's prime minister and closest confidant. In a nation that for two generations had been closely allied to France and was even more obsessed with Frenchness than the Russian nobility (let's not forget that Christina had beckoned the great French thinker Descartes to her court, where he had died, alas, of pneumonia), the Fersens were considerably more French than other families. *Père* had fought on the French side in several conflicts, most notably in the Seven Years' War. We spoke exclusively French at home and teased each other much about the mistakes we made in our native tongue, which we spoke only to our domestics. As our mother complained, "In our country one can barely manage to think in Swedish." My brother Axel wrote both his memoirs and his journal (the latter of which he began when he was fourteen) in French. If I live long enough his journals will also be published someday, and its editors might well joke about the fact that a famous Swede's diary had to be translated into Swedish from its original French!

But our Francophilia was not singular. His Majesty Gustavus III, the greatest king of eighteenth-century Sweden and a close family friend, a man much admired by Voltaire, Condorcet, and other Enlightenment luminaries, spoke his native language with a faint French accent. After being shot by a political enemy, he even spoke French at the moment when he thought he was about to die, uttering the following words: *"Je suis blessé, arrétez le et tirez moi d'ici!"* Would a czar have spoken anything but Russian, in that society noted for its Frenchness, at what he thought was the moment of his death?

FORGIVE THE DIGRESSION. I write these pages, above all, to tell you of Axel's childhood and youth. For my brother centered his own memories too extravagantly on that Austrian flirt who brought him so much misery, who kept him from ever marrying and having a family; dear God, here's what he wrote me once when he was approaching the age of thirty-five: "I've made up my mind, I don't wish to ever get married, it is contrary to my nature. . . . I can't belong to the one person I wish to belong to, the only one who truly loves me, so I do not wish to belong to anyone." In my early years, I cursed that Viennese sorceress every day of my life.

So, back to our family. Axel and I had a younger brother, Fabian, and an older sister, Hedda, but from earliest childhood on we focused so intensely on each other that Hedda and Fabian were almost excluded from our daily life. How close Axel and I were! I was nearly as tall as he, and we looked strikingly alike, almost like twins. Our siblings didn't partake in our childhood games, of which our favorite was to scare each other with tales of the mythological creatures that crowd our national folklore: each of us tried to upstage the other in the number of eerie visitations we received. There were the *skogsrå* or wood nymphs whose front presents a shimmering, ravishing white-clad creature but whose back is an ugly black hollow plumed with a large tail, and the *Vita Frun*, another malevolent white-garmented lady who haunts palaces, both of whom we often pretended to have seen in our respective rooms. But most especially we lived in the world of trolls, supernatural creatures of small stature and ugly mien—drooping jaws, warty noses, tangled straw for hair—who inhabit caves or the roots of trees, who come into human homes to steal money, which they greedily hoard, who kill any humans who seek them out to recover their lucre. We made much of the fact that trolls only have power over those who are afraid of them, and that they terrified most children. "I'm less afraid of them than you are!" Axel would shout. "No, you boob, I'm less afraid than you," I'd enjoin. By this time *Père* might have come into our room, annoyed by our din, urging us to grow up and give up on such silly tales—"the folklore of our peasantry," he'd call them. However much we loved him, we thumbed our nose at *Père* and resumed our dramas of ghostly visitors.

Père may have been against folklore, but he was a fairly religious man, or as religious as one could be while being an ardent follower of Enlightenment ideals. As Swedes we are all members, by birth, of the Lutheran state church, and at our home religious holidays were strictly observed. We're the descendants of those Vikings who sacrificed to the sun god to hasten his return; and at the beginning of the winter season we commemorated with particular fanfare the shortest day of the year, Santa Lucia Day, as the harbinger of brighter days to come. A symbol of light—*lux, luce*, observed on December 13—Lucia is more festively celebrated in Sweden than any other saint in the calendar. Candles are placed in every window to honor her attributes—benevolence, charity, good fortune. The religious service that celebrates her takes place in the early morning, and as children Axel and I ran home as swiftly as we could to devour the sweets traditional to that day, X-shaped saffron buns decorated with raisins. Shortly afterward there came Christmas, which in our country demands particularly strict discipline on the part of children; for the tree is hung with sweets—hard candies, tightly sealed cookies—which we were not allowed to enjoy until the day of Kurtz, January 13, twenty days after Christmas. Then, after dancing around the tree, Axel and Fabian and Hedda and I fell upon it and plundered it of all its goodies, often ending up with terrible bouts of indigestion, before throwing the tree out into the snow.

Père saw to it that we carefully observed several other traditional holidays: Easter, for instance, which for some reason was associated with witches. To deter their arrival, on Maundy Thursday the sign of the cross was painted on our foreheads, on the walls of houses and public buildings, even on the cattle's noses, and on Easter Eve Axel and I made huge bonfires to chase any witches away. Our next big holiday was Midsummer's Eve in the third week of June, the year's longest day, when everyone in Stockholm watches the sun setting on the horizon at 2 a.m., knowing it will rise again in a half hour, thinking of their compatriots in northern Sweden, where the sun remains in the sky for over a month. Every girl would want to be in love at such a time, I thought to myself as a teenager every Midsummer's Eve, but I was happy enough to love my brother Axel, and walk with him down Stockholm's embankments in the full daylight of midnight, our arms around each other's waist. . . . At all of these holidays, particularly the winter ones that we spent in one of our country houses, there was much friendly calling from our neighbors. *Père* was as prodigally hospitable as Axel would later be. Numerous candles were lit at the entrance of our estate, and our servants stood at the gates, handing steaming mugs of *glögg*—red wine heated with ginger, cinnamon, and other spices—to visitors arriving on their open sleighs.

One such visitor who arrived on a winter day of my seventeenth year was Count Piper, a tall, powerfully built fellow with a thick red neck and features too coarse to be called handsome whose principal topics of conversations were stag hunting and the yield of wheat crops on his estates. He had a booming, stentorian voice that reminded me of the Swedish proverb *Tomma tunor skramlar mest*, "The empty barrel made the loudest noise." I shied away from him for the simple reason that he seemed particularly drawn to me, and also because throughout my life I would only be attracted to men of Axel's like—elegant, sensitive men with strong intellectual passions. Within a half dozen of Piper's visits I realized that my father had chosen him to be my husband. Like innumerable girls have done for thousands of years I wept, I begged, I implored *Père* to let me wait until a man came along whom I had chosen to love. He would come very soon, I promised (lying through my teeth, since I had never been drawn to any man), I promise you, Papa, I will find some nobleman who will please you, whom you will be honored to have in your family. But *Père* would not budge. He had settled on Piper—his high rank, his wealth, his large land holdings, made him, in his eyes, the perfect spouse for me. I kept thinking of Santa Lucia, who had preferred to have her eyes gouged out with spears rather than marry the man imposed upon her by her father, and I confided in my tender-hearted brother. He gently made me realize that little could be done: going against a father's will, in my situation, would tarnish the family name. "You're a very beautiful woman, and in time," he said, "you will find another man who will love you purely, selflessly, and you will return his love and know decades of happiness."

And so I tied the crown of myrtles around my brow and went to the altar accompanied by my ladies of honor—my sister, Hedda, and my closest friend, Charlotte, Duchess of Södermanland, the pretty girl who'd been hopelessly in love with Axel since her teens. Swedish weddings are three-day-long events; and as my maids, on the second day, buttoned me into my first black dress—symbol of the rite of passage into the marital status—this custom I'd always looked on as inane suddenly seemed fitting: how appropriate to wear black to betoken the gloom of being married to Count Piper! I shall not elaborate on the horrors of my wedding night. Suffice it to say that the count's sexual habits were as overbearing as his appearance and general demeanor. "I shall ride you," he said with a coarse laugh, "ride you like a bull." And so he did. And in the next seven years I had three children with Piper. By that time he had gone through several mistresses; I told Axel I'd had enough, and as he had predicted, I took a lover of my own. His name was Evert Taube, and (wouldn't you know it?) he was my brother's closest friend, a man of probity, depth, and tenderness equal to Axel's. As my brother had foretold, our union lasted many decades; I lost him only a few years before I lost my beloved sibling.

WHENEVER I LEAVE SWEDEN and feel *Hemlängtan*—nostalgia for the home country—I think of water, of the constant presence of water in our native land. I dream of Stockholm, the "Venice of the North" as it is often called, built on twenty-two islands, its sherbet-hued buildings shimmering like mirages on the still water of the city's canals. I think of the marine view I had from my childhood bedroom in our home, which looked out on the bay where hundreds of sailboats were moored, swaying on the water in the gentle breezes that always waft through our city. Walking through the narrow medieval streets of Gamla Stan, Stockholm's largest island and the site of its earliest settlements, there are few corners from which one can not see the gleam of a canal, the outline of a fishing boat setting off on its daily journey.

It is with water too, that I associate the buildings of our youth: the Fersen Palace, our winter home in Stockholm, was a jewel of a dwelling directly facing the royal palace, and designed by the same great architect, Carl Harleman, who designed part of the royal residence. Come summer we spent much of our time at Steninge, some thirty-five kilometers north of the capital, a golden yellow mansion of luminous simplicity, overlooking a large stream, which is considered the finest example of Swedish baroque. Or else we went to Löfstad, several hours by coach south of Stockholm, an equally superb dwelling that hovers over a large lake and a wealth of pine forests. Not far from Löfstad we owned yet another great castle, Ljung, which we favored for winter holidays.

To return to my brother Axel, a few last words: whichever of our palaces he was living in, whatever country he was visiting, he eschewed many pastimes traditional to the nobility: hunting, for instance, which, loving animals as much as he did, he adamantly refused to engage in. His energies were focused on music, for which he had a considerable gift. He played the piano and the flute excellently, and had a powerful, lusty baritone. His portable clavichord accompanied him on most of his voyages. He also painted very beautifully. And only I know him well enough to say this: it is a pity that our family's high ranking in the Swedish aristocracy disqualified him from choosing an artistic vocation and giving free vent to his great talents.

CHAPTER 3

Axel:

GUSTAVUS III, MY KING

IT WOULD NOT BE fitting to speak any more about myself without first portraying the king who reigned over our nation during much of my adult life, my dear friend Gustavus III.

By the time he had reached the age of eighteen, Crown Prince Gustavus was a very slender man with handsome though irregular features and large, penetrating blue eyes. A slight depression on his left temple, caused by a midwife's ineptness, made the left side of his face appear oblique and a tad eerie. His left hip was a bit higher than his right one, causing a slight limp, which he tried to disguise by graceful motions of his cane. His delicate frame and the hairlessness of his face gave him a somewhat effeminate appearance. Yet I realized early on in our friendship that this delicacy was deceptive—his energy and determination were formidable, and he could work for days on end with little food or sleep without any apparent strain.

At the time of Gustavus's birth his father, a gentle, mild-tempered man, bore the title of Crown Prince Adolphus Frederick, son of Christian August of Holstein-Gottorp. However, his very brilliant mother, Ulrica, a sister of Frederick the Great, was as meddling, power-hungry, eccentric a woman as ever plagued the planet. Ulrica forbade her son to play boys' games in fear he would perspire too much. She insisted that he be fed only soups, creams, and vegetables because it was her opinion that solid food dulled the mind. From his childhood on, she kept him up until long after midnight so that he might not "sleep his wits away." Gustavus greatly desired to learn English, which in addition to French was taught to many young aristocrats, but French was the only language she allowed him to study. Mathematics was not permitted either. Louisa Ulrica's only wise decision was to choose as Gustavus's tutor Carl Gustaf Tessin, the son of the great architect who had designed Stockholm's royal palace.

Tessin, who deeply regretted not having been an actor, used to illustrate historical feats through grand theatrical gestures, and this may have incited the passion for drama that absorbed Gustavus throughout his life. In Tessin's reports to Crown Princess Louisa Ulrica, he depicts his pupil as a petulant but industrious and honest boy. Early in his instructions, Tessin also perceived that the precocious young Gustavus, who enjoyed playing with dolls and loathed such traditional male pastimes as hunting or even riding, had a vivid imagination and an amazingly retentive memory. His mastery of the dramatic arts and his grasp of ancient history were particularly notable. Aged ten, he composed a tragedy on the death of Julian the Apostate. Aged eleven, he began to write plays in French. By his midteens there were few French books he had not read; Voltaire shed tears of joy when the Swedish ambassador to France, Creutz, reported that the prince knew the philosopher's epic poem *La Henriade* by heart before he was sixteen.

But it was the stage that most absorbed young Gustavus. Upon seeing a play that enthused him, he committed long portions of its dialogues to memory, especially those recited by beautifully clad female characters. As a young child—I was nine years younger than he—I remember seeing him pace his room for hours after he was supposed to have been in bed, rehearsing his favorite feminine roles, decked out with sheets and towels that served as the trains or headdresses of his dramatic personae. In his adult years he would occasionally remain in disguise all day long, speaking and acting according to role and demanding that his entourage do the same. As one of the families closest to Prince Gustavus, all the Fersens had to get on stage at some point to act in his theatrical ventures—I took turns playing a jockey, a shepherd, a giant, and a medieval knight, the latter of which caused me to suffer through the day from the weight of a twenty-pound suit of armor.

In 1751, when Gustavus was five years old, his grandfather died at an advanced age, and his father ascended the Swedish throne under the name of Adolphus Frederick. As crown prince, young Gustavus's role models were Henry IV of France, Henry V of England, and above all the formidable Gustavus II Adolphus, father of Queen Christina, all monarchs far more authoritarian than his own benign parent. By his teens, Gustavus had assiduously cultivated that innate charm of manner that enticed me when I first met him, and that, he surely realized, made him so winsome to all. "One can not imagine greater ease, gaiety, tact, and politeness," so the French *saloniste* Madame du Deffand described the young crown prince upon meeting him during his first visit to Paris.

Since childhood Gustavus had ardently desired to go to France, and his opportunity came in 1770, when he was twenty-four. Accompanied by his younger brother, he arrived in Paris and instantly won the heart of Louis XV, who received the two princes as if they were his own sons. During their stay at Marly they were lodged in the apartments of the Children of France, a rare privilege. My prudish mother was shocked to hear of the manner in which Gustavus reciprocated the French king's kindness: he presented Madame du Barry's poodle with a diamond collar, which pleased Louis XV greatly. Ambassador Creutz also introduced the Swedish princes to all the foremost salons, and Gustavus would maintain a lifetime correspondence with France's most accomplished blue-stockings—Madame Lespinasse, Madame d'Epinay, and Madame Necker along with Madame du Deffand.

It strikes me that many pivotal events in the life of Gustavus, who was so stagestruck, would be in some way related to the theater. In February 1771, the crown prince was at the Paris Opera, watching a performance of Lampe's *Pyramus and Thisbe*, when a messenger appeared bearing the news that his father had died. Gustavus had much loved his gentle, indulgent parent. He hastened back to the Swedish embassy, where he remained in seclusion for the following four days, suffering great sorrow. Having been promised three hundred thousand livres by Louis XV to bolster his country's faltering finances, he went home to prepare for the business of being a king.

Soon after his coronation, it was announced that His Majesty Gustavus III had chosen Monday, Tuesday, and Wednesday afternoons as those times when his subjects could come to present their petitions and discuss their griefs with him personally. On the appointed hours the palace was thronged by crowds of every rank and age, and of both genders. The monarch listened with exemplary patience to the complaints of his humblest subjects. He bestowed favors as graciously as if he were receiving them. To some he offered money, to others he gave advice; every visitor was greeted with a friendly smile or a sympathetic word. The citizens were dazzled by their new monarch. To have seen the king and shaken his hand was looked on as the height of felicity, and he was lauded to the skies. My father, at the time, was still the head of the Hat faction, and he was immediately summoned by the king to open negotiations with the Caps. In June 1771 it was my privilege to see Gustavus, in full regalia and with the silver scepter of his ancestors in hand, formally open his first Riksdag, or parliament. His speech stirred deep emotions in those who heard it, all the more because everyone in attendance understood it: Gustavus felt close to his humbler subjects, and addressed the Riksdag in Swedish instead of French. It was the first time in more than a century that a Swedish king—and what an orator this one was—addressed a Riksdag from the throne in his native language.

After a moving allusion to his father's death, Gustavus proceeded to say: "Born and bred among you, I have learned to love my country from my earliest youth, and consider it the highest privilege to be born a Swede . . . to be the first citizen of a free people. . . . To rule over a happy people is my dearest desire, to govern a free people the highest aim of my ambition. . . . I have found that neither the pomp nor the magnificence of monarchy, neither the most prosperous economy, can ensure content or prosperity when a nation is not united. It rests with you, therefore, to become the happiest country in the world. Let this Riksdag remain forever memorable in our annals for the annulment of all party animosities, of all self-interested motives. I shall do all I can to reunite our diverging opinions, to reconcile your estranged affections, so that the nation may forever look back with gratitude on a parliament upon whose deliberations I now invoke the blessing of the Most High."

This encomium, delivered with the dramatic skill of a consummate actor, produced an extraordinary effect. If my own rigid, judgmental father was astonished and delighted by it, one can well imagine its impact on the entire assembly. It was unanimously decided, by all four estates, that the royal address should be printed in Swedish, German, and Finnish, and that a framed copy of it should be preserved on a wall of every parish in the realm. A translation of Gustavus's speech even appeared in the *Gazette de France* and was admired by many Parisians. Gustavus's reputation grew throughout Europe as he hired dozens of foreign and native architects to make Stockholm into an eminent cultural center. He built Stockholm's first opera house and a score of new theaters throughout the capital; founded the Royal Ballet and the Royal Dramatic Theater, where some of his own plays were performed; and established the Swedish Academy. In 1772 he created a highly progressive constitution that forbade him from declaring war without the consent of the Riksdag. And in time he worked toward social reform as few Enlightenment rulers would. He abolished torture, annulled the death penalty for many crimes, offered far greater religious liberty to Catholics and Jews, and proclaimed a limited freedom of the press that was equaled, at that time, only by Great Britain's. He was also a keen supporter of the American side in the 1776 War of Independence, writing about that conflict in the passage that follows:

"This might well be America's century. The new republic . . . may perhaps take advantage of Europe someday, in the same manner as Europe has taken advantage of America for two centuries. I can not but admire their courage and enthusiastically appreciate their daring."

On the military level of his own nation, one should note that it was Gustavus III who built up the Swedish fleet and made it into one of the three great naval forces in Europe, alongside France's and Great Britain's. It is all these political and cultural achievements that led his reign to be referred to as "the Gustavian age" and caused the arts he promoted to be known as "the Gustavian style."

But Gustavus had to struggle mightily with his parliament, the Riksdag, a combat that would have great consequences for the rest of his reign. I must explain that our parliament is not a liberal force, as it is in most other countries. On the contrary. Our Riksdag is composed of four estates—the aristocracy, the clergy, the burghers, and the peasantry. And the nobility then comprised a group of conservative nobles who much resented Gustavus's liberal measures, and his foreign policy. The king was singularly apprehensive of the power and ambition of Catherine the Great of Russia. She would happily have gobbled up Sweden upon the slightest provocation, and was then preparing to invade Turkey, with which Sweden had signed a peace pact nearly half a century earlier. In the 1780s, Sweden's principal ally was France, which was so weakened by its impending revolution that it could not possibly help Gustavus in any of his military ventures. Riding roughshod over his own constitution by not consulting the Riksdag, Gustavus engaged his navy in a naval battle with Russia in which both sides lost their most

important ships, but which essentially favored Russia. Gustavus realized that the Russian capital, Saint Petersburg, could only be attacked
by land. But he was prevented from engaging in any substantial conflict
by a massive mutiny of Swedish officers, who refused to do battle
because the king had not consulted the Riksdag concerning his naval
engagement with Russia.

Although he had far more support from them than from the nobility,
the lower estates also presented Gustavus with difficulties. The peasants
resented him for having taken away their right to distill their own
liquor; the Lutheran clergy was distressed by his policy of religious tolerance. After numerous confrontations with the Riksdag, in the summer of 1772, a few months after acceding to the throne, Gustavus staged
a canny coup d'état against the estates that much strengthened the
power of the Crown. On an August evening all the officers whom he
thought he could trust received secret instructions to assemble the following morning in the great square facing the arsenal. The following
day at noon, he met with his escort of several hundred high-ranking
officers and addressed them thus: "If you follow me, just like your
ancestors followed Gustavus Adolphus, then I will risk my life and
blood for you and the salvation of the fatherland!" A young officer
called out: "We're willing to sacrifice both blood and life in Your Majesty's service!" The king then had his officers take a new oath that
absolved them from their allegiance to the Riksdag and bound them
solely to his will. Meanwhile, the members of the Privy Council had
been arrested and the fleet secured. When, at the end of the day, the
king made a tour of the city, he was everywhere received by enthused
crowds, which hailed him as a liberator.

A few days hence, having assembled the estates at his palace, the
king took his seat on the throne and delivered a philippic that berated
the estates for their license and venality, and that would be viewed as
another masterpiece of Swedish oratory. He accused them of having

degraded the nation by "inciting hatred, inciting hatred to grow into revenge, inciting revenge to become persecution. . . . The ambition and lust for glory of a few people has damaged the realm," he continued, ". . . and the result of this has been the suffering of the people. To establish their own power base has been the estates' sole goal, often at the cost of other citizens and always at the cost of the nation." I was not a witness to this particular event, but I much doubt if Gustavus would have so readily met his political goals if he had not been one of the century's great orators—a gift inevitably linked to his devotion to the stage.

STRONGLY ASSOCIATED WITH Gustavus's sense of drama was his love of fashion. He took a passionate interest in women's clothes, noticing the smallest details of their costumes—the rosettes on ladies' slippers, the facings of their jackets. In the afternoons, after the business of cabinet meetings was over, he amused himself by drawing designs for new courtiers' vestments, most of them eccentric—I particularly remember black satin trousers trimmed with red ribbons, matched with a black-and-red hooded jacket, which made their wearers look like lobsters. Or else he embroidered bodices and belts for ladies of the court. To make himself taller, the king himself wore shoes with bright red high heels made for him in France.

Yet notwithstanding his fascination with their clothes, Gustavus had shied away from women and never displayed any interest in them. The only woman who had ever influenced him was his mother; and some members of his court soon began to sense that he might be homosexual. Alas for Crown Prince Gustavus, when he had turned twenty the issue of marriage had inevitably arisen. The bride imposed upon him by the Riksdag and his powerful courtiers was Sophia Magdalena, a daughter of Frederick V of Denmark and a granddaughter, on her mother's side, of George II of England. This princess could not have been more ill-suited to Gustavus. Pleasant-looking but not beautiful, diminutive in height, very pious, very shy, she loathed opera, theater, and all forms of dramatic art, and talked to me about her husband's artistic proclivities as being whimsical or profane. She did captivate many at the court, however, through her sweetness and generosity, even though her mother-in-law's entourage did everything they could to make her miserable. Every one of her moves was watched by the queen mother's spies. Oh, what a witch, what a harridan, that woman was; I've never met the likes of her! Queen Ulrica and her retinue did not even allow Sophia Magdalena to retain any of her Danish maids. They snubbed her for not taking part in theatricals, ridiculed her for not wearing rouge, called her stingy for refusing to gamble. And for years they teased her heartlessly about the fact that she was still a virgin.

For Gustavus had loathed the very notion of wedlock. He had been forced into his marriage by sheer public pressure, and had no plans whatever for consummating it. The couple had married in 1766. In the following decade Gustavus lived in palaces other than his wife's for a year or two at a time, not seeing or even talking to her, spending most of his time with his favorite, Gustav Armfelt. Predictably, eleven years went by without Sophia Magdalena showing any signs of pregnancy. Upon my scolding Gustavus about the indifference with which he treated his spouse, the crown prince turned on me in an unusually hostile and petulant manner and replied that his aversion to her was based on "the boredom that follows her wherever she goes." But his situation grew increasingly problematical in 1777, when he became king: Gustavus then began to worry about the continuation of Sweden's royal lineage. Meanwhile, his wife had grown increasingly shy and distant because of her husband's absences and the hostility incited by her scheming mother-in-law.

What to do? Enter one Munck, the king's first equerry, a young man of great physical power and tenacity, and of immense devotion to the king. Gustavus had a singular idea: he decided to engage Munck in the task of consummating his marriage and producing an heir. At first Munck demurred. According to one version of the episode, Munck helped the king to undress, led him to the queen's bedchamber, and withdrew to a nearby room; but twenty minutes later he was rejoined by the king. The astonished Munck asked his master what had come to pass, and upon the king's remaining silent and shamefaced, Munck wasted no more words. He picked him up as if he were a baby and carried him to the royal bedchamber, locked all its doors, and didn't return to fetch the king until five in the morning. This comedy was repeated for six consecutive nights, until Munck realized that Gustavus was totally paralyzed by the notion of making love to a woman.

It then became easier for Gustavus to persuade Munck that it was his, Munck's, citizenly duty to cohabit with the queen in order to produce a royal heir. Munck accepted the assignment, and within a few months, eureka! Queen Sophia Magdalena finally displayed signs of pregnancy. A healthy male heir, Gustav Adolf, was born in 1778, another one, Karl Gustav, who would live less than a year, in 1782. Ignorant of the intrigue devised by the king and his amiable conspirator, the nation rejoiced at the birth of Crown Prince Gustav Adolf. Meanwhile the king also married off his own personal favorite, Gustav Armfelt, to a cousin of mine, a de la Gardie, assuaging the court's concern pertaining to the sexual proclivities of Armfelt, who was actually an ardent womanizer.

Oh, Gustavus, how difficult it was to tactfully, amiably resist your own advances to me! How fearful I was of losing your treasured friendship, the joys of your warmth and generosity, the charm of your enlightened conversation and wit! You were thirty, and I twenty-one, when this confrontation came to pass, and you were sensitive enough, even then, to realize the degree to which I adored women, and to remain my close friend.

. . .

I RETURN TO THE ACTIVITIES of my own youth. In the spring of
1773, the year of Gustavus's accession to the throne, I had been sent
abroad with my tutor—I was eighteen—to begin my grand tour. I had
first gone to Italy to be introduced to Maria Carolina, queen of Naples,
sister of the then Dauphine Marie Antoinette. Naples had one of the
most superb theaters in Europe, the San Carlo, with its six floors of loges
and an excellent group of musicians whose singing delighted me. In this
city I was also received by the British ambassador, Sir Alexander Ham-
ilton (soon to be linked with the notorious Emma), a man of immense
culture and a gifted archaeologist whose collection of Etruscan vases he
would offer to the British Museum. I then voyaged on to Piedmont.
Apart from the fine museum of Turin, which I visited assiduously and
which owned a particularly fine collection of Bronzinos and Parmi-
gianos, I found Piedmont's atmosphere to be very coarse. I may be
considered priggish for saying that the Piedmonteses' conversation is
shockingly lewd, and that they talk to women in language that French
grenadiers would be ashamed to use with prostitutes. It was while in
Turin that I learned of Gustavus's coup d'état. Without a drop of blood
being shed, he had rid himself of the Riksdag's stranglehold on the
country! Voltaire celebrated him in these verses: "*Jeune et digne héritier
du grand nom de Gustave Sauveur d'un peuple libre et roi d'un peuple brave.*"

Having finally arrived in Paris in November of 1773, I met the
woman to whom I attribute my sexual awakening, the Marquise de
Blacas. Ah, *chère* Marguerite, what shall I remember best of your wondrous body, of the ecstasies you taught me? The long dark head of hair
that swept across my chest as you lay on top of me, your milky thighs
weaving about my waist as you displayed your superb mastery of the
male body? The great bushy twat I loved to bury my head in, making
my tongue as delicate as a cat's as it gamboled about your orifice? The

full round nipples I bit as you hovered over me, withdrawing from my penis in a slow gentle motion, then thrusting it back into yourself with great violence, whispering "*Oui, oui, comme ça mon chéri, comme ça,*" this not only addressed to me but also to some god of carnal love who was clearly your friend? Or those moments when I simply stared at you as you lay naked on your divan, looking at me with your sly, mocking gaze, hand held in mock modesty over your bush, reminding me, oh so gloriously, of Titian's *Venus,* needing only a black servant with a parasol, a white pup scampering at your feet, to become a replica of that masterpiece? Or else those times when I lay on top of you, mouthing your shoulders, neck, breasts, sliding slowly into you as if to erase every inner wrinkle of your silken path? All this and heaven too you taught me, dear professor of desire, as you turned the shy young Swede into a sexual athlete—one who henceforth tried not to display his swaggering confidence.

But it is at the very height of our gamboling that I went to that opera ball and met the chaste young woman who would become my life's central passion. Few men have known as well as I the discrete difference between profane and sacred love.

CHAPTER 4

Sophie:

MY BROTHER AT WAR

IT WAS HARD FOR ME to understand why my gentle brother would ever desire to take part in armed conflict, would ever be able to aim his rifle at another human being. But since his adolescence he'd aspired to be a soldier and experience battle, and he also tended to be very anti-British. In 1778 France decided to side with America's rebellious colonists; great numbers of distinguished French citizens—most notably the twenty-four-year-old Marquis de Lafayette and his brother-in-law the Vicomte de Noailles—crossed the ocean to join America's colonists in their struggle for independence from Great Britain. The example of such illustrious men influenced thousands of Europeans to volunteer in that war, and my brother was one of the very first to enlist in the French Expeditionary Force. By order of the king, this force could not exceed five thousand, and it is a sign of France's enthusiasm for the American cause that thousands of citizens eager to join the conflict were turned down.

But was Axel's decision to fight in the Revolutionary War solely dictated by his martial ambitions and his admiration for the American cause? Could it be that it also had to do with the queen's tender feelings for him, which she was expressing with increasing candor? I believe that all three factors contributed to his resolve to engage in the conflict.

Here is what Ambassador Creutz had to say about their relationship in a letter to our monarch, Gustavus III:

"I must let Your Majesty know that the young Count von Fersen was held in such high esteem by the queen that a few at court were made uneasy by the evidence of her regard for him. I confess that I myself saw too much clear proof of her penchant for the count to doubt it. Young Count von Fersen's conduct in this case was admirable for its modesty and moderation, as displayed by his decision to go to America. By taking his distance he prevents all danger. Truly, to surmount temptations in this manner takes a strength of character far beyond his years. During his last days at court the queen could barely take her eyes off him, and grew tearful each time she spoke to him."

Count Creutz is very accurate in his esteem for my brother's conduct. Axel was as prudent and discreet in his relations with the queen as he had been with the young Duchess of Södermanland, and the various other women who had been enamored of him. It is his ambition, I believe, as much as his delicacy of character, that has always led him to scrupulously avoid the least taint of scandal. Upon learning that Axel was leaving for America, one of the queen's more impolitic ladies-in-waiting, the Duchesse de Fitz-James, had the effrontery to address him thus: "Well, sir, is this the way you abandon your conquest?" His reply was a model of tact. "If I had made one, I would not abandon it," he answered. "I leave as a free man, and, unfortunately, without any regrets." Indeed, I do believe that his enthusiasm for joining the war prevailed over any chagrin that his separation from the queen might have caused him.

And so it was with joy in his heart that in April of 1780 Axel left for Brest, Brittany, to join the very general under whom he had yearned to serve in America, Comte de Rochambeau, a hero of the Seven Years' War. In part because of his excellent command of English, Axel was given the post of Rochambeau's first aide-de-camp. The ship they sailed on was the *Jason,* on which he had managed to get a private cabin where he would spend most of his days reading while at sea.

Axel wished to spare our parents any worries he could possibly cause them. This led him to be an excellent correspondent. He wrote *Père* dutifully every few weeks, whenever he could take time off from his military duties. These missives from America are documents very treasured by our family, and it is a joy to share some excerpts of them.

Brest, April 4, 1780

My dear Father . . . Our embarkation is getting on; the artillery, ammunition, and commissariat are already on board, and we shall be busy now with the troops. The first regiment arrives today, and all will be embarked by the 8th. M. de Rochambeau wants to be in the harbor by the 10th so as to set sail the 12th or 13th. I'm so happy I don't know what to do with myself, but my joy will not be perfect till we are off Cape Finistère. . . . We have provisions for four months at sea, and three months ashore.

August 5, 1780. Newport, in Rhode Island

May 4, left Brest . . . June 20, off the Bermudas, met five English vessels and fought them two hours without doing ourselves much damage. We intended to head North and anchor in Chesapeake Bay; but July 4, when we were only thirteen leagues away, we sighted eighteen vessels which we took to be men-of-war; this induced us to change our course and sail for Rhode-Island, where we arrived safely on the evening of the 11th and anchored in the harbor.

. . . We wish to join General Washington, who is only 25 miles from New York. . . . I don't yet know if this junction can be made. . . . We're expecting General [Sir George] Clinton at any moment; he has sailed from New York with 10,000 men; we're ready to confront him, all dispositions are made. I hope he may come, but I can hardly believe he would commit such a folly.

I WAS IN STOCKHOLM during the years Axel was in America, bringing up my children and enjoying the company of Evert Taube; and we rushed to whichever of our residences *Père* was living in—Lövstad, Steninge, Blasieholmen, the latter of which was named after the area of Stockholm it was on—to pore over Axel's letters and his descriptions of the American Revolutionary War.

> *Newport. September 8, 1780*
>
> We have not left our island; we occupy it peacefully, and with the best order, in a very healthy camp. . . . The strictest discipline is maintained; our men take nothing from the inhabitants without paying them ready money; we have not yet had a single complaint against the troops. Such discipline is admirable and astonishes the inhabitants, who are accustomed to the pillage of the English and even of their own troops.
>
> . . . You know Frenchmen, my dear father, and what passes as courtiers, well enough to judge of the despair of our young men of that class, who see themselves obliged to pass the winter tranquilly in Newport far from their mistresses and the pleasures of Paris; no suppers, no theaters, no balls; they are in despair.
>
> The general [Rochambeau] went to the mainland a week ago. I was the only aide-de-camp who accompanied him. We stayed two days and saw one of the finest regions in the world—well cultivated, inhabitants prosperous, but without luxury or display; their clothes are simple, but good, and their morals have not yet been spoiled by the luxury of Europeans.

. . .

MY BROTHER SENSED THAT America was a country that would be very happy if it could enjoy a long peace, and if the political parties that now divided it did not make it suffer the fate of Poland and so many other republics.

Newport, September 14, 1780

I have no interesting or very good news to send you. There are some that are very grievous to us: the defeat of the American General Gates by Lord Cornwallis in South Carolina on the 10th of August. An American, with whom I talked this morning, told me . . . that much of the militia under General Gates went over to the English at the beginning of the action. If that is true, what reliance can be placed on such troops? A man is much to be pitied for having to command them.

Newport, October 16, 1780

My dear Father, I am certain this letter will reach you. . . . It goes by a frigate that M. de Rochambeau is sending to Europe.

I went with M. de Rochambeau, about two weeks ago, to Hartford, which is forty leagues from here. . . . An interview was to take place with General Washington. M. de Rochambeau sent me in advance to announce his arrival, and I had time to see that illustrious, not to say unique, man of our era. His noble and majestic, yet gentle and honest, face agrees perfectly with his moral qualities; he has the air of a hero; he is very aloof, speaks little, but is polite and civil. An air of sadness pervades his whole countenance, and makes him all the more interesting. . . .

It was on his way back from Hartford that General Washington heard of Benedict Arnold's treachery. The latter was one of his best generals; he had suffered two gunshot wounds and his conduct had always been excellent. General Clinton had bribed Arnold to deliver up West Point, which he commanded. . . .

[When] General Washington had arrived at West Point from Hartford he had sent his aides-de-camp to General Arnold to say that he would dine with him. . . . The aides-de-camp had found Arnold at breakfast with his wife. A moment after they had sat down someone had come and whispered into Arnold's ear; upon which Arnold rose, spoke in a low voice to his wife, and went out. The words were "Goodbye forever." Mrs. Arnold fainted. The aides-de-camp succored her without knowing what was happening; but a while later a courier arrived carrying the news of Arnold's treachery. The traitor was pursued. . . .

If Arnold's plan had prevailed and the British had succeeded in seizing West Point, Axel commented, they would have been masters of the whole Hudson River; they could have prevented all communication and junction of the French forces with those of the Americans. And Washington, who was camped between West Point and New York, would have been caught between two fires and would certainly have been destroyed before the French could have assisted him. It might have been all over for America, the French themselves would have suffered the shame of coming here to be mere spectators of their allies' ruin. Happily, the plot failed. . . .

Through Axel's letters to us we also learned much about the great George Washington, including delightful details such as the name of his many dogs (Downey, Pilot, Mopsey, Sweetlips, Drunkard, Vulcan, Jupiter, Trueloose). Axel reported that a group of his colleagues—de Broglie, Montesquiou—went to see Martha Washington, whom they described as "a nice fat lady with no pretensions."

Newport, December 7, 1780

You see, dear Father, that we are still in Newport; we do not even think of leaving it. We are living tranquilly in winter quarters. Washington's army went into theirs two weeks ago. . . . Colonel Ferguson has been defeated by the Americans; his corps of fourteen hundred men was almost destroyed; this has obliged Lord Cornwallis, who commands the English troops in that region, to retire to Charleston with his corps of four thousand men, most of whom are dying of fatigue and of disease. . . .

Mr. de Rochambeau has just made a little journey of six days on the mainland. I went with him . . . and we did not see a fine country or pleasant people; they were, as a rule, lazy and selfish; with those attributes, how is it possible to be useful in war?

As he expresses it in the following letter, my brother did not have a great admiration for the American people for whose independence he was fighting. He found them to be materialistic, self-serving, and unduly obsessed with money. This disappointed many of us; our enthusiasm for the Revolutionary cause had led us to believe that Americans were of fine, idealistic character.

Newport, January 9, 1781

The spirit of patriotism exists only in the leaders and more eminent persons of this country, who are making great sacrifices; the others, who are greater in number, think solely of their personal interests. Money is the prime mover of all their actions; they think only of the means to gain it; each citizen is for himself, and few are for the public good. Because the English pay them well, the inhabitants along the coast, even the best Whigs, offer provisions of all kinds to the English fleet, which is anchored in Gardiner's Bay. They fleece us pitilessly; the price of everything is exorbitant; in all the dealings that we have with them they treat us more like enemies than friends. Their cupidity is unequaled; money is their god; virtue, honor, seem nothing to them compared to the precious metal. I do not mean that there are no estimable people of noble and generous characters—there are many; I speak of the nation in general; I think [their failings] are derived more from the Dutch than from the British.

We have just received some very sad news concerning the desertion of the Pennsylvania "line"—that is how they call the twenty-five hundred men raised in that State; they went over to the English because of their discontent at lacking everything. They had neither coats nor shoes; and they were left without food for four days. . . . This desertion sets a very dangerous example; it proves how little reliance can be placed on such troops.

Axel was often called upon to resolve differences between the American and French generals. This led us to think that he would make a wonderful diplomat. We'd always wanted a diplomat in the family.

Newport, January 14th, 1781
There is a coolness between General Washington and M. de Rochambeau; the displeasure is on the side of the American general; we are ignorant of its cause. Rochambeau has charged me to bring a letter to take to General Washington, who Anglicizes my name and calls me "Ferchin." I am to inform myself as to the causes of his displeasure, and remove them if possible. . . . So you see, my dear father, I am entering diplomacy; it is my first attempt, and I shall try to come out of it well.

Axel, who had engaged in this conflict in hopes of seeing armed action, was at first disappointed by the lethargy of the war's beginning.

Newport, May 17th, 1781
We have had too much inaction, mortifying inaction. It would have been more useful to America if we had sent her the money we are

costing the king here; the Americans would have employed it better. We ought to have had an army of 15,000 men on this continent; only 5,000 were sent, who have been in garrison in Newport for a year, and of no use whatsoever, except to eat up provisions and make them dearer. I hope we shall soon get out of this sloth and be active.

I say nothing of my own affairs, dear Father. . . . I begin to be tired of being with M. de Rochambeau. He treats me with discrimination, and I'm grateful for it. But he has a distrustful, very disagreeable, and sometime insulting manner. He has more confidence in me than in any other of my comrades, but even that is paltry; his general officers are much displeased, as are his superior officers. They have the good sense, however, to conceal their discontent for the good of the cause.

Like most of his Swedish compatriots, my brother was enamored of France, and so he was quite naturally anti-British, a predilection he expresses in the following letter.

Newport, June 3, 1781

Nothing has happened in these parts since my last letter. The English are making progress in the South; they burn or plunder everything; but they spend money to acquire new friends; before long they will have conquered the whole of that part of America; then the English will recognize the independence of the Northern states, or at least, will treat them as independent, and will keep the South for themselves. Imagine how glorious that will be for the arms of France!

Axel was too modest to boast about his military valor, but in fact he did often engage in hazardous armed conflict, which led to great worry on our Part. Poor *Père*'s head trembled whenever he opened a letter from Axel.

Yorktown, October 23, 1781

. . . We are going into winter quarters in the neighborhood, at Williamsburg, a villainous little town that looks like a village.

On the night of the 11th and 12th it was resolved that we would attack [the British]. . . . Four hundred grenadiers and infantrymen, supported by one thousand other soldiers, attacked their fortifications. . . . We captured only thirty-four prisoners and three officers. The Americans carried the other battlement; they worked all night to continue the trench, and by the morning of the 15th it was well covered.

On the 17th, the enemy put up a truce flag, and Lord Cornwallis asked to capitulate. The generals were engaged the whole of the 18th in settling the articles; on the 19th the capitulation was signed and the troops laid down their arms. There is every indication that we shall next be laying siege on Charleston. The English will not fail to send troops from New York to that part of America, so I think we may have an active war. . . . M. de Rochambeau has asked for reinforcements and the taking of Savannah . . . and of Charleston may well be its result, and crown the work we have now so well begun.

All our young colonels belonging to the French court are departing to spend their winter in Paris. Some will return; others will stay there and will be much surprised if they are not all made brigadier generals after fighting at the siege of Yorktown. I shall stay here, having no reason to go to Paris other than for my amusement and pleasure, and those I must sacrifice. My affairs can get on without me; I would spend a great deal of money, and I'd rather be careful with it. I prefer to engage in another campaign here, and to finish what I have begun.

That last passage made me appreciate all the more a trait of my brother's that I'd always admired since his early youth: his consistency, his lack of frivolity, his capacity for total dedication to a cause—qualities further enhanced by his participation in the Revolutionary War.

Williamsburg, March 25th, 1782

The last letter I had the honor of writing you, my dear father, was from Philadelphia. I left there on the 9th with the Chevalier de Luzerne, and we arrived here on the 17th. We made a charming journey and the provision boxes he brought with him, well furnished with pâtés, hams, wine, and bread, prevented us from experiencing the misery that reigns in the inns, where there is no bread, and nothing is found beyond salt pork. In much of Virginia the people eat nothing but cakes made of Indian corn flour, which they bake by the fire; that hardens the outside a little, but the inside remains uncooked dough. They drink nothing but *rum* (a sugared brandy) mixed with water. They call it *grog*. 250 miles from here, in a part of Virginia that they call "the mountains," it is quite different. The country is richer, and there they cultivate tobacco; the soil also produces wheat and all sorts of fruits. The principal product of Virginia is tobacco; this State, which is the largest of the thirteen, is capable of other cultivation, but the laziness of the inhabitants and their conceit are great obstacles to industry. It really seems as if the Virginians were another race of men; instead of occupying themselves with their farms and making them profitable, each landowner wants to be a lord. No white man ever works, as in the West Indian islands; all the work is done by Negro slaves, who are ordered by the whites, and by overseers under them.

In Virginia all persons engaged in trade are regarded as inferior to landowners, who say they are not gentlemen, and they do not choose to socialize with them. These Virginians have all the aristocratic instincts, and it is hard to understand how they came to . . . accept a government founded on conditions of perfect equality. But the same spirit that has led them to shake off the English yoke may lead them to other actions of the same kind, and I would not be surprised to see Virginia detach herself, after the peace, from the other States.

While encamped in Virginia, Axel's regiment was visited by a group of Iroquois, very devout Catholics who loved Mass, which seemed to serve them as a theater; they loved the shrimp the French troops offered them for dinner, but declared they preferred the taste of a British cook they'd recently consumed.

Back in Sweden, Stockholm's artistic life was thriving, thanks to King Gustavus's passionate interest in the arts. This very year he had founded Sweden's first opera house, the most technically advanced one in Europe. It was also the first opera house outside of Italy in which performances were sung in the local language, and not in Italian: at the Stockholm opera, singers sang in Swedish. These cultural events helped to allay the sadness and concern caused by Axel's absence from our midst.

Williamsburg, May 27, 1782

We are in great consternation because of a battle between the fleets in the West Indies. According to the first news we received we had won the advantage; but yesterday we heard more through . . . a New York gazette, which reports that our ship "Ville de Paris," 110 guns, was captured, with six other vessels, and that we were totally defeated. . . . We do not bear this reversal well; I see that we are easily depressed. . . . This defeat . . . is considerable, and could invalidate our whole campaign; it gives the British the upper hand in the West Indies; they can do us great damage there, and if they get reinforcements from Europe we may well lose our conquests.

This last letter worried me because my brother had always been such an optimist (I suppose it fueled his courage). He seemed deeply discouraged every time the British scored a victory.

Philadelphia, August 8, 1782

My dear Father . . . I came here with M. de Rochambeau, who had a rendezvous with General Washington to confer on the campaign's progress. The result of the conference was that I was sent on the 19th to Yorktown, Virginia, with a commission that was then secret; it was to ship as soon as possible our siege artillery, which we had left at West Point, and bring it up the Chesapeake Bay to Baltimore. This operation required great secrecy and much promptitude, for we had but one forty-gun ship to escort the convoy, and the English with two frigates could have kept us from leaving the York River, or else have captured some of the convoy. Our army is to leave Baltimore on the 15th to come to Philadelphia, and go hence to the Hudson River. . . .

This particular missive displays the great confidence Axel's superiors had in him. The most delicate, sensitive missions were always assigned to him because of his great capacity for tactfulness and discretion.

During the years Axel was in America my marriage was quickly deteriorating. My husband's numerous affairs—with scheming courtesans as well as with noted society women—were deeply humiliating to me. And yet I preferred not to divorce Piper, in part for the sake of our children, in part because it would taint the family name.

And so I found my principal solace in the affection of Evert Taube. Axel's correspondence also cheered me greatly when it intimated that the war might be drawing to an end, and he would soon come home to us.

Philadelphia, August 17, 1782

It appears as though peace were near. England appears to be much inclined if France is modest in her demands. The Americans desire nothing else, now that the King of England has declared them independent. . . .

The English . . . have sent all prisoners back from England, without demands for their exchange. General Carleton, who commands New York, has informed General Washington, in a very polite letter, that the King, his master, has granted the independence of America; that he has sent a man to Paris with full powers to negotiate; and he proposes to General Washington an exchange of prisoners. All this seems to indicate peace; we all think that if it is not already signed, it certainly will be in the winter, and that we shall embark in the spring. This causes universal joy; it gives me inexpressible pleasure; I have hopes of seeing you again soon, my dear father.

We all jumped for joy at the prospect of a peace being signed in the following year. Our Axel would finally be out of danger! His frugality, his indifference to physical comforts, continued to amaze me.

Camp at Crompond, October 3, 1782
Though we have not seen the enemy, our recent campaign has been a very rough one. We suffered much from heat, and now the cold weather is making itself keenly felt. I, for one, bear these changes well, and have never been in better health. This year I have a tent and a straw mattress. I'm not that well covered, but my cloak is a help.

My brother made many other interesting comments on American society that I did not have a chance to include in these excerpts, such as the following: the president of Congress offered him turtle soup for dinner. Axel was amazed to learn that Americans were allowed to do little on Sundays but read the Bible—a Frenchman trying to play his flute on the Sabbath almost caused a riot. He found America boring because of its lack of museums. He was puzzled to observe that everyone washed so often, used soap on their hair instead of powder, drank too much tea and thus lost their teeth early.

I was happy to hear that during the course of the conflict my brother changed his mind about General de Rochambeau. He ended up admiring him greatly.

Boston, November 30, 1782

We parted with M. de Rochambeau with sorrow; everyone liked to be commanded by him. M. de Rochambeau, with his precious sangfroid, was the only man capable of commanding us here, and of maintaining that perfect harmony which has reigned between two groups of citizens so different in manners, morals, and language, and who, at heart, do not like each other. . . . Our allies have not always behaved well to us, and our stay on their shores has not led us to like or to esteem them. M. de Rochambeau himself has not always been well treated; but in spite of this his conduct has been perfect. . . . The stern orders he gave our army . . . enforced that rare discipline which won the admiration of the Americans and English troops. The wise, prudent, and simple conduct of M. de Rochambeau has done more to conciliate the Americans than the winning of four battles ever could.

Boston, December 21, 1782

We are all going on board tonight; the ships are ready, and if the wind is fair we shall sail tomorrow morning. As soon as we reach the West India islands I will send you my news, dear Father, and shall have the pleasure of assuring you of my respectful attachment.

THAT WAS MY BROTHER'S last letter. Upon leaving Williamsburg in the first months of 1783 his regiment was sent to Porto Caballo, Venezuela, to join Spanish troops in the invasion of some British Caribbean islands. But the attack was canceled upon news of the peace treaty being signed by France and Great Britain. Axel suffered much from the tropical climate, contracting a microbe that led him to suffer recurrent fevers for the rest of his life, and permanently damaged his health.

"I want your news," he wrote me. "It's the only consolation we have in this vile country. We're dying of boredom here; we're becoming thin and dried up, growing old and yellow with heat and boredom. . . . Men are not made to live here, but rather tigers, bears, and caymans."

Having no one but the queen in mind, Axel was eager to return to Paris, and had to placate our father because he had no intention of going back to Sweden that year. To appease *Père* he hinted that he might be ready to settle down. "Despite the little inclination I have for this sacrament," he wrote him, "I'm at an age when marriage may become a necessary thing." He wrote Miss Leyel to ask her if she had changed her mind about marrying him, but soon learned that while he was away she had married the Earl De La Warr. He considered another marital prospect, the immensely wealthy Germaine Necker. "This project depends entirely on your wishes," he wrote our father; "I have no interest in it but yours. . . . I've only seen her once in passing. . . . I only recall that there was nothing disagreeable about her." But this notion also came to naught, for he found out that Mademoiselle Necker had been proposed to by his compatriot and old friend Erik de Staël. And so to Axel's great relief, all talk of marriage ceased for a while.

I'M PROUD TO LIST ALL the honors my brother was awarded for his fine conduct in the War of Independence.

Louis XVI named him Chevalier of the Order of Military Merit and appointed him second colonel of the Regiment Deux-Ponts. At the request of King Gustavus, France granted Axel a pension of twenty thousand francs a year; he was also made proprietary colonel of France's Royal Swedish Regiment.

King Gustavus promoted him to the ranks of titular colonel in the Swedish army, and made him a Chevalier of the Order of the Sword. ("Young Count Fersen," Ambassador Creutz had written the king, "was always present at the thickest of the battles, either at the spearhead of the attacking forces, or in the trenches, and displayed the most valiant courage.")

CHAPTER 5

Axel:

LOVING JOSEPHINE

COULD ANYONE IMAGINE that I would not instantly rush to see the queen upon my return from America? Although she had been militantly opposed to the American Revolution, which in her eyes countered all principles of the Divine Right of Kings, she had resigned herself to the fact that I had joined the French Expeditionary Force because I admired the American cause. And we had corresponded during my absence, but each letter took months, months to arrive, and our separation had been made all the more painful by the long wait between missives.

My ship having arrived in Brest on July 17, 1783, I reached Paris on the twenty-third. I dropped off my satchels at my flat; and by the time it took me to ready my coach and have new horses harnessed—a matter of hours—I was off to Versailles. I'd had no time to warn the queen of my arrival. Her guards remembered me well. I ran up the stairs alone to her apartments and cracked the door to her salon, hoping to surprise her. She was alone, as I'd hoped she'd be, and she was playing the harp. Three years! We were now both twenty-eight years old. My domestics in Paris had told me that I'd aged a great deal during my time at war, and indeed I found her quite altered also. She had had two pregnancies since I'd last seen her, and had grown plumper; her arms were rounder, her breasts more prominent. I felt a pang of regret: I'd left a lovely girl, and was now looking at a handsome, imposing woman. But as she sat there on her little gilt stool before her harp, plucking an air of Gluck's, I was again carried away by the graceful carriage of her head, by the beauty of her abundant dark blond hair—she was in morning dress, attired in a vaporous white chiffon gown. I stood there for several moments, contemplating her, before speaking those words so unrelated to the tender intimacy of my emotions. *"Votre Majesté!"* I exclaimed. I'd indeed managed to surprise her. She stopped abruptly in the middle of a chord, sprang up, and rushed to me, grasping both my hands in hers. *"Vous, c'est vous,"* she whispered. *"Toi, c'est toi!"* I murmured inwardly, my heart aching from our formalities. We stood there, holding hands. She simply stared at me, her eyes, those uniquely deep blue eyes, looking at me with immense affection and excitement, and then started questioning me, in that same girlish, impulsive way she'd queried me when we had first met nine years earlier at the opera ball. *"Comment est-il, ce George Washington,"* she asked. "Is it true that his teeth are made of ivory tusks?" Had I met any *peaux-rouges*, redskinned people? Is it true that they're cannibals? She interrogated me thus for a few minutes, shaking my hands at each query. She had grown so womanly, so statuesque, and yet retained her girlish spontaneity. Her little white dogs suddenly invaded the room, barking at my heels, sniffing the traces of my own spaniel Odin. She drew me to a sofa, and we sat down to speak further, our hands still in each other's. I asked her in turn about her family. Her older child, Marie-Thérèse, I learned, had recently been very ill, and she had been at her bedside all the while, allowing no one else to nurse her; the death of her mother, Empress Maria Theresa, had caused such deep depression that she had locked herself into her apartments in total seclusion for several weeks; this loss had left her more isolated and lonelier than ever; she now found her chief solace in her second child, the dauphin, who was now a year and a half, and in the bloom of health; as for the king, *"ce pauvre homme,"* doctors had counseled him to lose weight so as to avoid major cardiac problems, but alas (this with a resigned smile), he was as much of a glutton as ever. . . .

In the following weeks we saw each other as often as we possibly could. We played backgammon, at which she continued to beat me. We brought our dogs together, as of old. I gave her Saint Augustine's *Confessions*, one of my favorite books, to read, and we discussed it at length. Toinette loved to act, and I attended the plays she staged at the Petit Trianon's little white-and-gold theater, where she charmingly played Colette in Rousseau's *The Village Soothsayer*, and Rosine in Beaumarchais's *Marriage of Figaro*. The amount of time we could afford to spend together, even riding horseback, was limited; in growing older we had become more prudent, more wary of gossip and possible opprobrium. We settled for seeing each other a great deal at the opera—the queen had a loge into which she was in the habit of inviting half a dozen friends; I could easily be there as one of her chums, bantering with the Duchesse de Polignac or Madame de Fitz-James. We smiled slyly at each other when we heard Dido sing to Aeneas, "Ah I was well inspired / When I received you at my court."

One evening, while sitting alone with me in her opera box—her other guests had left to consume ices—she confessed her love for me. She slipped her finger into my hand and spoke in a low whisper while vigorously agitating her fan. "I love you, Axel, I love you, what else can I say?" She quickly withdrew her hand, and continued to whisper: "What else can I tell you, what else can I say?" I responded by scribbling her a tiny note on one of my visiting cards. "I too," I wrote, "I love you desperately." She read the card gravely, and then tore it into tiny bits—fourths, eighths, sixteenths—dropping the shreds of paper into her purse. What opera were we seeing that night? Rameau's *Les Indes Galantes*, I believe. That summer, as we walked the footpaths in the woods near the Petit Trianon, we often sat down on park benches, by the side of brooks or under heavy trees, to exchange embraces. Our mutual desire was throbbing, urgent, desperate. We talked a lot about opera, about how it reflected our relationship, about the impossible loves that were the central themes of most operas, about those operatic passions that led to tragedy and death.

We finally consummated our love some two months after my return from America, on a July night when Versailles was relatively emptied of courtiers, and the king had gone for a two-day hunting trip to Saint-Cloud. There was a small octagonal chamber above the queen's apartments that had been built just the year before, in which a few of her favorites—Lamballe, Polignac—had already stayed. It contained a large sofa set into a curtained alcove, and was reached by a secret staircase.

I am wary of disclosing too many details of those blessed hours. Let me just say this: I'd never felt truly *loved* before. I ask male readers to answer the following questions: Have you ever felt totally consumed by the intensity of a woman's love? Have you ever had the sense—it is sublime—that you were the first to fulfill her sensual needs? All this and heaven too I experienced. But the sweetest of all was to feel Toinette's purity, the guilelessness of her virginity. For a woman to be penetrated does not necessarily alter her chastity, which I look upon as a state of mind, and in her case, a state of grace. As she lay below me, her dark gold hair undone, looking at me with tenderness, but also with a never-before wonder caused by the novel sensations that washed over her; as all restraints fled and her body unfurled as into a sail that transported her to regions she'd never before traveled; as I mouthed her large erect nipples, as she finally moaned her pleasure with a kind of desperation, I finally knew the delight other men have experienced when deflowering a very young girl. For chasteness is a condition of the psyche that would always remain hers, that no man, not even I, could alter. And the greatest marvel of it was her ability to retain her purity while communicating her passion: by the manner in which her arms wandered over my nakedness, by the endearments she whispered, with an almost sisterly tenderness—*"Mon ami, mon âme, mon adoré."*

The following morning I wrote a note to Sophie, ending it with this phrase: "I've more than one reason to be happy." I commemorated that day—July 15—for the rest of my life. I find the following phrase in a diary note written decades later, many years after the royal family's tragedies, on July 15 of 1798: "I recall the day when I came to her privately for the first time," *"Je me rappelle le jour ou je suis allé chez Elle la premiere fois."* For "Elle," with a capital *E,* was one of the two code names I gave her from then on, to hide her identity from the eyes of curious valets or other possible foragers of my papers. The other code name was "Josephine," Josepha being one of her middle names.

A few weeks later that summer—I was trying to gather the courage to inform Elle about my imminent departure for Sweden, where I had not been for seven years—I wrote the following words in a note to Sophie: "I'm very pleased Miss Leyel is married. I've made up my mind. If I can't belong to the only person I wish to belong to, the only one who truly loves me, I do not want to belong to anyone." How else could I put it? Elle was not only my lover, she had become my closest friend, my confidante, the very texture of my life. One can imagine how much I dreaded to tell her of my return to Sweden. But how charming and generous she was, even about that. "Of course, of course you must go," she said, weeping gently, clutching my hands as ever, "of course you must see your family, you must see your father." She was somewhat assuaged by my promise of returning in the spring, and spending the entire following year with her.

AND SO I SET FORTH IN September on my way to Stockholm, traveling my usual route, through Germany. But the unpredictable happened: a few days into my journey I received word that I should remain in Germany in order to join Gustavus III, who had just started on a long trip to Europe. I was to meet him in Rostock, on the Baltic, and accompany him on a voyage that would wind southward through Europe and continue on through Italy. What could I do? He'd appointed me captain of his bodyguard.

I had to write to *Père*, again dreading his grief at my many years' absence.

I myself was furious at the king's imposition. It is not as if he had chosen me alone for his company. Gustavus was to be escorted by a whole retinue of courtiers, all of them tall and handsome, like most men with whom he enjoyed traveling. They included Baron Armfelt, his chief chamberlain; Baron Sparre; my sister's lover, Evert Taube; and a sizable group of Swedish sculptors and painters.

The king was in bed, sipping on hot chocolate, when I met him at the inn in Rostock where he waited for me. He welcomed me with effusion, laughing and weeping with joy as he murmured endearments. "Ah, my *långe* Axel! My most beautiful Axel! My beloved Axel!" I was used to the exuberantly affectionate manner he always had toward me, and tempered it as well as I could. This trip to Italy was not an end in itself, Gustavus explained to me when he'd calmed down. It was just a preliminary to his real aim, which was to obtain the French Crown's support for his "big deal"—the invasion of Norway. The way he was playing his cards, his arrival in France, some months hence, would merely seem to be the last stage of a European journey. He would try to remain incognito on this trip, taking on the *nom de voyage* of Count de Haga.

Our first major stops in northern Italy were Turin, Milan, Vincenza. However admirable his knowledge of art history, the king's pace of travel was utterly exhausting. He had to see every important church, every notable painting, admire every significant bit of architecture. In the Turin Cathedral he spent a long time in the Chapel of the Holy

Shroud, the altar of which contains the cloth in which Christ's body was wrapped after His deposition from the cross. Gustavus displayed a Christian piety, on this trip, of which we had never been aware. He knelt at length before the sacred cloak, frequently making the sign of the cross, occasionally weeping. We went on to Milan, where he was particularly entranced by the church of San Simpliciano, said to be founded by Saint Ambrose in the fourth century, and reputed to be pivotal to the conversion of Saint Augustine. (Gustavus's big lecture here on the details of Augustine's conversion, on his hearing a child's voice singing "*Tolle, lege,*" instructing him to "Take up and read" the Holy Book.) When visiting the museums with which these Italian cities are studded, we were also struck by the king's adulation of the Holy Virgin, who is barely mentioned in our Lutheran religion: Gentile da Fabriano's *Madonna with Angels*, Tiepolo's *Immaculate Conception* in the Museo Civico in Vicenza, Veronese's *Madonna with Child and Saints*, incited such reverence in him that he knelt on the floor in front of these paintings, sighing with veneration and whispering to himself. "Is he going to pull a Christina on us?" Taube whispered to me during one of Gustavus's prostrations. He was referring to our country's seventeenth-century queen, who had converted to Roman Catholicism early in her reign, resigned her kingdom, and moved to Rome to practice her new religion in peace.

We went on to Vicenza, Palladio's city; how could Gustavus not have been enthused by the Olympic Theater, the very first covered theater constructed since Roman times? What plays were performed there, he wished to know, when did this great Palladio die, where is he buried, I want to see his tomb. By this time, in order to better sate Gustavus's voracious curiosity we had hired a guide to accompany us on our Italian journey. In Piacenza, we admired the vast Gothic portal of the Church of San Antonio; in Parma, the Correggios (more genuflections in front of the Virgins Mary); in Pavia, at San Pietro in Ciel d'Oro, the tomb of

Saint Augustine (more signs of the cross, more quotes from that great writer, "Oh, save me God, but not quite yet"). We went on to Brescia, where the king spent hours in the exquisite Renaissance cloister in Santa Marie della Grazie; to Cremona, which led the cause of the Holy Roman Emperor in the thirteenth century (lecture here on the struggle between the Guelfs and the Ghibellines). All these treasures were lingered at for hours, commented on at length—what a good professor Gustavus could have been! By this time every member of the king's retinue was utterly worn out. Limping about, Taube feigned a sprained ankle and stayed in his room throughout our stay in Piacenza. Armfelt remained indoors in Cremona, pretending to have a serious migraine. Sparre took an emetic and vomited in front of the Brescia Cathedral in order to have his proper rest. Only I, as captain of the king's bodyguard, could not afford to drop out, although I pleaded a headache every few weeks in order to have time to write to my family, and my queen.

To make things worse, we were all deeply embarrassed by the gaudy costumes our king had imposed on us—canary-yellow culottes, gilt-edged sky-blue jackets, black shako hats topped with blue and yellow plumes—which made Italian citizens stare at us with wonderment. In several of the sites we visited—Cremona, Brescia—we encountered Emperor Joseph II, the brother of my beloved, whose austere dress and simple, forthright courtesy made my king's gaudy dress and mincing manners all the more outlandish. Joseph II, who in former years had ruled in consort with his mother, the late Maria Theresa, now that was a king! He had instituted many of the same reforms Gustavus had in his youth—freedom of the press, religious tolerance, abolition of serfdom, emancipation of the Jews. His talents included many familial virtues—one remembers that it is he who had enabled France's royal couple to finally share a bed properly. But alas, he disliked my king because of his preference for men. "Small, miserable, a dandy in front of his mirror," so he described Gustavus to his sister Marie-Christine. We finally reached Florence, and there I was to meet a beauty who might have sealed my fate. . . .

But first, of course, the "Comte de Haga" in Florence: we had to visit Santa Maria Novella, Santa Croce, the Duomo, some ten times apiece. Every stone touched by Brunelleschi was expounded on. At the Duomo, Gustavus asked for a chair and sat for hours in front of the bronze doors of the Baptistry, expounding on every detail of that great work. He lingered an equally long time in the interior of the Duomo, ecstatic before Lucca Della Robbia's *Ascension* and Uccello's heads of the prophets; these incited such fervent enthusiasm in him that he knelt down before them for much of the afternoon. Christina? We worried again. With this man everything was possible.

As for the Florentine beauty I have mentioned, she was Lady Emily Cowper, a relative of Lord Cowper, a British expatriate who entertained us royally. Ah, Emily, superb green-eyed Emily! Her hair was of the most marvelous reddish blond and, since she was but fifteen, still hung to below her shoulders, a smoldering curtain of gleaming amber silk. Upon one of her brother's many evening receptions I took her outside to a park bench and kissed her deeply on her mouth—it was the first time the child had been thus embraced, and she responded with fire and ardor, as if it were second nature to her. Upon subsequent caresses in the park, I unlaced her bodice and suckled her breasts at length, biting her tiny pink nipples as she cried out her pleasure. . . . Oh, what a delicious lover she would later make! I let my hand wander under her vestments, up her leg, to the tiny spot in front of the vagina—it is also called *klitoris* in Swedish—the fondling of which women are so partial to. Thus with my mouth on her breast and the other on her private parts I was able to bring the child to orgasm without deflowering her, and *la petite coquine*, the little scoundrel! She ended up stretched out on the park bench, crying out her delight so loudly that I had to put my hand over her mouth lest members of our group might hear her. We repeated our games several evenings in a row, and each time the exquisite little machine that was her body trembled more wildly, more tremulously than ever. Needless to say, I had my own difficulties remaining physically composed. I had experimented with a new kind of sexual play, always a delight for me. (I'd rather not be thought of as a rake, just as an average, venturesome sexual athlete.)

The dear little girl was very taken with our trysts, and while not admitting to our forbidden games, talked to her brother of her romantic feelings toward me. The duke even broached, ever so amiably, the possibility of marital intentions. I politely deflected his suggestions, saying I was determined to remain a bachelor, and asking him to console his sister with that explanation. Ah women, women, my life's plague and chief delight!

TRAVELING FURTHER SOUTH in the Italian peninsula, we reached Rome, where Gustavus had asked for an audience with the pope. Our fears were awakened again: he was the first Swedish ruler since Christina who had asked to see the pontiff! But it was not our shrewd monarch's newfound piety that drove him to the Vatican—he had ulterior motives of a political nature. Pius VI was an amiable, unimpressive little man who was made notable by his secret fondness for the Jesuits, who were currently seeking refuge in Russia after having been banned from most of Europe by a previous pontiff. Our king was perfection itself at the audience, advancing toward the pope deeply bowed and at a snail's pace, prostrating himself at all the right times, kissing the papal ring like the earth's most devout. And he readily charmed the pontiff into trading favors: he obtained Pius VI's permission to have a Lutheran chapel built in Rome, in return for promising to build a Catholic church in Stockholm. We stayed in the Eternal City for several weeks, the king dallying ecstatically amid its dozens of churches and museums, and refusing to make up his mind whether to go south to Naples or head back north to Paris. From Rome I described my impatience in a letter to my father: "We suffer from an exorbitant principle of disorder and indecision, we change plans twenty times a day, each of them more outlandish than the last. I'm in despair about participating in his trip. . . . It obliges me to daily witness odd and novel extravagances."

Gustavus finally decided to go south to Naples, which was ruled by yet another sibling of my beloved's, Queen Maria Carolina. A large, violently authoritarian woman, she totally dominated her husband, Ferdinand IV, who himself was no delicate chap. Massively built, loud-mouthed, with a huge nose that led to his being named "*nasone,*" he devoted himself entirely to fishing, cleaning and skinning his catches himself. Dressed as a sailor, he sold his produce at the public market, always surrounding himself with companions of the lowest possible provenance. The coarseness of the couple would lead me to be all the more amazed by the refinement and grace of their nearest kin, the French monarchs. Maria Carolina became smitten with Armfelt. There were many gay, puerile entertainments at her court, such as costume parties at which the queen dressed as Ceres, and her ladies-in-waiting as Neapolitan peasant girls who showered the guests with roses, while Armfelt, who loved masquerades, impersonated a bear.

And then we headed north toward Paris, the true goal of this entire journey that the "Comte de Haga" had so deviously planned. Once arrived, we faced some disappointments. Many of our old friends were gone. Our former ambassador to Paris, Creutz, had been recalled to Stockholm to be minister of foreign affairs. Baron de Staël had replaced him. Moreover, everyone at the French court dreaded Gustavus's visit because as Louis XVI's favorite minister, Comte de Vergennes, put it, "This prince will hardly renounce a costume that will expose him to derision everywhere he'll go." To make it even more awkward, Gustavus arrived at Versailles unannounced. It was June 7, 1784. Louis XVI was spending the day at Rambouillet and was about to sit down to dinner. Informed of the arrival of his royal visitor, he ordered up his horses and hastily dressed. So hastily, in fact, that to the queen's despair he greeted his guest wearing totally dissimilar shoes: one had a red heel and a gold buckle, the other a black heel and a silver buckle.

Once the royal formalities were over, Gustavus set out to explore Parisian culture, and would not allow any member of his retinue to miss one significant event. He saw every play performed at the Comédie Française, heard Gluck's *Armida* and a score of other works at the opera, and twice attended *The Marriage of Figaro*. There were occasions on which we were forced to attend two or three spectacles a day. "We're constantly occupied and constantly in a hurry," I wrote my father. "This kind of hassle very much suits the Comte de Haga, but I'm exhausted by it. He'd rather skip food, drink, and sleep than not be at spectacles all day long; it's an obsession."

My king, alas, was not popular with the French. Thirteen years before he had been a slightly effeminate young man, but now he made no bones about being homosexual. Everyone at court joked about his not attending brothels, as most every visiting dignitary did. The queen snubbed him because of his outrageous costumes and his unmistakable sexual orientation. Louis XVI found him pedantic and yawned at his conversation because of its abundance of art historical details. Nevertheless, magnificent parties were given in Gustavus's honor. Perhaps for my sake, Toinette, always an exquisite hostess, overcame her prejudices against my king and gave him one of the greatest fetes ever held at the Trianon. The supper was served at little tables dispersed among the bushes of the park, which was lit by many hundreds of candles. The queen went from one table to the next, standing at length behind the king of Sweden's chair, Taube's, Armfelt's, and mine, to speak to each of us in turn. "It was an enchantment, truly an Elysian spectacle," Gustavus wrote home to Sweden.

My king's pace was as feverish as usual—he had to see every site of note in the Île-de-France, as he had in Italy. Even I feigned a headache every few days to drop out of his retinue and have my essential moments of tenderness with Toinette. Gustavus would be more than enchanted by his stay in Paris. Over the weeks, the queen grew to appreciate his love of France and his remarkable culture, and ended up being quite fond of him. In exchange for granting France new trading concessions in Sweden, he obtained a colony he had desired for a long time, the island of Saint Barthélemy in the Caribbean, whose capital, I hope, will always remain named Gustavia.

This time I had to follow my king back to Sweden. It is with the greatest sorrow that I took leave of her again. My father was ill, and I had to spend the winter with him in Stockholm, where I had not been for nearly seven years. I was able to return to Paris very briefly in May, bringing Toinette a portrait of the Swedish crown prince, and we enjoyed a few sweet and passionate encounters.

IT HAS ALWAYS been a sorrow to me that I was in Sweden in the first months of 1785, when the queen suffered one of her life's most difficult episodes, the event known as the Diamond Necklace Affair. The greatest royal scandal of the century, it featured Marie Antoinette and a supporting cast of swindlers and charlatans of legendary proportions, and undermined Louis XVI's reign as no earlier event had. At the center of the imbroglio were the country's highest prelate, the notoriously frivolous and popular Cardinal de Rohan, grand almoner of France and scion of one of its wealthiest and most venerable families (whom I'd always suspected of being a total cad); a deeply indebted Paris jeweler, Monsieur Böhmer, who had set out to sell the world's most expensive diamond necklace to Marie Antoinette; and a gang of thieves led by a rapacious adventuress named Jeanne de La Motte, the illegitimate daughter of a member of the ancient Valois family, who was determined to gain fame and fortune at the cadaverous court of Versailles. Quite understandably, the flamboyant Rohan had been detested by Marie Antoinette's family during his tenure as ambassador to Vienna; the queen shared her relatives' intense dislike for him; and La Motte's plan was to capitalize on the cardinal's ardent desire finally to gain the queen's favor.

To this end La Motte, who had been Rohan's mistress, persuaded the prelate that she was a close friend of Marie Antoinette (upon whom, in reality, she had never laid eyes) and that she could help him secure the queen's esteem. Pretending to hand Rohan's missives to her "dear friend" Marie Antoinette, forging letters that promised the cardinal an eventual audience, and emptying his pockets at every turn, La Motte arranged a trumped-up encounter between Rohan and the queen: she hired a cocotte who, shrouded with thick veils, successfully impersonated my poor beloved queen, and offered the deliriously happy prelate a brief evening meeting in the gardens of Versailles.

Enter August Böhmer, a prominent jeweler, often employed by the French court, who at a time of deepening financial crisis was more desperate than ever to unload a certain necklace: it was a *"rivière"* of 579 diamonds, 2,800 carats' worth of them, which he had originally designed for Madame du Barry (due to Louis XV's sudden death, she had never been able to buy it). Böhmer had turned to La Motte for help. Couldn't she persuade her "dear friend" the queen to buy the trinket? La Motte was shrewd enough to know that a national debt of unprecedented proportions, and the country's increasing alienation from Louis XVI, would deter the king from spending 1.6 million pounds on yet another trifle for his wife. But La Motte circumvented that difficulty: she persuaded Rohan to consolidate his new friendship with the queen by offering her the necklace himself. She produced a supposed letter from the queen—La Motte's forgery of my beloved's handwriting— that authorized him to make the purchase. The shimmering trinket was then brought to the cardinal; besotted by the prospect of finally gaining the queen's good graces, he handed it to a minion of La Motte's who pretended to be the queen's own messenger; whence it passed, of course, into the adventuress's own hands. She had the necklace dismantled, sold its component stones in London, and for a few months lived like a multimillionaire, acquiring a grand chateau and so many luxurious furnishings that it took forty-two coaches to carry them.

But La Motte eventually faltered because she had underestimated the jeweler's diligence. Böhmer went to visit Marie Antoinette to deliver some far more modest items she *had* ordered from him—in view of the public opinion mounting against her, my darling friend was trying hard to be less ostentatious. During their meeting, Böhmer asked the queen about the diamond necklace she was purchasing with Cardinal de Rohan's help. "*What* necklace?" Marie Antoinette asked, immediately suspicious of the detested prelate. The queen and the jeweler did not take long to realize that they had both been the victims of a staggering swindle.

The denouement of "the Diamond Necklace Affair," as it came to be known throughout Europe, was as extravagant a coup de théâtre as any event of the century. My poor Toinette, not realizing that Rohan had been as duped by La Motte as she, begged her husband to arrest the cardinal. I need not tell you how subservient Louis was to his wife's wishes. On August 15, 1785, which was the queen's name day as well as the Feast of the Assumption, Rohan was scheduled to say High Mass in front of the assembled court. The royal couple called for the cardinal to come first to their private apartments. They were in the company of their favorite minister and adviser, my friend Baron de Breteuil, an avowed enemy of Rohan's. The detestable cardinal admitted that he had been a pathetic dupe. The king replied that since the prelate had defamed the queen's name, he must be arrested. The four luminaries then went into the Hall of Mirrors, where thousands of courtiers were waiting for Mass to begin. Breteuil stood next to Rohan, who was dressed in scarlet cardinal's regalia. "Arrest the cardinal!" the minister ordered the captain of the guards, his eyes sparkling with pleasure. The crowd was stunned. No Mass was said that day at Versailles. The hugely popular cardinal was hauled off to the Bastille like a common pickpocket. Once there, he enjoyed such a profusion of luxuries and privileges—a large retinue of servants attended him, oysters and champagne were brought him daily—that for reasons of security the daily walks allowed the occupant of the neighboring jail cell, the Marquis de Sade, were suspended for the duration of the prelate's stay.

Nine months after the necklace episode its chief participants would be brought to court before the Parlement of Paris. The jurors, after a sixteen-hour deliberation, acquitted Rohan by a vote of 26 to 22; La Motte was found guilty and sentenced to life imprisonment. But my cherished Toinette also received a life sentence of sorts. As Rohan emerged from his trial at the Parlement, as huge crowds voiced their support with shouts of "Long live the Cardinal!," the queen wept bitterly in her apartments. She was shrewd enough to sense that her husband's reign had been dealt a blow from which it might never recover. However trumped-up the charges against her, the scandal had exposed the feebleness of Louis XVI's rule, her own former frivolity, the corruption of the entire court. Philanthropy and prison reform being the fashion; it became very chic to visit La Motte in her jail cell. Two years after her conviction, the swindler escaped from prison and fled to England, whence she launched a vituperative propaganda campaign against Marie Antoinette that found an eager audience in France.

From the summer of 1786 on, the criticism focused on the queen grew barely tolerable. She was being blamed for every ill that plagued France, including the country's increasingly shaky finances. Shortly after Rohan's trial, it was learned that Louis's government had had to borrow over one million pounds from foreign powers. The woman disdainfully referred to as "L'Autrichienne" (it was pronounced with the emphasis on the last syllable, *chienne*, French for "bitch") now became known as "Madame Deficit." The slander was often laced with sexual innuendoes. Score upon score of lampoons published in the following years accused my chastest of friends of having gone to bed with dozens of persons of both sexes, including Cardinal de Rohan; the king's younger brother Comte d'Artois; her friend Duchesse de Polignac, whom she had appointed to be governess of the royal children; and Jeanne de La Motte herself.

The first time the queen appeared at the theater after Rohan's exoneration, she was greeted with such loud hisses that from then on she tried to stay out of public view. She ordered large additional cuts to be made in Versailles's budget. She stopped buying jewelry and new garments, coming close to sacking Mademoiselle Bertin. In addition, more than 170 courtiers who depended on her financially were sent packing. There was an end to masked balls. Several royal chateaus were put up for auction, or demolished to avoid the cost of maintenance. The queen even banned gambling—a potent symbol of royal frivolity, but also her principal refuge from depression—from the palace.

WHEN I VISITED Paris in 1786 my beloved friend was still smarting from the opprobrium cast upon her by the odious necklace episode. And her morale was made all the more wretched by the illness of her oldest son, the dauphin. At the age of three he had stopped growing, and had begun to suffer from frequent convulsions. The king and queen, as devoted parents as any royal couple I know of, spent many days together at the child's bedside. He recovered by year's end, but these were the first symptoms of the tuberculosis and other ailments that would carry him off a few years later.

My correspondence with the queen—I traveled back and forth a great deal between Paris and Stockholm in the following years—was made all the more ardent by our frequent separations. Since the French police had a department solely devoted to intercepting all mail, including diplomatic dispatches, secrecy was in order. So we wrote our letters in invisible ink and gave them to trusted couriers who carried them in biscuit boxes, or in the hems of their garments. I cannot quote from them, alas, for a decade's worth of these missives—those of the 1780's—were destroyed during the forthcoming Revolution. We had become like old lovers now, or like a married couple—so I liked to think of our relations—made passionate by frequent absences. In our missives, endearments alternated with much fussing over domestic details. I cared deeply for the royal children, and a good part of our correspondence concerned them. Toinette forwarded me designs for jackets she wished me to add to my wardrobe. We sent each other music scores to study for our next reunion. She asked me to buy her a dog in Sweden, and we had long negotiations about what kind of puppy she wished.

By the time the little white dog I'd bought for her arrived at Versailles, the queen had had another child, Louis-Charles, Duc de Normandie. Both of us were aware that the child was born nine months, almost to the day, after the great fete she had offered King Gustavus at the Trianon the previous year, when we had managed to steal a few hours of intimacy with each other. Could it be possible, I would wonder for the rest of my life, that the Duc de Normandie was my son? Never marrying, never having any other illegitimate children, I remained particularly obsessed with the boy for the rest of my days. Immensely gay, bright, and robust, he had none of his older brother's health problems, or any of his sister's chilly aloofness. He was undoubtedly the favorite of Marie Antoinette's children: she called him *"chou d'amour,"* "fruit of love," a phrase that might have denoted her own hopes that he was my son. It was also significant that the king displayed less affection for

Louis-Charles, at first, than for his other children; Louis's diary entry concerning Normandie's birth, which came to light after his death, might intimate that he suspected the boy not to be his child: "The queen was delivered of the Duc de Normandie at half past seven; everything happened as it had with my son, the dauphin."

While continually shuttling between France and Sweden, when in Paris I was careful to attend a great many of the queen's card games, and of her close friends' supper parties; they bored me immensely but made me appear to be just another member of her entourage. In 1786 I again had to return to Stockholm to fulfill my duties as captain of the king's bodyguard. My sweet friend was still smarting from the wretched Rohan's rehabilitation, and from the French citizenry's growing deprecation of her. Moreover, she was now plagued by the increased power of her old enemy Philippe d'Orléans, the king's first cousin, who had recently inherited an immense fortune from his father. The Duc d'Orléans had total control over the Palais-Royal, whose numerous pamphlet shops specialized in spreading yet more libelous gossip about the queen. Having never regained the popularity she enjoyed during the first decade of her reign, her kindness and compassion never recognized, she was now more detested than ever. Furthermore, the queen was pregnant again, and this particular pregnancy was one that she had not desired. Soon after my return to Sweden, in June 1786, I was informed of the birth of her fourth and last child, a girl called Sophie (the name was chosen because of my sister, with whom she now had a warm, tender correspondence, but she could readily plead that the child was named after one of the king's favorite aunts, Madame Sophie).

As France's finances plummeted—they had been vastly depleted by the nation's participation in America's War of Independence—the queen was increasingly referred to as "Madame Deficit," even though she had cut her budget by yet another three million. Seventeen eighty-seven brought her more sorrows: Shortly after I returned to France that year, her ten-month-old daughter, Sophie, fell seriously ill. She died in June, and the queen wrote heartbreaking letters to a few of her close friends amid European rulers, including Gustavus. The summer of that year was wretched for both of us. I was stationed with my regiment in the town of Maubeuge, near the Belgian border. King Louis, faced by growing political tensions and deprived of the counsel of his favorite minister, Vergennes, who had recently died, began to suffer from a depression that bordered on a nervous breakdown. The king's depression led him to depend increasingly on the queen's advice—"He trusts only the queen," I wrote Gustavus, "and it is quite clear that she does everything." It also incited him to indulge more gluttonously than ever in food. "When the king returns from hunting," Mercy wrote Emperor Joseph II, "he eats such excessive meals that they cause absences of his reason, and a kind of rough carelessness that is very distressing for those who have to witness it." He was indeed witnessed to have eaten, for breakfast alone, four veal cutlets, a chicken, a plateful of ham, half a dozen eggs, and a bottle and a half of champagne. It is at this point that the king's enemies began to refer to him as "the fat pig."

In early October of 1787 I wrote my tender friend that I would try to return in a few weeks, and that she should stoke my stove with logs: for I would again be lodging on the top floor of Versailles, in that alcove above her apartments that always brought back such poignant memories. But we shared only a few joyous months together. I was recalled to Sweden again in 1788, to join my king on a disastrous campaign against Russia, which was trying to seize control of Finland. And it was in Stockholm that I was apprised of the worsening conditions in France, of the calamities that would lead up to that demonic event known as the French Revolution.

CHAPTER 6

Axel:

THE END OF THE WORLD
AS WE KNEW IT

EVEN THE WEATHER in the year 1788 was a disaster. In July a hail-storm flailed through much of France, ravaging wheat crops and causing the price of bread to soar. The winter of 1788–1789 was the coldest in decades. After I returned to Paris from Sweden that January the city remained covered with many inches of snow, and the icy ground was so treacherous to horses that I preferred to cross the frozen Seine on skates rather than traverse its bridges by coach. The frozen river hampered the provisioning of Paris, and there was great fear of a famine. The year's political events had been equally unfortunate: conflicts between parliamentarians and the Crown had already come to a head in the spring of 1788. Attempting to resolve the nation's dire financial crisis, Louis XVI had tried to force the Paris Parlement to levy a new tax stamp. The Parlement had replied that only the Estates-General—a representative assembly that had not met since 1614 and represented the three societal orders of clergy, nobility, and commoners, the latter of which was known as the "Third Estate"—had the right to levy new taxes. Increasingly desperate, Louis was reported to have gone to the queen's apartments every day to weep at the critical state of the kingdom. I knew all too well that the tenderhearted king was easily given to tears, but his recent bouts of grief seem to have been more pronounced than usual.

Having failed to convince Parlement on the issue of the stamp tax, he irately ordered that assembly recessed and arrested two of its dissenting leaders.

All of the nation's regional parlements declared solidarity with their Parisian counterpart, and antiroyalist demonstrations began to spread throughout the kingdom's major cities. They drew from all classes of society, from peasantry to nobility. In July 1788, the demonstrations grew particularly violent in Grenoble, whose royal governor resigned after his men were assaulted by rioting mobs; Grenoble's regional parlement hence called for a meeting of the Estates-General, a demand soon echoed by every parlement in the nation and ultimately, resentfully, agreed to by the king. Brittany's uprisings were equally fierce: when a delegation of Breton gentry came to present their grievances, Louis could think of nothing better to do than to jail them in the Bastille. Even graver tumults occurred in Paris in April of 1789, a few days before the opening of the Estates-General. On the twenty-seventh of that month a mob attacked the factories of Charles Réveillon, a wealthy paper manufacturer who had recently infuriated the working class by advocating lower wages as a means of reducing the national debt. Réveillon's headquarters were in the Faubourg Saint-Antoine, a few blocks from the Bastille, a traditional area for demonstrations of popular dissent.

On the first day of the riot a band of rebels paraded the millionaire's effigy through the city's streets, then ceremoniously burned it in front of the Hotel de Ville. The anti-Réveillon mob announced that it would continue its protests the following day. But the Paris police, though fully informed, took utterly pathetic measures: it sent thirty men to deal with the riots, a pitiful number with which to confront a thousand pillagers. On the twenty-eighth, Réveillon's own home was sacked, and the holdings of its famous wine cellars were drunk to the last drop, along with bottles of house paint, which made some of the rioters extremely ill.

Meanwhile the Paris police, finally alarmed, had sent two thousand Swiss Guards. The rioters, armed solely with stones, killed a few of the soldiers, and government troops responded with a fusillade that killed close to a hundred rebels. The Réveillon incident infuriated Paris's citizens, and led them to center their hopes all the more ardently on the event they had been looking forward to for the past year—the opening of the Estates-General.

On May 3, 1789, on the eve of their first meeting—I had just returned to Paris from Stockholm—I stood at a window overlooking the avenue de Versailles watching the 1,200 deputies to the Estates-General make their solemn procession toward the palace. Most of Paris had come to watch the spectacle. Thousands of women dressed in their most sumptuous finery stood on the balconies of the avenue's houses; windows, even roofs, were filled with citizens. The king led the procession, followed by the queen, followed by the Swiss Guard and a group of mounted royal falconers, each with a hooded falcon attached to his wrist. Next in line were the deputies to the three estates: the black-clothed priests of the common clergy and three hundred prelates in their sumptuous scarlet robes; three hundred nobles bristling with plumes and swords; the heralds who accompanied the nobles, dressed in purple velvet, mounted on white steeds, and blowing silver trumpets. I was particularly struck by the dignity of the Third Estate's five hundred members, who followed the nobles: merchants, men of letters, a great number of lawyers, whose simple black coats contrasted starkly with the satins and gold lace of the nobility. Observing these delegates, one could not help but be struck by the leonine, heavily pockmarked features of the Comte de Mirabeau, the greatest orator of the time: one of the few nobles to have been elected as a deputy from the Third Estate, this aristocratic radical was considered by many to be a traitor to his class, and was particularly hated by Marie Antoinette. "Mirabeau's huge head of hair distinguished him from everyone else," Madame de Staël would note in her description of the Estates-General's opening. "It was as if his strength derived from it, like Samson's; his face gained in expressiveness from its very ugliness, and his whole person suggested a strange power."

I should note that I was happy not to be in the queen's company that day. She had been relentlessly hostile to the convocation of the Estates-General. Whereas I, coming from a nation in which a parliament, the Swedish Riksdag, had held powerful sway since the Middle Ages, saw the estates as potentially helpful to the peaceful survival of the French monarchy. And our discussions of that issue had verged on the acrimonious. But notwithstanding our differences I was shocked and grieved by the crowd's reaction to the deputies' procession. Understandably, the greatest enthusiasm was granted to the deputies of the Third Estate. Of the nobles, only the shrewd Duc d'Orléans, fourth in line for the throne, who with typical deviousness had walked close to the Third Estate's ranks in order to be identified with them, was enthusiastically cheered. As for the queen, she had been met early on by shouts of "*Vive le Duc d'Orléans!*," as if the populace expressly wished to offend her by acclaiming her greatest enemy. The insult indeed affected her deeply; she was already greatly weakened by the grief caused by her older son, the dauphin, who would die the following month. Her steps faltered and she came close to fainting; her ladies-in-waiting had to hold on to her with all their strength. But with the help of the Princesse de Lamballe she soon recovered, and stared at the crowd with a firm, disdainful gaze. Oh, Toinette, whatever your sorrows, how out of touch you were with your adopted country, with its most urgent needs!

That was May. The most significant event of the following month was the clergy's decision to ally itself with the Third Estate, which represented 98 percent of the population. It had renamed itself "National Assembly," and had already won the support of many liberal nobles. In response to these new alliances, and against the advice of his minister of finances, the progressive Jacques Necker (whose daughter I'd once thought of marrying), Louis XVI had ordered the Estates-General's meeting place closed. On June 20, finding the doors of their assembly hall locked, the deputies moved on to the royal tennis courts nearby, the Jeu de Paume. There, led by France's greatest astronomer, Jean-Sylvain Bailly—whose specialty, I'd heard, was the moons of Jupiter—the delegates swore not to adjourn until they had drafted a constitution for France. In another misguided response, the king ordered the royal guard to disband the Estates-General. But a group of aristocratic deputies that included Mirabeau and France's most popular military leader, General Lafayette, placed their hands on their swords to signal their support of the Estates. "We shall only leave our places under the threat of bayonets," Mirabeau announced. My poor friend Louis had to back down once more, and made yet another faulty decision. Wishing to intimidate the National Assembly, and facing growing insubordination from his own troops, Louis secretly assigned sixteen extra regiments— most of them Swiss and German mercenaries—to surround Paris and Versailles. On July 10, in response to Mirabeau's protest against this massing of foreign troops, the king stated that they were merely meant to maintain public order. The following day, having markedly disagreed with Necker's advice to show greater support for the National Assembly, Louis sent the minister a letter of dismissal. Necker was idolized by the French people, and Parisians' reaction to his downfall was tumultuous. Green cockades, the color that traditionally symbolized the concept of liberty, immediately appeared on citizens' hats. Mobs assailed the Hotel de Ville, grabbing ammunition. Out of curiosity, I followed the crowds as tens of thousands of citizens marched through the city parading busts of their heroes, Necker and the Duc d'Orléans.

In the following days the bourgeois militia recently formed to protect the Estates-General from royalist attack—it was being called the National Guard and was led by Lafayette—would be further reinforced by defecting government troops. On the morning of July 14 a crowd decided to march on that symbol of royal despotism, the Bastille, where the troops guarding the fortress consisted of 110 men, 80 of them retired invalids. Shortly after noon, upon amiably inviting a delegation of demonstrators to visit the prison, the Bastille's governor, Marquis de Launay, promised not to attack any rioters unless his soldiers were fired on first. But the band of rebels lingered in the fortress; the crowd grew impatient, suspecting a trap. When a second group of citizens entered one of the fortress's interior courtyards, seeking news of their comrades, de Launay thought he was being attacked and ordered his men to shoot. Ninety-eight persons were killed, and seventy wounded. News of the carnage spread swiftly through the city, and from then on there was no way of stopping a bloodbath. Several detachments of Lafayette's National Guard marched on the Bastille with cannons it had seized from the government. In midafternoon, de Launay surrendered his fortress to the mob, which rushed into the bastion to liberate its seven remaining inmates: they consisted of four forgers, a libertine nobleman, and two lunatics, one of whom was an aged man with a waist-length beard who called himself the Major of Immensity and asked for news of Louis XV's health. De Launay had been promised safe passage to the Hotel de Ville but was killed on the way, at place de Grève, where a young pastry cook hacked off his head with a pocket knife and placed it on a pike. By the evening of July 14 the capture of the ancien régime's most formidable emblem had spread terror among France's privileged classes. Most princes of the blood, including Artois, made plans to leave Paris in the following days to seek refuge abroad, as did many of the nation's most powerful nobles. (The queen's friend, Duchesse de Polignac, governess of the royal children, was among the first to leave the country.)

As for the king and queen, safely sheltered in the spectral routine of Versailles, throughout the day of July 14 they had remained totally ignorant of what was happening in the capital. It was an aristocrat of liberal sympathies, Duc de La Rochefoucauld-Liancourt, who woke Louis XVI a bit after midnight to break the news to him.

"Is it a revolt?" the king asked Liancourt upon being told of the seizure of the Bastille.

"No, sire, it is a revolution," Liancourt replied.

MUCH HAS BEEN said about the king and queen's decision to remain at Versailles after July 14, and not travel, as most of their friends and relatives had, to some more secure site. The most popular of suggested cities was Metz, in northwestern France: close to the border of the Austrian Netherlands, it was one of Europe's most powerfully fortified towns. Marie Antoinette had approved of the idea of moving there, and had even begun to pack. But the king, at first undecided, eventually heeded the advice of his brother Comte de Provence, who had stayed put in the Parisian area, and had advised him to do the same. Some years later the king told me that he greatly regretted not having left Versailles on July 14. "I should have gone then and I wanted to; but what could I do when Monsieur himself [Provence] begged me not to go, and the Marshal de Broglie, commander of my troops, told me: 'Yes, we can go to Metz, but what shall we do when we get there?' " The king then repeated sadly: "I missed my opportunity, and it never came again."

I remained in Paris throughout much of that year. Within a week of the capture of the Bastille there developed paranoid rumors in France that hordes of homeless brigands sympathetic to the Revolution were roaming throughout the country, pillaging property and murdering members of the more privileged classes. My family's panic concerning "the Great Fear," as it came to be called throughout Europe, was acute. Since they were concerned that as one of the royal family's closest friends I might come to harm, I wrote more often than usual, in the following months, to my father, and also to my king. I told them that all carriages were stopped in Paris, and everyone was forced to go on foot. All was confusion, disorder, consternation. The Comte d'Artois and his children, and the Princes de Condé, Conti, and Bourbon, among many others, had fled under assumed names to protect themselves from the mob. Every day numerous citizens were leaving the city, and unless quiet was restored, by winter it would be deserted.

July 22, 1789

Riots are taking place in all the cities of the kingdom. . . . The prisons have been opened, and it is that kind of rabble who creates the disorder. The bourgeoisie immediately armed itself, and that may help to restore tranquillity. The brigands, the *canaille*, are spread throughout the country; they're pillaging . . . all the abbeys and châteaus; they're hunted everywhere, and yesterday, in one spot, we captured one hundred and nineteen of them; many more will probably be taken.

That, my dear father, is this country's sad news; it is in a state of violent crisis; we must now see what the Estates-General will do; but at this moment all bonds are broken; obedience has disappeared in the army, and I doubt if it will be as easy to restore order as it was to overthrow it.

ON AUGUST 4 another uprising began. Stones were thrown at the windows of the archbishop of Paris. A few nobles considered particularly hostile to the Revolution were shot and hung up on streetlamps. In order to quell the disarray that ensued in the Assembly, the king, with extreme reluctance, signed the Declaration of the Rights of Man drafted by Lafayette (it goes without saying that it had been written with the American model in mind—the American ambassador, Thomas Jefferson, had even added to it a few grace notes of his own). To the queen's despair, Louis XVI also acceded to having the blue, white, and red cockade that was the revolutionaries' principal symbol attached to his hat. As for many members of the nobility and the more privileged bourgeoisie, they embarked on an orgy of dispossession. My former comrade in arms Vicomte de Noailles suggested the abolition of all feudal dues. The Vicomte de Beauharnais decreed that all citizens would have equal rights of admission to any military or civil office. To the horror of much of the clergy, the Duc du Chatelet proposed the abolition of church tithes. The Marquis de Saint-Fargeau propounded the extinction of all exclusive rights to game—henceforth peasants could kill any animals interfering with their crops, or needed for their own nourishment. The customers of my favorite café, the Procope, also frequented by Danton, were equally inflamed with this passion for altruistic giving: they filled a tub with silver buckles from their shoes and carried them to the Assembly. In the following weeks, a delegation of painters' wives, including Mesdames David, Vernet, and Fragonard, appeared before the Assembly to offer it their jewels, one of them saying that they "would blush to wear these baubles when patriotism incited all citizens to self-sacrifice." After a vote of gratitude, the ladies were given a torchlight procession to the Louvre with an honor guard from the Academy of Painting, while a band played an old tune, much fancied by my mother, that was becoming a cult song of the Revolution, "Where Better Could One Be Than in the Bosom of One's Family?" Meanwhile disorder was increasing throughout the country. Paris was the focus of trouble, and everyone was in haste to leave it. Numerous vagabonds and deserters were taking refuge there. They were being taken into the new militia—the National Guard—which was under the command of the Marquis de Lafayette.

The king's authority remained null. Paris trembled before forty to fifty thousand bandits and vagrants established at Montmartre or in the Palais-Royal. Members of the urban bourgeoisie were intoxicated with the notion, long expounded by the philosophes, that all men are equal; and the abolition of feudal rights (voted so glibly by the National Assembly in a three-hour session) had persuaded citizens that they had nothing to pay anymore. I wrote my father that summer, from my army post at Valenciennes, to sum up these events.

Valenciennes, August 15th, 1789

Any man in the nation can volunteer for the National Guard—mere valets can become lieutenants overnight. They have better pay than in our regiments and every effort is made to entice them. According to the war office, since July 13th there have been 12,570 deserters. The king's authority is totally annulled, as is that of the parliaments and the magistrates; the Estates-General themselves tremble before Paris, and this fear greatly influences their deliberations. In this kingdom there are no laws, order, justice, discipline, or religion anymore; all bonds are broken; and how can they be reestablished? Such are the effects of Anglomania and philosophy. France is ruined for a long time to come.

Valenciennes, September 8, 1789

Everywhere the rabble are committing frightful excesses against the châteaus of the nobles, which they pillage and burn along with deeds and papers; they even maltreat the owners if they find them there. . . . In urban centers insurgents have broken into the offices of tax collectors and driven them away. The taxes cannot be collected. The king will soon be unable to meet his financial commitments, and bankruptcy is imminent. The nobles are in despair; the clergy is going out of its mind, and even the Third Estate is wholly dissatisfied: it is the *canaille* who reign, and they are satisfied because having nothing to lose, they can only gain. No one dares to command, and no one is willing to obey.

Such is France's state at this moment. One shudders at the sight of these events, and it is impossible to foresee how they will end. All this makes me very unhappy. I share with you, my dear father, the attachment you have for France, and I cannot witness its ruin without sorrow. Many regiments have mutinied; some have even attacked their chief officers. In our regiments things have not yet gone so far, but our soldiers did force open the gates of the town and for three days went out to drink in the country, where they committed horrible excesses. On the third day they would certainly have pillaged the town and set it on fire if citizens had not stopped them. Aided by the bourgeois militia, we have now reestablished order and quiet.

Less than three months after the capture of the Bastille—on October 5, 1789—another dreadful rebellion took place. Angered by the king's continued defiance of the National Assembly and above all incited by the high price of bread, Parisian working women organized a march on Versailles that within a few hours would turn as violent as the fall of the Bastille.

The queen had been at the Petit Trianon the earlier part of that day. I had arrived at Versailles a week earlier, to spend the winter in a house I'd acquired in town. We had spent the morning in one of the bowers she so loved, reading to each other from Rousseau's *La nouvelle Héloise*. The king was shooting in the woods above Meudon. I returned to Versailles with the queen in time for dinner; but a half hour after we'd sat down the Comte and Comtesse de Provence rushed into her quarters in a state of great agitation, followed by an emissary from the Comte de Saint Priest. Several thousand Parisians, they announced, were marching on Versailles. The queen immediately demanded that guardsmen be sent to find the king, and bring him home.

The band of women, most of whom came from the Faubourg Saint-Antoine, the same festering Parisian area in which the events of July 14 had taken place, had gathered at the Hotel de Ville and headed for Versailles before noon. Armed with pikes, sickles, and guns, they were undaunted by the pouring rain and the muddy roads. Versailles, as one can imagine, was in turmoil. We courtiers were unarmed that day, for at the palace none of us were allowed to carry more than a decorative sword. However, the Versailles National Guard and the Flanders regiment stood with their backs to the gates of the royal courtyard, ready for battle. Upon being brought news of the women's march the king immediately left for home, galloping all the way up Versailles's Grande Avenue; he arrived at three, and cloistered himself in the Council Room with the queen and his ministers. A series of agitated discussions, the queen told me later, took place concerning the royal family's preparation for the expected invasion. Would it be more secure to decamp to Rambouillet, twice the distance of Versailles from Paris and far more secure? The king was determined to stay. Marie Antoinette also rejected the idea of leaving, wishing to remain at her husband's side, as she had during the July uprising. A message that Lafayette and his National Guard were on the way relieved the royal family. But no decision on how to deal with the protests had yet been made by the time the market women arrived.

The first of them reached Versailles at about four o'clock. Drenched to the bone by rain, most of them took refuge at the Assembly, while a delegation of them—half a dozen women—hastened to find the king. When they reached the antechamber of Louis's quarters, the Oeil-de-Boeuf, he was still conferring with his ministers. Exhausted by the long, wet march and dazzled by the splendor of the palace, many of the women were overcome by timidity when confronted with their monarch. One of them, the king later reported, fainted. Another, bolder one, who had been assigned to do the speaking, harangued the king concerning Parisians' need for bread. The king told her that he would order the directors of two granaries to release all possible stores, and gave her a copy of the order in writing. The women left, some satisfied, some still murmuring angrily, some threatening that they had worn their aprons in order to carry the queen's entrails, with which they intended to make cockades.

An additional mob of women arrived at 8 p.m., after nightfall, and all of us heard them howling, "Bread, bread, bread!" The king was still conferring with his advisers. A group of courtiers—I was among them—joined him in his study. There were more pleas on our part that the royal family leave for Rambouillet, or Normandy. Paralyzed, as usual, by indecision, Louis kept repeating, "A fugitive king! A fugitive king!" He asked to speak privately to the queen, and after a few minutes recalled his advisers and ordered that his carriages be prepared. Marie Antoinette hastened toward her children's quarters. "We're leaving in a quarter of an hour, hurry," she told their new governess, Madame de Tourzel, the kind, calm widow who had been appointed to take care of the royal children when Madame de Polignac had left for exile abroad.

But as soon as the crowd, many of whom were bivouacked in the place d'Armes, saw the carriages being led out of the stables, they were enraged. "The king is leaving!" the cry rang out. A mob assaulted the carriages, cut the harnesses, and led the horses away. Panicked, the king and queen decided not to leave after all. By then it was 10 p.m. Marie Antoinette conferred with Madame de Tourzel. They decided that if there were to be any cause for alarm, the dauphin and Madame Royale should seek refuge in the king's apartments. The royal family was somewhat reassured when General de Lafayette arrived on his great white horse, splattered with mud. He reassured the king that Parisians would not turn violent. The king and his friends were relieved by his words, and entrusted him with the security of Versailles; Louis decided to retire, and urged the queen that she do the same. I left the palace shortly after 1 a.m., along with the rest of the courtiers. By two in the morning, everyone at Versailles had gone to bed.

Meanwhile some of the Parisian invaders had found shelter in stables, churches, and taverns; but most of them camped out on the Place d'Armes in front of the château. Groups of men and women sat around bonfires, eating, drinking, and singing. But shortly before dawn there were drumbeats, signifying a call to action. Several women had noticed that the gates into the chapel courtyard were open. The crowd started for the palace, some assembling under the king's window, while others ran up the queen's stairway. They massacred one of the queen's bodyguards on the way; another was killed at the entrance to the queen's apartment.

The queen had been awakened shortly before six by a noise coming from the terrace. Her chambermaid reassured her that some of the Parisian women were probably assembled there. But suddenly a voice called out from the guardroom, "Save the queen!" Marie Antoinette jumped out of bed, put on a dressing gown, and ran down the stairs to the king's bedroom, which was empty. The king, in fact, had put on his robe and rushed to the queen's quarters. His guards reassured him that their paths must have crossed. The king next set out to the dauphin's quarters and returned to his apartments, the child wrapped in his arms. It was still totally dark, his candle went out, and he told his attendants to hold on to his robe. Finding their way through the dark as best they could, his retinue reached the dining hall, where the queen had just arrived. She was worried about her daughter and rushed down an interior stairway to get her; within moments the entire family was reunited, joined by Madame Elisabeth, the king's sister, and the king's aunts, *Mesdames Tantes*. Soon General de Lafayette reappeared, having just saved some thirty of the king's body guards who had fallen to the mob.

As the gang of women approached the royal apartments the queen stood in front of a desk, between her daughter, Madame Royale, and Madame Elisabeth, the king's sister. The four-year-old dauphin—the former Duc de Normandie, whom I cherished—stood in front of her, tugging at his sister's hair and repeatedly saying, "Maman, I'm hungry." Louis XVI was still consulting with his ministers in a neighboring room, but Lafayette returned and convinced the sovereigns to step out onto the balcony. So the royal family came out and faced thousands of their citizens, the queen holding her daughter by the hand and clutching the dauphin in her arms. I was standing with the shouting mob, a few hundred feet away from my cherished friend; how I wish I could have given her a sign of reassurance! "No children!" a voice suddenly shouted. Marie Antoinette took the children back into the king's room and faced the crowd all alone. She made a deep curtsy, her hands crossed on her chest. It is to this moment that I trace the emergence of the great latent strength in the queen's character that had remained muted during the sovereigns' years of prosperity. Those in the crowd who had been jeering her moments earlier seemed to be awed by her simplicity and dignity. For the first time in years Marie Antoinette heard shouts of "Long live the queen!"

But there were even louder shouts of "To Paris, to Paris!" For by this time the mob's original objective of securing food had been replaced by the determination to transfer the royal family to the French capital. The queen walked back into the palace. "They're going to force us to go to Paris," she said tearfully, "the king and me, preceded by the heads of our bodyguards on pikes." The clamor outside grew increasingly menacing. After a few more minutes of discussions with his ministers, the king, the queen, and Lafayette went out together onto the balcony. "My friends," said the king in his loudest, most assertive voice, "I shall go to Paris with my family; I entrust what is most precious to me to the love of my good and loyal subjects." Great applause followed as the royal family went inside.

After returning to her quarters, the queen assembled her jewels to bring them to Paris, while the king, in his study, hastily gathered his most important papers. Lafayette had the carriages readied again and prepared all details for the family's departure. They began to leave at one o'clock. Most of the crowd had dispersed; the palace precincts were more or less tranquil. The queen and king, their children, Madame Elisabeth, and Madame de Tourzel got into the same coach and set off toward the capital; they were surrounded by a mob made tumultuous by yet more wine, some of whom carried pikes surmounted by the decapitated heads of the queen's bodyguards. The queen's face showed signs, Madame Elisabeth reported, of "violent grief." From time to time the king covered his face with his handkerchief to hide his tears. At the front and rear of the immense cortege was the National Guard. The royal carriage was escorted by Lafayette and followed by hundreds of coaches filled with delegates to the National Assembly and whatever members of the court of France who had remained in Versailles and not fled abroad. Behind them was a train of wagons and carts filled with flour from the royal bins. I traveled in a carriage a few hundred feet in back of the royal family. Trying to avert my gaze from the sight of the slain bodyguards' mutilated heads, I hoped against hope that someone in the queen's carriage would keep her from seeing the same horrifying vision. "We're bringing back the baker, the baker's wife, and the baker's little boy!" the mob walking alongside the royal coach shouted loudly throughout the twelve miles that separate Versailles from Paris.

The royal family had been advised that they would not be living at the Louvre, home of several ancestors of Louis XVI, but at the Tuileries, a huge 386-room building overlooking the Seine that had originally been built in the sixteenth century by Catherine de Médicis. They were met at the Chaillot tollgate by the mayor of Paris, Jean-Sylvain Bailly, who offered the king the keys to Paris on a velvet pillow. It was eight o'clock, already getting dark. However ardently the royal family wished to get to their new quarters at the Tuileries, they had to go first to the Hotel de Ville, where they again had to appear on a balcony, and were acclaimed by yet another excited crowd. How I would have wished to accompany my friends to their new home, and help them settle in as comfortably as possible! But it would have been madness on my part to thus compromise the queen. I left the royal procession a few minutes before it reached the Tuileries. And a few days later I wrote a brief note to my father about the day's dreadful events, the news of which, I was sure, had spread throughout Europe.

Paris, October 9th, 1789

All the newspapers have probably told you, my dear father, of what happened at Versailles on Monday 5th and Tuesday 6th, and of the King's coming to Paris with his family. I witnessed it all and I returned to Paris in one of the carriages of the King's suite; we were six and a half hours on the way. God keep me from ever again seeing anything as afflicting as the events of those two days.

The people seem enchanted to see the King and his family; the Queen is much applauded, and she can not fail to be when they get to know her, and do justice to her goodness and the kindness of her heart.

Toward the end of the year 1789 I rejoined my regiment at Valenciennes. I quelled a rebellion that had arisen in its ranks, and punished its leaders. I then received orders from Gustavus to return to Paris and to remain there near the king of France in order to facilitate communication between the two sovereigns. For my monarch was clearly alarmed by the impact that the French Revolution might have on other European nations, and greatly feared similar uprisings. Although I myself was terrified of the Revolution's impact on the French king and queen, I sought to allay his panic as best I could.

To His Majesty, the King of Sweden

January 7, 1790

. . . The detailed manner in which Your Majesty has approached the affairs of Sweden and France are a new proof of kindness by which I am deeply touched. France's situation is distressing, and Y.M. has grasped it from the right point of view. I believe, as you do, that M. Necker is very guilty, and that nothing short of a civil or a foreign war can restore

France and the royal authority; but how is that to be brought about, with the King a prisoner in Paris? It was a false step to allow him to be brought there. Now it becomes necessary to try to get him out of it. . . .

Once out of Paris, the King ought to be able to create a new political order. . . . His party is already much increased in the Assembly and in the provinces; the courage, firmness, and good conduct of the Queen have brought many back to her. All the nobles, except a few who are not worthy of being such, are devoted to her, as is the clergy. . . . Only the *canaille* is still stirred up by the famous words "despotism" and "aristocracy."

The noble, compassionate, and generous manner in which Y.M. expresses Himself on the situation of the King and Queen of France is worthy of Y.M. The letters that Y.M. sends to the King and Queen can only touch them—one is always more sensitive to kindness when unhappy. The assignment that Y.M. offers me is so appealing I could not fail to fulfill it.

I came here from Valenciennes two days ago to see about Taube. . . . I'm not satisfied with his state of health.

I am, Sire, with the most profound respect, Your Majesty's very humble and obedient servant and faithful subject.

CHAPTER 7

Axel:

AT THE TUILERIES

OBEYING GUSTAVUS'S ORDERS, I returned to Paris at the end of January 1790 and remained there for another year and a half. So I witnessed the royal family's adjustment to their new quarters at the Tuileries Palace, which had seldom been inhabited since Louis XIV (he had briefly lived there for a few months before moving to Versailles in 1682). Three decades later it would be occupied by Louis XV when he was still a minor, from 1715 to 1722. Since then the enormous building had been divided into apartments and assigned to courtiers, and to Parisian artisans and artists; they were all instantly evicted on October 6 to make room for the royal family. "Maman, it's so ugly here!" the dauphin had exclaimed upon entering the Tuileries. But within a few weeks the edifice was made relatively comfortable. Furniture was moved from Versailles to make the place cozier. The queen had three rooms on the ground floor, and a little library upstairs next to her daughter's bedroom. Louis XVI and the dauphin shared an apartment above the queen's, connected to it by a small private staircase. Madame Elisabeth and the Princesse de Lamballe lived in the Pavillon de Flore, where they had a view of the Seine. The remaining rooms were distributed among Madame de Tourzel, the courtiers who had accompanied the royal family, and the domestic servants.

These close quarters, unusual for any royals, created a very close family life. Marie Antoinette spent the morning attending to her children's lessons, and the king frequently joined them, making Marie-Thérèse and the dauphin recite what they had learned that day. The royal couple dined en famile with their daughter and Madame Elisabeth; Marie Antoinette then played billiards with her husband to give him a limited amount of exercise. In the afternoons she wrote letters or did needlework until supper, at which the royals were joined by the Comte and Comtesse de Provence. The Tuileries gardens remained open to the public, as most of the Versailles Palace had been, and Parisians flocked there, displaying immense curiosity toward the royal family. The king and queen, in turn, instructed their children to be unfailingly amiable toward visitors and to the National Guards, even though they did not trust the latter. The four-year-old dauphin tried hard to carry out his parents' wishes, running to his mother and whispering, "Was that good?" when he spoke to one of the visitors.

Yet notwithstanding this new intimacy, most court rituals were maintained. Though etiquette was more relaxed than at Versailles, the monarchs still continued the ceremony of the *lever* and *coucher*, and the tradition of lunching in public a few days a week. However, balls and concerts were banned, and the sovereigns tried hard to dramatize their captive state. The king refused to go out of the palace, and for the first time since his adolescence abstained from riding and hunting. The queen also restricted herself to the Tuileries, never attending any operas or plays, and rarely showing herself in public. This reticence was interpreted as proof of her coldness and haughtiness; within a few months both monarchs grew aware of their subjects' disapproval, and ended their isolation to a degree. They visited such institutions as foundling hospitals and glass manufacturers in the Faubourg Saint-Antoine. The king reviewed the troops. Marie Antoinette took her children out for drives around the city again.

However, the queen did not trust her new guards, and at first was wary of receiving visitors in her new quarters. Although she maintained a cheerful front for the sake of her children, she was deeply unhappy in her new life, as she confided on December 29, 1789, in a letter to Madame de Polignac, who was exiled in Switzerland.

"Our troubles, those of our friends, and those of everyone around us, make a load too heavy to bear. And if my heart were not so bound to my children, and to you . . . I would often wish to die. . . . The *chou d'amour* is charming, and I love him to distraction. . . . He's very well, growing strong, and no longer throws tantrums." In a postscript to this missive the queen cryptically added: "I have seen him. After three months of grief and separation . . . the person and I managed to see each other safely once. You know us both, so you can imagine our happiness."

She was of course referring to me, and we had indeed shared a day of blissful reunion that Christmas week. "At last on the 24th I spent the whole day with Her," I wrote my sister. "Imagine my joy."

Sophie and her lover, Evert Taube, were the only persons in the world to whom I had confided my love for Marie Antoinette. I had restrained from similarly informing Gustavus. My king, notwithstanding his great qualities, was such a chatterbox that although I always praised the queen in my letters to him I referred to her with formality and circumspection.

A POLITICAL HIGHLIGHT of the year was the monarchs' decision to consult the all-powerful Mirabeau, who was eager to convince the king to accept a constitution, and had been writing the sovereigns copious notes about the political situation. Louis XVI had originally refused to meet with this libertine radical, whom he considered to be one of those responsible for the Revolution. However, the queen, being far more

cunning than her husband, consented to a secret conference with Mirabeau even though she had always found him repellent and referred to
him as "a rascal" whose "whole existence is deceit, cunning, and lies."
She met the tall, courtly, heavily pockmarked nobleman at night, in her
apartments, and the meeting lasted for nearly an hour. Mirabeau did
most of the talking, imploring Marie Antoinette to not heed the partisans of the counterrevolution, who were exiled in Belgium and other
countries and led by Artois. She listened to Mirabeau with immense
attention, and he was enormously impressed with her courage, wisdom,
and sagacity. As he was taking leave of her, the queen held out her hand
to him with that graciousness unique to her; "The monarchy is saved!"
he whispered as he knelt down to kiss it. "The king has only one man
with him—his wife," Mirabeau wrote to a friend after their meeting.

That summer of 1790, the royal family was allowed to move to Saint-
Cloud, where the queen's spirits improved considerably. She invited
actors and musicians to the château, and she sang again, accompanying
herself on the clavichord. I had taken quarters at Auteuil, not far from
Saint-Cloud, and joined her in her apartments on most evenings. Were
we throwing caution to the winds again? Tongues wagged, but she did
not seem to care. I was almost arrested one night, when I was leaving
the park of Saint-Cloud at three in the morning. The Comte de Saint-
Priest warned the queen that my nocturnal visits could prove to be dangerous. "Tell that to him," she replied impatiently. "As for myself, I
don't care." Never had my feelings for the queen been more tender. "She
is the most perfect creature I know," I wrote to Sophie. ". . . She is
extremely unhappy and very courageous. She is an angel. I try to console her as best I can, I owe it to her, she is so wonderful to me. My only
sorrow lies in not being able to fully console her for all her misfortunes,
and not making her as happy as she deserves to be."

As for my relations with the king, they can best be described as a
watchful amity. How aware was he of my true relations with the queen?

I know that he totally trusted, and was most grateful for, my loyalty and devotion to his cause. And even though I deplored his political judgments, I respected, and was deeply moved by, his integrity and the goodness of his heart. The queen, meanwhile, had used all her feminine wiles to convince the king that her relationship with me was totally innocent. While intimating that I was the only friend whom they could blindly trust, she was forthright to her husband about all the public gossip concerning our affair, and offered to stop seeing me, which Louis refused. Although he never gave any overt sign that he either suspected a liaison or was troubled by it, I imagine that in truth the unfathomable king was aware of his wife's love for me. Louis's friends were so few that he may well have realized he could not afford to lose the support of a man known for his zeal and his devotion to the royal cause. Or might it be possible that the king concealed his jealousy for many years, and made use of my talents with the intention of sidelining me at a later moment?

I SHOULD RIGHT NOW admit that I was not exclusively absorbed, at this period of my life, by my love for the queen and my deep concern for the fate of the royal family. In the fall of 1789—the first months of the monarchs' seclusion at the Tuileries—intimacy with my beloved Toinette had become harder to come by. And I'd become the prey of an aggressive beauty called Eleanore Sullivan, a voluptuous Italian-born brunette with milky skin and large onyx eyes who had spent her early years as a dancer and trapezist with an ambulating actors' troupe. She had already passed through the arms—and beds—of many prominent men. First came the Duke of Württemberg, to whom she bore a daughter. Next in line was Emperor Joseph II, Marie Antoinette's brother, though that liaison was made brief by Empress Maria Theresa's irate demand that Eleanore leave the country. Upon moving to Paris, Eleanore had married an Irish diplomat, Mr. Sullivan, who took her to India, where he was seeking to increase his fortune. It was in India that she met Quentin Craufurd, a very rich Scotsman who had made his money in the British colony of Manila through his dealings with the East India Company (he was referred to as "the nabob of Manila"). Craufurd swiftly captured Eleanore from the inconsequential Sullivan in the early 1780s and brought her back to Paris, where they settled in a large house on the rue de Clichy. It was graced with Craufurd's sumptuous paintings and furniture, which soon came to be looked on as one of Paris's most reputed art collections. His intelligence, wealth, and notoriously fine eye for art endeared him to many of Paris's preeminent aristocrats. The Duc de Lauzun, the Vicomte de Noailles, and Talleyrand, to whom he often loaned money, were among his friends. His two-volume history of Indian civilization, translated into French by the Comte de Montesquiou, had been exceedingly well received. A British comrade of his, the Marquess of Hutley, had introduced him to Marie Antoinette, who took a great shine to him and always referred to him as "*ce bon* Craufurd." In sum, Craufurd was one of Paris's most distinguished expatriates.

I met Craufurd in 1789 at the Club de Valois, a gentlemen's association I belonged to at which we played many a game of backgammon. He invited me to his home to meet Eleanore, and I very soon became her lover, a pleasure that remained unknown to Craufurd for some years to come because of his very frequent trips to London. Being devoted to the queen, my sister worried a great deal about my relationship to Eleanore. "I'm warning you, dear Axel, for the love of Her to whom it would cause a fatal blow if she heard the news. Everyone is watching you and talking about you. Think of unhappy Her. Spare her the most fatal pain of all." Such kind cautions, for the time being, remained unheeded. Both of my new friends—Craufurd and Eleanore, the latter of whom had loving memories of her tryst with Joseph II, were ardent supporters of Marie Antoinette. Ah Eleanore of the engulfing mouth and round, invasive arms. . . . Much more about you later on. I merely wished to record another aspect of my life during the years in which I continued to write my father about France's worsening crisis.

Paris, February 1, 1790

What a frightful situation this kingdom is in! It is complete anarchy. All bonds are dissolved; there is no obedience to laws, no respect for religion, which does not exist except in name. The people have learned to use its strength, and is doing it with ferocity. The nobles, clergy, and parliament, who set the first examples of disobedience and resistance, are the first victims; they are ruined and their châteaus burned. The upper bourgeoisie, who were also seduced, now repent, but it is too late. Workmen, manufacturers, and artisans are all ruined and dissatisfied, for purses are closed. . . . Numerous persons incited by hatreds, jealousies, and private revenge have conducted themselves badly toward the king and have forgotten their obligations to him. . . . They are inciting the *canaille* with the great words "liberty," "despotism," and "aristocracy."

The National Assembly continues its folly. The provinces are in greater ferment than ever, and the king is a prisoner in Paris. His position—and above all that of the queen, who suffers from their captivity much more keenly than he does—is dreadful. The queen has shown and still shows a courage, character, and conduct that have won her many adherents.

THE QUEEN HAD TO suffer another great grief in that wretched year of 1790—the death of her beloved brother Joseph II. The emperor's health had been failing in recent months, but he had continued to do everything possible to help his younger sister. "I'm so cruelly tormented about her fate," he had written after the march on Versailles of October 5, 1789; "the dangers the Queen faced and still faces make me shudder." A few months later he had prevented an armed incursion into Provence by the Comte d'Artois and a force of émigré army officers, which would have been a calamity for the royal family. During his final days he had written his sister that one of his most bitter regrets about dying was to leave her in such a cruel position, and not be able to prove the deep love he had always felt for her. He passed away on February 20, 1790, a week after he had sent her that last letter. The queen sequestered herself in her apartments for several days, weeping. Joseph was succeeded by his younger brother Leopold, Grand Duke of Tuscany, whom Marie Antoinette had not seen since she was ten years old; and though he instantly offered her his support, he would prove to be untrustworthy, and would only live for another two years.

I continued to write my father about the events in France.

Paris, April 2, 1790

Little change. . . . Poverty and discontent are increasing; they are beginning to affect the people, especially Parisians, who now find themselves without resources owing to the diminution and annihilation of fortunes occasioned by the Assembly's decrees. There are persons who have lost 40,000 to 50,000 francs a year, and others their whole revenue, because of the abolition of feudal rights. Most of the workmen and artisans are reduced to beggary. The best workmen are leaving the Kingdom, and the streets are full of paupers. One and all they blame the Assembly. . . . The royal treasury is exhausted; there is neither credit nor confidence; money has disappeared, everyone hoards it. That, my dear father, is the present state of things. God knows how it will end. Necker's state is worse than ever; his health is quite destroyed, and I don't believe he will live long. He'll be regretted by very few.

Paris, June 28, 1790

You will read about the state of the army in the newspapers; there is no longer any order or discipline. Soldiers form committees, they dismiss, break, judge, and sometimes execute their officers. Every day we hear of new horrors, and there is no longer any pleasure in serving. My regiment [the Royal Swedish] has behaved marvelously well up to now, even though everything has been done to seduce it. There has not been the slightest insubordination, and I hope this may continue.

Although the queen's spirits had revived upon moving to Saint-Cloud, she was bound to find the first Feast of the Federation, which commemorated the fall of the Bastille, to be a depressing event. I described the episode to my father.

Paris, July 16, 1790

The famous Feast of the Federation, which had inspired such fears and driven so many persons out of Paris, has just been celebrated. The ceremony, which might have been very august, very fine, and very imposing, was made ridiculous by its disorder and indecency. It was held at the Champ de Mars; you will see a description of it in the papers. But what the papers will not tell you is that no one was in his right place; the soldiers, who ought to have guarded the area, obeyed no one; they ran about hither and thither, dancing and singing. Before the arrival of the king and his troops, they took a priest and two monks from the altar, and, putting grenadiers' caps on their heads and muskets on their shoulders, they marched them around the amphitheater, singing and dancing like savages do before they eat Christians. People also sang and danced during the Mass, and no one knelt at the moment of the elevation of the Host, which led many persons who were present to declare that the Mass was not said at all.

In order to remain near the queen, I spent the rest of the summer at Auteuil, near Saint-Cloud, in the house lent to me by my friend Valentin Esterhazy. I saw my Toinette nearly every day, and was most unhappy at the end of October when I had to return to Paris ("that vile cesspit," as I described it to Sophie). But there was a great deal to do; above all I had to urge the king to reassert his authority. For the Assembly had decreed the abolition of the nobility, and nationalized all Crown property; church lands were being sequestered and sold off to speculators; the deficit was still speedily rising, which led the now discredited Jacques Necker to resign. The ministers whom Louis appointed in his place proved to be equally unable to help the nation, and there were violent protests throughout the country. The Civil Constitution of the Clergy, which wrenched the French church away from Rome, dictating that bishops and other clerics would be directly elected by French citizens and owe their ultimate allegiance to the state rather than the king, had just been decreed, and was sure to be vetoed by Louis XVI. Yet another danger was being caused by the king's brothers: Comtes d'Artois and de Provence, exiled in Koblenz, were raising an émigré army with the ultimate intention of invading France from the Austrian border and restoring the ancien régime by force, which might well have led to the execution of the royal family.

Paris, November 5, 1790

Disorders increase daily [I wrote my father]. . . . Poverty is felt everywhere; coin has disappeared; *"assignats,"* the paper money that has replaced it, have little or no credit; in many of the provinces the people will not take them at all. The merchants sell nothing; manufactures are at a standstill; provisions grow dearer. Paris is full of thieves; one hears of nothing but robberies committed, and since there is little law and order they remain unpunished. This state of things can not last, and the growing discontent will slowly lead to some kind of change; when the dissatisfaction will have greatly risen, the new order of things will be as quickly overthrown as the old order was; such is the volatility of the French.

I was made happy that winter by the increasingly tender emotions that had developed through the correspondence between the queen and my sister, who asked me for a lock of the queen's hair, which she wished to set into a ring. "Here is the hair you asked for," I wrote Sophie; "if there isn't enough I'll send you some more. It is *She* who gives it to you, and she was deeply touched by your request. She is so good and so perfect, and I seem to love her even more now that she loves you."

My father, however, was still grieved and angered by my long absences from Sweden. And I often had to placate him by explaining the royal family's urgent need of me, and my intense emotional need to remain with them, as I did in the following letter.

February 15, 1791

My position here is different from that of everyone else. I have always been treated with kindness and distinction in this country by the king and queen and by their ministers. Your reputation, my dear father, has been my passport and my recommendation. . . . My discreet conduct may also have won me approbation and esteem. I'm attached to the king and queen, as I ought to be because of the immensely kind manner with which they always treated me . . . and I would be vile and ungrateful if I abandoned them now. To all the many kindnesses they've offered me, they have now added a flattering new one—that of confidence; and it is all the more flattering because it is limited to four persons, of whom I am the youngest.

If I can serve them, what pleasure I shall have in returning part of the numerous favors they have done me; what sweet enjoyment to contribute to their welfare! You can not but approve of me, dear Father. . . . This conduct is the only one that is worthy of your son. . . . In the course of this coming summer, the situation here must surely change, and decisions be reached: if it evolves badly and all hope is lost, nothing will then prevent me from returning to you.

. . .

IN APRIL OF 1791 the Comte de Mirabeau died. Many thought that he had been poisoned, and the Duc d'Orléans, who was out to undermine the king's power by any means he could, was suspected by some. The great orator had made a few pro-royalist speeches in the Assembly that proved highly popular, and his passing ended the king's chances of restoring order through peaceful means. That spring, the king and queen asked me my advice concerning their situation, and I gave them my opinion in a long missive. I reiterated, as I had numerous times in past months, that it was imperative for them to leave Paris, that their only way of surviving those increasingly monstrous revolutionaries was to flee the country. And I offered to be in charge of planning their escape. I'd already given the project much thought. According to the evasion route I'd devised, the royal family would head toward the town of Montmédy, on the border of the Austrian Netherlands, and there establish a rallying site at which they would be joined by émigré forces and those army regiments that had remained loyal to the king.

General Marquis Louis de Bouillé, the superb military tactician and hero of the Seven Years' War, would be in charge of the royalist troops. Marie Antoinette's brother Emperor Leopold was sure to offer all the help he could with his army. So was my king, Gustavus III, who had begun to be appreciated by the French monarchs at the end of his last visit to Paris, and who was one of the few persons, along with the Austrian emperor, to be apprised of this hazardous but imperative venture.

CHAPTER 8

Axel:

THE FLIGHT TO VARENNES

I DO BELIEVE THAT the escape plan I devised for the royal family was superbly programmed, and would have been highly successful if I'd had my way. Trace your finger east of Paris on a map of France and you will easily find the route I chose, and the towns I'd designated as the principal relay stations: eastward from Paris, traveling through the department of the Marne, you pass through the towns of Châlons and Pont-de-Somme-Vesle, then on to Sainte-Ménehould, Varennes, and Montmédy, the latter of which I'd decided was the best place for the family to cross into Belgium, part of the Austrian Netherlands, where our allies would rally behind them.

But the king began to sabotage my project—bless my cherished friend, it was as usual with the most benign intentions—by insisting that his entire family travel in one coach. In order for the royals to be less noticeable, I had originally planned for two modest-sized carriages, one for the queen and her daughter, the other for the king and the dauphin, with attendants, governesses, etc., distributed among the vehicles. But Louis, usually so amenable, insisted with most unusual, adamant firmness that he wished his entire family to remain together. Thus I was unfortunately forced to arrange for the kind of coach known as a *"berline,"* a carriage large enough to accommodate six persons inside it and three on the top box. In order not to awake suspicion, I ordered it in the name of Baronne de Korff, the Swedish-born widow of a Russian general, a family friend of mine who was devoted to the monarchs and eagerly accepted to help with their journey. The coach's interior fittings, as specified by Marie Antoinette, were of the most luxurious kind: white velvet upholstery, taffeta curtains, two iron cooking stoves, several chamber pots of burnished leather. Moreover, this large, flamboyant green-and-yellow vehicle required six horses, and I feared from the start that it would attract far too much attention along the roads of a nation undergoing a revolution.

There was another major problem: money. This venture needed a lot of it, and like many monarchs of his time, Louis was penniless—he'd never had any private resources, his immediate needs being paid by the French treasury. The queen was equally insolvent: her only valuable possessions were her jewels; just imagine the ruckus the sale of those gems would have caused. So as a first step in the fund-raising I gave up every penny I had and asked my close friend Evert Taube, Sophie's lover, to borrow all he could against his eventual inheritance. How to play it safe, even within a small circle, when the secret is so huge? I also turned to Madame de Korff and her sister, ardent royalists who donated much of what they had. Without hesitation, Eleanore Sullivan and Quentin Craufurd, both of whom were deeply attached to the king's cause, also contributed the handsome sum of three hundred thousand pounds. Equally important, they offered to shelter the royal family's *berline*, which would be far less visible in their stables on the rue de Clichy than at my own lodgings, which were at the corner of rue du Faubourg Saint-Honoré and avenue Matignon.

How many outstanding minds could I count on to help plan this hazardous escape? Only one, General Marquis de Bouillé, who would bring a dozen or so officers into his confidence, using his intuition as to which of his men could best keep a secret. An alarming amount of incidents kept delaying the evasion, which had originally been set for May. In the preceding weeks one of the dauphin's ladies-in-waiting was judged to be untrustworthy because her lover was a National Guardsman. She was discharged but kept postponing her departure, only leaving on the twentieth, forcing various officers scheduled to man relay stations on the road from Paris to Montmédy to keep altering their plans. Last but not least, there was the problem of the sixth place in the royals' carriage. The fifth was to be occupied by the king's twenty-seven-year-old sister, Madame Elisabeth, whom he did not have the heart to leave behind. Bouillé had wished the sixth place to be taken by a competent, able-bodied officer who might assume control if trouble arose, and had chosen me for that role. But the week before the departure, Louis started insisting that the dauphin's governess, Madame de Tourzel, take that place instead. Oh, Louis, had I argued more firmly I might have won you over, and the course of history might have taken a different turn! It would later be said that the king only wanted French citizens to accompany him to safety; it was also intimated that he might not want his wife's lover to have that honor. Would that I had been bolder, less awed by Your Majesty! No man is more stubborn than a weak-willed one who suddenly wants to show his strength.

As for the second coach in the royals' cortege, Toinette had demanded that a place be reserved for her hairdresser, Léonard, a kind but emotive fibbertigibbet who would play an important role in the demise of my venture. Dear Toinette, however more frugal you'd become in recent years, how naive and vain you still remained! So assured were you that the escape would be successful, you wished your tresses to be perfectly coiffed when you met your friends and relatives at the Belgian border.

But ultimately it was my dear royals' passionate devotion to their children that sabotaged my project: bourgeois solicitude undermining their safety, they insisted on traveling together in that one large, ostentatious *berline*. Neither did it help that Toinette entrusted all her jewelry to the hapless Léonard, who upon being told that he was to leave on this journey lapsed into one of his familiar hysterical fits, sobbing and moaning that the Countess of This and the Duchess of Whom were awaiting him the following day to have sailboats and garden bowers set into their coiffures.

The date finally set for departure—after much haggling, much postponement—was midnight of June 21, the longest day of the year. To allay any suspicions of my collaboration with the royal family, I had taken all of my meals, for the previous week, at Eleanore Sullivan's, who was scheduled to leave Paris on the same night with Craufurd. On the afternoon of the twenty-first I went to the Tuileries to check on last-minute details. The monarchs received me in the king's study. The queen's nerves were threatening to give way—she wept intermittently during our hour's visit. Dear Louis took my hand in both of his—what warm, cushionlike hands he had—and upon tenderly embracing me said, "Monsieur de Fersen, whatever might happen I shall never forget all that you have done for me." The principal detail to iron out that afternoon was the handling of the *berline*, which I'd arranged to be parked at Quentin Craufurd's stables; it would have to be driven out of the Paris gates and reparked in a small street off the road to Metz. I had already arranged for an ordinary hackney cab to be placed at the place du Petit Carousel near the Tuileries; once the royal family had taken their places in it I would drive it myself out of Paris, dressed as a coachman.

Throughout that last day, my friends followed their habitual routines with admirable punctilio. The king received several deputies from the Assembly and gave various commonplace orders to his household staff. In the afternoon the queen took her children for a walk in the public gardens of the Luxembourg. Having been mercifully liberated, upon moving to the Tuileries, from the ritual of dining in public, the family sat down for their evening meal at the habitual 8:45 p.m., in the queen's salon. There the Comte de Provence and his family, who were scheduled to leave Paris that very same night, dined with them, as they customarily did one night out of two. (Wisely traveling in two small, inconspicuous carriages, they would make it to the frontier with no trouble whatever.) The queen then began to engage in the riskier preliminaries to the journey. She went into her daughter's apartments and informed Marie-Thérèse's lady-in-waiting of the evasion plan. She went on to her son's room and upon waking him told him that they would be going to a place where "there would be a lot of soldiers." The dauphin—my beloved little friend—leaped out of bed and grabbed his toy sword. "Quick, quick, let's hurry!" he exclaimed. "Give me my boots, let's go!" Great was his grief when his valets swiftly attired him in girls' clothes, though he calmed down when his mother told him that he was going to "act in a play" and that his stage name would be Aglaë. May I note that the royals had decided to include both the dauphin's and the princess's principal attendants in their party. The fugitive family's retinue now included three maids, a governess, three equerries, a hairdresser—the group was becoming conspicuously large.

Close to 11 p.m., the queen had to engage in the first hazardous step—leaving the Tuileries. Holding her daughter's hand, followed by the dauphin and Madame de Tourzel, she managed to make her way safely to the cour des Princes, and saw me in my coachman's uniform, whistling and smoking as those men do, wearing a wide-brimmed hat that hid most of my face. The plan was for the queen to go back to the palace's salon, where she habitually played cards at that hour; I was to take the children to the carriage parked at the place du Petit Carousel and watch over them until she managed her second exit from the Tuileries. As Toinette returned to the palace it was 11 p.m., and the Provences were making their farewells; it was time for the king's *coucher*. Lafayette was present at the ceremony that night and would later report that although the king was as affable as ever, while chatting with his entourage he glanced often, and in an unusual way, at the sky—clearly, he was checking on whether conditions were propitious for the voyage. They were: the night was dark, the sky overcast. The king then knelt for his prayers, was divested of his clothing by the noblemen of his household, and went to bed.

As soon as his courtiers and valets had left, the king slipped out of his bed, drawing the thick blue curtains tightly about it so as not to arouse immediate suspicions. Waiting in his dressing room was one of the trusted attendants I had recruited a few days earlier to help the royals get into their disguises and assume their roles. The dauphin's governess, Madame de Tourzel, was to travel as Baronne de Korff, the Swedish-born aristocrat in whose name the carriage had been ordered; the dauphin and Madame Marie-Thérèse were to pose as Baronne de Korff's daughters, Amélie and Aglaë, and the queen as their governess, Madame Rochet. The king's sister, Madame Elisabeth, would play the role of Rosalie, Baronne de Korff's lady companion. Louis was designated to be Baronne de Korff's valet, Monsieur Durand; and to get ready for the excursion he put on a plain brown jacket, a green overcoat, and a brown wig topped by a hat.

His Majesty then walked by the sentinels posted by the Tuileries' gates without impediment, being taken for one of the retainers who had participated in his *coucher* earlier that evening. Five minutes later he had joined me at the place du Petit Carousel, where I waited in the hackney coach, watching over the sleeping children. That is when we began to worry: according to my plans the queen should have arrived before the king, at about 11:30, but came midnight and she still had not appeared. We would be increasingly anxious for the next half hour. . . . She finally swept into view, dressed in the plainest gray dress and a black shawl, and explained her delay. Just as she was going through the main gate of the Tuileries, Lafayette's carriage, escorted by torchbearers, had driven by her. She had flattened herself against one of the gateposts, terrified. The general's carriage passed so close to her that its wheels brushed against her skirts. The episode so unnerved her that she took a wrong turn, bearing left where she had been told to take a right, and lost her way in the maze of little streets that crisscross that area of the city. Mishap after mishap continued to plague us. The *berline* had been hidden so carefully by my aides that we spent a good hour searching for it, finding it much farther on the Metz road than we'd expected. I quickly tucked the family into the vehicle, got on top of the coach, and whipped the horses. Dawn would begin to break in less than half an hour. The size of the king's *berline* necessitated six horses, and three more were needed for the attendants' carriage that followed it; I continued to worry that such a number of animals were also bound to arouse attention.

I was scheduled to leave the royal family at the first relay stop, Bondy. My apprehensions were boundless. "I shall continue on the road to the Belgian frontier," I'd written my father the previous day, "and meet the king at Montmédy, if he's lucky enough to get there." I don't wish to presume any supernatural intuition, but I had a strong sense that my presence was needed for the evasion's success. While the horses were being harnessed I again approached the king for his permission to accompany him, and with great kindness he again refused. So I pondered this nightmare scenario: an indecisive king who, with the sole exception of going to Reims for his coronation, had never in his life proceeded beyond Paris or Versailles, and barely knew a square meter of the country he ruled; an equally sequestered queen with delicate nerves who had never even set foot in a public conveyance. My failure to successfully plead my case would haunt me for the rest of my life.

Nevertheless, I tried to maintain my composure. As the coach was ready to leave Bondy I doffed my hat to Madame de Tourzel, loudly exclaiming, "Adieu, Madame de Korff!" Just before the windows were closed the queen quickly reached for my hand and thrust a gold ring into it. I mounted my horse and galloped back to Paris. After twenty minutes, feeling safely out of sight, I stopped to look at the ring, and read its inscription: *"Lâche qui les abandonne,"* "He who abandons them is a coward." Tears in my eyes, I cantered on. Several different parties were speeding toward frontiers that very night: the Provences riding toward Switzerland, Eleanore Sullivan and Quentin Craufurd fleeing to the Netherlands.

As THE QUEEN AND Princess Marie-Thérèse would later report—the rest of my account is drawn from both their recollections—an hour or so after I'd left them, when they'd entered the valley of the Marne, the royal family felt far safer, and began to truly relax. They devoured with relish the provisions I'd prepared for them. Louis read aloud from his letter to the National Assembly, scheduled to be delivered that morning, which justified his departure from the capital. What had been the result of all the concessions extorted from him through threats of violence? he asked in his missive. "All authority defied," he had written, "private property destroyed, anarchy abroad in the kingdom." The only solution, so his letter summed up, was to purge the kingdom of the intrigues and disputes that were making Paris intolerable. "After he'd read that letter, gotten it off his chest," Marie-Thérèse later recalled, "Father suddenly seemed much happier. 'Believe you me,' he said a few times, 'once my butt is back in the saddle I'm going to be a new man!'" According to the queen, as his carriage sped eastward from Paris the king also indulged in his passion for geography. He had brought a large map of France with him, and happily ticked off the name of each village through which they passed.

But then the monarch began to commit some imprudences. By the time the party reached the relay at Fromentières he had grown restless and begun to suffer from the low spirits that always beset him whenever he was denied physical exercise; so he emerged from his coach and fell into conversation with a band of local folk gathered at the relay.

Loquacious as he could be only with humble people, he talked to them about their favorite topics—the year's harvest, the rotation of crops, the kind of cattle being bred in the village. The queen was much upset by the risks he was taking, and his chief attendant, Mourtier, tried to persuade him to return to the carriage and continue to remain anonymous. "Oh, I wouldn't worry about anything," the king replied, radiant about finally being able to converse with his subjects. "We're out of danger now; we're among the good people of France."

What a naive optimist my cherished Louis was. By the time the royal coach lumbered eastward to the next posting station, Chaintrix, it was two o'clock in the afternoon; they were awfully late—that was the time they had been expected to reach Pont-de-Somme-Vesle, which was still three hours away. The royals' insouciance about these delays was caused, in part, by the deep joy this journey was bringing the king, in part by Marie Antoinette's habit of being late to most of her appointments. And it was at Chaintrix that the king was first recognized. The son-in-law of the posting master had been to Paris the previous year and had seen the king at the Feast of the Federation. With joy and trepidation, he invited the royal family into his house to take refreshments. The children were exhausted, the afternoon was hot, and the family much enjoyed the excellent consommé he offered them. "You see how good our subjects are in the *real* France," Marie-Thérèse heard her father whisper to her mother, "the real France outside of Paris!"

The posting master insisted that his son drive the royals' coach to the next relay, and to show off his skills the young man whipped the horses so furiously that a wheel of the carriage flew off the road; another half hour was spent repairing the damage. By the time the party reached the next posting station, Châlons, the flat, dusty town at which Attila, as legend has it, was defeated by the Romans, they were three hours late. And this was the very town that General de Bouillé and I most worried about—an active little commercial town with a sizable garrison of

National Guardsmen and a committed Jacobin Club. Yet the royal couple felt so sheltered within the cocoon of their carriage that the king put
his head out of the window to once more enjoy the sight of his subjects.
"We were looking forward so much to our meeting with the Duc de
Choiseul, whose troops were waiting for us, and up to then my mother
had kept exclaiming 'We are saved!' " Marie-Thérèse would relate later.
"But it was here that we were openly recognized."

Indeed, Châlons's citizens, alerted to the identity of the *berline*'s passengers by the proud young posting master's son, were in a state of turmoil, arguing the pros and cons of reporting the king's identity to ensure
his arrest, or else to ensure his safety by keeping quiet. They chose the
latter option. But it was then that the most ominous apparition of this
trip appeared. As the royal family left Châlons a solitary rider, swathed
in a flowing cape, a hat drawn over his eyes, galloped up to their carriage, drew close to its window, and shouted the following phrase: "Your
plans have gone awry! You will be stopped!" And he sped away ahead
of them. Was this mysterious adventurer an emissary of the last town,
Châlons, sent ahead to forewarn the passengers? Or was it a republican
militant sadistically predicting the turmoil that lay ahead of them? "A
joker!" the king exclaimed. "A hapless joker!" But Marie-Thérèse did
not look upon him as lightly as her father. For the rest of her days, she
later told me, she would remember him as a sinister harbinger of fate.

I ASK YOU NOW to put yourself in the place of the Duc de Choiseul, a
committed young nobleman of deep royalist convictions who'd recently
received his regiment by birthright, and who, unlike his father or General Bouillé, had neither the temperament nor the training to take on a
risky assignment. He had been instructed to provide a military escort
when the royal coach reached Pont-de-Somme-Vesle, the first in a series
of escorts that would accompany the king and his family on their way to

safety in Montmédy. Having to inform one of his subalterns of the purpose of his mission, Choiseul had shared the secret with one Aubriot. Aubriot too would later relate his impressions of the royals' flight. And his words attest to the deep mystical awe with which the French monarch was still held by his subjects.

"My whole body began to tremble," Aubriot said, recalling his emotions upon learning that he would help to save the king. "My legs gave way under the weight of my body. Sparks of fire began to flash through my veins. In short, the secret threw me into such a state of disorder that I was momentarily unable to answer Monsieur le Duc. . . . When my senses were at last calm I swore with all my heart that I would defend my king and his august family and that I was ready to sacrifice myself for their sacred persons."

So Choiseul and Aubriot, accompanied by forty hussars, had gathered since noon at Pont-de-Somme-Vesle, where the royal coach was expected to arrive at 2:30 in the afternoon; how could they know that the king, who was gauchely referred to by many officers as "the Treasure," was still many hours away? Assembled before the posting station, Choiseul's party anxiously scanned the horizon for the cloud of dust that would presage the king's arrival. As they waited the town's peasants began to assemble angrily about them. By one of those many accidents of fate that foiled my escape plan, they were convinced that members of the Choiseul party were emissaries from a local absentee landowner, the Duchesse d'Elbeuf, who had been trying to collect tithes from her delinquent tenants. Certain that Choiseul's soldiers were her men, come to get their money, they brandished muskets and pitchforks as they gathered about the royal party, growing increasingly menacing by the hour. Choiseul kept explaining that his troops were meant to escort "a treasure" that was arriving at any moment from Paris.

This explanation was equally awkward. I'd disliked that word and had vetoed it all along, for one of the most persistent rumors that plagued Marie Antoinette concerned the possibility that she often shipped French gold to her brother in Austria. The word "treasure" was another factor that could have fueled the hostility of the local crowds: here was proof that she'd been robbing the nation! The inexperienced young Choiseul, threatened by bands of enraged peasants, now made a disastrous mistake. He scribbled notes for the leaders of the detachments stationed farther ahead on the escape route, on the road between Pont-de-Somme-Vesle, Sainte-Ménehoud, and Montmédy. The success of the entire venture had depended on all of these detachments falling in behind the king. But in his notes, Choiseul wrote that the "treasure" was not expected to pass that day, and that he would send fresh orders on the morrow. And whom did he entrust with this already calamitous message? None other than the queen's hairdresser, Léonard, one of the few royal retainers sent ahead to meet Choiseul. Léonard had barely stopped weeping and deploring his fate since he had left Paris. As the master coiffeur tearfully trotted eastward toward the next stations of the escape route, Choiseul himself, after waiting yet another hour for that chimerical cloud of dust, abandoned his post. It was then 5:30 p.m. He guided his men onto a path that he thought was a shortcut to Varennes, but the route led him instead into the depths of the Argonne Forest. By nightfall his group was hopelessly lost—they would not find their way out of the woods for another twenty-four hours. The angry farmers of Pont-de-Somme-Vesle had dispersed when they had seen Choiseul disappear. Thus the town was empty when, half an hour after Choiseul's defection, a cloud of dust down the Châlons road finally appeared, presaging the long-awaited arrival of the king's coaches.

THE FOLLOWING EVENTS are so painful to relate that however calmly the queen and Marie-Thérèse, a very cold-blooded girl, reported them, I still suffer pain at every word.

That wretched Léonard again! Carrying the messages Choiseul had given him to bring to General Bouillé, he arrives in Varennes. Bouillé is stationed at the first relay stop on the escape route beyond Varennes, Stenay, waiting for the king with a complement of troops. Idiot Léonard! Upon leaving Varennes for Stenay he takes a wrong turn. He heads east rather than north, toward Verdun, and never reaches Bouillé, who if he'd received the message might well have saved the day by moving his militia back to Varennes. So Bouillé and his aides, having received no directives, decide to await developments in Stenay and get some rest. They retire to their rooms at the Hotel du Grand Monarque and go to sleep. They are wakened two hours later by the clanging of the tocsin, and shouts of *"Aux armes, aux armes!"*

For while they were slumbering the king's coaches had arrived in Varennes. To the royal party's discomfiture, the sleeping town was empty. General Bouillé and his troops, who were supposed to accompany them to the second-to-last relay on the road to safety, were nowhere in sight. The passengers got out of their coaches and started walking through the town, looking for Bouillé. The search was futile; they returned to their carriage and tried to convince the postilion to take them to the next relay station, Stenay, where they suspected Bouillé might be waiting for them. The postilion, emphasizing his horses' exhaustion, adamantly refused, turning down bribes and all possible modes of persuasion. By then an important citizen of Varennes, postmaster Jean-Baptiste Drouet, had been wakened by the din of coaches, and now he galloped up to the royal carriage. He had seen the queen at Versailles some years ago while serving in the Royal Cavalry, and he had no doubt whatsoever that the woman in the plain gray dress sitting in the carriage was Marie Antoinette. As for the big hulking man dressed as a valet by her side, Drouet furtively took a fifty-pound bill from his pocket and checked out the image of the king's face printed on it: its similarity to the passenger's face removed all possible doubt.

Arrives the deputy mayor of Varennes, a grocer named Jean-Baptiste Sauce. He asks to check the passengers' documents, and finds them in order. But Drouet, dazzled by his epiphany, tries to convince Sauce that this is indeed the royal party. The town is now wide awake; armed guardsmen and angry crowds carrying torches fill the cobbled streets. Sauce, still apprehensive, not totally trusting Drouet but aware that he could be accused of treason for not stopping the royals, invites the family to rest at his house, where he sells candles and other provisions. He crowds the six passengers—the royal foursome, Madame Elisabeth, and governess de Tourzel—into a tiny second-floor room hung with sausages and hams; and he helps the queen, alias governess of Madame de Korff's children, put the exhausted youngsters to sleep. Madame de Tourzel, alias Baronne de Korff, sits on a chair beside the sleeping children. The king, introducing himself as Durand, valet to Madame de Korff, paces the room, chatting with his habitual amiability with whatever citizens or officials wander into the room. But around midnight an elderly retired judge name Jacques Destez, who had once lived at Versailles, is led in and recognizes the monarch. Overwhelmed by the king's presence, he falls to his knees, uttering the fatal words, "Oh, sire!" *"Eh bien,"* says Louis, "I am indeed your king." Louis then goes about the room, tears in his eyes, embracing Destez, Drouet, Sauce, and whatever other local citizens surround him, most of whom are also awash in tears of emotion and awe.

This is the kind of scene that also makes me, Axel von Fersen, still weep. These were the people with whom Louis had always felt most at ease, with whom he would always be at his warmest and most outspoken. . . . Such public tenderness, however, was not Marie Antoinette's style, and she sat more morosely than ever by her sleeping children as she watched her husband weeping in the arms of butchers, grocers, and candlestick makers.

How incongruous is it, I ask you, that the Capetian dynasty, the royal descendants of Saint Louis, came to an end in a grocer's shop in a small village in the Marne?

WITHIN AN HOUR some 4,500 members of the National Guard arrived from the villages of the surrounding countryside. Choiseul, having finally found his way out of the Argonne Forest, clattered into Varennes and joined the royal family in the room hung with hams. Two couriers arrived, sent by the National Assembly in Paris, bearing a letter signed by Lafayette which stated that the king was not permitted to continue on his journey. Louis read the Assembly's letter and let it fall upon the bed where his children were sleeping. "There's no longer a king in France," he whispered. Marie Antoinette swiftly picked the letter off the bed and threw it to the floor. "I will not have such an object taint my children!" she exclaimed. Meanwhile the crowds in the streets below were growing more inflamed. "The king to Paris!" they roared. "The king to Paris!" "We'll drag them by their feet if need be!" a voice arose. "To Paris, or we'll shoot them all!" another cried. The royal family was playing for time, hoping against hope that General de Bouillé and his troops would arrive to rescue them. But by 7 a.m., with no Bouillé in sight, they realized it was time to leave. In single file, they descended the stairs they'd ascended a few hours earlier. Princess Marie-Thérèse, although she never liked me, would much later admit to me that just before leaving the room her mother had taken Choiseul aside and asked: "Do you think Monsieur de Fersen is safe?" I had, in fact, fled to Belgium as soon as I heard of the disaster—that was what the queen had ordered me to do in case the escape failed.

In the chorus of accusations that arose after the Varennes debacle—Choiseul blamed Bouillé, Bouillé blamed Choiseul, both denounced Léonard, etc.—one voice alone was not heard: the king's. In his habitually charitable manner, Louis tried, to the contrary, to allay the remorse of those who might feel they had failed him. Nothing more clearly displays the king's immense kindness than a letter he wrote to General de Bouillé a few weeks after his return to the capital, a letter that absolved him of all responsibility for the debacle. "You must stop accusing yourself, monsieur," he wrote. "You risked everything for me and you did not succeed. Fate was against your plans and mine. Circumstances paralyzed my will, and your courage and all our preparations came to naught. . . . Accept my thanks, monsieur, I only wish it were in my power to offer you some token of my gratitude."

The return to Paris—this was best described to me by the queen—was the most frightening aspect of the entire Varennes episode. At the beginning of the three-day journey, a terrible heat wave was plaguing northeastern France. The horses dragging the royal coaches were foundering on the road. In every hamlet and town crowds of vociferous citizens jeered at the sight of the carriage. In one pathetic display of royalist devotion, a Comte Val de Dampierre, whose estate was nearby, attempted to ride up to the coach and salute the king. He was dragged away by a group of National Guardsmen and hacked to death. At another stop a man leaned into the carriage window and spat at the king, whose hand trembled visibly as he wiped away this evidence of his citizens' rancor. When the royal family stopped at an inn to refresh themselves, Marie Antoinette's dress was badly ripped by the savage crowd, many of whom were drunk. The women were particularly hostile. "Stop, pretty little lady," one cried out, shoving the queen as she was stepping back into the coach. "Your life's on the line!"

When two deputies sent by the Assembly to accompany the royals back to Paris arrived, the king and queen welcomed them with joy, hoping they would protect them. One of the deputies, Jérôme Pétion, who would soon become the mayor of Paris, was a dour, militant republican and an outspoken enemy of the king and queen. The other was twenty-eight-year-old Antoine Barnave, known as "the Tiger" because of his ferocious diatribes against the royal couple. He was a notably eloquent speaker, a soulful, idealistic man with chiseled features and beautiful blue eyes who in 1789 had been among the deputies elected to represent his province, Grenoble, at the Estates-General. To make room for the two men in the crowded *berline*, the queen, who sat between Barnave and her husband, took the dauphin on her lap, while Marie-Thérèse sat on her aunt Elisabeth's. And within a few hours both republican deputies were conquered by the friendliness and warm simplicity of the royal passengers. The king called his sister "Babette." The six-year-old dauphin asked his father for his chamber pot, which the king handed him without the least embarrassment. Then my cherished little prince noticed the revolutionary motto on the brass buttons of Barnave's coat— *"Vivre Libre ou Mourir,"* "Live Free or Die"—and, showing off his reading skills, pronounced the words. Barnave was impressed, and complimented the royal couple on their son's precociousness. This pleased the queen no end. Pulling up her veil, she started talking with Barnave about children's education, and they were soon having an animated conversation. Barnave was awed by the royal prisoners' familial, unpretentious manners, which appeared to be absolutely similar to those of his own bourgeois milieu. Instead of the aloof, domineering Catherine de Médicis kind of woman Marie Antoinette's detractors alleged her to be, so Barnave would later write, he found "a pale, shattered woman," a remarkably gracious human being who was bearing her difficult plight with admirable dignity. Despite her increasingly wasted features, my Marie Antoinette still had a charm, a grace of bearing, that sensitive men such as Barnave and I could find irresistible. . . . As for Pétion, he started flirting shamelessly with Madame Elisabeth, amusing himself with the notion that she might grow enamored of him; her gaze having softened after an hour of conversation, he would later boast to his colleagues that she had fallen passionately in love with him.

Outside the *berline*, however, the crowds grew increasingly malevolent as the royals approached Paris. Many women howled for "the queen's head" and asked for her intestines to be distributed among them. To appease them Marie Antoinette tried to lift the dauphin to the window, but one woman shouted, "Take him away! We know that fat hog isn't his father!" In suburban streets bands of enraged citizens defaced or smashed shops and inns that bore the king's name. Terrified of the mobs' ire, Barnave ordered the National Guardsmen to better protect his passengers from such insults.

The royal coaches lumbered into Paris on June 25, three days after their departure, through the Champs-Elysées. Here the avenue was lined by huge, eerily silent crowds. The Assembly had warned Paris citizens that "whoever insults the royal family will be beaten; whoever applauds them will be shot." This excommunication of silence—the city's stillness—was broken only by the slow beat of muffled drums. National Guardsmen crossed their rifles in the air as a show of defiance. Citizens had been ordered by the Jacobin Clubs to keep their hats on their heads as a show of disrespect for the royal family. At the Assembly, that very day, the militant thirty-five-year-old deputy Georges-Jacques Danton had described Louis XVI as "a traitor or an imbecile" for having engaged in the escape attempt. But he received little support for his proposal to replace the king with an executive council. Even the Assembly's most militant figure, Maximilien Robespierre, argued that the new constitution had already given France the best of both worlds, "a republic with a monarch." Revolutionary leaders were also anxious about the probability that deposing Louis XVI might lead to war with Austria, which most members of the Assembly were still eager to avoid. But it was clear that the king had become an utterly powerless member of the body politic. As the royal family drove up to the Tuileries they saw huge placards placed against its gates that read *"Maison à Louer,"* "House for Rent."

As for Marie Antoinette, when she had rested a bit and had had time to ponder the Varennes catastrophe, she sent for her principal chamber-maid, Madame Campan, the first person to whom she would relate details of the piteous voyage. It was Madame Campan who told me that during the three-day ordeal Marie Antoinette's golden hair had turned snow white, "like that of a woman of seventy."

"All is lost, dearest father," I wrote my beloved parent when the news of the debacle reached me in Brussels, "and I am in despair. Just imagine my grief, and pity me."

A few days after her return the queen wrote me two hurried notes, which I received in Belgium.

"I exist," she wrote, "but how worried I've been about you; I know you must be suffering much not to have heard from us! Will Providence allow this to reach you? You must not write me, for that would endanger us. Above all, do not come back here on any pretext. They know it was you who got us out of here and you would be doomed if you were to return. We are watched night and day. But you mustn't worry. Nothing will harm me. The Assembly wishes to treat us leniently. Adieu . . . I can write you no more."

"I can only tell you that I love you and I barely have the time to do that," she wrote me a few hours later. "Don't worry about me. . . . Send me letters through your valet. Advise me as to whom I should send the few letters I'll be able to write you, for I can't live without writing you. Adieu, the most beloved and loving of men. I kiss you with all my heart."

PART II

CHAPTER 9

Axel:

THE WAITING GAME

WHAT WRETCHES THE king's brothers were! Informed by Bouillé of the royal family's arrest, the Comte de Provence could hardly conceal his satisfaction. "There wasn't a tear in those eyes as dry as his heart," Bouillé would report. "All one could discern was their customary expression of falsity across which darted a few sparks of perfidious satisfaction."

By this time Provence had already established his own government at Koblenz, which along with Brussels was the capital of French émigré life. He had settled in a palace given him by one of his uncles, and had appointed his brother Artois lieutenant governor of his realm. He had even had the audacity to draw up a constitution that made him regent of France and stripped Louis XVI of his sovereignty. Meanwhile the Comtesse de Provence, more given than ever to her lesbian amours, was enjoying a passionate liaison with an English woman who was said to be a spy. It was clear that the princes of the blood, perfidious as ever, were as hostile to the French monarchs as the most radical members of the National Assembly.

As for my own king, Gustavus III, at the time of the Varennes debacle he had been at Aix-la-Chapelle, waiting to celebrate Louis XVI's deliverance. The news of Louis's arrest put him into a terrible state of shock. The French monarchy's most loyal supporter, he had been the only sovereign to grasp the horrendous implications of the French Revolution for the rest of Europe. The events of June 1791 clearly unhinged him: once renowned for his liberalism, he made a radical about-face, shedding all his progressive ideals and pledging to uphold the divine right of kings. He even proposed an armed invasion of France that would involve Russian, Austrian, Prussian, and Swedish troops. An armed venture was also being demanded by Louis XVI's brothers, though they differed with Gustavus, who wished his coalition to be led by Sweden. Gustavus's intention was to invade France via Normandy and "throttle the Hydra in its lair." Put into the paradoxical position of having to curb his zeal, I talked him out of this absurd venture, which equally terrified the queen of France and me: what solely obsessed Gustavus was to uphold the principle of absolute monarchy, and it had not entered his mind that such an invasion would greatly threaten the lives of Marie Antoinette and Louis XVI. In dearth of wise support, I thought of Quentin Craufurd, and persuaded Gustavus to appoint Craufurd as emissary to the king of England, from whom he would solicit funds for the French Crown.

As for Marie Antoinette, in the summer of 1791, shortly after the Varennes debacle, she began a complex and duplicitous relationship with Barnave. Soon after her return she contacted the deputy through the mediation of one of her favorites, the Marquis de Jarjayes, who came from the same area of France as Barnave, the Dauphine, and whose wife was one of her ladies-in-waiting. "Tell Barnave," she said to Jarjayes, "that I was much struck by his character and by the frankness I found in him during those two days we spent together. I should very much like him to advise us as to what we are to do in our present position." As out of touch as ever with the details of real politics, the queen wished Barnave to intercede with the Assembly on behalf of the royal family. As their correspondence progressed, Barnave—whose moderation I was grateful for, however much I resented his close friendship with the queen—wrote Marie Antoinette long reports on the political situation. Like Mirabeau had before him, he tried to persuade the queen that the king had to accept the constitution, and support it firmly and "with sincerity." In addition, he advised her that she and Louis had to publicly condemn the counterrevolutionary movement led by the king's brothers, and also demand the return of those princes and of other émigrés. This ingratiating little dolt, Barnave, had even acquired intolerable influence on the queen's daily life. "Your Majesty should go to the opera more often," he'd tell the queen. "I'll go to the opera tomorrow," she would meekly reply.

It should be made clear that Marie Antoinette disliked the constitution even more than the king did, considering it unworkable, and was forthright in stating her disdain for it to Barnave. She was not alone in this regard. Her objections to it were even shared by many revolutionaries, such as Camille Desmoulins, who called the constitution "a veritable Tower of Babel" because of its numerous contradictions. Yet even though she looked on the Constituent Assembly, which had drafted it, as "a heap of blackguards, madmen, and beasts," she promised Barnave that she and the king would "steadfastly" support it. However, during all this time she was conniving with Barnave, she was also conspiring with me and several allied rulers on an alternative plan—an armed congress. She clearly had taken the keys to the kingdom from her increasingly passive husband, who, deeply depressed by the Varennes episode, spent most of his time reading and sleeping.

I never knew that my Toinette, usually so guileless, was capable of such double-dealing! Under Barnave's guidance, for instance, she wrote a letter to her brother Leopold II, asking him to support the new French nation, and to renounce all military ventures against it. Yet soon after mailing him that missive she wrote a second one to the Austrian ambassador, Mercy, telling him that her letter to Leopold had been extorted from her by Barnave. She concluded this message, however, with a kindly report on Barnave and his disciples. "Although they're tenacious in their opinions I have never seen anything but the greatest decency in them . . . and a genuine wish to restore order and . . . the authority of the Crown."

The remaining months of 1791 were equally steeped in duplicity. Toinette was deceiving me through her secret relationship with Barnave; I was hoodwinking Gustavus by assuring him that the queen shared his enthusiasm for an armed congress. Barnave, of course, was double-crossing the Assembly through his dealings with the royal family; while Leopold of Austria, though saying yes yes yes to his little sister, had no intention whatever of coming to the French royal family's rescue in the event they needed it. Neither did the king of Prussia have any similar intent, even though he too had pledged his support of the French Crown. Meanwhile Provence and Artois, who could barely conceal their elation over the Varennes debacle, were duping the Assembly by expressing hypocritical concerns over their brother's fate.

In the midst of all these double-dealings, how did I react, one might well ask, to Toinette's relationship with Barnave? Although it was rumored that she was sleeping with him I did not believe a word of it. Only I knew the extent to which the French tended to sully her reputation through loathsome gossip; only I knew that she was not that sexually driven, that she could only be aroused by someone with whom she was deeply in love. However, I was concerned enough about her relationship with the blackguard to write her the following words of caution: "Do not open your heart to those madmen; they're all scoundrels who will do nothing for you. . . . The nobility whom you would thus abandon would no longer feel it owes you anything. You would debase yourself in the eyes of the powers of Europe, who would accuse you of cowardice." "Set your mind at rest," she replied to me; "I'm hardly joining the *enragés*. If I see them or have relations with some of them, it is only to utilize them. They inspire too much horror in me; I would never go over to them."

But the immense correspondence the queen was maintaining with diverse factions in her effort to save the Crown—with Barnave, with me, with her brother Emperor Leopold, with several other allied sovereigns whose support she was seeking—was clearly draining her. The young woman who had once exasperated her mother with her frivolity and laziness was often at work until 2 a.m. "I'm exhausted from writing," she wrote me in one of her letters, which she sent to me in food tins, or in the hems of clothes. "I've never done work such as this before and I'm always afraid of forgetting something or making some stupid mistake." And in another letter she phrased her weariness in the following manner: "Please understand my position, and the role I'm obliged to play all day long. Sometimes I barely recognize myself and I have to pause to realize that this person is really me. . . . When I'm at my saddest, I take my little boy in my arms, I kiss him with all my heart, and that momentarily consoles me."

IN JULY AND AUGUST OF 1791 I considered it more prudent to not write the queen at all. For I spent those months in Vienna, trying to convince the Austrian and Prussian monarchs to join an armed venture that would restore Louis XVI to his former power. Yet if I'd anticipated the anguish my silence would cause poor Toinette I might have reconsidered my prudence. It appears that several of her letters, including the one in which she called me "the most loving and beloved of men," were intercepted, and they reached me only years later, after her death. Not aware of these interceptions, she was hurt by my muteness. "My heart is full of grief," she wrote our mutual friend Valentin Esterhazy, "for I have no real friends here in whom I might confide my sorrows. . . . To have no news of him is unbearable. Should you write

HIM tell him that many miles and many countries can never separate hearts." A few days later she sent Esterhazy another note, in which, he reported, she enclosed two rings. "The one that's wrapped in paper is for HIM," she wrote him. "Send it to HIM for me. It is exactly his size. I wore it for two days before wrapping it. . . . I don't know where he is. It is dreadful to have no news of those one loves and not even know where they are." Alas, I never received the ring.

I wrote the queen in late summer, after I'd finished my consultations with the Austrian emperor and the king of Prussia (whose pledges of support I did not in the least trust). It was a propitious time to write the queen; for in September of 1791 Louis's decision to accept the constitution, which I now realize to have been essential to the survival, however temporary, of the monarchy, unleashed much indignation among Europe's royalists. Gustavus was so outraged by Louis's intention to sign this document that he threatened to entirely withdraw his support of the French Crown. Catherine of Russia was as incensed as Gustavus. Even more vociferous than those sovereigns were the king's brothers, who were still holding their make-believe alternate court in Koblenz. Their verbal abuse, predictably, was directed at Marie Antoinette, whom they accused of being the one who had convinced the king to ally himself with what was now called the National Constituent Assembly.

Meanwhile the royal family's life at the Tuileries, in the aftermath of Varennes, had become a kind of imprisonment. Menacing crowds often swarmed close to the palace, shouting threatening phrases such as "Death to the king!" or "Kill the queen!" Thousands of National Guardsmen camped in tents next to the château. Anyone wishing to enter the Tuileries was searched, and had to present a note signed by Lafayette himself. The king and queen could not even move about freely in their own apartments. Four officers escorted Marie Antoinette when she went to see the dauphin in the boy's quarters. One of them knocked on the prince's door and shouted, "The queen!" The sentry on duty at the dauphin's rooms opened the door for the queen, and her four guards would remain with her while she visited her son. The same procedure was followed when the young prince went to visit his mother. Equally painful, Toinette wrote me, was her lack of privacy at night. National Guardsmen were posted right outside her bedroom door, which she was not allowed to shut, even when she went to sleep. They often entered her room to make sure that she had not fled, and one night a guard even had the temerity to sit himself on her bed to "have a good talk" with her.

The Tuileries' aura also remained hostile when the royal couple were alone with Madame Elisabeth, for the king's sister served as her émigré brothers' secret agent, fully supporting their belief in counter-revolution. "It's hell at home," the queen wrote me. "All conversation is impossible. . . . My sister-in-law is so indiscreet, and surrounded with so many intriguers, that if we spoke to each other at all we would argue all day." In her letters to me, the queen gave full vent to her growing resentment of the French, and I fully concurred, calling them, to her delight, "wretches," "monsters," "a cursed race." Our correspondence, as ever, was written in invisible ink, and coded. Our codebook in those years was *Paul et Virginie*, Abbé de Saint-Pierre's 1788 novel, and we were careful about our couriers, mostly using the queen's secretary, Goguelat, or else Eleanore Sullivan's housekeeper.

ON SEPTEMBER 13, 1791, the Salle du Manège where the National Constituent Assembly met was packed as the king came to take his oath to the constitution. When Louis stood up, took off his hat, and began speaking the first words of the oath, he noticed that the deputies, breaching all protocol, had sat down and had failed to take off their own hats. Feeling deeply humbled, Louis continued to read the document while sitting down. In spite of the loud cheers that rang out when he had finished speaking, the king was distinctly dismayed by the event. On his return to the Tuileries, he broke down and wept in the arms of the queen. "Why did you come to France to see me so humiliated?" he asked. But the monarchs were heartily cheered again when they went to the theater that night, and indeed the surveillance imposed upon them was somewhat relaxed after the constitution had been signed.

The threat of counterrevolution, however, continued to menace the Assembly, and it asked the king to sign additional, more contentious decrees. In December 1791 the Assembly voted several ordinances concerning émigrés, and "refractory" priests who had not taken the oath to the constitution. The émigrés, including the king's brothers, were threatened with the seizure of their assets if they did not return to France within two months; in addition, Louis was to ask all European princes who had welcomed the émigrés to expel them from their domains. As for the refractory priests, they were threatened with deportation if they did not take the oath to the constitution. The king did not mind signing the decrees that concerned his brothers and other émigrés. But his great innate piety, and his deep allegiance to the church of Rome, led him to veto the statutes concerning refractory priests. Although the monarchs placated the Assembly by attending daily masses celebrated by state clergy who had taken the oath, they would secretly make their Easter duties in 1792 at a predawn service celebrated by nonjuring priests. However, the Assembly, suspecting the king's support of refractory priests, threatened to abolish the right of veto originally granted him by the new constitution. Accusing the queen of having pressured her husband into resisting the Assembly's ordinances, deputies began to call her "Madame Veto," and she lost whatever small degree of popularity she had regained in previous months.

Meanwhile the king was being increasingly pressured by his brothers to take armed action against the new French government. The extent of the king's opposition to such a civil war is expressed in a letter he wrote to his brothers in Koblenz. "France at this moment is on the verge of total collapse," he wrote, "and her ruin will only be hastened if violent remedies are added to the ills that already overwhelm her. . . . The use of force can only come from foreign armies. . . . Can a king such as I allow himself to take his nation into war? Is the remedy not worse than the disease? Such an idea must be abandoned at once. . . . I have been greatly grieved by the Comte d'Artois going to the conference at Pillnitz without my consent. I'd like to emphasize that in acting independently of me he undermines my plans."

The conference at Pillnitz to which the king alluded had to do with his brothers' habitual deceitfulness. In the summer of 1791 Artois had met with the Austrian and Prussian rulers at Pillnitz, in Saxony, and tried to persuade them to sign a statement that threatened to restore the king of France's former sovereignty through armed force. The Austrian emperor, Leopold, and the king of Prussia, Frederick William II, both of whom equally disliked Artois, did sign a short, noncommittal statement deploring the "disorders" in France, and stating their hope that other European powers would give such help as might be asked of them. Since Great Britain had adamantly stated its neutrality, this bland declaration would have remained insignificant if the Comte de Provence had not rewritten it. He drew up a long statement of his own, which he described as an "interpretation" of the manifesto signed by the Austrian and Prussian monarchs. This "interpretation" was a bellicose document that bluntly threatened the French nation with armed attack if Louis XVI's original powers were not restored. The document, read before the outraged Assembly and distributed throughout France, was held up by many as evidence of the queen's treasonable collusion with her brother the Austrian emperor. I was with the queen when she read

Provence's manifesto. "They have murdered us!" she exclaimed, referring to her brothers-in-law. I then heard her use the following word
about the detestable Provence: "Cain!"

In the late fall of 1791 the National Constituent Assembly was dissolved and was replaced by a new assembly—the Legislative. Those
who had sat in the first congress were ineligible for election to the new
one, with the result that Barnave, along with the majority of the centrist
Constitutional party, lost their offices and were replaced by new, more
radical deputies. And by December it was clear that the Constitutionalists as a whole were as threatened as the Crown. Realizing that the situation was rapidly deteriorating, Marie Antoinette decided to once more
consult Barnave, who in view of his party's demise was planning to
leave Paris and retire to his native Grenoble. This was a dangerous
meeting for both of them, but she managed to see him alone at the Tuileries at the end of January 1791; and Barnave's parting words to the
queen intimate that he had premonitions about his eventual fate. "I'm
certain to pay with my head for the interest that your misfortunes have
inspired in me and for the services I wished to render you," he quotes
himself as telling the queen in his memoir of that meeting. "I only ask
you for the honor of kissing your hand." Marie Antoinette, with tears in
her eyes, extended her hand to him. Barnave would go to the scaffold in
October of 1793, just two weeks after the queen.

In order to clarify the quandaries facing France's royal couple, I
must now pause and give the reader a brief glimpse of European dynas-
tic politics in the early 1790s.

The king of Prussia was then Frederick William II, a nephew of
Frederick the Great, the latter of whom had died in 1786. By 1790 the
grossly fat Frederick William, a relentless womanizer, had acquired
three wives in addition to numerous mistresses. And all these women,
along with their husbands and lovers, pressed the voluptuary king
for various personal ends, creating a morass of contradictory political

policies. However, even this weak-willed leader was very distressed by the Varennes debacle, and its general impact on the French Revolution. He allied himself reluctantly with Prussia's traditional enemy, Austria, against the new French government, hoping that an anti-French incursion might help him gain some precious territories, suck up a chunk of Flanders.

As for the ruthless, brilliant Catherine the Great of Russia, she held to one goal throughout her reign: her nation's territorial aggrandizement. Her ambitions, in that decade, were particularly centered on Turkey and Greece. Shortly after the beginning of the French Revolution, Catherine invaded Turkey with the help of Austria, whose territories also touched upon the Ottoman Empire. In view of their plans for carving up Turkey, the leaders of the two nations were thrilled to witness the collapse of France's power, knowing that it was now far too unsettled to interfere with their ambitions in the Near East.

But the Austrian-Prussian alliance was undermined by the craft of Frederick William's brilliant prime minister, Hertzberg: he stirred up revolts in several Austrian possessions, particularly Hungary, where Magyar nationalist strivings were strong, and Belgium, part of the Austrian Netherlands, where the peasant class allied itself with clergymen eager to weaken the impact of Enlightenment ideals. In March 1790 a great pillage occurred in the Austrian Netherlands, sparing only those houses that displayed a picture of the Virgin Mary. Leopold II, Marie Antoinette's sibling, who had just acceded to the Austrian throne after the death of their brother Joseph II, had to abandon his invasion of Turkey to quell these revolts.

Having wrought havoc in Austrian lands, some months later Prussia turned its attention to Russia's principal possession, Poland, and pledged to support it if it rose against its Russian occupiers. Poland, the country that connected Catherine the Great's empire to Europe, was pivotal to her foreign policy. Unable to grab much land in her earlier incursion, when she had had to share part of the Polish loot with Austria and France, in her next assault she wished to seize all she could. She hoped that Austria and Prussia would be too involved in their armed actions against France to meddle with her policies. But a council of the Austrian government held in January 1792, at the very time I was in Vienna pleading for Austria's support for an armed congress, threatened to thwart her plans. It stated that "to sacrifice Austria's gold and blood to restore the Bourbons' power would be as great an act of madness as Austria could possibly commit." So my own mission to Leopold was aborted: he asserted that he would not participate in an armed congress unless all the European powers—Russia, England, Prussia, Spain—agreed to support it.

I was trained to be a soldier, not a diplomat, and I must pause and admit to the pathetically naive, trusting attitude with which I addressed these intricacies of European diplomacy. It was not in my nature to comprehend Frederick William's and Catherine the Great's Machiavellian machinations. Neither was it in my nature to have predicted Emperor Leopold's crass indifference to his sister's fate. I told the queen that her brother was "a real Italian," by which I meant a duplicitous liar.

In contrast to the heartless and hypocritical heads of state I've just referred to was Gustavus III, who had conceived yet another escape plan, which he asked me to propose to the French monarchs. According to this new rescue strategy the French royal family, occupying separate coaches, would travel from Paris to Normandy, whence they would escape across the Channel to England with the help of twelve thousand Swedish soldiers. And in January of 1792 I wrote the queen that I was coming to Paris to speak to her and Louis XVI about this "affair of state." However much she missed me (we had not seen each other for seven months, since the evening before the flight to Varennes), Marie Antoinette, concerned as ever for my safety, ordered me to remain in Brussels, the capital of the Austrian Netherlands. I would face certain death if I was caught in France, she warned me. Upon my insistence she finally relented, and in February, telling me that conditions were somewhat safer, she wrote to say she would welcome my arrival. I immediately began to plan my departure, acquiring false credentials—I feigned that I was a Swedish diplomat who was making a brief stop in Paris on his way to Portugal.

I reached Paris on the evening of February 13 with my orderly and dropped off my baggage at the Hotel des Princes, on the rue de Richelieu. From there I took a cab to the home of the Baron de Goguelat, the queen's secretary, who, though under surveillance since the Varennes venture, was able to move freely about the Tuileries. He took me to the queen's apartments shortly after 9 p.m. I would not leave her until 6 p.m. the following evening, when I was planning to visit the king in his own quarters.

How can I—how can any man—write with serenity, even fifteen, twenty years later, about his very last night of intimacy with the love of his life? I'm emotionally incapable of sharing the details of our final hours. I also would rather not speak of my dark premonitions—I seem to have had them about many crucial events of that decade. But on this occasion I felt that my beloved too strongly sensed that this was to be our last meeting. I can only say that we spoke to each other as ardently, as nostalgically, as we made love. We recalled all of the happy times we had shared over the years: our silly, youthful conversation on the night we first met at the Paris Opera; our secretive horseback rides in the forest of Saint-Cloud, the way she got annoyed when I gave her a handicap for racing our horses to the finish line; our backgammon games, which she always won; the way we used to dodge Ambassador Mercy to minimize his intrusion into our lives; our first trysts, in the little alcove over her Versailles apartment.

In between bouts of lovemaking we also talked, of course, about Varennes—it was from her that I first received a detailed narrative of that episode: the king's naive enthusiasm about seeing his country for the first time; the absurd flirtation, on the way back to Paris, between Princess Elisabeth and Deputy Pétion; the decency and humaneness (by this time I had ceased resenting him) of Barnave; the poor noble- man who, during the monarchs' return to Paris, was put to death for saluting the king. We recalled the books and plays we had read aloud to each other—Laclos's *Liaisons dangereuses*, Voltaire's *Candide*. We spoke too of our merrier moments, of the operas we'd enjoyed together— Gluck's *Iphigenia*, Rameau's *Les Indes galantes*, Mozart's *The Marriage of Figaro*. Sitting there in bed, we even sang "*Là ci darem la mano.*" We were together for twenty-one hours. A few hours before we parted, Toi- nette gave me a gold watch, precisely similar to one she had, on whose surface were carved our initials, A and F.

The day after my arrival, when the clock in Toinette's drawing room rang the hour of 6 p.m., I knew I had to move on and see the king: for I had come, ostensibly, to offer him the new escape plan devised by Gus- tavus. As we exchanged a last embrace she controlled her tears, perhaps to allay mine. "*Sois toi-même,*" she whispered to me. "Be true to your- self," she repeated gently as she gave me one last kiss. It was the first time she had spoken that phrase to me.

Louis XVI, his eyes dreadfully sad and resigned, grown even fatter by the bouts of overeating he indulged in during his deepest depressions, welcomed me with his habitual warmth and affability. But he refused to so much as discuss the evasion plan proposed by Gustavus. After Varennes, the king explained to me, he had promised the Assembly that he would never again try to leave Paris. "His scruples restrained him," I would jot down in my journal the following day, "because he is an honorable man." Louis, with his habitual humility and candor, was forth- right about the mistakes he had made, the possibilities he had wasted. "I know now that I missed the moment," he said. "I should have left on July

14 and I wanted to; Monsieur himself begged me to leave. I missed the moment and I've never found it since." The king buried his face in his hands and remained silent for a minute; then he raised his head again, and added: "I've been abandoned by everyone." The sorrow in his eyes, as he spoke that phrase, was barely tolerable. Shortly afterward the king took his leave. He had made it impossible for me to do anything more for him.

I had another hour alone with Toinette; she asked me where I was going. I told her I was going southwestward, to Orléans and Tours, toward the Spanish frontier, to do a diplomatic errand for my king. This was the same lie I'd told to Taube and Gustavus himself. "*Sois toi-même*"—Toinette's phrase kept tormenting me as I exited the Tuileries into the freezing, snowy night and hailed a cab to get to my next destination. For I had decided not to ride that southwestern road toward the Spanish frontier. Instead, I drove directly to Eleanore Sullivan's home on the rue de Clichy.

This is where I fear my readers will begin to dislike me, to loathe me even. Here goes the fickle Don Juan, they'll say, from the bed of his great love, who lies in mortal danger, to that of a strumpet. How reprehensible. How base. The scoundrel, the cad, the rotter. I accept all these censures. Fifteen years later, in my prudish, ascetic fifties, I berate myself for my callousness. But there it was—Eleanore had been my mistress for over three years. Not only did I lust for her, she had shown remarkable devotion to the French monarchs during the preparations of the Varennes venture. It was she, along with the baronne de Korff, who had gone to the carriage maker to order a green *berline* that could accommodate nine persons, and who had paid for it. It was she who had gone to the Russian ambassador, Simolin, to arrange for the monarchs' passports. So besides my affection for her I owed her great gratitude.

Moreover, I'm a voluptuary, and an aesthete. I longed for Eleanore, as I did for her wondrous house, furnished with such taste by Quentin

Craufurd, filled with Watteaus and Poussins and glorious Renaissance furniture. Upon my arrival she greeted me with open arms, as ever; when had she not? She was wearing a dress of red cut velvet that brilliantly offset her milky skin, her silken dark hair, her copious white shoulders. She sat me down and immediately asked me about the queen, for whom she had always had the most intense, loyal concern. She wept when I told her of my last conversation with the royal couple, of their adamant refusal to leave the country. "They're lost," she whispered between tears, "they're lost." "Joseph would never have allowed this," she added, referring to her former lover, the Austrian emperor, Marie Antoinette's oldest brother. "Never, never would Joseph have abandoned his sister this way."

She said this over dinner, weeping, in her superb wood-paneled dining room, where a group of Craufurd's Botticelli drawings hung over the mantelpiece. She went on to describe what our living arrangements would be for the following days. Craufurd traveled a good deal and went to the theater almost every night, she explained, as he had this particular evening—he owned a stake in several Paris theaters and liked to attend at least one play a day. He usually came home at around midnight. I could dine with her on the nights Craufurd was out; but whenever he was home I would have to hide in the maid's quarters she had provided for me on the top floor of her house. She took me to my room directly after dinner.

How lovingly she had arranged this little nest for me! There were logs by the fireplace, which had already been lit. There were flowers, a bowl of fruit, a dozen novels and historical works stacked upon the bedside tables. Although I was worn out, emotionally drained by what I sensed had been my last meeting ever with the queen, Eleanore and I made love. But making love with Eleanore was not an exerting experience; she did the bulk of the work. She was a fleshy, large-breasted woman (yes, I do love breasts) with a bounteous belly that reminded me of the Venus de Milo's. Her favorite position—one should keep in mind that she was once a circus dancer—was to mount a man and exert all kinds of fascinating, exotic practices upon his body. She performed, at a variety of angles, many nuances of entrances and withdrawals. Her legs wrapped around me as I sat at the edge of the bed, she alternated exquisitely slow and excitingly speedy motions. Standing up, as I cradled her in my arms and she kept her plump white limbs wrapped around me, after some stupendous exertions we ended up sharing our orgasms on the floor. This all happened in my little room, whence we could always hear the front door opening and closing, and remained warned of Craufurd's comings and goings.

Craufurd was a very large man, about my height—six feet four—but wide shouldered and big boned, with the beginning of a paunch. He had a Vandyke beard, swift, expressive hazel eyes, handsome features marred only by a slightly bulbous nose caused by his great liking for spirits. He was known for his fierce temper and physical strength, and the thought of his learning of my trysts with Eleanore terrified me.

So when Eleanore told me that Craufurd would be at home during my stay with her, I was happy to abide by the rules she had set for me. I hid in my room, taking care to keep my shoes off at all times because Craufurd's study was directly below. When Craufurd was spending the evening at home my meals were sent up to me clandestinely on a dumbwaiter, at the very time the Craufurds were supping in their dining room or having a reception in their salon. (Eleanore, by the way, had told her servants that I was one of the illegitimate sons she'd had by the Duke of Württemberg, of whom Craufurd was very jealous.) I offered myself an excellent education during the days I was sequestered at Eleanore's: I reread my beloved Saint Augustine, whom I'd much enjoyed since my youth; perused a few articles on the Bounty mutiny and a slough of Voltaire's plays; and wrote a great deal in my journal. When I was sure that Craufurd was not in his study, I paced my room swiftly for an hour at a time, the way prisoners do, to activate my circulation. The most amusing nights were those when Craufurd went to the theater. On those evenings I dined with Eleanore downstairs and went to my room an hour later, and Craufurd, when he came home at midnight, would be offered the leftovers of our supper.

But notwithstanding the cheerful intrigues of my sojourn at the Craufurds', I can't say that I was happy there. I was far too concerned about Marie Antoinette. My anxiety about her future kept me up much of the night, and in daytime not an hour passed without my thinking, worrying about her. At times, when I compared the queen to Eleanore, I experienced a sense of disdain about the latter: her loud, full-throated laugh, which verged on the vulgar; her thick, somewhat coarse limbs; her overly agitated manner. The Prince of Wales, upon meeting her in Craufurd's company, had compared her to "an apple vendor." I kept thinking back to Toinette's delicacy, the exquisite lightness of her gliding walk, the aura of warmth and gentleness she perpetually emanated, and missed her more desperately than ever. Craufurd himself had written about her "infinite grace," her "very rare aura of benevolence." Plagued by my longing for the queen, on a day in late February, I sensed it was time for me to end the charade with Eleanore and return to Brussels. I made an official visit to Craufurd. Leaving the house by the back stairs, I walked around the block a few times, and then rang Craufurd's bell and was ushered into his house through the front door. "My dear fellow!" he exclaimed. "Always a delight to see you!" Craufurd was enchanted by my visit, and instantly asked me to stay for tea, and for supper. The next morning, I went back to Brussels.

THE SPRING OF 1792 was cursed by two disasters. The first was the death of Marie Antoinette's brother Leopold II, who passed away after a brief illness in March, after a two-year reign. The queen had been disappointed by his reluctance to lead an armed congress against revolutionary France, but she had hoped that his equanimity and wisdom might help her in the future. Leopold was succeeded by his twenty-four-year-old son, Francis, whom the queen had never even met. Two weeks later we were dealt an even greater blow: on March 16, Gustavus III was shot at a masked ball in Stockholm, and he died two weeks later of his wounds. It was an ironic death for a man who had always been so passionately drawn to theatricals and masquerades. The events that led to his demise would have a long-lasting impact upon the fate of Sweden.

Gustavus had long been hated by the Swedish nobility because his numerous edicts and reforms had favored the clergy, the burghers, and particularly the peasant class at the expense of the aristocracy. He had passed a law, for instance, that allowed the peasantry, for the first time, to purchase land owned by nobles or by the Crown. Moreover, he started wars with Russia and with Denmark without the permission of the Riksdag; and although Sweden's army and navy eventually prevailed against Russia, the conflicts put a disastrous strain on the nation's economy. In 1789 he had arrested many aristocrats for opposing his edicts, and the wars he had started. During a meeting of the Riksdag that same year, at the end of a speech in which he censured the nobility, Gustavus ordered all of the nobles to leave the Hall of State, where the Riksdag was being held. Never before had such an order been given. Many of the aristocrats who resisted the king's decrees were exiled to the island of Saint-Barthélemy, which Sweden had acquired from France a few years earlier. Several others were condemned to death. Most of these sentences were commuted to prison terms, but one particular officer, Colonel Johan Hästesko, was publicly beheaded. Huge crowds attended his execution. When his head rolled into the basket, one of his officer friends, thirty-year-old Captain Johan Anckarström, swore he would avenge his comrade's death.

Johan Anckarström, whom I'd always detested, came from a well-to-do and cultivated family and in his younger years had been a page at the Swedish court. He joined the army and rose to the rank of captain, becoming known as a tough-minded fellow who readily came into conflict with his peers. He left his army career when still in his twenties to become a farmer, but quarreled mightily with his neighbors and other landowners. Like those of many well-to-do Swedes, his fortune was vastly diminished by the financial crisis caused by our war against Russia. In 1791 he was accused of insulting the king, an offense punishable by death. While in his cups, Anckarström had publicly criticized the king's conduct of Sweden's war against Russia, which he thought would end badly. His vilification of Gustavus was reported to the authorities, he was taken to court, and the possibility of a death penalty tortured him. In his rage, he blamed all his setbacks in life, his economic failures, and those of the entire nation on King Gustavus.

Anckarström's ire against Gustavus came to the attention of other army officers who wished for the king's demise. Particularly important in the plot against the king were the noblemen Claes Fredrik Horn and Adolph Ribbing, the latter of whom would later become a lover of Madame de Staël. This conspiratorial group decided that the best occasion upon which to assassinate Gustavus was a public event attended by a large number of people. They knew of Gustavus's predilection for masked balls, and chose a ball that was to be held on March 16, 1792, on the stage of the opera house built by Gustavus at the beginning of his reign. Captain Anckarström dressed as a harlequin—he wore a white mask and a false black beard, and carried a pistol loaded with tacks and sharp fragments of metal.

On that evening the king dined with a few friends in his private chambers. He had received a letter that very evening warning him that an attack on him was being planned. But although his friends suggested that he wear a protective vest he laughed at the idea—he knew that much of the nobility hated him, and he had received many such letters of warning before. After he finished dining, the king fussed about what costume he would wear to the masked ball—the art of costume had always been of great concern to him. He decided to wear a Venetian cape of black taffeta that hung loose over his shoulders, so that the Grand Star of the Seraphim—a decoration that only the Swedish monarchs and a handful of nobles could wear—could be clearly seen. He also put on a black tricorn, decked with white plumes, to which his large black mask had been sewn.

Anckarström saw the king approaching through the crowd, surrounded by his masked guests. He cocked the pistol at the king, aiming at Gustavus's back. *"Bonjour, beau masque,"* one of Anckarström's co-conspirators said, placing his hand on the king's shoulder. The king had been expected to turn around, but did not do so—he simply turned to his left a little to speak to one of his friends. Anckarström pressed the trigger. The shot entered Gustavus's body just below his cummerbund. He startled and winced, but did not fall. The pistol's report had hardly been heard; except for the king's friends the crowd was oblivious of what had happened. *"Ay, je suis blessé, arrétez le et tirez moi d'ici!"* the king said to one of his companions, speaking French, as he had all his life ("I am wounded, arrest him and get me out of here"). As the king, still able to walk, was whisked away by his friends, Anckarström thought he had failed. He let his pistol fall to the floor, then pushed his way into the crowd and shouted, "The building is on fire!" Panic did not arise as he had hoped. Upon learning that the king had been shot, a high-ranking officer ordered all doors shut and forbade everyone to leave.

Stockholm's commissioner of police was soon on the scene. Within the next hour he had listed the names of all the guests present at the ball, and the pistol was found. The king had been taken to the castle and put on a divan in his room. His brother, Karl, Duke of Södermanland, came swiftly to his side, as did members of the court, the leading functionaries of the realm, and ambassadors from many European countries. The king was smiling bravely, greeting all, finding a special word for everyone. But in the following days his wound hurt increasingly; it became more and more difficult for him to move. His surgeon poked about and removed a number of tacks, but could not get them all. The wound festered, Gustavus developed a fever, and then pneumonia set in. Gustavus's family and closest friends remained at his bedside. He writhed with pain, but continued to joke and make small talk, bearing his suffering with remarkable courage. In his last days he wished to speak of ancient heroes. "Come then and, like another Anthony," he said to Armfelt, "let us show Caesar's bloody garments so that his enemies might be crushed." But in his very last hour he spoke more plainly. "The Jacobins in Paris will rejoice when they hear this news," he whispered to Armfelt. He died thirteen days after being shot, at the age of forty-six.

By this time the murderer, Anckarström, had been captured, and had confessed to the crime. Swedish executions are gory events: after being whipped for several days on a square in Stockholm, Anckarström was taken to the traditional place of execution at Skanstull—somewhat similar to Paris's place Louis XV—where he was guillotined. His body was then quartered, his head was nailed onto a pole, and the quartered parts of his body were attached to a wheel. These remains were left on public display for several weeks.

Several other conspirators were arrested, Ribbing among them. They were sentenced to death, but their sentences were then commuted and they were sent into perpetual exile, forbidden to ever return to Sweden. As one of Gustavus's supporters remarked, "never before had the assassination of a king been punished so mildly."

I was in Brussels when I heard of the king's death. I was in such despair that I did not leave my room for three days. Gustavus, my benefactor, my frequent traveling companion, one of my closest comrades . . .

"You have lost a firm supporter and a good ally," I wrote to Marie Antoinette. "I have lost a protector and a friend. It is a very cruel loss."

Gustavus's successor was his thirteen-year-old son, who would later rule as Gustav IV Adolf. Until the crown prince's eighteenth birthday, Gustavus's brother, the Duke of Södermanland (yet another man I disliked), would reign as regent.

Adjoined to the grief caused me by Gustavus's death was a concern for my own fate. Would my status as Swedish agent in Brussels be renewed by the regent? At Gustavus's bequest I'd occupied an official position, with all the remuneration and privileges that went with it. Should the regent abolish my post I'd find myself without revenue or employment. Writing Marie Antoinette, I assured her that even if I was deprived of my position, I'd sell my furniture and move to more humble accommodations in order to continue living in Brussels, and remain accessible to her. My worries soon came to an end: in mid-April, the regent renewed my appointment.

But by the time I received this good news another calamity had taken place: war had been declared between France and the German powers, a war that still rages as I compose these recollections. The first to suffer from this new conflict were the French royal family, who in a few months' time would be moved from the Tuileries and imprisoned in a far grimmer place.

CHAPTER 10

Axel:

WAR AND DEATH

"*Dulce et decorum est por patria mori*"? Not in this case. As with most pivotal events of the Revolution, the origin of the war that broke out in the spring of 1792 lay not in such noble motives, but in partisan political disputes. In March of that year the Girondin party had succeeded the Constitutionalists as the leading faction in the Assembly; and they were hell-bent on plunging France into war in order to prove themselves indispensable to the nation. Ironically, the war was also championed by Marie Antoinette, who held to the delusional belief that the Austrian-Prussian coalition would liberate Paris in a matter of months. She did not even seem to realize the increased personal dangers the war would bring her: more than ever, she would now be looked on as the inimical "*Autrichienne*," an enemy alien who incited increasingly hostile public sentiment. Her Austrian patriotism, in fact, did verge on treason when she revealed to me some French military plans she had overheard at a council meeting: "They plan to attack through Savoy and the Liège country and hope to gain something this way because the two flanks can not be protected," she wrote me. "It is essential to take precautions on the Liège flank." Not that the queen would look at this indiscretion as a treasonable act: in her view, the revolutionaries were as much of a threat to the French nation as they were to her personally.

Neither did Marie Antoinette realize that the war would make her personal life, and her communications with me, more difficult than ever. Eleanore Sullivan and Quentin Craufurd, who had provided our principal means of contact, had fled to Brussels after the declaration of war; before leaving, Craufurd had gone to pay his last respects to the queen, whom he found affable but sorrowful. "I have no illusions; there is no more happiness for me," she said to him as they parted. She was fortunate that the Craufurds had a dependable housekeeper, a Madame Toscani, who had remained in Paris, and it was through her that the queen's missives were now dispatched to me, smuggled out of the Tuileries.

Ever since the Varennes debacle the royal family had been obsessed by the possibility that they would be massacred. On June 19, 1792—just before the anniversary of Varennes—the king learned that the Paris mob was planning to invade the palace the next day. Certain that his end was near, he sent for his confessor. "I am through now with men," he wrote that day in his diary. "I must turn to God. . . . I shall have courage." He constantly reread the history of Charles I of England, who had been decapitated on grounds of incompetent rule. He had recently entered into a state of despondency so deep that on one occasion he did not utter a single word in ten days, not even to his family, except during the backgammon games he played with his sister, when he spoke the few words necessary to the game. Louis was right to be afraid. On June 20 a mob of some thirty thousand Parisians wearing the Jacobins' "*bonnets rouges*" burst into the Tuileries, screaming imprecations against "Monsieur and Madame Veto." Bearing pikes and firearms, even cannon, the intruders flocked toward the center of the palace in search of the king. Just before the crowd had entered the palace, the monarchs had fled to different quarters. The king had gone upstairs to his study in the Oeil-de-Boeuf. The queen, her children, and a few of her ladies-in-waiting had sought refuge in a small secret passageway on the ground floor. The queen hid there, terrified, for over an hour, hearing nearby doors being broken by hatchets, and men's voices crying out for her blood. "They're going to kill me," she whispered to one of her women. She set out across a corridor for the Oeil-de-Boeuf, wanting to face death with the king. But a man she did not know—a royalist called the Chevalier de Rougeville, who would reenter her life later in dramatic circumstances—did not allow her to pass; he warned her that she would have to make her way through the mob to meet the king, which could be fatal to her. He persuaded her to accompany him to the Council Room, which the mob had not yet reached, and with the help of a few reliable grenadiers he moved a heavy table into a corner of the room.

Protected by a few men, and barricaded behind this table, the terrified queen and her children waited for the mob to reach them. Two hours passed before the invaders arrived. When they did, a citizen assuming the role of barker placed himself in front of the Council Room, urging the crowd to "come in and see the queen and the dauphin." One of the mob's leaders, Santerre, saw to it that order was maintained. And many citizens who had come to insult Marie Antoinette were won over by her courage and gentleness of bearing. One intruder shouted at her: "You are a vile woman!"

"Have I ever done you any harm?" the queen asked her.

"No, but you're the cause of the French people's unhappiness."

"So you have doubtless been told, but you've been misled," Marie Antoinette said. "I am the king's wife and the dauphin's mother. I am French. . . . I was happy when you loved me."

"I can now see that I was wrong, and that you're a good woman," said the woman, bursting into tears.

Santerre pushed her away. "She's drunk!" he said.

Upon orders from Pétion, who was currently the mayor of Paris, after eight hours the crowd finally dispersed. The palace was in shambles, doors smashed, floors covered by shattered glass and fragments of furniture.

After the June 20 invasion, Marie Antoinette, certain that she and her children would be killed upon the next such insurrection, did not sleep at night anymore; instead, she took short daytime naps when she was sure that either the king or her sister-in-law was awake and watching over her children.

"I still exist, but it's by a miracle," she wrote me shortly after the invasion of the Tuileries. "The 20th was a dreadful day. It's no longer against me that they're most bitter, but against my husband's very life. . . . He showed a firmness and a strength that impressed me for the moment, but the dangers could arise again at any time. . . . Adieu, take care of yourself for our sakes."

Throughout July of 1792 the queen's missives to me took on an increasingly urgent, desperate tone as she worried about the advance of the allied troops. When would they reach Paris to save her and her family? "Tell them to hurry with the help they've promised for our deliverance," she wrote. A few weeks later: "Tell Monsieur de Mercy that the lives of the king and queen are in the greatest peril and that the delay of so much as a day could cause incalculable harm. . . . The band of murderers is growing by the hour."

Yet the insurrection of June 20 had not been the success the Jacobins had hoped for. A petition supporting Louis XVI was signed by some twenty thousand Paris citizens. The same citizens demanded Mayor Pétion's arrest, and the whole of the province of Picardy voted to offer assistance to the king. But the monarch did not take advantage of this amicable popular mood. One of his aides, Bertrand de Moleville, suggested that he ride out openly from Paris with his guards to greet his citizens—public indignation over the June 20 riots would make such a trip safe. But Louis, with his usual caution and indecisiveness, demurred. Moleville also insisted that escape was the wisest action to take. "Oh, I don't want to flee a second time," the king answered. "It clearly put me in a bad position. I clearly saw that they wanted to kill me." "I don't know why they didn't manage it," he added with his usual fatalism; "another day I shan't escape them. . . . It doesn't matter whether one is assassinated two months sooner or later." When Moleville reminded the king that he should flee with his family to ensure their safety—the threats against the queen were growing increasingly severe—he replied that his family would not be increasingly endangered if he was killed. In those months Louis's lethargy was compounded by many similarly mistaken judgments, and he could be surprisingly insensitive to his family's fate.

BACK IN BRUSSELS, I received accounts of the events of June 20 that made me shudder, and also heard rumors that the Jacobins planned to move the royal family out of Paris. At the end of July I wrote Marie Antoinette: "Your position torments me ceaselessly. . . . Above all try to not leave Paris. That's the essential. . . . The Duke of Brunswick's plan is to reach you there." Brunswick was a gifted royalist general who commanded the Prussian and Austrian forces. (In an attempt to save herself and her children, the queen had persuaded me to compose the "Brunswick Manifesto," a proclamation signed by the allied nations threatening reprisals against France's revolutionary government if the royal family was harmed. I'm the first to admit that in retrospect this was a very bad strategy that increasingly estranged the royal family and their intimates from the rest of the nation.)

The queen replied to me: "Our position is dreadful but don't worry too much. I have courage and something tells me we'll soon be happy and safe. Only this idea sustains me. . . . Adieu. When shall we see each other again?"

A few days later: "Don't torment yourself too much about me," she wrote me in code, adding, in reference to Russia's promise of aid: "Hasten, if you can, the process of intermediation for our deliverance."

But there was no sign of Prussian, Russian, or Austrian troops: France had declared war in mid-April, it was now the end of July, and there was still no military movement on the Prussian or Austrian frontiers. The Austrian nobility was far more interested in the coronation of Marie Antoinette's nephew Francis I, which was being held that summer, than they were in the war. There was another reason for Austria's hesitation to engage France. The Austrian high command feared that Prussia was currently too busy helping Russia carve up Poland, and wished to wait until Prussia could contribute more men and arms to the French venture.

Finally, in early August, Brunswick began to march toward France. And I suddenly grew apprehensive about a conflict that I'd initially desired. "The moment of crisis has finally come," I wrote Marie Antoinette when Brunswick's troops began their advance, "and my soul shudders at the thought. May God protect you all."

At first, the allied armies marching into France met with little resistance. My earlier fears were allayed. I grew certain that Brunswick would reach Paris and rescue the royal family in a matter of weeks. How naive I was! So certain was I of a quick allied victory that I wrote the queen suggesting a few cabinet appointments upon Louis XVI's return to full power. The war ministry should be given to La Galisonniere, I proposed, foreign affairs to Bombelle, etc. The queen, understandably, reacted with pique at my suggestions, making me realize how out of touch I was. She told me of the Marseillais' arrival in Paris, of the collapse of the National Guard, of riots all over the city. "In the midst of so many dangers it is difficult to focus our attention on the choice of ministers," she wrote me with some annoyance; "for the time being we must think about how to avoid daggers and try to struggle against the conspirators who surround a throne that is about to vanish. The rebels no longer conceal their plan to massacre the royal family." As she was writing these words, Brunswick continued to score consecutive victories against the French revolutionary forces.

I should insert a few words here about the men designated as "rebels" by the queen: they were the Revolution's two most influential leaders—Georges-Jacques Danton and Maximilien Robespierre—who would now dictate the royal family's destiny.

Danton, a huge strapping fellow, born in 1759, trained as a lawyer, served as advocate to the royal councils before the Revolution, and opposed the Assembly's decision to maintain Louis XVI on his throne after the Varennes debacle. One of the Jacobins' most brilliant orators, this particular swine, known to love money and to be notably purchasable, instigated the decrees calling for the arrest of refractory priests, and initiated the movement demanding the king's deposition.

Robespierre, another bloody lawyer, was elected deputy to the Third Estate from his native Pas-de-Calais region, and would eventually be elected president of the Jacobin Club. Referred to as "the Incorruptible" because of his allegedly strict moral conduct, he was suspected of having dictatorial ambitions, a charge that would turn out to be accurate. In the king's forthcoming trial, he would intervene eleven times to demand Louis's death without delay.

Marie Antoinette was right to have been pessimistic in the summer of 1792. Paris erupted again on August 10, and in a far more violent manner than it had six weeks earlier. As Parisians were apprised of Brunswick's steadfast advance toward Paris, their emotions rose to the boiling point, and Danton capitalized on their anger. Controlling Paris's ablest armed factions, he staged a coup d'état that simultaneously toppled the Assembly and the Municipality of Paris. Through Danton's seizure of the Municipality, known henceforth as the Commune, the Parisian population became France's rulers.

The insurrection that began during the dawn hours of August 10 made the uprising of the previous June 20 look like child's play. All through the night the king and queen had heard the bells that for centuries had raised the alarm of invasion or fire—the same bells that two hundred years earlier had presaged the massacre of Saint Bartholomew—booming at the Church of Saint-Germain l'Auxerrois. They were followed by the tocsins of Saint-Antoine, of Saint-Jean and Saint-Gervaise, of Notre-Dame. And then, just before dawn, there began to be heard the bugle call with which the French mobilize their forces, the sullen fury of drums, the clattering of horses' hooves upon the pavement. The king had not undressed that night, but had paced the floor, lying down from time to time for a brief nap. The queen had wandered from room to room. One hope remained: the king's Swiss Guard was still loyal. And it was possible that the National Guard stationed at the Tuileries could be convinced to defend the palace. As for the Paris militia, it had, alas, succumbed to the revolutionaries: Danton had ordered their commander murdered, and the militia, from then on, took its orders from him.

Just before dawn the queen called for Madame Elisabeth, and they stood by a window from which they could see the sunrise. It was promising to be a bright, very hot day. The sun began to rise in a red mid-August sky.

In Brussels, thirty hours away by coach or horseback, I must have felt intimations of the disaster to come; for that very day I wrote Toinette in a tone far more pessimistic than my earlier letters. "I'm profoundly worried about you. I haven't had a moment's peace and my only comfort is to have my anxiety shared by M. Craufurd, who only thinks of you and of ways of helping you. . . . " This was my last letter to Marie Antoinette, and she never received it. It survives in a copy I made of it.

Meanwhile, back in Paris: at 7:30 in the morning, even before any shot had been fired, Louis, alarmed by the night's events, decided to abandon the Tuileries and to seek shelter with his family at the Manège, the nearby building where the Assembly met. Accompanied by an armed guard and their closest intimates—Madame de Tourzel and the devoted Princesse de Lamballe, who had left a comfortable exile abroad to return to her friend's side—the royal family walked down the main stairway into the garden, which they crossed on foot to reach the Manège. The king walked in front of the retinue, murmuring from time to time that the leaves had begun to fall very early that year. The dauphin, holding the queen's hand, trotted by her side and amused himself by pushing away those same dead leaves with his feet, until he grew weary and one of the royal guards lifted him into his arms. Once at the Assembly they were taken to a small box, behind the president's chair, which was habitually occupied by the Assembly's stenographers. They would be confined in this hot and airless space—some ten feet square— for fifteen hours, without anything to eat or drink.

As Marie-Thérèse later related it to me, at last a compassionate guard brought them some biscuits and a bottle of wine bought with his own money, but all the queen would take was a glass of water. From inside their closet, the royal family could hear their fate being discussed by the deputies. From the direction of the garden, they heard the sound of cannon and musket fire heralding the attack on the Tuileries. The last order that Louis was to sign as king of France was a fateful one: thinking that further defense of the palace was useless and that the Swiss Guards could gain amnesty by laying down arms, the king hurriedly wrote them a note to cease firing. But in fact this dictate served as a death warrant for the Swiss Guards and for many of the palace's inhabitants. For soon afterward the rebels invaded the Tuileries and began their carnage: the Swiss Guards and the entire domestic staff of the palace, to whom the invaders were particularly merciless, were slaughtered with the mob's habitual sadism. Every man, from the head chefs to the humblest scullion, perished.

Louis and his family spent that night in a cell at the nearby Convent of the Feuillants. On the following day they again returned to the Manège, where they heard the deputies abolish the institution of kingship and dissolve the Assembly: the new body that replaced it was to be called the National Convention, which would give Danton a higher number of votes than was received by any other deputy, and made him the most powerful man in France. The royal family also heard a long discussion about their future residence. Many deputies proposed the Luxembourg, but the Convention's strong men—Danton and Robespierre—decided that the royal family should be sent to the Temple, a seventeenth-century building in the Marais, not far from the Bastille, that had once been the residence of the Knights Templar.

I had visited the Temple once, as a young man, on my grand tour. A vast, austerely elegant compound, it had many dependencies that had been built in earlier centuries, and one of these, at the far end of the Temple's gardens, was a dungeon known as the Temple Tower. A square, turreted building some sixty feet high, of grim and foreboding appearance, with ten-foot-thick walls, its interior was composed of four identical floors connected by a narrow stairway. Having been entertained in the splendid rooms of the Temple by the Comte d'Artois, at dinner parties after the opera, Marie Antoinette was well acquainted with the Temple proper. (Shuddering at the sight of its bleak tower, she had often asked Artois to demolish it.)

Upon arriving in their new residence, the royal family were served an elaborate meal in the Salle des Quatre Glaces, where Artois had habitually received the queen. What they did not yet know as they sat down to dinner was that they were destined to be lodged in the tower of the Temple, not in the Temple proper. The mayor of Paris, Jerome Pétion, the same Pétion who had flirted with Madame Elisabeth on the way back from Varennes, was in charge of them that day; a man not devoid of compassion, he lacked the courage to tell the royals that their home would be in the dungeon. So he went to the Hotel de Ville that very evening and suggested to the deputies of the Commune that the prisoners be incarcerated in the Temple Palace rather than in its tower. But the rest of the deputies did not share Pétion's empathy. The royal family, the Commune insisted, must go to the dungeon. Madame de Tourzel and Madame de Lamballe were to be sent to the prison of La Force. Two of the king's and dauphin's valets, Hue and Cléry, were briefly detained but then released, and were allowed to accompany the royal family to the Temple dungeon.

The "Capets," as the family was called after the institution of kingship was officially abolished (I've refused to use that name), soon began a routine that would not change in the following five months. Marie Antoinette and Madame Elisabeth spent the morning instructing Princess Marie-Thérèse, and after dinner they worked at their embroidery or read aloud to each other (the princess reported that Fanny Burney's *Evelina* was one of the queen's great favorites). As for the king, he knelt down for a long time to say his prayers early each morning, and then instructed his son—an unusually bright, receptive boy—in essentials such as Latin, history, and geography. Lessons finished at about two. Louis and the dauphin sat down for dinner with their family, after which the king and queen might play backgammon while the dauphin and his sister flew kites or played ball with Cléry in the garden. In his spare time the king read his breviary for several hours of the day and also read a great deal from the prison's well-stocked library. The guards vigilantly surveying the royal family at every moment of the day were the only drawback to a not unpleasant existence.

After months spent at the Tuileries under perpetual threat of attack, at first the king and queen were relieved by this new mode of confinement. By the Commune's order, they were cut off from all communication with the outside world. So they lost sense of the menace still posed by the Parisian mob. But the next uprisings, known as the September 3 massacres, reminded them all too brutally that the Revolution was still raging unabated. The immediate incentive for the September 3 massacres was an impulse to avenge those patriots who had died during the insurrection of August 10, three weeks earlier. The Parisians' rage was also prompted by new reports of the Prussian army's success, particularly by the unexpected defeat of French troops at Longwy at August's end. Moreover, there were rumors of plots being hatched within the prisons: it was feared that if enemy troops reached Paris, they would open the doors of these jails and, aided by the former convicts, cause an even greater massacre of patriots.

Early on the morning of September 3, Parisians learned that Verdun was about to fall to the Prussians. The Commune decreed a *levée en masse*. And soon thereafter the slaughter in the jails began. Among the first to be attacked was the prison of L'Abbaye, where scores of prisoners—prominent aristocrats, priests, judges, royal bodyguards—were killed by a group of some fifty neighborhood patriots that included jewelers, butchers, and café owners. There followed the onslaught on the prison of Bicêtre, where more than 1,700 beggars and other harmless castoffs were killed, among them thirty boys between the ages of twelve and fourteen. At the Salpetrière, girls of ten were murdered. At the Carmelite prison, more than two hundred priests were massacred by a crowd who sang the hymn "Dies Irae" as they went about their slaughter. The murderers moved on to the prisons of Saint-Firmin and La Force, where they killed Madame de Lamballe in a particularly sadistic manner. A total of more than two thousand innocent citizens thus met their demise.

On the afternoon of September 4, soon after the onslaught on La Force began, the king and queen had started their after-dinner game of backgammon when they heard a growing roar below their window. They then heard a terrible shriek. It was from the valet Cléry, who came rushing into the monarchs' room to close its curtains: the head of Madame de Lamballe was being paraded in front of the queen's window. Municipal guards next appeared in the room. One of them bluntly told Marie Antoinette the truth: "It is the head of Lamballe, which they have brought here to show you and to make you kiss," he told the queen;

"this is how the people takes its revenge upon tyrants." Upon hearing these words, Marie-Thérèse reported, Marie Antoinette fainted. All through the following night the princess could hear her mother's sobs. The queen was lucky that the details of Madame de Lamballe's death were never reported to her: she had been disemboweled, her heart devoured, and her intestines trailed through the streets of Paris to the palace of her brother-in-law, the Duc d'Orléans.

A DISAGREEABLE, irascible couple called the Tisons had been assigned to watch over, and serve, the royal family during their incarceration at the Temple. In addition to their domestic chores—keeping house, overseeing the family's meals—they were ordered by the Commune to spy on the prisoners. The queen, according to her daughter, immediately realized that the Tisons were probably incapable of pity or compassion, and that she could never mollify them by any friendly deed or gesture. But there was another member of the Temple staff—twenty-nine-year-old Francois Turgy—who turned out to be more than kindly disposed to them, who was, in fact, an ardent royalist and a passionate admirer of the queen. Turgy, who had been employed as a scullery boy at the kitchens of Versailles, had moved on with much of the domestic staff to the Tuileries. Not having lived at the palace, he was spared the massacre of the servants that occurred there on August 10. A highly resourceful fellow, Turgy managed to get himself designated to the Temple kitchen through a series of subterfuges, telling Commune members that he had been sent there by the Assembly, and telling his section leaders at the Assembly that the Commune had appointed him there. Turgy's job was to set the table and serve the royal family their meals. And despite the vigilance with which the king and queen were surveyed by their guards—roast meats and even rolls were torn into pieces to make sure that they did not contain messages—Turgy managed to communicate with them. As he mounted the winding stairwell toward their floor, for instance, he might insert a note in the stopper of a bottle. Moreover, when out of earshot of the Tison couple he was occasionally able to whisper a few words to Madame Elisabeth or the queen, and eventually he established a code of finger signals with which he could transmit to them news of the outside world. "If the Austrians are successful on the Belgian frontier," so Turgy later described details of his sign language to me, "place the second finger of the right hand on the right eye. . . . When they are within fifteen leagues of Paris . . . place it on the mouth."

Another potential champion of the royal family's was Citizen Lepitre, the owner of a small boarding school who was a skilled Latinist; he had only joined the revolutionary forces for reasons of personal survival, and soon made it clear to the former king and queen that he sympathized with them. Upon one occasion, seeing Louis reading his copy of Virgil's *Aeneid,* he asked the king if he could borrow the book, and addressed the request in perfect Latin. Louis, amazed that one of the guards was so familiar with the classics, gave it to him with great pleasure; Lepitre would eventually engage in the rescue efforts that would attempt to liberate Marie Antoinette.

At first the news communicated by Turgy was heartening. Brunswick met with no resistance as his troops advanced toward Paris. From Verdun they marched into the Argonne and captured Stenay, where a year beforehand, in June 1791, the royal family had hoped to be rescued by Bouillé. But a bit farther on, at Valmy, a few miles off the road I'd planned for the royal family to take to Varennes, the course of the war was abruptly reversed: the allied armies were resoundingly defeated by the French revolutionary forces. Valmy, one of the world's most decisive battles, was commented on by Goethe, who witnessed the event, as the beginning of "a new era in the world's history."

The ragtag army of the penniless French Republic defeating the

well-drilled regiments of several wealthy European countries, and seal-
ing the fate of my beloved royal family? I never would have thought it
possible, and I doubt if historians will ever explain it. I was in Brussels
with Eleanore Sullivan, Craufurd, and the Comte de Mercy when I
learned of Brunswick's rout. We were not only horrified but totally
puzzled by the news: his defeat seemed inexplicable. It was attributed to
a variety of causes: a violent outbreak of dysentery among his forces
was one; another, more ideological reason, was that patriotism instilled
into the newborn French Republican army an esprit de corps, a savage
valor, that was mightier than any physical force. Rumors also spread
that Brunswick, who was known to be greedy and corruptible, had
been bribed with five million francs by a wealthy republican to lose the
battle. His retreat, unlike his leisurely advance, was very hurried. On
November 6 Eleanore Sullivan and I, accompanied by the Russian
minister, Monsient de Simolin, were taking a walk in the forest outside
Brussels. Suddenly, coming from the west, we heard the faint sound of
artillery fire. Over dinner that night at Craufurd's, the Comte de Mercy
assured us that the sound was nothing more than a celebration of Saint
Charles's Day. But in the middle of the meal a courier arrived with an
urgent message for Mercy to report to the palace of Archduchess Maria
Cristina, Marie Antoinette's sister. She informed him that the Austrian
army had suffered a crushing defeat and that the French were arriving
in Brussels in a matter of days.

Eleanore, Craufurd, Simolin, and I left for Düsseldorf two days later.
We did not reach our destination until the third week of December;
it took us five weeks from Brussels because of the mayhem on the roads.
We often made do with the humblest circumstances as we rode southward through Germany, sleeping on straw pallets on stable floors. The
roads were dense with fleeing émigrés—merchants and aristocrats, the
rich and the poor—walking toward freedom, carrying their possessions
on poles slung over their shoulders. Once settled in Düsseldorf, we

began to hear of the horrors committed by revolutionary troops as they surged through France. The country's treasures were being methodically plundered by Jacobin functionaries and by thieves. *Liberté, Égalité, Fraternité*, indeed! What a hypocritical slogan! The most shameful sacking took place in churches, where reliquaries and crucifixes were picked of their precious stones and melted down, and where masterpieces by such artists as Van Eyck and Van der Weyden were destroyed. Few leaders of the revolutionary troops were more outraged by this rampage than their commander in chief, General Dumouriez. Dumouriez, a Girondin by conviction, was already offended by the fact that the French war ministry had fallen to the extremists—the minister of war was now in the pay of the rabble-rousing Marat. When he learned that arms and ammunition that should have been directed to the French army in Belgium were being diverted to Marat's private army, he made his own plans for the future: he would eventually defect to the Austrian side.

Upon our arrival I heard that the Convention was bringing Louis XVI to trial. I was in the deepest torment, all the more so because I initially feared that the queen was going on trial with him. My dear, gentle Louis! Writing to Thomas Jefferson, Gouverneur Morris, the American ambassador, gave an excellent estimate of the king. "It is strange that the mildest monarch who ever sat the French throne, one who was precipitated from it precisely because he would not adopt the harsh measures of his predecessors, a man whom one can not charge with one criminal or cruel act, should be prosecuted as one of the most nefarious tyrants who ever disgraced the annals of human nature."

Once a large majority of its deputies found the king guilty, the Convention deliberated from the eighteenth to the twentieth of January concerning the nature of his punishment. The American-born deputy Tom Paine suggested that Louis be sent to the United States, where he might be rehabilitated as a good patriot. "Ah, citizens," Paine cried out, "give not the tyrant of England the triumph of seeing the man perish on the scaffold who aided my so much loved America to break its chains!" He was shouted down on the grounds that Paine's religious sect—he was a Quaker—was notorious for its opposition to the death penalty. A few deputies voted for banishment, many for death with a reprieve, and a narrow majority of fifty-three for immediate death. The vote was cast on the twentieth of January 1793; and needless to say, that swine, that rotter the Duc d'Orléans, who had taken the nom de guerre of "Philippe-Égalité" upon being elected deputy to the Convention by his Paris district, voted for his own cousin's demise. Even some of the hard-line revolutionaries were appalled by d'Orléans's ballot. "Miserable wretch," Danton muttered to Robespierre; "he of all people could have refused to vote."

Louis XVI had been separated from his family on December 11, a few weeks before his trial. This had been a fresh source of sorrow for the queen. In this gauche, ungainly man she had once derided with her frivolous friends she had recently discovered many precious qualities—his courage and fortitude, the gentleness, calm, and patience he maintained in the most perilous circumstances. I suspect that her tenderness for him had turned into love—no, more, into passion. She had made his bed herself, had sat by him round the clock whenever he fell ill. In the thrall of this new devotion, she announced that she wished to die with him, that she would henceforth refuse all nourishment. Soon after their separation one of the family's guards took such pity on her that on one particular night he arranged for the royal family to have supper together. Marie-Thérèse reports that the queen displayed immense delight upon this prospect, weeping with joy and passionately embracing her children and her sister-in-law. Even their most ferocious guardian, the cobbler Simon, burst out: "In truth, I think these damned women are capable of making me cry!"

The king, in turn, living in unprecedentedly close quarters with his wife, came to esteem her own brand of courage, and treasure as he never had before her extraordinary familial devotion. Their parting may have been all the more painful because each of them had just begun to cherish qualities they had never perceived in each other during their twenty years of marriage. On the eve of his death, the king seemed to have finally experienced, after all these years, the sweet certainty of knowing he was loved. "Alas," he said to his confessor in his last hours, "it shall be worse because I love so deeply, and am so tenderly loved in return!"

On Christmas Day, the king would compose his last will and testament. I have read that extraordinary document many times, have marveled at its generosity and clemency, have been increasingly touched, over the years, by those words that relate to Marie Antoinette: "I beg my wife," he wrote, "to forgive me all the pain which she may have suffered for me and the sorrows that I may have caused her during our union." And then there comes that enigmatic phrase: "Should she have anything with which to reproach herself, may she feel sure that I hold nothing against her." Reproach herself for what? For those froths and follies of her youth that had led her to be calumniated as no previous consort in French history, and had played a part in leading her husband to the Temple? Or did the words allude to a more specific issue—Marie Antoinette's liaison with me?

"Poor woman!" Louis said to one of his counsels during his last weeks. "She was promised a throne, and it has come to this." Talking to his lawyers, he often referred to the ill will the French people had borne Marie Antoinette, to the pernicious influence of a recklessly hedonistic court, to the fact that she had been only fourteen when she arrived in its midst. They minded his words, for few persons who met the king during his solitary confinement—National Guardsmen, municipal officers, even members of the Commune—did not come to esteem and pity him. We have it on Cléry's word—I know his memoirs by heart—that a local citizen from the Faubourg Saint-Antoine had a keen desire to meet the monarch. Cléry managed to arrange a visit. "What, sir, is this the king?" the citizen said to Cléry after the meeting. "How good he is! How he loves his children!" . . . "Ah," he went on to say, striking his chest, "never could I believe that he has done us any evil!" For the king, affable as ever in his captivity, conversed at length with every one of his visitors and guardians, asking them about their childhoods, their work, their families, their children. Family was that focal point upon which these men, coming from radically opposite circumstances, found a common ground. Those citizens who came to know Louis, moreover, could not see the sense of his being separated from his nearest and dearest. What harm could have been brought by merely familial talk? Each time the king spoke of his wife and children his guards were very moved. "Today is my daughter's birthday," he said to them on December 19. "It's her birthday, and I can't even see her!" A few of these men broke into tears. Those who did not might well have repressed them.

The king would not be allowed to see his family until the night before his execution. But the queen could hear his steps as he left the Temple daily for the Convention hearings, and every evening she would hear him return accompanied by his lawyers and armed guards.

During the weeks of the king's solitary imprisonment, the queen's health began to fail. Always a picky eater, she now ate next to nothing, and her request for a dressmaker who could take in her clothes was granted.

On the twentieth of January, the eve of his scheduled execution, the king asked for a three-day reprieve during which he might better prepare to meet his God. His request was refused, and his execution remained fixed for the next morning. On the queen's floor that same evening, a guard came in at eight o'clock and told the royal family that they could go down and see the king one last time.

They stayed in Louis's quarters for almost two hours. The king, seated with his emaciated wife on his left and his sister on his right, drew his son toward him and made him stand between his knees. In one of his last instructions to him, he asked the child to never avenge his death; and since the boy had never pledged an oath before, the king took up his little hand and made him vow that he would keep his promise. He then pressed his wife to his shoulder while his daughter, who passionately loved her father, clung to him and gave way to bitter tears. Marie Antoinette knew that Louis desired them to leave, and said, "Promise that you will see us again."

"I promise," he said, "at eight tomorrow morning, before I go."

"Please come earlier," she begged.

"All right, half an hour earlier."

"Promise me."

He repeated his promise. The two women and two children left through the great nail-studded oak door, and walked up the winding stairs. The queen threw herself fully dressed on her bed after she had put her boy to sleep, and Marie-Thérèse could hear her weeping for the following many hours.

As soon as his family had left, the king told his guards that in spite of his promise, his family should not be told of his departure for the scaffold the next morning, for it would make them suffer all the more. He then ate a substantial supper, which included half a chicken, a beef roast, and a bottle of champagne, and slept very soundly. He woke at 5 a.m., and heard Mass said by the priest permitted him by the Convention, a half-French, half-Irish curate called Abbé Edgeworth de Firmont, who had been educated in a Jesuit seminary in Toulouse. Louis received communion from the abbé, and proceeded to dress. At 8 a.m., a group of delegates from the Convention arrived. He asked them if Cléry might cut his hair to spare him the indignity of having it cropped on the scaffold, but permission was denied. Noticing that the deputies all wore their hats, he asked for his. He then took off his wedding ring and gave it to Cléry, saying, "You will give this to my wife, and tell her that our separation causes me much sorrow." He also handed Cléry, to give to his son, the dauphin, the seal of France, thus transmitting to him the principal symbol of kingship.

Louis was offered his coat. He said he did not need it. He was wearing a brown jacket, black trousers, white stockings. As the delegates, who were led by the brewer Santerre, a leader of the June 20, 1792, attack on the Tuileries, continued to shuffle around him, Louis gave the definitive order. "*Partons!*" he said. Accompanied by his captors, he walked from the dungeon to the palace of the Temple, turning several times to look back at the prison where his family still waited for him.

It had been barely six in the morning, in the January dark, when the queen had heard steps coming from the king's room. Her hopes for Louis's visit had risen . . . but it had been merely a guard who had come to fetch the king's missal. She had waited until eight, at first light, and still the king had not made his promised appearance. Some moments later she had heard the sound of many men walking toward the Temple's first floor; she then knew that they were coming to fetch him.

In front of the Temple palace Louis XVI got into his coach, which was of the same dark green color as the one he had ridden out of Paris on his way to Varennes. It was to take him to the place Louis XV— odiously renamed the place de la Révolution—along the widest streets, which even on this bitterly cold morning were lined with citizens and troops. According to Abbé Edgeworth, during this trip of over two hours he never looked out of the coach's window, keeping his eyes fixed on his breviary.

It was ten minutes past ten when the king arrived at the place Louis XV. There was a total silence on the part of the crowd, which was some twenty thousand strong; all one could hear was the continual roll of drums. The king warmly thanked his confessor, and took off his hat and jacket himself. All of a sudden, he grew agitated. The noise of the drums seemed to anger him. "Silence, silence!" he cried out. And then, as the drums quieted down, "I am lost! I am lost!"

The executioner, Sanson, wanted to tie his hands. He resisted him, glancing at his confessor as if to ask his counsel. "Sire," Abbé Edgeworth said, "this last outrage is yet one more trait in common between Your Majesty and your God, Who will be your recompense." The king lifted his eyes to the sky and ceased resisting. "Do whatever you wish," he told his executioners. "I will drink the chalice down to the dregs."

The steps to the scaffold were very steep, and the king leaned on his confessor. Having reached the last step, he freed himself from the abbé and ran to the other side of the scaffold. "Frenchmen," he shouted at the crowd, "I die innocent of all the crimes of which I am charged. I pardon those who have brought about my death."

The drums rolled again. "Do your duty!" citizens were yelling at the executioners.

Louis's last words were interrupted by the guillotine itself. "May my blood strengthen the happiness of the Fr—"

"Son of Saint Louis, ascend to heaven!" Edgeworth cried out as the twelve-inch blade came crashing down. The king's dripping head was held up to the crowd by the executioner. A few seconds passed; then came loud shouts of "*Vive la République!*"

Louis's body, placed in a basket, was taken to the cemetery of the Madeleine. There it was put into a plain wooden coffin of the kind that was used for the poorest citizens; it was buried ten feet deep, and covered with lime. As soon as his body was carried away a huge crowd rushed to the site of execution to dip their kerchiefs, linen, and swords in puddles of the king's blood. A group of British citizens stood at the bottom of the scaffold, shouting that they wished to purchase relics of this new martyr. Among revolutionaries there would be an immediate effort to make regicide look commonplace, so much so that the Sèvres industry produced demitasses with an image of the king's severed head rendered in dainty gold paint.

But the effect of the king's execution on the French population at large was not at all what the Convention had hoped. Those who witnessed the event testify to the "mournful air" that hung over Paris. Most windows remained shuttered; citizens stayed inside their houses. I heard that there were many suicides that day: a woman threw herself into the Seine; a wig-maker cut his throat; a librarian went mad; a retired officer died of shock. A few days later, the Convention received a letter from a man who asked that he be given Louis's corpse, so that he might bury him next to his own father. "The late king of this country died in a manner becoming his dignity," Gouverneur Morris wrote to Thomas Jefferson. "The majority of Parisians mourn the fate of their unhappy prince. I have seen grief similar to that evoked by the untimely death of a beloved parent. Everything here wears an appearance of solemnity which is awfully distressing."

Upon hearing that the king was to be executed, I kept fearing that Marie Antoinette might be guillotined alongside him. "My dread is unimaginable," I wrote my sister Sophie on January 24, before I'd received any official news, in a series of letters in which I poured out my grief. "Poor, unfortunate family, poor queen! Why can't I save her with my blood? It would be the greatest happiness for me, the sweetest joy for my soul. Ah! . . . think then how wretched I am and how dreadful my position is. Yes my dear Sophie, it's almost unbearable. . . . I don't know if I can tolerate my emotions."

"I spent the whole day in uncertainty and in a dreadful state," I wrote a few days later from Düsseldorf. "Ah, how much I loved *Her*, and how much I suffered! This evening the director of the imperial mail came to see me. . . . He had been told that the king was executed and the whole family massacred."

A few days later, in a missive made barely coherent by grief: "My tender, kind Sophie. Ah, pity me! Only you can know the state I'm in. I've now lost everything in the world. You alone and Taube are left for me—ah, don't abandon me! *She* who was my happiness, she whom I loved—yes, my tender Sophie, because I have never stopped loving her, not for an instant, and I would have sacrificed absolutely everything for her, I fear that at this moment, she whom I loved so much and for whom I would have given a thousand lives, is no more. . . . She no longer lives! My grief is overwhelming and I don't know how to stay alive. Nothing will ever efface my sorrow, she will always be present in my memory and I shall weep for her forever. . . . Ah why didn't I die at her side and for her—for them—on June 20. I would have been happier than dragging out my miserable existence in eternal sorrows, in sorrows that will end only with my life, because her adored image never will be effaced from my memory. . . ."

"We received the definitive news of the king's execution," I wrote Sophie a day later still. "My heart is so torn I haven't the strength to tell you more. There is no word about the rest of the family, but I'm still in great dread. Ah my God! Save them and have mercy on me!"

Eleanore Sullivan and I wept much when Louis's execution was officially confirmed, and my rage at the Jacobins grew apace. "Tigers, cannibals, savages!" I wrote Taube. "Oh, accursed nation! If there exists a God, this impious, sacrilegious, barbaric horde should be damned by him. It is to be annihilated, exterminated. . . . It should be overwhelmed by all evils: starvation, disease, misery." I knew that the French monarch had been obsessed with the fate of his British counterpart, Charles I. But what a difference between the two men's demise! Charles had been decapitated in a lordly manner, in the courtyard of his palace, surrounded by a few dignitaries; Louis had been slaughtered like a common criminal, before a crowd of tens of thousands. The lack of news concerning Marie Antoinette gave me hope that she and her children were still alive. But for how long? "Alas, my dear Axel," Sophie wrote me in mid-February, "she is not yet dead, but destined for fresh sufferings. . . . How it grieves me. . . . There are no words to describe the horror of her situation and my fears and my griefs."

Another rumor tormented me the following month: the dauphin, it was said, would be declared a bastard; the queen would have her head shaved and be shut up in the Salpetrière prison. "My soul is so tormented and rent . . . by the loss I have just suffered and my fears for the future, that I can hardly think about anything else," I wrote Sophie. "In vain I try to console myself, in vain I want to hope. . . ."

A fortnight later I was calmer: "I'm beginning to have a little hope about the fate of the queen and her family; there is no talk of either her or her trial."

The great majority of European citizens reacted with horror, as Gouverneur Morris had, upon hearing of Louis XVI's execution. Overlooking the regicide that his own compatriots had committed a century earlier, Prime Minister William Pitt referred to Louis's beheading as "the foulest and most atrocious deed which the history of the world has yet had occasion to attest."

CHAPTER II

Sophie:

LA REINE DE FRANCE

SOPHIE PIPER HERE, continuing to edit my brother's memoirs. The task has been in turn joyful, painful, moving. Who else could have been capable of the kind of loyalty Axel offered the French monarchs? What steadfastness, what compassion! But there is a strange gap in Axel's memoirs: it struck me as most curious that he left out the nine months that passed between the king's execution and that of Marie Antoinette. What were the grounds for this omission? Might one perhaps see it as an act of self-protection? He who had so loved her could not tolerate the pain of describing her dreadful last months. So I've set out to chronicle them, with the help of any evidence I've been able to collect.

As the reader may have gathered, I had not initially appreciated the French queen, having heard much about her frivolity, her spendthrift ways, her disdain for that holy man, her husband. But as time went on I learned that she had a great heart; that she was capable of immense acts of thoughtfulness and generosity; that she was as remarkable a mother as one could hope to find in any walk of life. And I began to realize, as the reader might have, that there were three separate and distinct Marie Antoinettes: the first was the flighty, capricious girl called "Featherhead" by her own brother; the second was the woman who, especially after the Varennes debacle, became impassioned with European politics, and attempted to play a role in them as conscientiously as she could; and last, there was the bereaved, imprisoned widow, "La Veuve Capet" as those barbaric revolutionaries called her, who became, in my eyes, a saint—in her fortitude, her gentleness, her largesse toward anyone who had even less than she.

Let's start chronicling those last months of hers with the morning of the king's death. Upon hearing the terrible cry that signaled his execution, "*Vive la République!*," the queen, her daughter Marie-Thérèse, and Madame Elisabeth engaged in a traditional ritual of obeisance: they bowed deeply before the new king, seven-year-old Louis XVII, saluting him as France's new monarch. From that day on little Louis-Charles would sit at his father's place at the dinner table, and be served first— the only tribute his mother and aunt could offer him in their humble circumstances.

And from then on the boy's health and happiness would become the central preoccupation of Marie Antoinette's life. For after her husband's death she sank into a terrible depression. She spent most of her days seated in a faded green chair, knitting, thinking, occasionally reading. She refused to go down the Temple's familiar curving staircase to take air in the garden, for she feared that the sight of her late husband's room would deepen her sorrow. Only her children's company, especially that of the little king, could allay her torpor. She worried much about his character—the charming, unusually engaging boy had a lively imagination, and tended to gossip and exaggeration. As for the dauphin's education, the queen tried to continue the teaching schedule—mathematics, the rudiments of Latin and history—Louis XVI had partaken in with the boy, but found herself sorely deficient in that task. She made sure that he engaged in as much outdoor exercise as possible, sending him out to the Temple garden to play ball with the friendlier guards. Above all she insisted he treat the Tison couple and the guards with unfailingly good manners, bidding him to say "Bonjour, monsieur," "Bonjour, madame," upon every one of his encounters with them.

On the day following Louis XVI's execution a dressmaker came to Marie Antoinette's quarters at the Temple, as she had requested, to fit her with the simplest of widow's weeds: black stockings and shoes, a black dress with austere white trimming about the neck, even a black fan.

But notwithstanding her pitiful looks and threadbare clothes the Widow Capet, the emaciated gray-haired woman who looked decades older than her thirty-seven years, had retained much of that charm, that hypnotic graciousness of manner, that had captivated men since her youth. Months before Louis's death, during the first weeks of the royal couple's incarceration at the Temple, there had appeared a man—one of their guards—who seemed determined to save them. A fellow with rough manners and a wild, unruly appearance, he was a bookstore owner, originally from Toulouse, appropriately called Francis Andre Toulan. There had been few more ardent patriots in Paris. Toulan was most probably part of the mob that attacked the Tuileries on June 20. He led a battalion when the palace was stormed on August 10. It was to reward his valor that the Convention had appointed him to be one of the men to guard the royal family at the Temple.

But however coarse his mien, Citizen Toulan was capable of compassion. Within a few weeks of guarding them, his original hatred for "the tyrants" changed into pity and concern. He was awed and moved by the patience and dignity with which the former king and queen bore their suffering and sorrow. While publicly continuing to fulminate against "the Austrian" and her consort, he began to give signs of his support for the royal family, who were at first distrustful. But Toulan soon found concrete ways of manifesting his sympathy for them. He was responsible, for instance, for setting up a newspaper vendor near enough to the tower that the family could hear him calling out reports of the day's events. After Louis's separation from his family, he made every attempt to carry messages between Louis and Marie Antoinette. The wild-looking Toulan, whom Marie Antoinette called "Fidèle," often displayed his devotion with great audacity. He managed to retrieve the king's wedding ring and seal, which the king had given Cléry on the morning of his death, and which had ended up in a chest in the guard-room. Shortly afterward Toulan, on a day when he was alone in that room, smashed the chest, swiftly grabbed these mementos, and brought them to Marie Antoinette.

Some months later, after the king's death, when he was out of the Tisons' earshot, Toulan asked the queen whether she would be willing to attempt escaping from the Temple. The queen demurred, as I and any other devoted mother would, saying that she would never accede to any escape plan that did not include her children. Toulan replied that his scheme was equally safe for four people, but that he needed an accomplice to make it work. The queen thought a bit, and came up with just the right man: the chevalier de Jarjayes, who had been her private secretary during her years at the Tuileries. He was married to one of her former ladies-in-waiting, and the previous year, upon the tribulations of August 10, he had promised Louis XVI to remain in Paris in case his services might be needed by the royal family. Upon the king's death, however, he felt liberated from that promise, and decided to emigrate. But shortly before his scheduled departure he received a visit from a mysterious, hirsute man—Toulan—who after identifying himself as a guard at the Temple declared that his conscience tortured him: the sor-row displayed by the queen had moved him greatly; he felt that he had been most unjust toward fine, innocent people; and he now wanted to make amends by helping the queen to escape.

In those days all of us royalists remained very suspicious of anyone displaying sympathy for the queen; as my brother put it, we had to remain constantly in dread of being duped. Toulan ultimately gained Jarjayes's trust by handing him a note from the queen, whose handwriting Jarjayes knew all too well. "You can trust this man," the queen had written; ". . . his feelings are well known to me and they have not changed for months."

Jarjayes, who like most members of her former entourage was devoted to Marie Antoinette, was so moved by the queen's note that he was close to tears. After moments of considerable emotion he regained composure. Toulan convinced Jarjayes that Marie Antoinette's life was in imminent danger, and the two men began to discuss escape plans with a great sense of urgency. But Jarjayes felt he could not join the project without first speaking with the queen, and they had to devise a scheme whereby Jarjayes could enter the Temple prison.

Toulan concocted another ruse to achieve that end. He decided that Jarjayes would impersonate the lamplighter who came to the Temple every night. Playing to the lamplighter's patriotism, he told him that a patriot friend of his wished to visit the Temple Tower in order to see the Widow Capet in her humiliated state. The lamplighter, knowing of Toulan's reputation as a committed revolutionary, agreed, and Jarjayes, dressed as the lamplighter, was able to visit the queen. They had little time to talk, but Marie Antoinette reassured Jarjayes that she would consent to any escape plan he might propose.

Jarjayes's plan was auspicious, for in recent months the prison guards had grown far more relaxed about their duties, and the Convention had even diminished the amount of sentinels assigned to the dungeon. One more man was needed for the rescue plot to work, and the queen was asked to choose him. She decided on Lepitre, the professor of Latin who had guarded the royal family when Louis was still alive, and had signaled his sympathy for the royal couple by asking the king for his copy of Virgil. Many other clandestine signs of esteem had convinced the queen that Lepitre could be trusted.

Lepitre acceded, at first, to the queen's request for his help; but over time he grew worried about what would happen to his wife if the venture failed, and only agreed to participate in it in exchange for a sizable sum—the contemporary equivalent of twenty thousand dollars, to be paid in advance. Rather than raise suspicions by borrowing the money from a bank, Jarjayes, at the risk of depleting his entire fortune, paid Lepitre out of his own funds.

Once Lepitre had been purchased, the details of the evasion were planned: the Tison couple, who used a great deal of snuff, would be drugged by a narcotic put into their tobacco. The young king would be carried out by Turgy in the bottom of a laundry basket. Marie Antoinette and Madame Elisabeth would leave the Temple in male disguise, dressed as municipal officers. Marie-Thérèse, also in masculine costume, would impersonate the son of the lamplighter, who often came to the Temple with his father. Once they had left the Temple dungeon the four prisoners would enter three small carriages waiting for them a block away. In the company of Lepitre and Toulan, they would travel to Le Havre, where a friend of Jarjayes had provided a boat that would take them to England.

But Lepitre, whatever his devotion to the queen, grew increasingly worried about the plot's possible failure. It was his appointed task to acquire passports for her from the Convention, which would have been easy for him, since he was president of its Passport Committee. But he was terrified of taking this crucial step. He would daily arrive at the Temple with yet another excuse for not having gotten the documents. Marie Antoinette grew desperate and bribed him with a lock of the late king's hair; Madame Elisabeth knitted him a bonnet. He still demurred. The day set for the evasion slipped by. And shortly afterward France suffered a serious setback when General Dumouriez, commander of the French Republic's army (described by my brother as "a typical Frenchman, vain, gullible, and fickle"), defected to the Prussian-Austrian side. Faced with many additional problems—rebellions in the Vendée, Brittany, and Normandy, a worse shortage of bread than any Parisians had ever experienced under the monarchy—the Convention decided to close the capital's gates and to stop issuing any further passports.

Undaunted, Toulan, Jarjayes, and Madame Elisabeth persuaded the queen, against all odds, to flee alone, arguing that it would benefit her children to have her free. But she changed her mind in a matter of hours. As the mother of three, how well I understand her emotions! Looking at her son sleeping in his bed, she exclaimed to her sister-in-law: "It's impossible! I can't leave!" Feeling guilty toward the two men who had risked so much for her, she wrote Jarjayes a short note that ended with these phrases: "I'm very moved by all the emotions that have attached you to my fate . . . but were I to leave my children I would enjoy nothing in life." So Jarjayes left France as he had earlier planned, having promised to do a few favors for the queen: to bring the king's seal to the Comte de Provence, and the king's wedding ring to Artois. There was another important errand she asked him to do: concealed in her jail cell was a signet ring that had some personal association with my brother Axel, which he might even have given her. Inscribed on it was the image of a dove bearing an olive branch, and the motto *"Tutto a te mi guida,"* "Everything leads me to thee." She made a wax impression of the ring on a piece of paper, and asked Jarjayes to bring it to Axel, and to tell him that "this motto has never been more true."

ALTHOUGH THE NUMBER of French troops that followed Dumouriez was negligible, his treason considerably helped the allied side. By July allied troops were again marching across the border onto French soil. My brother, who often displayed unwarranted optimism, had one such moment of preposterously unfounded hope. "I've heard on good authority," Axel wrote my dear friend Taube, "that at this very moment they're heating the apartments of the royal family at Versailles." "I consider the whole business closed and am delirious with joy," he wrote a few weeks later. "According to all reports there's nothing to fear for the royal family. . . . Don't be surprised if in a short while I tell you that they're being carried in triumph through the Paris streets." As Axel was writing this, the Convention was making secret proposals to Austria for an armistice, intimating that it would consider releasing the royal family in exchange for peace. But now that France was on the run Austria had no desire for an armistice. So in that summer of 1793 all diplomatic possibilities for the release of the queen and her children ceased to exist.

My brother and I had several other reasons to be apprehensive: the Comte de Provence, having announced himself to be the representative of the French Crown abroad, had appointed himself regent for his young nephew; and he was once more spreading all sorts of calumnies concerning Marie Antoinette to the courts of Europe. Worst of all, we heard it said that young Louis XVII had been separated from his mother, and that the queen was to be taken to the Conciergerie and tried by the Revolutionary Tribunal. "My soul is torn apart when I think of her grief and suffering," Axel wrote me; "my inability to help her makes my situation all the more terrible."

I would later hear, from Turgy, a detailed account of the queen's terrible separation from her son. There had been no warnings to that effect. It was evening, and the princess was reading aloud to her mother and her aunt. The two women listened to her while mending the children's clothes. The little king slept in his bed in the same room; his mother had draped a shawl over his eyes to dim the light. As the princess read on, her elders suddenly heard the sound of steps on the floor below. The door opened, and they saw a group of men whose presence they could not explain—one of them, a former lemonade vendor called Michonis, had been one of the guards who had shown sympathy to the royal family before the king's death. Marie-Thérèse stopped reading; the women stared at the visitors. One of them stepped forward, saying, "We have come, by order of the Convention, to tell you that it has voted to separate Capet's son from his mother."

The former queen lost all of the composure she had retained in her life's earlier crises. She had often been petulant, raising her voice against citizens' delegations, throwing the Tuileries' keys at Lafayette's face after the return from Varennes. But until her son was torn from her she had never lost command of herself. This time she stood by his bed and shrieked accusations, implorations, threats.

"Take my son away from me? Never! You can not do it!"

I call on all mothers: mightn't some of us have been even more violent? Marie Antoinette's daughter and Madame Elisabeth joined in the queen's imprecations. The dauphin had gotten out of his bed and clung to his mother as for dear life, repeating, "Don't let them take me, don't let them. . . ." She kissed him repeatedly and hung on to him as if no one could take him away without also taking her life. The men hesitated, standing at the door.

The scene, according to Turgy, lasted the better part of an hour. At last one of the deputies cried out to the queen, "Why do you make such trouble? No one wants to kill your son! Let him go freely, otherwise we'll take him by force."

Marie Antoinette, suddenly resigned, began dressing her child, lingering over him with repeated, prolonged benedictions. A few of the men, impatient, started murmuring threats. She herself loosened the boy's little hands from her dress, saying, "Come, you must obey." Then he was taken away. The women, trembling beside his bed, could hear his waning voice pleading with his captors, and then as the door clanged below all was silent again.

For three days Marie Antoinette could hear her son weeping in the room below hers, the same room that her husband had occupied. His crying eventually abated, but this did not diminish her suffering, for she heard that the dauphin's keeper and "tutor" was the cobbler Simon, one of the Temple's roughest wardens. He had been directed by the Commune to "turn the Capet boy into a good *sans-culotte*"; "Citizens, it's true that the wolf's cub is insolent," he had told the deputies, "but I'll know how to tame him." From then on, Marie Antoinette found her only solace in those occasions when, through a chink in her prison wall, she could see her son being taken to the platform at the top of the Conciergerie tower to get fresh air.

It is just as well that the queen never learned of the indoctrinations little Louis XVII underwent at the hand of his captors. After a few days of weeping and missing his doting female relatives, the boy had begun to enjoy his freedom from them; dressed in the loose clothing of a patriot, a red bonnet on his head, with no more women fussing over him, he came to relish roughhousing with the guards and learning their salty lingo. This singularly attractive and engaging child had always enjoyed making people laugh, and he soon found that the guards were vastly amused when he made republican remarks in blasphemous language. One day as he was playing checkers with a guard he heard the sound of chairs being moved upstairs in his family's room. "Haven't they guillotined those whores yet?" he asked impatiently. The guard himself was deeply shocked.

Simon had decreed that the seven-year-old be given plenty of wine and brandy to drink, and the boy seemed to enjoy that too. Simon had another perfidious plan in mind. He remembered the little king's hernia, which had caused doctors to visit him in past weeks, and decided that the ailment might help the Convention extract false confessions from the child. On October 6, a committee composed of the mayor of Paris and a few other officials, looking for new evidence that might be used in the queen's trial, came to the Temple to cross-examine Louis XVII, his sister, and his aunt. Seated in a big armchair, swinging his little legs, which did not even touch the floor, upon being questioned the child asserted that he had been taught to masturbate by his mother and aunt. He obligingly declared that "several times they had amused themselves watching him repeat these practices in their presence," so went the report filed by the officials, "and that very often this took place when they made him go to bed between them." "He made it clear," the report added, "that his mother once made him come close to her; that this resulted in copulation and a swelling in one of his testicles, for which he wears a bandage, and that his mother advised him never to speak of it; that this act took place several times."

On the following day, Marie-Thérèse was questioned by the same officials, who were now joined by the painter David, a member of the Committee of General Security. The princess adamantly denied that her mother and aunt had ever lain in bed with the boy between them. Madame Elisabeth was next summoned, and was read her nephew's statement concerning the indecencies he had mentioned. Elisabeth was appalled. She insisted that masturbation was a habit the child had indulged in for some time, and that he must surely recall the occasions upon which she and his mother had scolded him for it. The little king was pressed to reply to his aunt's statements, and insisted that both women had initiated him into this practice. Hapless, ill-starred child! His testimony would have a crucial impact on his mother's life.

WHERE WAS MY BROTHER all this time? He had returned to Brussels, obsessed by the problem of how to liberate Marie Antoinette and her son. Since the French Republican forces were fully engaged in their effort to stop the allies, Axel wished to raise an army of volunteers who could march directly on Paris and free the queen and the dauphin. But Ambassador Mercy talked him out of it. Unlike Axel, he was a pessimist. "It is with regret that I say this," so Axel reported Mercy's words, "but if the queen of France was climbing the scaffold that atrocity would not move the allies in the slightest." Axel then devised a ransom plan to liberate the Queen. But shamefully, the Austrian emperor would not even contribute any money to a venture that might have bought his aunt's freedom. This refusal was particularly reprehensible because the money would have come from a large sum that Louis XVI had sent to Austria just before the flight to Varennes. Mercy had brought these funds to the Austrian emperor, whereupon it was pocketed by the Austrian treasury.

Axel's scheme to ransom the queen had been fairly promising, since it was based on his plan to approach Danton. Danton was eminently purchasable, and he was capable of compassion. Unlike most of his peers at the Convention, he had no particularly wrathful feelings toward the Widow Capet; he had recently married, and his young wife often talked with commiseration about the widow imprisoned in the Temple. Moreover, Danton hoped to sign peace treaties with England, Prussia, and Austria, and knew that it would be essential to liberate the royal captives to pursue such diplomatic goals. But because of his relative moderation, Danton had many enemies at the Convention. He aroused their ire, for instance, when he sent two agents to Italy to secure the neutrality of Naples, Florence, and Venice in exchange for the queen's release. On their way south the agents were captured by Austrian forces and jailed. When Danton's involvement in this covert mission became known he was expelled from the Committee of Public Safety. He would be beheaded some six months after Marie Antoinette.

It was at this time that the Tison couple, who had been guarding the royal family since their arrival at the Temple, started to play a role in the queen's fate. The Convention had begun to suspect Toulan and Lepitre of being sympathetic to her, and sent two delegates to question the Tisons. The Tisons, at this time, were furious because their only child, a winsome fourteen-year-old whom they adored, and who was allowed to call on her parents daily, had suddenly been forbidden by the Convention to visit them. Upon talking to the mayor of Paris, Pétion, during one of his visits to the Temple, the Tisons accused Toulan and Lepitre of bringing letters to Marie Antoinette. Having signed a paper officially corroborating their denunciation, they were allowed to see their daughter.

But even borderline monsters such as the Tisons can occasionally feel remorse. Such was the case with Madame Tison. After weeks of suffering deep feelings of guilt—as a devoted mother she strongly identified with the queen's sorrow at being separated from her child—she burst into Marie Antoinette's cell and flung herself at the prisoner's feet. The scene was witnessed by Turgy, upon whose account my retelling is based.

"I implore Your Majesty to forgive me!" Madame Tison cried out. "I'm a miserable, unhappy woman, for I'm causing your death and that of Madame Elisabeth! Forgive me, I beg you!"

The former queen did all she could do to calm the woman, taking her by the waist and raising her to her feet. But Madame Tison continued to holler and rant accusations at herself, and again fell to the floor in convulsions. It took eight men to carry her away. Shortly afterward she was taken to the hospital of the Hôtel Dieu, where she was diagnosed as insane. She would never return to the Temple. For her remaining months Marie Antoinette displayed considerable concern for Madame Tison's state. "Is Tison's wife as mad as they say?" she would ask Turgy. "Are they taking good care of her?"

MY NEVER SEEN BUT BELOVED FRIEND, my token sister-in-law, how fully I understand her suffering! When her son was taken from her Marie Antoinette sank into a depression far deeper than any she'd yet known. Her health was also very poor: she was suffering from severe uterine hemorrhages, and was so weak from the loss of blood that she often could not stand without someone's support. Her morale was so low that she did not even register any emotion when policemen came on August 2 to tell her that they were moving her to the Conciergerie on the Île de la Cité (it was Paris's oldest prison and was known as "the Antechamber of Death," being the temporary lodging for those awaiting execution). Helped by her daughter and Madame Elisabeth, she packed a little satchel of clothes. Once dressed she was requested to empty her pockets: the men allowed her to retain a bottle of smelling salts and one handkerchief. They missed seeing a little gold watch that she wore on a chain around her neck, a gift from her mother that she had brought from Austria twenty-three years earlier. After embracing her daughter and sister-in-law, she went slowly down the Tower stairs, accompanied by the police, her hand on the wall for support. As she finished descending the stairs, she hit her forehead against a lintel set over the door. One of the guards asked her if she'd hurt herself. "No," she murmured, "now nothing can hurt me anymore."

The coachman who drove Marie Antoinette to the Conciergerie later reported that the seat of his carriage was full of blood when she exited the vehicle. She was brought to her cell by the warden of the prison, a Monsieur Richard, and was briefly joined by Madame Richard and her maid, a young woman called Rosalie Larmorlière, whose compassion would henceforth be her only solace. They all departed, but left two guards who would be in the same cell with her, round the clock, for the following two and a half months.

The cell was some twelve feet square. Since it was half belowground and near the Seine its stone walls dripped with damp and slime. A camp bed with a filthy, worn blanket and dirty sheets, two chairs, and a small table, were its only furnishings. The guards never left the room, not even when the queen went about her bodily functions. The cell's only amenity was a screen that Madame Richard, a kindly woman, had placed beside the bed so that the queen could undress out of the guards' sight. The two men, Sergeant Dufresne and Gendarme Gilbert, who were armed with sabers and muskets, spent most of their time playing backgammon, smoking, and drinking—each of them consumed a bottle of wine and a pint of brandy a day. They were amiable enough, and Gilbert even bought the queen flowers. To distract her, Madame Richard once brought her youngest child for a visit, a handsome little boy who was about the same age as the dauphin. The queen took the boy into her arms, covered him with kisses and caresses, and began to cry. She constantly spoke of her own son, whom she thought of day and night, Madame Richard later reported; she wore a portrait of him hidden in her bodice, along with a lock of his hair.

The fetid cell was intolerably hot for the next summer weeks. When autumn came it grew terribly cold, and the poor captive's shoes soon grew moldy. Not allowed any needles or thread, she could not mend her old black dress. But one of the police commissioners, Michonis, who had already proved to be friendly to the royal family when he guarded them before the king's death, brought her some belongings Madame Elisabeth had prepared for her at the Temple—a white wrapper, some stockings, a pair of shoes, a box of face powder. There was no chest of drawers in her cell, but the kind Rosalie brought her a cardboard box in which to keep these precious belongings. Rosalie later recalled that Marie Antoinette received this box "with as much satisfaction as if it were the world's most beautiful treasure."

Many other prisoners at the Conciergerie were allowed far greater privileges than the queen was. They were permitted to walk about the corridors and courtyards chatting with each other. Women wore full toilette in the mornings, and changed into chic evening gowns in the late afternoon. Small luxuries such as warm blankets, fresh linen, and plentiful candles were readily available to them. But the queen was not offered such freedom or amenities. The worst aspect of her last months was her solitude and lack of occupation. At first she was allowed some travel books—*The Travels of Captain Cook, A Voyage to Venice, A History of Famous Shipwrecks* (she confided to the prison warden that she "read of the most terrifying adventures with pleasure"). But later she was denied access to books, and was not permitted pen or paper; the only thing she could do in daytime was to watch the guards playing backgammon, a game at which she had been very skilled. Her days' main events were the meals, which I admit were simple but excellent—dinner offered soup, a ragout of beef, chicken, or duck (her favorite), a plate of vegetables, and a dessert. The food was of the highest quality. For upon being told for whom it was intended, market women offered the best they had; and although she had always been a picky eater the queen seldom left any vegetables on her plate. When she grew weary of watching the guards' backgammon games she played with the two rings she still wore on her fingers, and which had not yet been confiscated by her guards—she would take them off, put them on again, and pass them from one hand to the other several times in one minute. She had wept terribly when her mother's little gold watch had been taken from her—it was her last link with her mother and her youth.

One wonders whether the stream of visitors allowed into Marie Antoinette's cell—there were several a week, mostly persons of royalist beliefs, and a majority of them British—annoyed her or gently allayed the terrible tedium of her days. The visits were made possible by heavy bribes and the cooperation of Michonis, whose income was thus nicely supplemented. My brother, who was still in Brussels, was offered a description of one of these visits that he found most painful. It was from an Englishman who claimed to have paid twenty-five louis to enter the queen's prison. "He found the queen seated with her head lowered and covered by her hands and extremely poorly dressed. She did not even look up."

Upon hearing accounts of her life at the Conciergerie, Axel wrote me the following letter from Brussels: "I no longer live, because ... suffering all the pain I suffer is not living. . . . To be incapable of doing anything for her is dreadful for me. . . . I would give my life to save her and I can't. My greatest happiness would be to die for her and to rescue her. I would have this happiness if cowards and villains had not deprived us of the best of masters [Gustavus]. He alone would have been capable of liberating her. . . . He would have dared everything and conquered all."

"I even reproach myself for the air I breathe when I think she is shut up in a dreadful prison," he wrote a few days later. "This notion is breaking my heart and poisoning my life, and I'm constantly torn with grief and rage." A few days later still: "Why did I have to lose all means of serving her?"

ON A PARTICULARLY hot late August day, as Michonis entered the queen's cell on his usual rounds, he was accompanied by a rather short man in his midthirties with a round, pockmarked face who wore two carnations in his buttonhole. Marie Antoinette startled, trying not to show her surprise. It was the Chevalier de Rougeville, the man who had saved her life in June of the previous year by persuading her to stay away from the mob when it invaded the Tuileries. Rougeville himself was amazed by the sight of this old woman who now looked like "a deformed specter." As described later by Michonis—fortunately for hapless scriveners such as I, all these men wrote memoirs—Rougeville, a consummate actor, betrayed no emotion. He took the carnations from his buttonhole and threw them behind the screen that stood in the queen's cell. Having found a subterfuge to be alone for a minute without her visitors or guards, she saw that the flowers contained notes, which she quickly perused. "I'll always seek to show you my devotion," one note read. "If you need three or four hundred louis to give to the men about you I'll bring them." The other note mapped out a well-thought-out plan for her escape. She summoned the two visitors back, on the pretext that she wished to complain to Michonis about the prison food. And while Michonis diverted her guards she spoke to Rougeville.

"You're risking too much for me," she said.

"Don't worry about me," Rougeville answered. "I have money, men, and the means to get you out of here."

"I'm not concerned about myself. I'm only anxious about my children."

"Is your courage low?"

"If I'm weak and downcast," the queen answered, placing her hand on her heart, "*this* is not."

"Take courage, we'll save you. I'll come back the day after tomorrow, and bring you the money you need for your keepers."

"Look at me, look at my bed," she added in parting, "and tell my family and my friends about my condition."

Michonis's scheme might well have been successful, for his reputation as a good patriot was impeccable, and he had a fairly high-standing rank in the police. His plan was to get to the Conciergerie late in the evening, wave some official-looking documents at the concierge, Richard, and say that upon orders of the Convention he had come to escort Marie Antoinette back to the Temple. Guards would then take them to the carriage in which Rougeville would be waiting for them. They would be whisked to Madame de Jarjayes's secluded country château near Paris and hence, some days later, to Germany. The keystone of the plan, however, was to obtain the help of the queen's two principal guards, Gilbert and Dufresne, both of whom seemed to respect her, and also might be amenable to bribes.

The queen approached Gilbert and offered him an immediate reward of fifty livres, which, she promised, would later be increased by larger sums. She also gave him a note written in pinpricks—some friendly soul must have loaned her a needle—which she asked him to give to

Michonis and Rougeville. It asserted her trust in Rougeville, and agreed to the escape plan.

The first steps of the rescue strategy, engaged in on the night of September 2, went according to schedule. The queen and Michonis passed through a number of prison gates without any problem. But as they were about to walk through the door that led onto the street, one of the queen's two guards, Gilbert, prevented the prisoner and her friends from going any farther. The rescue plan was thus sabotaged: Gilbert's patriotism had prevailed over his greed. The following day, when Michonis returned to the Convention, which was investigating reports of the plot, he denied any complicity, but was arrested. Rougeville, in order to avoid retribution, instantly fled Paris for Belgium.

As a consequence of this pitiful attempt Marie Antoinette was moved to an even smaller and darker cell. The Richard couple was dismissed and replaced by one Monsieur Bault and his wife, who were threatened with the guillotine in case the prisoner tried to escape again. My heart breaks at the details of the queen's last weeks of captivity. She was no more allowed a screen behind which she could change her clothes; she was not permitted a lamp or candle; and no one, neither the guards nor the Baults, was authorized to speak to her. Rosalie's gentleness and silent respectfulness were her only solaces. "I prolonged the various preparations for the night so that the solitude and darkness imposed on my mistress might be delayed as long as possible," Rosalie would write in her reminiscences. "She noticed these little attentions, which were the natural outcome of my loyalty and respect, and she thanked me for them with a friendly glance as if I had done more than my simple duty."

There was another solace in Marie Antoinette's last weeks: she received a visit from a Mademoiselle Fouché, about whom little is known aside from the fact that she had arranged for a nonjuring priest, Abbé Magnin, to visit the queen. The queen received him with joy, and upon his third visit the prison warden allowed him to remain with the queen for an hour and a half. Abbé Magnin would later relate that he twice heard Marie Antoinette's confession and brought her communion at the Conciergerie.

According to my brother, who wrote me almost daily from Brussels, there were a few men on the Committee of Public Safety who still hoped to use the former queen as a bargaining chip with the allies. One of them was Cambon, after whom one of Paris's most elegant streets was later named. But as it grew clear that Marie Antoinette's nephew, the Austrian emperor, took no interest in saving his aunt's life, the *enragés'* demands for the queen's trial grew more strident. The most violent of these men was one Jacques-René Hébert, a particularly brutal instigator of the Reign of Terror. He had a pathological hatred for Marie Antoinette, and was the editor of a guttersnipe publication called *Le Père Duchesne*, which promulgated some of the most scabrous pornographic lies about the chaste queen. Upon the denouement of the Carnation Plot, he demanded that she be brought to trial by the Revolutionary Tribunal as soon as possible. "I've promised the head of Marie Antoinette to my readers," he shouted at a meeting of patriots. "I'll go off and cut it off myself if there's any delay in giving it to me." This time his wishes were fulfilled. When the public prosecutor Fouquier-Tinville was sent for, he demanded to fill the Tribunal's rank of jurors and judges with men of his own choice. On October 3, Fouquier-Tinville was officially ordered to prepare a case against the Widow Capet.

MY BROTHER, still in Brussels, was cast into despair by the news that Marie Antoinette was about to go to trial. "All will be lost if this trial takes place," he wrote Taube; "we can hope for nothing with these scoundrels who invent nonexistent evidence and condemn people on flimsy accusations and suspicions. No, my friend, let's not hope for anything. Let's resign ourselves to the Divine Will. Her death is already decided and we must now prepare ourselves for it and gather enough strength to endure this terrible blow. I've been trying to do so for some time. . . . God alone can save her now. Let us pray for His mercy and submit to His decree."

Mercy d'Argenteau, spurred on by my Axel, decided to make his own appeal to the allies. "Now that [the queen] has been handed over to a bloodthirsty tribunal it should be our duty to take any step that is capable of saving her," the ambassador wrote the Austrian emperor. "Future generations will hardly believe that Austria's armies did nothing to prevent so enormous a crime, which took place only a few steps away from them."

"Is the emperor going to allow the queen to perish without even trying to snatch her from her executioners?" Mercy wrote Francis I soon afterward. "Aside from political considerations, are there not *private* intentions owed by Austria to Maria Theresa's daughter, who is about to suffer her husband's fate? Is it fitting to His Majesty's dignity or interest to witness the fate with which his august aunt is menaced, and do nothing to save her from her executioners?" But Mercy received no reply to these pleas. The Austrian emperor and his advisers had been studying the French situation, and had decided to let the French destroy themselves; with shocking heartlessness, they saw Marie Antoinette as just another of the Revolution's victims. "A great purge should be effected in France," wrote the ruthless Austrian chancellor, a man appropriately named Thugut. "The human species must be looked on as a tree that is ceaselessly pruned with an invisible hand—blood is the fertilizer of that tree."

Mercy easily resigned himself to the notion that his pleas were useless. Axel was deeply upset by Mercy's apathy. "Mercy has always made it clear that he was only devoted to the queen because of her mother," he wrote, "whereas he should have been devoted to her because of her generosity and her trust in him."

Meanwhile, at the Convention, Fouquier-Tinville was hard-pressed to find any documents that could be used against the queen beyond the transcripts of the interrogation that had followed the Carnation Plot. These interrogations had aimed to lure Marie Antoinette into expressing unpatriotic thoughts. But she did not fall into any traps, answering Fouquier's questions with great skill.

"Were you pleased with the success of our enemies' forces?" Fouquier asked the queen.

"I only sympathize with the success of my son's country."

"What is your son's country?"

"Surely there can be no doubt. Is he not French?"

Fouquier had gotten so little from these exchanges that he decided to submit the queen to a preliminary examination on the two days that preceded her trial.

The examination took place in the Palais de Justice, that had once been the Grande Chambre of the Parlement of Paris; its vast, bare rooms were stripped of the exquisite fleur-de-lis tapestries and Dürer paintings that once decorated its walls, and were now hung with posters of the Declaration of the Rights of Man. The queen, who had suffered a particularly heavy hemorrhage that morning, had been wakened in the middle of the night, ordered to dress, and taken to the Palais de Justice by a group of guards. The questions asked of her there prefigured the four principal accusations that would be brought against her at her trial: that she had squandered French money on festivities and pleasures; that she had always sacrificed French interests to those of Austria and had sent huge sums of gold to her brother, the emperor; that she had been responsible for the decision to leave France that resulted in the flight to Varennes; that she had intrigued with foreign powers against France during the Revolution, and at home had "intrigued against liberty." (In the following months, this same elastic accusation of "intriguing against liberty" would send to the scaffold most of Marie Antoinette's worst enemies at the Convention, including Hébert and Robespierre.)

The queen answered such queries with poise and aplomb, and often caught her questioners' mistakes. When the examining magistrate asked her why she did not keep her brother from making war on France, she reminded him that it was France, not Austria, that had declared war. At the end of this long, exhausting session, she was asked if she wished for counsels. She said she did. Two men—Citizens Doucoudray and Chauveau-Lagarde, the latter of whom had defended Charlotte Corday earlier that year—were appointed to be her lawyers. They had only some twenty hours to prepare their case.

"Like Messalina, Brunehaut, Frenegonde, once called queens of France, whose names are forever odious,"* so began the indictment which the lawyers would study that day, "Marie Antoinette, widow of Louis Capet, since her arrival in France has been the curse and the leech of the French people." Comparing her to a "vampire" who had fed on French blood, the indictment elaborated on her "criminal intrigues" and "abnormal pleasures."

Having less than a day to prepare their defense, the queen's lawyers persuaded her to ask the Convention for a three-day delay. She wrote a letter to that effect, and asked that it be brought to the prosecutor Fouquier-Tinville so that he might deliver it to deputies of the Convention. In fact, this missive was never delivered to the Convention. *Gode Gud!* The following detail makes me despair of the male gender: having consulted the queen's doctors, Fouquier did not wish the queen's trial to be delayed, wanting it to be held during her menstrual period, when she was at her weakest. He kept Marie Antoinette's missive, and after her death gave it to Robespierre, who hid it under his mattress, where it was discovered after his own execution the following year.

---

* In fact Messalina, notorious for licentious behavior and for instigating murderous court intrigues, was not a queen of France, but the third wife of the Roman emperor Claudius I. Brunehaut and Frenegonde, equally contentious women, were princesses, not queens, of Merovingian France.

As Axel kept pointing out to me, Marie Antoinette's trial was a most unusual event in European history: it marked only the second time that a monarch's wife was brought to court and executed (I have Anne Boleyn in mind—Mary Queen of Scots was herself a ruler). Equally unusual, almost every charge against the queen could be traced to the slander that her own peers, and particularly her in-laws, had spread about her when she had first arrived at Versailles. It was not the French people, but her husband's odious aunts, "Mesdames," who had first referred to her as "*L'Autrichienne*" and thus branded her as a potentially hostile foreigner. It was her perfidious brother-in-law Artois who had started the gossip about her being a lesbian. It was the despicable Comte de Provence who had invented tales about her "lovers," and had spread rumors about the orgies and debaucheries held at the Trianon, in revenge for the fact that he was never invited there.

The jurors chosen by Fouquier-Tinville included a wig-maker, a cobbler, a surgeon, a café owner, a hatter, and two carpenters. The trial, as the queen's lawyers reported it to me, proceeded uneventfully through the morning of its first day. At one point the *tricoteuses* (lower-class women who took a sadistic pleasure in attending trials and executions, and worked at their knitting while watching the proceedings) shouted to Marie Antoinette that she should stand while answering the questions posed to her, so that they could hear her better. "Will the people ever be weary of my hardships?" she murmured. Drama came to the courtroom in the afternoon, when Hébert created a sensation by announcing that the guard Simon had "surprised the young Capet in indecent self-defile-ments, bad for his constitution." When Simon asked him who had taught him such bad habits, Hébert related, young Capet replied, as he had a few weeks earlier when interrogated in the Temple, that he had learned them from his mother and his aunt. According to Hébert, the boy further revealed that the two women often made him lie between them, and that there then took place acts of "the most uncontrolled debauchery." "According to what the young Capet said," Hébert ended his testimony, "there is no doubt that there was an incestuous relationship between mother and son."

This is where I, Sophie Piper, grow so enraged that I need to draw a breath and pause, and collect myself again. I ask the following question to all mothers who might read these pages: What worse suffering could those ruffians have imposed on the queen than they did through these scabrous accusations? What villainy, and above all, what sadism! Upon hearing about these moments of the trial, my brother Axel stood up and beat his fists against the wall, shouting, "The swine! The scoundrels!"

One is left to imagine how the queen herself must have felt when she heard Hébert invent these lies about her *chou d'amour*. According to witnesses, she withheld any show of emotion. There was no telling gesture on her part, no change of gaze. She sat as if in a trance.

"There is reason to believe," Hébert continued, "that this criminal intercourse was not dictated by pleasure but in the calculated hope of dominating the child, whom they still thought as destined to be a king. As a result of the efforts he was forced to make, the boy suffered a hernia, for which a bandage was needed. But since the child has been taken from his mother his constitution has become robust."

The queen might well have replied that her son was already suffering from a hernia when her whole family was at the Temple, and that it had been caused by his using a stick as a hobbyhorse, which put too much pressure on one of his testicles. But she may have been too shocked, and too weak, to compose such a reply.

"I have no knowledge of the incidents Hébert speaks of," she quietly said.

Fouquier-Tinville seems to have been troubled by Hébert's accusations, for he tried to change the thrust of the examination. But one of the jurors stood up and complained that the queen "had not answered the charge made by Citizen Hébert on the subject of what had passed between her and her son."

At this point the queen rose from her chair. The stenographer recorded that she appeared "very moved." "If I did not reply," she said, "it is because nature recoils from such an accusation against a mother." She then turned toward the public gallery where the *tricoteuses* and other women visitors sat. "I appeal to all the mothers in this room!" she exclaimed.

Upon this pandemonium broke out in the visitors' gallery. How I wish I'd been there! Many of the *tricoteuses* broke out into applause. Others shouted that the proceedings should be stopped. Several women fainted. For a few minutes the meeting had to be suspended.

M.-J.-A. Herman, the presiding judge, a protégé of Robespierre brought up in Arras, the same town as the Incorruptible, rang his bell and demanded order. Trying to redress the balance in favor of the court, he asked the queen a series of questions about Varennes. Who had provided her with a carriage in which she had gone away with her family? "It was a foreigner." Of what nation, Herman asked. "Swedish." Was it not Fersen, who was living in Paris on the rue du Bac? "Yes," the queen quietly replied. A few whispers were heard in the spectators' gallery. My brother's liaison with the queen had by this time become common knowledge.

The trial's first day ended with various absurd charges, among which was the accusation that wine bottles had been found under the queen's bed on the night of August 10, evidence that she had enticed her guards to get drunk. She was also accused of having intended to murder the Duc d'Orléans: having learned of the plot, so went the demented tale, Louis XVI ordered that his wife be searched, upon which two pistols were found on her; he punished her by confining her to her apartments for a fortnight. "It may be that my husband ordered me to remain in my apartments for a fortnight," the queen responded disdainfully, "but it was not for any such reason."

That very evening, Robespierre, upon hearing, over dinner, of Hébert's charges concerning the queen's incestuous relations with her son, and of the *tricoteuses'* support of her, grew furious. "The fool!" he shouted, slamming his fork on his plate. "Can't he be satisfied with the Capet woman being a Messalina, instead of giving her a public triumph?"

TUESDAY, OCTOBER 15, a rainy, windy day, the second and last day of Marie Antoinette's trial, was the birth date of Saint Teresa, the feast day of Marie Antoinette's mother, and also of her daughter. She woke early, paid special tribute to the saint during the long time she spent in prayer, and was brought to the Tribunal at nine in the morning. One of the first witnesses, who caused a sensation in the courtroom, was the Marquis de La Tour du Pin, who had been a minister of war under Louis XVI, and who, the prosecutor hoped, might help him prove that the queen had meddled in affairs of state. When asked whether he knew the witness he bowed deeply to the queen and replied, "I have indeed the honor to know madame." La Tour du Pin denied that Marie Antoinette had engaged in any significant politicking. For that bow and for his respectful approach to her, he was to lose his own head a few months later after his own appearance at the Revolutionary Tribunal.

The sitting was suspended after seven and a half hours, and during the recess Rosalie tried to bring Marie Antoinette some soup. "I went up to find the queen," Rosalie later recalled, "and was about to enter the room when a police superintendent snatched the bowl from me and gave it to his mistress, who was young and covered with finery. 'This young woman is very eager to see the Widow Capet,' he said. 'This is a *charming* opportunity for her.' Whereupon the woman carried it away, spilling half the soup."

After the recess the queen's lawyer, Chauveau-Lagarde, gave a two-hour defense of the accused, emphasizing the lack of any evidence against her. When he was finished Marie Antoinette, who was sitting next to him, whispered: "How tired you must be, monsieur. . . . I so appreciate all the trouble you've taken." But Chauveau's vigorous defense enraged Fouquier, who had the lawyer arrested then and there. After the queen's second attorney, Doucoudray, made his own plea, he was also arrested. It is a marvel that they should have lived to tell the tale; for the following accusation against them appeared the following day in Hébert's hugely popular periodical, *Le Père Duschene*, couched in his inimitably scurrilous prose: "Is it possible that there should exist scoundrels bold enough to defend her? And yet two babblers from the law courts have had that audacity. . . . Those two devil's advocates not only danced like cats on hot bricks to prove the slut's innocence, but actually dared . . . to say to the judges that it was enough to have punished the fat hog, and that his whore of a wife should be pardoned."

The queen had to submit to another painful experience that day: the packet of belongings seized at the Temple when she was transferred to the Conciergerie was opened before her. A clerk of the Tribunal, one Fabricius, read the inventory of the items aloud, asking her to identify them.

The clerk: "A packet of hair of various colors."

The queen: "They come from my dead and living children and from my husband."

The clerk: "A paper with figures on it."

The queen: "It is a table for teaching my son how to count."

The clerk: "A little wallet filled with scissors, needles, silk, thread, etc. A little mirror, a gold ring with some hair in it, a paper on which are two gold hearts with initials, another paper on which is written 'Prayer to the Sacred Heart of Jesus; prayer to the Immaculate Conception'; a portrait of a woman."

Herman interrupted. "Whose portrait is that?" he asked.

"Madame de Lamballe's," the queen replied.

"A small piece of cloth on which there is the design of a flaming heart pierced by an arrow," the clerk Fabricius continued.

Fouquier interrupted and announced that this item, a scapular (a symbol of Christian faith then considered to be counterrevolutionary), had been worn by most of the "conspirators with whom the law has justly dealt by striking them with its sword." (It is a mark of his hypocrisy that Fouquier himself, according to his daughter's later testimony, wore this religious emblem well hidden under his judge's robes.)

The clerk carried away these mementos of Marie Antoinette's loved ones. Soon thereafter, the examination shifted to the issue of the Trianon and of the Diamond Necklace Affair, as Herman tried to trap the queen into admitting that she had been a friend of Madame de La Motte, the villain who instigated the scandal.

"Where did you get the money to build and furnish the little Trianon, where you gave parties at which you were always the goddess?"

"There were funds especially for that purpose."

"These funds must have been large, for the little Trianon must have cost immense sums?"

"It is possible that it did, perhaps more than I would have wished."

"Was it not at the Trianon that you knew the woman La Motte?"

"I never once saw her."

"Was she not your victim in the famous affair of the necklace?"

"She can not have been, since I did not know her."

"Do you persist in denying that you knew her?"

"I have told the truth and will persist in telling it."

When the defense lawyers had finished their presentation Herman questioned the queen about the fact that she had the dauphin sit at the head of the table after his father's death, and had served him first.

"Why, when you had promised to bring up your children in the principles of the Revolution, did you instill errors in them, for example by treating your son with a deference which made it appear that you still thought that he would succeed the former king his father?"

"He was too young to understand all that. I had him sit at the head of the table and served him the food he needed."

There was a recess. The second part of the hearing resumed after dark. The questioning went on for another seven hours, but at no time, so witnesses have told me, did the queen seem to weaken. Soon after midnight Fouquier turned to her and asked her if she had anything to add in her defense. "Well, no one has uttered anything against me," she replied. "I conclude by observing that being the wife of Louis XVI, I was bound to conform to his will."

Herman pronounced his indictment:

"Today a great example is given to the world and it will doubtless not be lost on the peoples inhabiting it. Nature and reason, so long outraged, are at last satisfied. Equality triumphs. . . . This trial, citizen jurors, is not one in which a single deed, a single crime, is submitted to your conscience. . . . You have to judge the accused's entire political life since she came to rule beside the last king of the French. But above all you must consider the maneuvers that she has never for a moment ceased to employ to destroy liberty, either at home, by her intimate connections with base ministers and treacherous generals . . . or abroad, by negotiating that monstrous coalition of European despots that Europe will ridicule for its impotence, and by her correspondence with the former émigré French princes."

After finishing his indictment Herman asked the jurors four questions:

1. Was the accused involved in intrigues and secret dealings with foreign powers that aimed at giving them monetary assistance,
enabling them to enter French territory and facilitating the progress of their armies there?

2. Is Marie Antoinette d'Autriche, widow of Louis Capet, convicted
of having cooperated with these intrigues and of having had these
secret dealings?

3. Is it established that there was a plot and conspiracy to start a civil
war within the Republic?

4. Is Marie Antoinette d'Autriche, widow of Louis Capet, convicted
of having taken part in this plot and conspiracy?

It was three in the morning. I hear that some spectators were confi-
dent that the queen would be acquitted, seeing that the trial had in no
way proven that she had obeyed orders from her mother and brother at
the expense of France; that there had been little concrete evidence of her
frivolity and extravagance; that there was no proof of her "double
game" of 1791 and her "treachery" of 1792. One spectator even exclaimed, "She'll get away with it. She gave her answers like an angel.
They'll only deport her!" This optimism was not totally unwarranted.
Citizens had not yet realized that the Terror—the death machine crafted
by Fouquier-Tinville—was just then beginning, with the queen's trial.
She was its first, its pioneering victim.

In a room adjoining the Grande Chambre Marie Antoinette waited
in company with Lieutenant de Busne, the guard assigned to her. At
4 a.m. she heard the president's bell tinkling in the distance. She could
discern Herman's voice, exhorting the crowd to remain calm. An usher
came to fetch her. She took her place on the platform. Her lawyers had
also been brought back into the hall.

"Antoinette," Herman said with shocking familiarity, "here is the
jury's verdict: 'Yes,' on all the questions."

She then heard Fouquier demand that "the accused be condemned to death, in accordance with Article 1 of the first section of the first chapter of the second part of the penal code, which reads: 'All intrigue, all intelligence, with the enemies of France tending either to facilitate their entry into the territories of the French Empire, or to deliver up to them towns, fortresses, ports, vessels, or arsenals belonging to France, or to furnish them aid in soldiers, money, food, or munitions, or to favor in any manner whatever the progress of their armies on French territory, or against our forces by land or sea, or to undermine the loyalty of officers, soldiers, and other citizens toward the French nation, shall be punished by death.'"

Punished by death! Those may have been the single words the queen could make out in that ponderous statement. As she sat on her chair, the only expression that she seemed to display was one of astonishment. "She did not give the least sign of fear or indignation," her lawyer Chauveau-Lagarde would relate later, "but she seemed stunned by surprise." After the verdict was spoken she rose and stepped down from the platform without a word or a gesture, crossing the Tribunal and raising her head with "very great dignity"—her lawyer's words—when she passed the spectators' gallery. As she went down the narrow stone stairway of the Palais's tower, accompanied by the gendarme Busne, her steps began to falter, and she whispered, "I can hardly see to walk. . . . I can go no farther." The gendarme offered her his arm, and helped her descend the last steps leading to the courtyard. On the grounds that he had offered her his arm, Busne, denounced by a fellow guard, would be arrested that same morning.

Upon reaching her cell, Marie Antoinette, however wearied by two days of trial, the second of which had lasted more than twenty hours, asked for pen and paper. And when these were brought her she wrote a letter to her sister-in-law. Dear reader, observe the thoughtfulness and poignancy of this letter, and consider the metamorphosis wrought by life's tribulations upon the once giddy, frivolous dauphine.

The 16th of October at four thirty in the morning

It is to you, my dear sister, that I write for the last time. I have just been condemned, not to a shameful death—that is only for criminals—but to one in which I shall rejoin your brother. As innocent as he, I hope to show as much firmness as he showed in his last moments. I am at peace as one only can be when conscience holds no reproach. I regret deeply having to abandon my poor children; you know that I lived only for them. And you, my good, kind sister, you who in the goodness of your heart have sacrificed everything to be with us, what a situation I'm leaving you in! I learned during the trial that my daughter has been separated from you. Alas, poor child, I dare not write her. . . . I hope that one day when they're older my children will be able to be with you again and enjoy your tender care, and that they will both remember the lesson I've always tried to teach them—that the carrying out of obligations should be the principal foundation of life, and that friendship and mutual trust should be its greatest happiness. . . . My son must not forget his father's last words, which I expressly repeat to him now: he must never seek to avenge our deaths. I have to mention something that hurts me greatly: I know how much distress this child must have caused you. Forgive him, dearest sister. Remember his age and remember how easy it is to make a child say things he does not even understand. The day will come, I hope, when he will feel even more deeply the value of your tenderness. . . .

I die in the Catholic, Apostolic, and Roman religion, that of my fathers, in which I was raised and which I have always professed. . . . I sincerely beg pardon of God for all the wrongs I have done during my lifetime. . . . I ask pardon of all whom I know and of you in particular, sister, for all the distress that, without intent, I may have caused you. . . . I say farewell here to my aunts and to all my brothers and sisters. I had friends. The idea of being separated from them forever, and of their grief, is one of my greatest regrets in dying. May they at least know that my thoughts were with them until the last moment.

Farewell, my good and loving sister. May this letter reach you! . . . I embrace you with all my heart, together with those poor, dear children. Oh, God, what an anguish it is to leave them forever. *Adieu! Adieu!* From this moment on I'll solely devote myself to my spiritual duties.

"*I HAD FRIENDS. The idea of being separated from them forever, and of their grief, is one of my greatest regrets. . . .*" Thus she bade farewell to my brother Axel, the love of her life.

Predictably, this letter never reached Madame Elisabeth. The queen gave it to Bault, the Conciergerie's warden, who in turn gave it to Fouquier-Tinville. Fouquier then passed it on to Robespierre, and after his death it was found under the Incorruptible's mattress, along with the letter Marie Antoinette had written asking for a delay in her trial.

AFTER FINISHING HER letter the queen, still in her black dress, lay down on her bed. When Rosalie came into her cell at dawn she saw that she had moved her pillow to the foot of her bed to keep her feet warm, and that she was weeping. Rosalie offered her some broth, noting that she had eaten nothing the day before. "I need nothing, my child. Everything is now over for me," the queen replied. But when she saw that Rosalie was also crying she accepted a few mouthfuls of soup, and then asked the girl to come back at eight to help her dress.

When Rosalie returned, the queen laid her clean chemise on the bed, slipped into the little passage between the bed and the wall, and started taking off her black dress. At her bidding, Rosalie came to stand before her, but the gendarme came forward and insisted on watching her undress. "Allow me to change my linen without witnesses, monsieur," the captive asked. But the guard curtly replied that he was ordered to keep an eye on her at all moments.

"With all precautions and modesty possible," as Rosalie put it, the queen took off her chemise, which was drenched in blood, and put on a clean one. Over it she slipped on the white negligee she usually wore in the morning, and a large muslin fichu, which she folded under her chin. She also carefully arranged a white bonnet on her head. Then she rolled up her bloodstained chemise, tucked it into one of its own sleeves, and, in Rosalie's own words, "looked anxiously about her." With an air of "ineffable satisfaction," she tucked the soiled linen into a crevice she had just noticed in the wall.

Soon thereafter Rosalie left her, and the Abbé Girard, a conforming priest sent by the Tribunal, came into her cell. He offered her confession and communion, which she refused.

"But, Madame," said the priest, "what will people say when they hear that you refused the help of religion in your final moments?"

"You'll tell them that God's mercy provided for it."

The priest asked if he might accompany her that morning. "If you wish," she answered. A few moments later she asked the gendarme: "Do you think the people will let me go to the scaffold without tearing me to pieces on the way?"

Soon after the priest's arrival Herman entered the cell with two judges. Marie Antoinette was kneeling by her bed, praying. "Pay attention," Herman said. "I must read you your sentence." The queen replied that this was useless, since she had already read it. "No matter," one of the judges said. "It must be read to you a second time."

The judge had just spoken the word "Republic," the last word of the sentence, when a hugely tall, corpulent young man entered the queen's cell. He was the executioner Henri Sanson, son of the recently retired executioner who had guillotined Louis XVI. "Hold out your hands," he ordered the queen. "To be bound?" she exclaimed. "Louis XVI's hands were not bound!"

At these words, Sanson brutally seized the queen's hands and manacled them very tightly behind her back. He then took off the bonnet she had put on a while ago and with a huge pair of scissors cut off her hair, which he put into his pocket. It was nearly eleven o'clock. Marie Antoinette and her grim visitors left the cell; the executioner held the end of the rope with which he had tied her hands, leading her like an animal.

There were many other indignities imposed on the queen that had not been inflicted upon her husband. When she was led into the courtyard of the Palais de Justice she saw the manure cart in which she was to be taken to what was known as the place de la Révolution. She had probably expected to be taken there in a closed carriage, as her husband had been! The vision of the open tumbrel drawn by two farm horses seemed to startle her terribly. She asked the executioner to untie her hands so that she could relieve herself. This she did, squatting in a corner of the prison wall. Then she offered her hands to Sanson so that he might tie them again. Once in the tumbrel, she tried to sit facing the horses, the way passengers in a carriage habitually do, but her guards made her sit with her back to the animals. Abbé Girard sat next to her, holding a small ivory crucifix, but she did not say a word to him.

Thirty thousand troops were lined up along the route. For a moment the cart stopped. A smiling child, held up by its mother, blew her a kiss. Her eyes filled with tears. But there were also yells of hatred. "Make way for the Austrian!" "Long live the Republic!" As the cart jolted and the queen almost lost her balance a derisive voice shouted, "Ah, those aren't your Trianon cushions!" After her brief bout of tears the queen remained impassive, expressionless. "The slut was audacious and insolent to the end," Hébert would write, furious about the dignity and courage she displayed throughout.

The cart turned onto the rue Saint-Honoré. How many times had she gone down that street on the way to the opera in her glittering finery and flashy Léonard headdress, sitting in a gold-and-silver carriage drawn by eight white horses! "Death to the Austrian!" a voice shouted.

The place Louis XV—I refuse to use its new name—was filled with a huge, noisy crowd by the time the tumbrel came lumbering in from the rue Saint-Honoré. When she looked to her left, the queen could see the Tuileries, where she had lived happy days with her family, where Axel had held her in his arms, in whose gardens she had played with her children.

The cart stopped in front of the scaffold. Not accepting any help, Marie Antoinette hurriedly climbed its stairs, with that same light, lilting step that had once so enchanted her peers. She climbed it so speedily, in fact, that she lost one of the little purple shoes Madame Elisabeth had sent her a few weeks earlier from the Temple. Limping a little, upon reaching the platform she trod on the executioner's foot.

"I beg your pardon, monsieur, I didn't do it on purpose."

Those were her last words. It was 12:15, a quarter past noon. According to witnesses, she shut her eyes as she was tied to the upright wooden plank. The plank was then tipped horizontally, and the heavy wooden collar was fixed around her bare neck. Another few seconds passed; one heard the guillotine's whistling whir and click; then the executioner's assistant held up her head by its white hair, carrying it around the scaffold to great applause.

Suddenly the gendarmes in the front row rushed forward and arrested a man who had crawled out from beneath the scaffold. He held a white handkerchief in his bloodstained hands and held a flower in his teeth.

While the deranged intruder was taken away, the crowd parted to make way for the cart that would carry Marie Antoinette's body to the Madeleine cemetery. There the executioners, noticing that no coffin or grave had yet been prepared, are said to have thrown her body on the grass, the head between the legs. No one knows how long her corpse remained lying there. It was not until November 1 that the grave digger sent in his bill for the burial: "The Widow Capet, for the coffin: 6 livres. For the grave and grave diggers: 15 livres, 35 sous."

Requiescat in pace, Maria Antonia Josefa Johanna of Austria-Lorraine. *Requiescat in pace,* my beloved, unseen friend.

CHAPTER 12

Axel:

LOVE AND GRIEF

I READ THE news of her death in a newspaper. What a dreadful way to have one's life transformed! As I sat at my club in Brussels, a valet brought me *Le Standard de Bruxelles*, along with the glass of port I take every evening before supper. And there it was, the banner headline, "*La Reine de France Éxécutée.*" I dropped the paper and let my head fall to my knees. A few acquaintances passed by, touched my shoulder to see if I was ill. I would raise my head, tell them fibs about a migraine, and let it fall again.

Thus prostrated, I began to wonder why I was feeling so numb, so void of all emotion. It's as if the grief were imbued with its own anesthetic. All I was experiencing was a deep sense of shock. I was surprised that I wasn't more upset. . . . I felt nothing; I was upset that I wasn't more upset. Yet I'd been thinking about her ceaselessly all day: of the dreadful circumstances of her last months; of her poor son—perhaps my own too!—and the torments to which he was probably being subjected; of her unhappiness at not seeing him in her last hours; of the doubts she may have had about my devotion to her.

Why were my emotions not even tinged with sorrow? I worried. Was I a monster? Apart from my grief at Gustavus's death I had never mourned before. My mother, my father, my beloved sister, were still alive; the whole process was quite new to me. Instead of sorrow I was beginning to feel great anger, rage. I was particularly indignant at the behavior of French émigrés in Brussels. The French were barely mourning a queen whom they should have adored. A typical brute, Monsieur de Courban, former page in the royal stables, wanted to give a play and a concert a few days after her death. What frivolity and insensitivity, I thought to myself, what a miserable, detestable nation! I was equally incensed about the lack of mourning on the part of the Viennese: Emperor Francis II held one memorial mass for his aunt at the Hofburg, and allowed the round of dinner parties and court theatricals to continue at their habitual pace.

As I received fresh details of her trial and execution, my anger grew. The fact that she was alone in her last moments without consolation, with no one to talk to, no one to whom she could transmit her last wishes, was horrifying. "The monsters from hell!" I wrote. "Without revenge, my heart will never be satisfied."

Indeed my rage at these indignities incited an increasingly strong desire for revenge, revenge against all those wretches responsible for the queen's death, for that of the saintly king, for the toppling of France's sacred monarchy. This need for reprisal was the only emotion that sustained me. I fantasized with enthusiasm, with great appetite, about the deaths of everyone of my Toinette's enemies. I imagined exquisitely dreadful tortures for Robespierre, Marat, Herman, even oafish, money-crazed, relatively merciful Danton, even for her erstwhile friend Barnave, who was executed soon after her. In the first few days this lust for revenge was the only emotion that devoured me.

The week I received the dreadful news I went riding daily in the chill autumnal rain to be alone, to figure myself out. I rode, I rode for hours, going deep into the forests that surround Brussels, remembering those times when Toinette and I had ridden together in the woods of Saint-

Cloud and Fontainebleau, when we'd raced each other and she'd grown annoyed that I'd given her a large handicap, or that I'd slackened my pace in order to let her win. While riding, while waiting for my emotions to settle, I pondered the nature of love.

I'd recently reread Saint Augustine. "My love is my weight, where it goes I go," he'd written. *"Amor meus, pondus meum: illo feror, quocumque feror."* Ah, what wisdom, to focus on the gravity of love; this is why I was feeling so unmoored, so floating-in-a-void—I'd lost the love-weight that had anchored me for all those years!

Saint Teresa of Avila was also masterful on the theme of love: she distinguished lasting unions from the "falling-in-love" kind, and described them thus: "It is as if water were falling from the sky into a river . . . and the river water can no longer be divided or separated from the water which fell from the sky."

There are two types of men: the kind who are happiest when they're possessed by another, and those who are happiest when self-possessed. In my youth I was sure I was one of the latter. It turned out that I was wrong.

Ah, the recurring drama of eroticism! Eleanore entranced me physically, but I believe in something called the soul, and my beloved queen held mine totally in her sway.

I rode on, remembering those times when we'd dismounted our horses and sat on a park bench and first kissed each other; remembering the further embraces exchanged in the pavilions of the Petit Trianon, the consummation of our love in that small octagonal chamber above her apartments at Versailles.

As these memories returned, grief began to assault me at last, like a tidal wave.

"Her suffering, her death, and my love can never leave my mind," I wrote in my journal eight days after her execution. "Oh my God, why did I have to lose Her and what will become of me?"

And two days later: "Every day my grief increases. Every day I realize all the more how much I have lost—I have lost all."

In early December: "I would have been much happier if I'd died on June 21, the night of Varennes. It would be cowardice not to admit how much I suffer."

On Christmas Eve I wrote to Sophie: "Losing *Her* is the greatest grief of my entire life, and my sorrows will only leave me when I die. Never have I felt so deeply the value of all that I possessed, and never have I loved Her so much. . . ."

In the first months of 1794 I began traveling all over Europe to find objects that had belonged to my Toinette—by that time antiquarians and collectors had snapped up every one of her possessions, even the few chairs and teacups she had been allowed to bring to the Temple. I found my principal consolation in touching things that her hands, her lips, had lingered on.

In Vienna I bought a marquetry cabinet by Boulle of gold brass and pear wood embossed with mother-of-pearl; a painting by Van Meytens showing my love at the age of nine, dancing with two of her brothers in a pantomime ballet, *The Triumph of Love.*

In Florence I purchased a four-foot-high jewel chest of ebony and gilded rosewood, with inlays of flowered Sèvres porcelain, an armchair upholstered in green flowered silk . . . oh the joy of sitting in the same seat she'd once used!

In London I discovered a Riesner table of mother-of-pearl and gilt brass, and andirons in the shape of large gilt bronze camels; I had noticed both of these treasures many times in her rooms while holding Her in my arms.

In Düsseldorf I bought a white porcelain bowl in the form of an overturned breast, its luscious pink nipple pointing downward, reminding me of my love for her breasts, the pleasure I took in fondling them.

In Naples I obtained Her harp! It was made for Her in 1774, the year we first met—nineteen-year-old kids—at the opera ball. How clearly I remember Her playing that harp. . . . She was playing it on that day in 1783 when I'd just come back from America, and surprised Her in her apartments.

I spent the first months of 1794 in an agony of sorrow and remembrance, acquiring and beginning to live with these objects. They would help me greatly in learning to live with my grief. Grief! After it had finally exploded in me, a few weeks after her death, it had continually grown deeper. I was startled, astounded by its turbulence. I began to take notes on what I was discovering about grief, hoping that writing about it could help bring me a measure of peace.

I was learning that it is slow, patient work, a meticulous process that must be carried out over a far vaster amount of time than society usually allots us; that it is crucial to retain links with the places, the belongings, once shared with the departed; that it is a slow, long, gradual process of severance. What happens if we don't allow the work of mourning to proceed on this stately course? Like those spirits of the dead in Greek literature who went to riot if improperly mourned—devastating crops, destroying whole cities—the psychic energies reserved for mourning, if suppressed, can cause grievous harm.

At some time in my first months of mourning I also reread Homer's *Iliad*. Here we are in books 5, 6, and 7, looking in on the clamorous terror of Homeric battle. Lances are being driven clear through eye sockets, livers, and genitals, brains pour out of mouths and severed heads, limbless torsos spin like marbles about the black-blooded earth, men catch their gushing bowels in their hands, crashing "thunderously as towering oaks" onto the blood-soaked ground, and throughout this mayhem there remains on both sides one obsession, one concern: to call an occasional truce that will allow each side to properly bury and commemorate their dead. By mutual consent and for this purpose only, all fighting stops, and on both sides the night is spent in lamentations, in washing and anointing the treasured corpses, in adorning funeral pyres with flowers and drenching them with wine, in honoring with cleansing fire the bones that will eventually be carried back to the warriors' homes. Mourning rites, Homer tells us, serve in great part to protect survivors from the excesses of their pain. Quite as treasurable as wealth and fame, he reminds us, is the honor of a proper funeral; and life's principal terror, to the Greeks, was the disgrace of being improperly mourned.

Well there was nothing I could do about the funeral rites denied to my beloved: she received the kind of treatment—thrown into a communal grave by Jacobin monsters—that the Greeks would have most feared. But at least I could engage for the rest of my life at the somber task that one might call the labor of grief.

MY FATHER HAD long begged me to return to Sweden. But I refused to leave the continent because I felt that I might still be useful to Marie Antoinette's children, if and when they would be released from jail. "This child [Louis XVII] still interests me; my worries about his fate increase my grief," I wrote Sophie about the boy who might be my son. "And this unfortunate girl, Madame, what will become of her? What horrors, what humiliations, will they not put her through—it breaks my heart to think of it."

Writing about the little king fifteen years after his mother's death, I am still filled with rage when I think of the fate meted out to my cherished boy. Shortly after his mother's execution young Louis XVII had been placed in solitary confinement in a jail cell of the Temple Tower, and he would die there a year and a half later, in the spring of 1795, in a heartbreaking state of physical and psychic degradation. His sister, who heard witnesses's reports, would describe his confinement thus: "He slept in a bed that had not been made for months. It was covered with lice and fleas, as were his clothes and body. His filth was never taken out of the cell. Since the window was never opened the room was filled with a noxious stench. They gave him no light, but he dared not ask for any although he'd always been terrified of the dark. . . . Even if he'd lived he might well have become an imbecile."

What the Jacobin functionaries who visited the ill-fed, rachitic boy in the Temple Tower found most striking is that Louis-Charles would not or could not speak. The ebullient child who a few months earlier had so enjoyed joking with his guards seemed to have become mute. My little friend's silence could be attributed to his sorrow over his mother's death, or to the remorse he felt about the terrible testimony he had given against her. Others claimed that the prince had either died in the first weeks of his imprisonment, or that he had been spirited out of the Temple and whisked abroad. In either case, another boy, a mute one, would have replaced him in the jail cell. The mystery of the young king's fate has not yet been solved, and may never be.

As for the women in the royal family: Madame Elisabeth was guillotined in May of 1794. Marie-Thérèse (or Madame Royale, as she was still called by royalists) was liberated a year and a half later, seven months after her brother's death. Still as practical and orderly as she was stubborn and prosaic, she had kept her quarters tidy, briskly paced her room for an hour of the day, and was thus in relatively good health when the revolutionary government freed her in December 1795.

For by that time she was of no more use to the National Convention. In the summer of 1794, when Robespierre lost its support, political conditions had changed drastically. The Incorruptible's end was as dreadful as I would have wished all revolutionaries' deaths to be: botching a suicide attempt, he had incurred a very grave wound by shooting himself in the jaw; and on July 29 (or Thermidor, as the French call it), he was sent to the scaffold with twenty-two of his acolytes. In order to remove all obstacles from the guillotine's path, executioner Sanson, who'd done his job on the queen nine months earlier, tore away the bandage that had been holding together the Incorruptible's jaw. Dreadful screams of pain issued from him as he was put upon the scaffold, silenced only by the screeching blade.

Power then fell into the hands of the so-called Thermidorians, revolutionary brigands like Barras and Tallien whose hands were by no means unstained, but who put an end to the Reign of Terror. This junta looked on Marie-Thérèse as something of an embarrassment. She had begun to be adulated by many Parisians as an innocent, persecuted martyr, "the Orphan of the Temple." Fearful that she might become an increasingly inspirational figure for royalists, the new leaders suggested to the Austrian emperor that she be exchanged for those members of the Convention whom Austria still held captive. Madame Royale—the aloof young girl I'd guided out of the Tuileries on the night of the flight to Varennes—was sent to Vienna in December of 1795. There a debate began concerning her marital plans. Wishing her fortune to remain in their hands, the Austrians wanted her to wed Emperor Francis II's younger brother, Archduke Karl. Her Bourbon relatives wished her to marry her first cousin, the Duc d'Angoulême, son of the Comte d'Artois. I shall return at length to Marie-Thérèse; suffice it to say for now that her French relatives would win out, and she eventually became the Duchesse d'Angoulême.

SORROW WAS FOLLOWING upon sorrow. In May of 1794 I received news of my father's death. Notwithstanding his frequent pleas for me to come home, and his declining health, I had not seen him for six years because of my attachments to the queen of France and, after her demise, to Eleanore Sullivan. So this particular heartbreak was tinged with a strong sense of guilt. I decided to return to Sweden for a while to deal with issues of inheritance, but I procrastinated throughout the summer: I first had to settle my relations with Eleanore, and also look after my financial problems. Eleanore was living in Brussels, as I was, and had always refused to visit Sweden with me. Throughout my first months of grieving for the queen, whom she had idolized, Eleanore had grieved with me and been my only consolation. And in my journals I couldn't help but occasionally compare the two women of my life. "Oh, how I reproach myself for the wrongs I did Her and how deeply I now realize I loved Her," I wrote in my journal that summer, referring to the queen and to my infidelity. "What kindness, what tenderness, what a fine and loving heart! Eleanore will not replace Her. . . . She doesn't have all those qualities, though I love her and she is my sole comfort and without her I would be very miserable." But I should add that within six months of the queen's death Eleanore ceased to concentrate on me and resumed her social whirl, attending every possible ball with her daughter (offspring of the Duke of Württemberg), who was now living with her and with whom I did not get along.

There are women who gain dignity, who become more alluring, with the advance of age, but Eleanore was not one of them. A Swedish diplomat who met her in Frankfurt in 1796 praised her beauty, yet added: "Madame Sullivan did not have a pleasant manner. Her gaiety was of the loud Italian kind; she shrieked when she should have spoken, and laughed a full-throated laugh. As long as Count Fersen was with her, she was silent and lost in observation like him. When Craufurd was home, things also proceeded decently; but when both these gentlemen were away, there were games and forfeits, kisses were bestowed, and there was enormous hilarity."

Yet Eleanore and Quentin Craufurd had all along offered generous support and financial aid to the French royal family, and for this reason alone my loyalty to them was unshakable, however complex our relations. Since 1789—the year Eleanore and I became lovers—I had been living in a ménage à trois with her and Craufurd. The situation was hardly ideal. Craufurd was often absent on business, but rumors about me reached him from the servants' quarters; and there were recurrent scenes of jealousy in which he could become very hostile, and which I found ridiculous: how could he imagine that a woman of Eleanore's temperament could remain alone for weeks or months at a time? Besides, Craufurd had occasionally needed me. A few years earlier I had arranged for him to be one of Gustavus's Paris agents, which flattered his vanity. And somewhat like Louis XVI, he seemed to be grateful that I was far more discreet than many other men whom his mistress could have chosen as a second lover. (I sometimes asked myself: Was I predestined to be the ideal rival?)

Moreover, I was a man of few friends, and in my solitude I had long looked on Eleanore as the only person who could console me. I had already written the following to Sophie the month after Louis XVI died: "I often curse the moment I left Sweden; I wish I'd never left our rocks and pines. I would not have had as much joy, but . . . I would have avoided much pain. I weep very often alone, dear Sophie, and together with E., when we are able to. She herself is too afflicted by what has happened to be able to comfort me. But at least I have the solace of weeping *with* someone. This good woman is excessively attached to the French royal family; she has made many sacrifices for them, and this is what makes me love her."

The following fall again I revealed my dependence on Eleanore as I contemplated the approaching demise of Marie Antoinette. "I shall have then lost three sovereigns, my benefactors and friends," I wrote. "There only remains one woman, whom I love and who loves me, but her character is very different from mine and she belongs to another."

I would be less than honest if I did not admit that I have an urgent, pressing need for women; that I am sexually very driven; that however reclusive I am, I dislike solitude. In sum, I like solitude *with another*. Thus notwithstanding Eleanore's and Craufurd's stormy temperaments, our ménage à trois was an arrangement I had to tolerate. "I must rediscover the kindness of E.'s character," I wrote in my journal, "behind the thousand brusque acts and the thousand slights that she afflicts me with and that I find hard to endure."

So however greater my love had been for my lost queen, between 1794 and 1799 I was very taken up by my attempts to win Eleanore away from Quentin Craufurd. My life was also governed by the need to allay the state of my finances, and that of a few others. I had given a considerable amount of money to the French royal family to implement the Varennes project. I was also contributing large sums—fifteen to twenty thousand pounds—to help numerous émigrés who had fallen into poverty, and were taking on menial tasks to feed their families. (I was having all my shirts made, for instance, by a woman from one of the most prominent noble families in France.) Moreover, I felt it a duty to refund the charitable citizens, particularly Madame de Korff and her mother, who had loaned nearly every penny they had to the royal family at the time of Varennes, and who were now living in dire poverty (I was helping out by paying them, out of my own pocket, the interest on this loan). In the face of such monetary quandaries, how could I possibly compete with the prodigal Craufurd, seeing the luxurious style of life Eleanore was used to? I explained these issues to my dear friend Taube.

"I have financial problems to take care of for myself and for others. I have to repay Madame de Korff the large sum that she loaned to the late king of France—it was almost her entire fortune. As for myself, their late Majesties bequeathed to me 1,500,000 pounds in 1791, at the time of their departure for Varennes, about which the world knows nothing, and which is in the hands of Count Mercy. I have their note, which I have not yet presented to him."

The fact is that I had a letter, signed by Louis XVI and Marie Antoinette on June 20, 1791, the day of their escape from Paris, which bequeathed to me the above amount. I had raised that sum from Madame de Korff and others, and from my own holdings, to cover the expenses that royalist troops would have incurred if the king's escape had succeeded. The monarchs' note, forwarded to Mercy along with the money, read thus: "We request that Count Mercy remit to Count Fersen all of our money that is in his [Mercy's] possession, about 1,500,000 livres, and we ask Count Fersen to accept his share of it as a sincere mark of our gratitude for everything that he has done for us."

This note caught Mercy by surprise. He had indeed received a considerable sum from the royal family but, alas, had turned it over to Marie Antoinette's sister Archduchess Maria Cristina, the regent of the Low Countries, who in turn seems to have handed it over to Emperor Francis II of Austria. Why had I not presented this request at the time I first came to Brussels in 1791? asked Mercy, who would die a short time later in London. I replied that it would have been highly indelicate of me to solicit these funds at a time when the French monarchs were still alive.

So the money, by that time, was said to be in Vienna, in Emperor Francis II's treasury. In the spring of 1794, shortly after Mercy's death, I wrote the Austrian chancellor, the gruff, odious Baron Thugut, about the sum owed me, and did not receive a reply for four months. Thugut's eventual response was highly elusive, and did not bode well: "It would have been more propitious for you had you decided to make use of the arguments that are the basis of your pretensions during the lifetime of the late monarchs." I finally realized that I would eventually have to go to Vienna to settle this debt. But this trip would be delayed for many months by the fact that I had to return to Sweden and settle my family affairs in the aftermath of my father's passing. As the eldest son, I had inherited a large share of his holdings, including the Fersen Palace in Stockholm, the estates of Steninge and Ljung, sizable other lands near the Finnish border, and his shares in the East India Company. My brother, Fabian, inherited the Mälåker manor on Lake Mälaren, and my mother retained the estate in Lövstad, which upon her death in 1800 would pass on to Sophie.

. . .

UPON THE FIRST ANNIVERSARY of my Toinette's death, October 16, 1794, I was already on a ship, traversing the Baltic on my way to Sweden. "Today is a dreadful day for me," I wrote in my journal. "It is the date upon which I lost the person who loved me the most in the world. . . . I shall mourn Her until the end of my days and whatever I feel for Eleanore can never help me to forget what I have lost." October 16 would indeed remain a day of mourning for the rest of my life.

I tried to be as inconspicuous as possible when I returned to Stockholm, but that was barely possible. The reappearance of a citizen who was known to have been the lover of Europe's most glamorous and controversial queen thrust tumult into our provincial Swedish society. Women, women again, my life's plague and joy! Adolescent belles and ripe older beauties came from all possible corners of Stockholm to seek me out. I was more than aware of the fact that I had greatly aged since my last stay in Sweden, that the griefs I'd suffered had lined my face as if with acid, that I looked far older than my thirty-nine years. But this did not seem to minimize the pandemonium of female attention I incited. To my surprise, I was impelled to take full advantage of these ladies' advances. It's as if my need for revenge had suddenly become a kind of aphrodisiac. Never had I allowed my sexual impulses to be so brutally released. I was driven to take to bed every woman who approached me. I made love savagely to each of them, enraged by the fact that she was not my Toinette. I made them lie down on their bellies, thrust at them furiously from behind. When bedded with bolder females, I pressed their breasts together and thrust my penis up and down between those delicious globes, ejaculating on their chests. I'm most attracted to noble, aloof women. My sex acts were tinged with the desire for revenge that had swept over me at the time of Toinette's death. I tied princesses', duchesses', countesses' hands to the rails of their beds, thrust at them from a great distance as ferociously as possible, bit their nipples until they bled.

All my captives were startled by my wildness; was I not supposed to be the reserved, proverbially gallant Count von Fersen? I relished their moans of pain or pleasure, and that exquisite shouting that occurs when the two sensations are admixed. Some were terrified by my antics and vowed to never come near me again; others could not have enough of it. I was at it almost every day, sometimes capturing five, six women in one week. I kept thinking of the refrain from Mozart's *Don Giovanni:* "*V'han contesse, baronesse, marchesine, principesse, / Ma in España, son già mille e tre.*"

The only woman I dared not dally with was Charlotte, Duchess of Södermanland, a close friend of Sophie's. Her husband was the regent for the adolescent king, Gustav IV Adolf, youngest son of Gustavus. Infatuated with me for years, garrulous, indiscreet, her foot constantly seeking mine under the table at official dinners, Charlotte would have been a perilous woman for me to tryst with, and I asked Sophie to calm her down. For the regent, Duke Karl, was all too aware that his wife had been in love with me for decades, and that his duchess, *faute de mieux*, was currently having an affair with my younger brother, Fabian. Another reason for the Duke of Södermanland's distrust of me was that his sympathies lay with the French Revolution: he was about to officially recognize the Convention, and considered me dangerous because of my notorious association with the French royal family. His suspicion of me was so pronounced, in fact, that he surrounded my house with spies.

There were other reasons for the regent's animosity: Sweden was rife with political intrigues: a bitter rivalry had arisen between the current regime, headed by the regent, and the Gustavian faction of which I was a leader, along with the late king's closest adviser, Armfelt. The regent wished to continue his dominance as long as possible; my faction hoped for the early succession of Gustavus's son. Armfelt had come to see me in Brussels, and I was particularly alarmed by his report that the Duke of Södermanland was isolating the young king from all those persons who had been devoted to his father, Gustavus III.

In 1795 I spent a happy summer with my sister Sophie and our friend Taube, who were now living together more openly than ever, Sophie's husband having died in May of that year. The three of us went to a spa on the shores of Lake Vättern, where Taube, whose health was frail, took a cure. How I envied them the perfect life they shared! When in their company I often wondered whether I would ever enjoy a happiness similar to theirs. Sated with the winter's sexual exploits, that summer I also spent serene days at my estate of Steninge, where the strawberries were just fruiting and the peas were abundant. I was happy with the condition of my farm, most satisfied with the work of my overseer. For the first time in many years I felt a deep attachment to the lands I'd inherited from my father, and began to long for a more leisurely pace of life that would allow me to spend more time at my country estates. My happiness at Steninge was deeply marred, however, by the news of young Louis XVII's death. My handsome, brilliant little friend, possibly my own son! "He was the last and only interest retaining me in France," I wrote Sophie; "the news is unbearably painful, and brings back heart-rending memories." I grieved much for the child, bitterly remembering the few happy times we had played together, the vigor with which he would kick a ball in my direction, his sparkling laugh, the joy he had taken at playing blindman's buff.

My departure from Sweden was incited by the news that Louis-Charles's sister, Marie-Thérèse, now eighteen years old, had been released from her prison at the Temple and sent to Vienna. I would be in lifelong mourning for her mother, the love of my life, and I felt very emotional about the prospect of once more seeing her daughter, Madame Royale.

There was also the unresolved issue of the legacy left me by her parents. I confess to having a patrician disdain for fiscal matters, and the effort to seek reimbursement—for myself or for others—was repugnant to me. My own finances had been improved by my father's inheritance; so were it not for my yearning to indemnify Eleanor and Craufurd, and Madame de Korff and her mother, the latter of whom remained in dire financial straits, I would have let the whole matter drop. But I was truly obsessed by the Korffs' dilemma. I had been informed by the Austrian emperor that the money I was soliciting belonged to Marie-Thérèse, so it was only by seeking her out in Vienna that I could hope to resolve the Korffs' plight.

ARRIVING IN VIENNA in January of 1796, the month after Madame's release, I was immediately informed by French refugees about the virtual imprisonment that had been imposed on the princess. Her Hapsburg relatives had apparently decided that she should have minimal contact with the world around her, and most especially no communication with her Bourbon relatives. Her entire French retinue had been dismissed, and replaced by titled Austrian women who were being employed as spies and informers. All her correspondence with her uncle the Comte de Provence was opened and censored; even the Prince de Condé, whom her uncle had sent to greet his niece upon her arrival, was forbidden to visit her. And French émigrés, who all longed to see her, could only get a glimpse of her on Sundays when she went to Mass at the Hofburg Palace.

My impressions of Vienna as a whole were mostly negative. I became caught up in a social whirl little suited to my tastes or habits. I gravitated to the company of the higher nobility, in which the most beautiful women and the greatest gallantry prevailed. In this circle I was again mobbed, and gave full sway, as in Stockholm, to my sexual appetites, finding

Viennese women singularly more naive than my female compatriots. Thrusting my tongue into the ravishing Princess Metternich, I learned to my surprise that she had never yet engaged in this delightful practice. Where in heaven's name had Viennese men been for all these centuries?

I blamed Vienna's lack of sophistication—sexual and otherwise—on the mediocrity of the imperial court. When I went to the theater, which I found very poor, I saw the Emperor Francis II and his Empress in their loge, looking like a couple of bourgeois. "How awkward of them at a time when royalty should try to impress!" I wrote in my journal. In the Prater, the emperor's carriage was like that of a greengrocer compared with the magnificent vehicles of the aristocracy. As for his sons, the five archdukes, none of them had any bearing, or manners, or talent for conversation. I was equally baffled by the Viennese's insouciance concerning the war against the French. "The whole day I heard nothing but talk of balls, celebrations, and divertissements," I wrote Sophie shortly after my arrival. "I'm struck by how little they think of the war." It was against this staid and dowdy couple, surrounded by a scatterbrained, constantly intriguing nobility, that France's revolutionary armies were scoring their greatest victories. As much as I hated their principles, it was clear that the revolutionaries' efficiency, drive, and convictions were bound to overwhelm the old order's apathy and frivolity.

A great delight of my stay in Vienna—there were few of them—was a concert at which quartets by Franz Joseph Haydn were played. His Sixth Quartet was especially beautiful. Haydn himself was there, performing on the violin. Not a good violinist, but a marvelous composer, this tiny, very shy man was in the service of Count Esterhazy. I was shocked to hear that this great artist had to take his meals in the kitchen, with the Esterhazys' domestic staff. Only at the residence of the Russian ambassador, Count Razumovsky, did I find grace and democratic ease. There the custom of an open table was maintained, at which persons of quality could dine every evening without invitation. In fact by the month of March I was practically living at Razumovsky's home, where his wife showed me nothing but kindness and warmth.

There was another important encounter in Vienna, one that gave me both joy and sorrow. I was visited several times by Louis XVI's former valet, the faithful Cléry, who had managed to escape to Vienna a few days after the king's death, and whom I embraced like a brother. He narrated to me, in the greatest and most painful detail, his master's last days and hours.

UPON MY SECOND WEEK IN VIENNA, emotion overcame me when I first caught sight of Marie-Thérèse. It was on a Sunday, as she was returning from Mass. I came close to fainting. I had not seen her since that night of June 20, 1791, when I placed her in the coach in which her parents attempted their ill-fated escape. I could not help but compare her to the queen. She was blond, tall, and well built like her mother, and had grace and nobility of bearing, but her features resembled those of Madame Elisabeth rather than those of the queen; and in comparison with Marie Antoinette, who glided so ethereally when she moved, she walked rather awkwardly, pigeon-toed. I longed to visit with her, but this desire was fraught with foreboding. She had so adored her father, and she must have known of my relationship with her mother, whom she'd disliked since childhood. How could she not have negative feelings toward me? As I saw her on that Sunday morning she gave me an amazed look as she passed by me, and blushed, and turned around to look at me again before entering her apartments. I flattered myself to think that she would have liked to give me some sign of recognition, however she may still have disliked me.

A few days later I saw her again at a reception. She was looking at the crowd the way her mother used to when she searched for people she knew, and when she saw me she came toward me, and greeted me in an amiable enough manner. "I'm so glad to see that you're safe," she said. Those words gave me great pleasure, and tears of sorrow kept springing to my eyes. I could not help but notice that she had inherited her mother's love of dogs: bouncing about her was Coco, her red-and-white spaniel, which had once belonged to her brother, and had shared Louis XVII's jail cell. Upon the little king's death, Cléry had told me, the dog found his way to Marie-Thérèse's quarters. Not yet knowing that her brother had died—she would not learn of his demise for months—she took the dog in and kept it, believing that it had gotten lost.

Princess Marie-Thérèse and I saw each other again at a few other social events. Occasionally, to my great emotion, she was affable enough to draw me aside: she wished me to describe her parents when I first knew them, when they were still very young. I told her of her mother's perennial graciousness; of the many times I brought my spaniel, Odin, to her apartments to play with her dogs; of her father's abiding amiability and of his confidence in me. Upon another meeting Marie-Thérèse, in turn, gave me some precious details about the trip to Varennes: she told me of the mysterious horseman who had galloped up to her family's coach and shouted, "You will be stopped!"; of the imbecile Léonard, her mother's hairdresser, who had taken a wrong turn upon leaving Varennes, and never delivered a crucial message to General Bouillé; of the grocer's rooms, hung with sausages and hams, in which her parents were arrested.

Madame's attitude changed dramatically, alas, when I began my financial quest. A few days after we had had that last conversation about Varennes I wrote her a letter stating my demand for the funds owed by her parents to Madame Korff and me; and as weeks passed I received no reply. I wrote her numerous times, and she never responded. On one occasion she sent me an invitation to come to her apartments, but upon arriving there I found some twenty other guests, and was unable to say a word to her in private.

After a few months of similar evasions on Marie-Thérèse's part, my attitude toward her radically changed. "I'm disgusted with her," I wrote Taube. "I can now understand why people become democrats. I've been unable to see Madame Royale in private and I doubt if I ever shall. It's yet another disillusionment, and another regret, but I'm used to those by now. I'm not really surprised because everything that has to do with those unfortunate sovereigns [the French royal family] is forgotten here. Predictably, my devotion to them is also forgotten."

Marie-Thérèse never invited me again to a private reception; and after a while—this hurt me terribly—she even ceased to recognize me among the courtiers who trailed behind her during her public appearances. It had been clear to me from the start that she had none of her mother's charm; it was also becoming evident that she did not have a trace of her father's kindness. On one occasion I managed to have a private conversation with her principal lady-in-waiting, Mademoiselle Chanclos, who told me that Madame Royale was heartless and stingy toward every member of her retinue, and that she hated her Hapsburg relatives as well as the French émigrés. And this led me to recall that her mother had often complained to me about her daughter's coldness and insensitivity. The lack of generosity or justice in Madame's behavior outraged me, and the failure of my attempts to visit her wounded me deeply. Might it be that Gustavus, Louis XVI, and Marie Antoinette were among the last royals to have the civility and empathy that had always justified, in my view, the divine right of kings?

CHAPTER 13

Axel:

DIPLOMACY

IN 1796, a few months after I'd left Vienna and returned to Stockholm, the young king of Sweden, Gustav IV Adolf, reached his majority and began to rule. Tall and thin, with a long neck surmounting narrow shoulders, his face marred by bad teeth and a pendulous lip, he hardly had the charm or winsomeness of his father, Gustavus III. However, there was dignity in his bearing, and without having Gustavus's oratorical brilliance he was a good enough speaker. Obsessed by the perils wrought by the French Revolution, which in Sweden was called "*le mal Francais*," he was highly conservative. He was as stubborn as he was vain; lest he adopt the contrary measure he had to be carefully approached with any request; and his distrust of others led to a brusqueness of manner that was not suitable to a monarch. He was also very stingy: all balls, operas, fetes, celebrations, were banned at his court; a decade into his rule he closed all state theaters, and even ordered the Stockholm Opera House to be razed to the ground, though he was eventually persuaded to keep it intact. His unease and diffidence toward the nobility may well have been caused by the mystery and intrigues that still surrounded his birth (his blood father, Munck, had recently returned to Sweden after a long exile in Italy, threatened to tell all if he was not allowed to recuperate all his possessions, and had to be paid high sums to remain silent). Notwithstanding his distaste for the aristocracy Gustav IV Adolf was well aware of the affection his father had had for the Fersen family, and was particularly well disposed toward me.

When the young king assumed the throne the issue of his marriage inevitably arose. The pro-Russian faction at the Swedish court had wished him to marry a niece of Empress Catherine the Great of Russia, a Princess Mecklenburg, and Gustav Adolf went to Saint Petersburg himself to sign the marriage contract. But at the last minute he had religious scruples concerning the fact that he was Protestant and the Princess was Russian Orthodox, and refused to go through with the wedding. Empress Catherine, who was present when he broke off the engagement, had a stroke shortly thereafter, and died in November of that year.

Some months later a new bride was found for Gustav Adolf— Fredrika Dorothea, a beautiful and accomplished Danish princess from Baden. Upon arriving at the Swedish court the young queen was horrified by its relatively relaxed sexual mores, and wrote her mother that the Duchess of Södermanland had "all possible tastes," hinting that she was having an affair with my sister, Sophie Piper. Because of the youngsters' total sexual ignorance—the king was nineteen, the queen fifteen—the consummation of their marriage proved to be as problematic as that of Gustavus's. The inexperienced young king had begun his bridal night reading the first act of Racine's *Esther* to his bride, and had then flung himself upon her with such ferocity that she fled, terrified, to her ladies-in-waiting, and refused his advances for weeks. A solution was finally found: the young king asked his bride whether she knew anything about the act of lovemaking; she replied that her mother had only given her one bit of advice—to spread her legs apart. To the relief of the court, whose members had grown much concerned, as I had, about the teenagers' quandary, this conversation helped the young couple solve their dilemma: until then they'd only tried it with their legs closed. They went on to have a most loving marriage marked by extremely active sexual relations, so much so that the queen had six children in eight years, and I thought it fitting to write a note to the king urging him to spare the queen's health.

At the time of Gustav IV Adolf's marriage I was living quietly in Frankfurt, still smarting from the painful fiasco I'd experienced with Marie-Thérèse in Vienna, and dallying, as usual, in a ménage à trois with Eleanore Sullivan and Quentin Craufurd. But I was suddenly thrust into public life again when Gustav Adolf assigned me to be his minister plenipotentiary at the Congress of Rastatt, which had been called to negotiate a peace treaty between the German principalities and France in the wake of the armistice recently enacted between France and Austria. (Rastatt had been the site of an earlier peace conference between France and Germany, in 1714.) The mission I was assigned perplexed me for several reasons: The king of Sweden had not been officially invited to send a representative to this council. He was imposing himself under the pretext that Sweden, some decades earlier, had initiated the Treaty of Westphalia, through which it had acquired the German principality of Pomerania. Moreover, I had never yet performed this kind of diplomatic function, and had to ask for an aide who was specialized in issues of German foreign policy.

I was only too aware that the rest of Europe was puzzled by Gustav Adolf's choice of me as a delegate to Rastatt. I was seen throughout Europe as a living symbol of antirevolutionary—thus anti-French—principles. This did not affect my daily life, since I lived in Frankfurt. But there were ugly rumors of nepotism, suggestions that my post had been suggested to Gustav Adolf by his close confidant Evert Taube, my sister's lover. Talleyrand, France's foreign minister, complained to the Swedish consul that he was shocked to see, negotiating with ministers of the French Republic, "a man well known for his hatred of us, and for his efforts to serve the enemies of liberty." He went on to suggest that Staël be sent in my place (it should be noted that Talleyrand owed his post as foreign minister to the machinations of Madame de Staël). But Gustav Adolf stubbornly held his own and persisted in his decision to send me to Rastatt.

When the Congress of Rastatt opened in December 1797, my own stupid vanity brought me yet more problems. Having learned that Russia was sending an ambassador to Rastatt, I persuaded my king to give me the same title. But shortly afterward Russia recalled its representative, and I found myself to be the only delegate with that designation, which some other delegates derided as pretentious. Seldom has my vainglory so tainted my reputation.

A WORD IS needed here about the political situation in France. The elections of April 1797, which resulted in a royalist majority, had raised my hopes. But shortly after the elections, a young republican military star, General Napoleon Bonaparte, defeated a group of royalists who had staged a rebellion against the National Convention in an attempt to restore the monarchy. Notwithstanding our totally opposite ideologies, Bonaparte had struck me as a brilliant, ambitious young man, one with whom it would be interesting to deal diplomatically. Eager to dissipate the tensions that had recently arisen between France and Sweden because of my king's loathing of republicanism, I called upon Bonaparte the day after I arrived in Rastatt. I knew that he wished Sweden to remain neutral, and dreaded any possibility of our alliance with Great Britain. Wishing to impress him with the splendor of Swedish style (another stupid mistake on my part) I arrived in a coach drawn by six white horses, in the company of domestics in full livery. Bonaparte's aides-de-camp accompanied me to the salon, where the general was pacing up and down the room, as was his custom, in front of the fireplace. At his side was Berthier, one of my acquaintances from the American Revolutionary War. Bonaparte was a small, slender, dark-haired man who coughed a lot and seemed to suffer from a chest condition. He bade me sit down and our conversation began. I was immediately annoyed by the fact that he addressed me as "Monsieur" or, only occasionally, "Your Excellency" instead of the properly ceremonial "Monsieur L'Ambassadeur."

"Have you come to Rastatt to arrange for King Gustav Adolf's marriage to Princess Fredrika of Baden?" he asked.

"No," I said, "I've nothing to do with this detail. Baron Taube is taking care of that. My king sent me here as ambassador to the congress."

Bonaparte seemed not to have heard, and asked: "Has Monsieur spent some time here?"

"No, I've been staying in Frankfurt."

"And have you a chargé d'affaires in Paris?" he queried.

"No, General, since the little misunderstandings that occurred between our nations we've had no one in Paris, but everything seems to be settling down now and we'll surely send someone soon."

This response seemed to annoy the general, who launched into a polemic against me.

"Sweden seems to take pleasure in choosing to be represented by individuals disagreeable to all French citizens. . . . The king of Sweden would not be indifferent to a minister who had tried to incite the people of Stockholm to revolt. . . . In the same manner, monsieur, the French Republic will not suffer seeing men who are only too well known to have had close links to the ancient court of France, men perhaps listed as émigrés, come to defy the ministers of the world's most evolved people. The French nation, before consulting its political interests, will above all consult the sense of its dignity."

I sat there, fuming, increasingly furious at this parvenu. How did this arrogant little upstart who thought it distinguished to be insolent dare lecture me this way? It took all of my patience and self-control to not respond to him as crudely as he deserved. He was clearly treating me as an émigré. (I later heard him to have remarked that Sweden should be ashamed to have sent to the congress "a courtier from the old order who had been Marie Antoinette's lover," and that I had struck him as a man "steeped in all the fatuities" of the Bourbon court.) I rose and took my leave, commenting that I would discuss our meeting with my king, who, I said, surely wished to conserve the most harmonious relations between our two countries. "After my visit with this so-called great man so small in his manners," I wrote in my journal, "I'll heartily say 'Amen' to whatever may befall him."

But I soon realized that the general's rebuff had ruined my standing at Rastatt. All of Bonaparte's public comments about persons disagreeable to the French regime seemed to have referred directly to me. Some delegates pretended not to recognize me at the theater. Metternich's door was closed to me. I was as if quarantined. Bonaparte stayed only five days at Rastatt, and after leaving the congress, sent as his representatives two Jacobin deputies named Bonnier and Treilhard. The delegates to the congress awaited them with curiosity, and were startled to see the two men unwashed, uncombed, and in every way uncouth, or as Metternich put it, "like bears come out of a forest." "One would die of fright if one met the best dressed of these riffraff in a wood," Metternich commented. Going to visit Treilhard to present my king's good wishes, I was met by a very drunk lackey; he led me to see his master, who was still in his bathrobe. I tried to clear my record, stating that I could not possibly have been an émigré or an enemy of the French Republic, since it had been established in September 1792, many months after my departure from France. But my appeal to Treilhard went nowhere: Talleyrand confirmed to all that the Directory had fully approved the general's rebuff of me.

Even during my absence, news of the incident could not help but spread to Sweden—all the more so because Gustav IV Adolf had reestablished the freedom of the press abolished by his father. The king was again criticized for having chosen me to attend Rastatt. After having been lionized much of my life, I suddenly found myself ostracized, and harassed by rumors aimed to discredit me. The French chargé d'affaires in Stockholm, for instance, who kept pressing for Staël's appointment as Sweden's ambassador to Paris, spread the word that my sister Sophie was scheming to have me appointed as chancellor of Sweden. The king finally consented to send Staël to Paris, on the condition that I could remain in Rastatt. But Talleyrand wanted me out. So the king asked me to retire to Karlsruhe, a town a few miles from Rastatt, under the pretext that I was to arrange the details of my king's marriage to the Princess of Baden. I was furious to lose face before Talleyrand and the Jacobins, who had always spread outrageous calumnies concerning me. And nothing was more odious to me than to be accused of plotting with the émigrés, who, in my opinion, had greatly contributed to the fall of the French throne.

"In view of the care I've taken concerning my conduct and my reserve," I wrote my king, "it is all the more painful to suffer from all these denunciations. . . . If I were to seek justification, my colleagues—witnesses of my demeanor, about which they've often complimented me—would vouch for me."

In Karlsruhe, where I could easily be apprised of the events in Rastatt, I found a pretty house on the outskirts of the city with a splendid view of the mountains. There I saw few people. I lived solely in the company of my domestics, meditating on my recent griefs and losses, on the glumness of a bachelor's life in advancing age, and on my longing for a stable home. While there I turned down my king's offer of an ambassadorship to Vienna. I was now ready to return to Sweden and accept some important post there, in part because my affair with Eleanore Sullivan was finally coming to an end. During my stay at Rastatt I had seen her in nearby Frankfurt, and found her suddenly aged. Her once extraordinary skin had darkened and grown murky, her absurdly curly head of hair resembled a poodle's, and she was given to wearing too many flamboyant diamonds.

As for Craufurd, too self-involved to respond to anyone else's needs, he was growing deaf and losing his sight. One evening after I'd left Eleanore and returned to my little country house, he paid me a visit and angrily showed me a letter which alleged that Eleanore was having an affair with a certain man whose initials were A.B. Amused by the thought that both Craufurd and I might have been cuckolded, I commented that anonymous letters should be ignored.

But in the following weeks the drama deepened. Eleanore had given her friend Simolin, the ninety-year-old retired Russian ambassador, two letters to mail, one to me and one to Craufurd. The venerable Simolin had confused the envelopes, sending me the letter destined for Craufurd, and mailing to Craufurd the missive destined for me, thus leading Craufurd to finally learn about my affair with Eleanore. My principal fear, ironically, was not that Eleanore would leave me, but that she'd be left by Craufurd, and would rely on me for support, demanding that I marry her. Seeing her bizarre and flashy conduct, my relatively modest means, and my position as a diplomat, she would hardly make an appropriate wife for me. And what would I do about her daughter, whom I could not abide? The notion that I might be obliged to marry a spendthrift, increasingly vulgar mistress because her letters had been improperly addressed horrified me.

I'd been expecting a furious scene with Craufurd, and I had one. Referring to the time I had arranged for him to be one of Gustavus III's agents in Paris, Craufurd absurdly accused me of having compromised him during the Revolution, of having put his life on the line to serve my own ambitions; he went on to denounce me for having abused his trust by making advances to his mistress. I rebutted that it was Craufurd, ever self-promoting, who had proposed his services to Gustavus, and that it was Eleanore who had made the first overtures to me. During our quarrel Eleanore sat in a corner, weeping. Simolin, tormented by the notion that he was responsible for the fiasco of misaddressed letters, had an attack of apoplexy that would lead him to die a few weeks later. After the shouting was over I took my leave, and never saw any of them again. My first great love had ended in tragedy. My second little love ended in burlesque.

Eleanore eventually married Craufurd, in 1802. By then they had become favorites of Napoleon and Josephine's, and the emperor, who had his puritanical side, bade them to marry, not approving of irregular liaisons in his circle of intimates. The Craufurds' home became one of the two or three most notable salons of the Empire. Craufurd's next book, a study of French literature, was very well received. Eleanore, now known as "that nice fat Mrs. Craufurd," had the pleasure of seeing her daughter marry the Comte d'Orsay, and of moving in the highest aristocratic circles. Good-bye to all that!

Soon after making my definitive break with Eleanore I had intended to return to Sweden. But my plans were again countermanded, this time tragically so. Evert Taube, whose health had always been frail, grew very ill, and in July 1799 Sophie and I brought him to Karlsbad to take the waters. "The doctors think he may have a few more days to live," I wrote Gustav Adolf as I sat by the dying man's bed. "The painful prospect of losing my only and closest friend, to whom I'm attached by a great conformity of feeling and of action, is most painful. His calm, his resignation, his sangfroid, are admirable; this is the death of a just and honest man; he does not cease to speak of Your Majesty and displays his attachment to you in the most touching manner."

The doctors had been too optimistic. Taube died just as I was finishing this letter. In his will he left the entirety of his considerable wealth to Sophie, and made me his sole executor. Rumors hence spread, among his relatives, concerning the causes of his death. Taube had confided to me that he had drunk "a suspect glass of Malaga" at the table of our compatriot Engeström, who was of the prorevolutionary party, and would have had every political reason to bring about the demise of a man of the opposite faction. But my sister Sophie was also accused of having poisoned him because of his great fortune. The absurd notion! Sophie, whom I'd seen at Taube's side for nearly a quarter of a century, nursing him through illnesses, sacrificing the company of her beloved children to be constantly with him, enjoying an intense relationship with her lover! Two days after his death we buried Taube's ashes in Karlsbad. For the rest of her life, Sophie would wear, in a locket that hung about her neck, the ashes of her lover's heart.

SOPHIE AND I took a ship to Stockholm. I was aware of all the rumors that were spreading throughout my city concerning the position the king might offer me. Upon my arrival, before even mentioning any post, Gustav Adolf bestowed upon me yet another title, that of Lord of the Realm. The designation had been created by Gustavus III. There were only twenty of us at any one time, and each of us was to be addressed as "Your Excellency." But notwithstanding the pleasure I took in this honor, upon my return I did not find Sweden agreeable. The brilliance of Gustavus's reign had much faded, as had the prevailing manners and style. The bourgeoisie, which had long kept its distance from the nobility, played an increasingly important role in society: minor officials, tradesmen, journalists, refugees from Finland and persons of other foreign origins, most of them rootless, were holding more and more powerful positions on city councils and other civic institutions. I readily admit to being a snob. I rigorously shunned members of this newly potent burgher class, finding uncouth their slipshod manners and their constant prattle about money. In recent years, as Sweden's finances grew strained, they had suffered some economic decline, and this made them all the more hostile to us, the ancient nobility. Foreign diplomats, in their dispatches, often stressed the Stockholm bourgeoisie's hatred of the aristocracy. A dislike for the rich and powerful prevailed among them far more than among the peasantry or the city's poor, and they had grown increasingly hostile as they grew literate and politically aware. From the little contact I had with them, I noted that their men tended to drunkenness; that their conversation was dim-witted; that their women dressed horribly and turned fat and wrinkled before their time. At dinner tables they consumed fruit jams with marinated fish, and after the meal the two genders separated into two different drawing rooms. All these factors made Stockholm life far less enjoyable. Moreover, French was spoken notably less well than it had been in my youth, and to my horror French phrases were constantly being admixed with Swedish words.

What did I do, once home, to escape this philistinism? I continued to collect rare books. I spent much time in artists' studios, buying the work of the younger, poorer painters and sculptors, attempting to revive the tradition of patronage that had flourished under Gustavus III. I often went to the opera, focusing on those works that Toinette and I had most enjoyed together—*The Marriage of Figaro; Orpheus and Eurydice*, which had been composed by my beloved's own music teacher, Gluck; *Dido and Aeneas*, which had been a great favorite of hers. What painful memories and longings filled my heart when I saw these spectacles!

IT WAS WITH some apprehension that I went to see the king, when he summoned me at the end of November, to learn what position he was going to offer me. Chancellor? Grand marshal? Minister of foreign affairs? There was one I was not willing to accept—the governorship of Stockholm—because I knew I was highly unpopular with the citizens of our capital, who would hasten to get rid of me. To my great surprise, he offered me something totally different: the chancellorship of the University of Uppsala.

"But, sire," I said, "I know nothing about the education of the young!"

"That's not what I'm looking for," said the king. "I need a firm, intelligent man to watch over the education of our future leaders."

I asked the king for twenty-four hours to think about this offer. As I left the palace, I began to see his train of thought: Sweden's student population had been much radicalized recently by the ascent of Bonaparte. When, the previous year, a false rumor had spread that Napoleon had died in Egypt, thousands of students had gone into mourning. A few weeks later, when his disembarkment in Fréjus was announced, there was dancing in the streets, and partisans of the Directoire government held a great celebration in a Stockholm restaurant. The feast lasted until 6 a.m., and a bust of Napoleon was carried about the room amid shouts of *"Vive la République!"* *Le mal Français* was being spread throughout the country by the young. . . . The king was making sense. He wished to stem the republican tide at Sweden's most distinguished university.

For the University of Uppsala had been founded in the fifteenth century. It had some six hundred students and employed dozens of the country's most distinguished professors. In view of the students' radicalism, my nomination for the post of chancellor, seeing my well-known reactionary views, was an extremely confrontational step for the king to take. Moreover, my long absences from Sweden were highly criticized. I was called *"L'Étranger,"* "the Stranger." The students deplored my reputation as a French émigré, and as a personal enemy of Bonaparte. Although some justified my distant manner ("Notwithstanding his deliberately cold, aloof conduct," one student wrote, "he was never discourteous toward us"), others were more harsh. "He pretended not to recognize any person he met," an antagonist wrote; "no insult is more offensive or irritating."

I made my first visit to Uppsala in December 1799, in the company of the king, who introduced me to the faculty. Its members, who could not countermand the king's wishes, nevertheless pretended to meet apart from us to discuss my fitness for the position Gustav IV Adolf had offered me. After an hour they came out, announcing that they had unanimously decided to accept me as their chancellor. I had to get up and make some kind of declaration to thank them. Oh horrors! I found I had forgotten much of my Swedish! I searched so frantically for words in my native tongue that I made my acceptance speech as short as possible, and was well enough applauded. I spent the rest of the day visiting the city's highlights: Uppsala's great Gothic cathedral, the Vasas' funerary chapel of white marble, and, inside the sacristy, the wooden statue of Thor, Nordic god of storms. As soon as I assumed my functions I concentrated on enriching the natural history collection, which particularly pleased me because it had been created by the great botanist Linnaeus. Before I arrived this collection consisted of some twenty thousand plants; I decided to much increase it. I also offered the university my father's splendid collection of medals.

In my first months I saw to it that the professors' salaries, and the scholarship funds for the poorer students, were increased. After two years or so the students not only tolerated me but rather liked me, finding me honest and fair, and looking on me as one of the more accommodating members of the university staff. The faculty were equally sympathetic, and were particularly impressed by the fact that I could converse fluently in Latin.

I should note that I did not have to reside in the very provincial town of Uppsala—I much pitied the inhabitants of that dreary city. My duties only engaged me to visit the university every few months, for two or three days at a time, and at the beginning of my appointment this suited me well, for there was again a romantic interest in my life. I had met, at a dinner in Stockholm, a beautiful Spanish woman, the wife of the Spanish ambassador, Marianne La Grua. She had declared her love for me, but I was perplexed by it, for her husband, a truly jealous and vindictive man, would not have had the relative tolerance of a Quentin Craufurd. I took her to the usual diversions one takes a mistress to—sleigh rides, oyster lunches, operas—but was wary of having relations with her, for she was just beginning a pregnancy.

On March 6, I made my way to Norrköping, the town on our northern coast that the king had chosen for his coronation, at which I was assigned to bear the great "Banner of the Realm" into the cathedral. Looking at myself in the mirror as I was leaving for the ceremony, I was quite pleased. The large white ermine mantle of the Order of the Seraphim, our nation's highest decoration, awarded to only twelve men at any one time and just recently bestowed on me, covered my jacket, which was encrusted with dozens of medals. A diamond necklace shone on my white lace collar, and my hair, which I wore quite long and was beginning to turn gray, was surmounted by a large feathered hat. I feared that the king, who made a point of dressing plainly, would feel a bit eclipsed by my presence, and indeed he barely said a word to me during the entire ceremony: tensions had already arisen between the monarch and my family over his disdain for protocol, when my brother, Fabian, protested the fact that Gustav Adolf had invited his secretary to an official dinner. Great was my relief when, after I had given the king the ritual bow and kissed his hand, he warmly pressed mine. A few days after the coronation, the Riksdag met. I may be too frivolous in my taste for ceremonial attire, but I was struck by how shoddy the representatives of the nobility looked. In other countries, any one of them would have been taken for a commoner: their filth, their stench, their reek of tobacco, which one could have cut with a knife, conveyed a poor notion of our aristocracy.

. . .

IN 1800 MY MOTHER DIED, a loss that I can't pretend afflicted me deeply, for we were never close. I had been far more sorrowful, earlier that year, about the health of my sister Sophie, who had been very ill with influenza, and whose demise would have killed me. Sophie and I had become even more deeply bonded since Marie Antoinette's and Taube's deaths. Since our childhoods we'd had no secrets from one another, had shared all sorrows and joys, and now we lived exclusively for each other. Sophie was my All. Her children, to whom I was devoted, might as well have been my own, and when her daughter Edwig, a maid of honor at court, found herself pregnant, I offered her a handsome wedding and provided the young couple with a good living. "Ah my tender Sophie," I had written her after Marie Antoinette's death, "since destiny assails us with its cruelest blows, let us live to recall our joys and console each other for our sorrows."

Sophie and I had decided to live at Blasieholmen, in the stately Stockholm home, directly across from the Royal Palace, in which we had spent our childhoods. We were much similar to each other physically: known as the handsomest woman in Stockholm, Sophie was almost as tall as I was, and, so it was said, equally haughty. Both of us were fastidious about our domestic surroundings, both of us were lazy about tending to anything that did not totally enthrall us, both of us were indefatigable travelers and not truly at home anywhere in the world. We were twin images of each other. Referred to as "*le couple* Fersen," we were looked upon with admiration or animosity, seldom with indifference.

King Gustav Adolf spent several months of 1804 traveling in Germany, and upon returning called me in to offer me the post of Chancellor of the Realm. The position, frankly, scared me. I feared that my assuming it might greatly harm relations between Sweden and the French

Republic. After so antagonizing Napoleon, how could I, Fersen, possibly deal with Sweden's foreign policy? Bonaparte was marching from victory to victory, and Gustav Adolf was planning to draw closer to France. Besides, I wished to preserve my freedom, and the position was too time-consuming; I would only accept one that would allow me several free months a year to travel. The king considered these objections for a few days, and called me back in. The courtiers waiting outside of the king's apartments fully expected the chancellor of the realm to walk out of the room; but instead they saw . . . the grand marshal of the kingdom.

I would later learn that the Duchess of Södermanland, who unlike her husband was fond of me, had doubted whether I was up to the job of being chancellor. "He loves his comfort too much to hold a post that demands that much time and application," she wrote. "Moreover, his clearly French manners would not be suitable."

I was fairly mortified by the duchess's words, but started working hard at my new position, which consisted of taking care of every detail of the king's palaces, down to the supervision of the royal stables and of household supplies. I went at the job with great diligence, as I had at my work at Uppsala, surveying financial accounts, tracking down thieves of royal silver, counting the coffee spoons of the royal dinner service, while dreaming of my next trip abroad. I thus had occasion to observe the king closely. He was growing more erratic, brusque, and rude than ever, most particularly toward the foreign diplomatic corps. I was startled by his indolence, his lack of ability for matters of state, and his refusal to abide by etiquette. Sophie and I were so struck by his uncouthness, in fact, that we had never once invited him to dine at Blasieholmen, which in retrospect might have been a serious mistake.

In the mid-1800s I left for another grand tour in the company of Sophie, her daughter, and her son-in-law. Among the domestics who accompanied us was a notoriously fine French chef, Pierre-Felix Berger, who would often write his family about the pride he took in serving a gastronome as reputed as I was. "I can not tell you how affectionate [my master] is with me," Berger would write about me in a letter to his brother. "He is Sweden's greatest lord, well known in France. . . . He loves me as if I were his own child. . . . [At his home] I am well lodged, well heated, served by my own domestic, who takes care of my clothes, cleans my room, makes my fire. . . . I cook at least fifteen courses at lunch and at dinner, other times as many as thirty or forty courses." Both Berger and I, understandably, suffered exceedingly from gout, and exchanged remedies for it in a spirit of great intimacy. I was as popular with my servants as I was unpopular with Stockholm's bourgeoisie, among whom I had an increasing number of enemies.

LET ME NOTE that amid all these travels, diversions, responsibilities, I never failed to commemorate the death of my cherished Marie Antoinette. "Losing *Her* remains the greatest grief of my life," I wrote in my journal a decade or so after the queen's death, "and my sorrows will only abate when I die. Never have I felt so powerfully the emotions I had for Her, and never have I loved Her as much."

While traveling with Sophie and her party I continued to pursue this beloved shadow, and took turns visiting all those of Marie Antoinette's sisters who still survived: Archduchess Elizabeth, the lofty abbess of a convent in Innsbruck; Maria Amalia, Duchess of Parma, who reiterated the gratitude she felt for my devotion to her sister; and Maria Carolina, future queen of Naples, the sibling Toinette had been closest to, and who received me with particular affability. They painfully evoked my great love through their proud, majestic carriage. I found that the towns and principalities over which they reigned, and others I visited, had been devastated by *le mal Français*. Traveling to Florence, which I'd seen flourishing years earlier under the reign of Marie Antoinette's brother Grand Duke Leopold, I found it pillaged by Bonaparte's troops. I proceeded to Rome, where I had an audience with Pope Pius VII, whom I found to be living in a state of great poverty, as were most of Vatican City's denizens, who foraged for bones and shreds of vegetables thrown out of windows by the privileged few. I was saddened and angered by the way in which Europe had been impoverished by the French Revolution, and continued to be deprived by the devil Bonaparte.

While in Italy love interests continued to take up my time. Marianne La Grua, now delivered of her child, appeared in Rome, and swore to me that I was the only man she held to her heart. I did not believe a word of this, but played along with her delusions until I met Princess Yekaterina Nikolaevna Menshikova, a Russian belle whose qualities matched those of any French woman I'd known. "Ketty," as I called you, what treasures I encountered in your arms! You were small and as delicately modeled as a Meissen figurine, but oh the softness, the creamy softness of your skin! Your golden hair, when you untied it from its formal braided chignon, cascaded to below your hips. I enjoyed wrapping those satiny strands about my private parts, thus providing an additional layer of silkiness for my exquisite entrances and exits. You put your mouth to my nipples, suckling them like a babe, and that too was a novel sensation I found paradisiacal.

I had seldom witnessed so many qualities—beauty, amiability, sensuality—united in one woman. But our liaison lasted only six months, for Ketty had to return to her husband in Russia. "I've always had to be separated from those I love," I wrote Sophie; "It seems to be part of my destiny to never be happy."

Returning to Stockholm after my last grand tour with Sophie, I found some consolation in a romance—a platonic one, for once!—with a neighbor of mine at Lövstad, Emelie Aurora De Geer. A few years earlier, when her mother had died, Emelie had renounced her position as lady-in-waiting at court to dedicate herself to her family estate, which adjoined mine. Emelie was a delicate, willowy brunette with huge, pale blue eyes and a waist so tiny that my hands could almost span it. I'd admired her beauty, intelligence, and dedication, and did all I could to help her with her domestic affairs. We were often separated by my frequent trips to Stockholm, and our relationship was close enough that we wrote each other almost daily when I was in the capital. Though I continued my lifelong wariness of marriage, the beautiful, virginal Emelie would consider nothing less. We became even more closely bonded when, upon her father's death in 1809, I was named one of her guardians. So there we were, vaguely affianced. For a variety of reasons, I kept postponing a definitive offer of marriage—emotional exhaustion, a fear of abandoning the sweet accumulated habits of a lifetime. . . .

Upon returning to Stockholm I found the king to have grown even more irrational. He kept talking about being visited by the White Lady, a spectral character of Swedish mythology whose appearances bode bad luck to those who saw her. Upon his bouts of foul humor, which could last for days, he lashed out at everyone and sought every pretext to be aroused. He became so enraged, for instance, upon hearing a page coughing in the vestibule that he wanted to send him to jail. Nevertheless, I had to accept a new and important charge from him: that of overlooking the education of his son, a frail child, Gustav, now three years old.

Yet despite this important duty I remained *"L'Étranger"* to most denizens of Stockholm. Notable citizens were barely civil to me at social gatherings, and even cut me off at dinner parties. I started pondering the fact that I had always tried to *impress* others, but had never in my life tried to be *liked*. I had never cared. This was part of the Fersen pride. My father had been the same way, haughty and aloof, and had led a magnificent life. . . . At times I thought I should try a new tack, be obliging, engaging, prepossessing. Those who had known me long and well, after all, had just that view of me. I took solace in a letter I was shown, written years earlier by the Duchess of Södermanland, who had this to say about me: "He is the most honest and loyal of friends. He's a true royalist and is ready to do anything for his king; he tried to rescue his benefactor Louis XVI and suffered much as a result. He is too proud to be intriguing, he expresses his opinions frankly and fearlessly, he suffers in silence and never utters a critical word. He is full of tact. . . . He is not any haughtier than anyone needs to be to inspire respect."

Amen and much gratitude, I say to a friend who truly understood me.

THE POLITICAL CLIMATE in Sweden was growing increasingly troubled. Gustav IV Adolf was becoming a more and more implacable, tenacious enemy of the French Republic, and one event particularly increased his ire: in early 1804, in revenge against an attempted royalist coup planned by the Comte d' Artois, Bonaparte masterminded the murder of the Duc d'Enghien. D'Enghien, son of the Duc de Bourbon-Condé, a cousin of Louis XVI, had emigrated with his father at the outbreak of the Revolution and settled in Baden. Upon hearing a false rumor that d'Enghien was preparing a coup to depose him, Bonaparte, then first consul, had him kidnapped by his police and brought to the castle of Vincennes, where a court-martial was hurriedly gathered to try him. D'Enghien was convicted of bearing arms against France, and was shot a few days after his arrest, thus putting an end to the house of Condé. This transgression of Bonaparte's caused his foreign minister, Talleyrand, who had opposed the prosecution, to make a typically sardonic comment: "It's worse than a crime, sire, it's a mistake."

The indignation provoked by d'Enghien's murder spread throughout Europe, and few monarchs were more aroused than Gustav Adolf, who swore vengeance against all things French. He ordered all French residents of Stockholm—including diplomats—expelled from the capital; all French books and magazines were burned; no event occurring in

France was allowed to be mentioned in the Swedish press. To make things worse, Gustav Adolf had fallen under the influence of a self-styled prophet who, basing himself on the Apocalypse, had persuaded him that Bonaparte was the Antichrist and that he, Gustav Adolf, was the prophet destined to abolish him. When, later that year, Bonaparte proclaimed himself emperor, the king of Sweden persisted in referring to him as "Monsieur Bonaparte," refusing to recognize him as monarch of France.

Although wary of such excesses, I kept advising my king to pursue resolutely antirepublican principles. And my own attachment to royalist causes would remain undiminished. In 1805 I began to see more of Louis XVI's two brothers, who had sought exile in various European countries. The Comte d'Artois received me with the greatest affection. The Comte de Provence, or Louis XVIII, as he called himself, was piqued at me because I'd discouraged him from settling in Sweden, which would have gone against our principles of neutrality; but he continued to flatter me, as he did most people whose help he might eventually need. I dined almost every night at the table of the "King of France," as Provence also referred to himself, and returned his invitations at my home with a magnificence that was well noticed. I found erudition and wit in Provence, but too weak a character for the kingly role he aspired to, and a tendency to drink too much. I esteemed Artois as somewhat superior to his brother, and found him very matured by his unhappy exile. However great the joy I experienced in visiting these princes, it was troubled by the memory of the tragedies visited upon their brother and sister-in-law.

IN THOSE YEARS Gustav Adolf's personal conduct continued to grow increasingly bizarre. He threw away his sword and his uniform, donned a bourgeois frock coat and gray trousers, and grew a mustache, which none of our kings had ever done before. He alienated the emperor of Prussia when he returned the Prussian Order of the Black Eagle on the grounds that the emperor had accepted the Legion of Honor from the French government. ("It is impossible to calculate the consequences of this insult," I wrote a friend, "which is in fact a harsh criticism of other nations.") Aware of the fact that he was greatly disliked in his capital, Gustav spoke of retiring to Moravia, or to the southern province of Scania. He began by seeking refuge in the royal castle of Gripsholm, where he kept total silence, not even speaking to his wife, and communicating with his aides solely by writing. He exclusively bonded with Gripsholm's inept, boorish caretaker, another self-styled psychic who spoke solely of ghosts and specters. Upon spending a few days at Gripsholm, I was dismayed by the funereal atmosphere of the court. Dinner was announced as a battle might have been, by a guard with a saber at his side. The dishes were few and poor, the women dressed in severe gray dresses; I recognized only one or two courtiers of Gustavus's time. How I missed my dear friend, that king! Even though he'd made some political mistakes, how nostalgically I recalled his intellect, his grace and polish, his faultless aesthetic, his charm and warmth and wit!

Like Gustavus III and unlike his son, Gustav Adolf, I insisted on great elegance at my homes. I owned some fourteen carriages and sleighs and, when moving from one summer residence to another—from Lövstad to Ljung, for instance—used no fewer than twenty-six horses. A staff of twenty-four domestics ran the house Sophie and I inhabited in Stockholm, and I took pleasure in being reputed to have Sweden's most magnificent table. I enjoyed entertaining groups of our most ancient nobility, continuing to shun the new burgher class that had gained much power in the last decade. As my chef Felix Berger has testified, notwithstanding my severe case of gout, fifteen courses were an absolute minimum at my dinners. I was perfectly capable of having a hundred persons for a lunch of oysters, and was admired by all for the excellence of my chef's inventions. This did not at all please my king. Stingy by nature and abstemious for political reasons, he was beginning to dislike me for entertaining so much more luxuriously than he, and for advising him to remain calm and prudent toward the beast Napoleon.

So here I was at the age of fifty, grand marshal of the kingdom: heading the regents' council whenever the king went abroad; attending the Riksdag attired in the ermine cape worn only by the twelve men anointed with Sweden's highest distinction, the Order of the Seraphim; as eagerly sought out by women as ever, equally pursued by noble ladies looking for wealthy son-in-laws; mildly flirting with the lovely Emelie De Geer; so heavily covered with medals that I had trouble, at times, rising from my chair; inhabiting my magnificent family palaces; listening to my beloved music; living with my handsome loving sister, whose attachment to me was as deep as mine to her. And yet notwithstanding all these honors, accolades, loyalties, I felt empty, utterly empty . . . with no purpose in mind beyond continuing to live an existence that I felt would grow increasingly vacuous, seeing that I was vain, self-centered, and morose.

On March 31, 1808, I discontinued keeping my *dagbok,* the journal I had begun to write at the tender age of fourteen. Could it be that I had lost much of my taste for life? I determined to devote myself all the more energetically to the memoir of my past times, my often glorious past loves, which I'm presenting in these pages.

CHAPTER 14

Axel:

A KING'S AND
A PRINCE'S FALL

I HAD INDEED lost much taste for life. My increasing melancholia, an innate trait, might well have incited me to cease writing my diary; and my depressions were aggravated by the terrible condition of my country. Gustav IV Adolf—moody, impetuous, inconsistent, constantly countermanding his own orders—had dealt great blows to Sweden through his idiotic foreign policy. When France and Russia made peace through the Treaty of Tilsit in 1807, Gustav Adolf stubbornly continued his war against both France and Russia. Denmark, an ally of France's, declared war on Sweden in 1808. Our king had earlier hoped for assistance from England, but it was then at war with Spain and could offer little help. When England finally did send a regiment of ten thousand men to Göteborg (I was there, attending a shareholders' meeting of the East India Company), Gustav quarreled with the British general and refused his aid. Sweden thus became totally isolated, with enemies in the east, south, and west. By the end of 1808, Finland, which had been occupied by Sweden for decades, would be lost to Russia, which would also conquer the Swedish fortress of Sveaborg, Sweden's largest military base. The Russian army advanced as far as Umeå, in northern Sweden. A bitter peace would be signed in 1809 at Frederikshavn, through which Sweden lost a third of her territory and a quarter of her population, forfeiting to Russia not only Finland, but also the Åland Islands northeast of Stockholm.

The winter of 1808 was in every way catastrophic. It was the coldest in many decades, and wood was barely available, since it had habitually come from Finland. The extreme cold, and the pulmonary epidemics it caused, killed several dozen persons a day; thousands of workmen stayed home to avoid the freezing temperatures. Moreover, the king refused to call a meeting of the Riksdag, which his uncle, the Duke of Södermanland, and others of his closest aides had repeatedly asked him to do. Instead, to the dismay of the nation, he ordered a war tax five times larger than the previous taxation and decreed a large levying of troops. And although he had no military talent or experience whatever, he announced that he would henceforth be commander in chief of Sweden's army. He did not have a chance to exercise these duties: in previous months a rebellion had been brewing among army officers; and in March 1809 Lieutenant Colonel Georg Adlersparre, the aggressively ambitious commander-in-chief of our troops on the Norwegian border, signed a private armistice with the Danish commander of southern Norway, and marched on Stockholm with the intent of forcing the king to sign an official peace treaty and call a Riksdag.

When the king heard of Adlersparre's plans he hurriedly left the castle of Haga, some three miles from Stockholm, where I'd been visiting that day to celebrate the queen's birthday. Leaving his wife and children in my care, he rushed to the capital with the intent of traveling on south to Scania, Sweden's southernmost province, in hopes of rallying troops there. Arriving in Stockholm, he found menacing crowds in the courtyard that faced his palace. Two of the nation's leading military men, Marshal Klingspor and General Adlercreutz, had assembled at the palace with other officials to convince the king to remain in Stockholm, and to convoke the Riksdag. Their pressure so exasperated Gustav Adolf that upon one particular argument with his dissenters he raised his sword threateningly against the aging Count von Stedingk, one of his father's closest friends, and had to be restrained.

The morning after the king's return, Marshal Klingspor, delegated by his peers, went to see Gustav Adolf and again exhorted him to remain in the capital. The king, furious, shouted insults at him, and upon hearing the imprecations General Adlercreutz and yet another esteemed military leader, the aggressively ambitious Colonel Silfversparre, rushed into the room. When he saw them enter, the king accused them of treason and brandished his sword again. Silfversparre managed to restrain him, but the king's personal guards arrived; while Adlercreutz conferred with them the king managed to escape, and was only caught after an antic chase through the palace corridors.

Upon more discussions with the monarch, who was now detained in his apartments and still adamantly refused to put an end to his war with Denmark, Adlercreutz and other high-ranking notables realized that their only recourse was to suggest that he resign. Silfversparre, who had been appointed to be the king's guardian, took the situation in hand, and asked him to abdicate. Gustav Adolf accepted with surprising ease, and soon went into exile abroad with his wife and children. But who could take his place? The notables settled on Karl, Duke of Södermanland, Gustav Adolf's uncle, and elected him provisional head of state. Even though this indolent, aging prince enjoyed living in his various country estates, lacked any political insight, and had no ambition whatever to rule, a few months later he was crowned as King Karl XIII. I played my habitual, preeminent part at the coronation ritual, and upon this occasion the king promoted me to the rank of general.

Karl XIII being childless and ailing, the next order of business, inevitably, was to decide on his successor. The choice of a crown prince was made all the more difficult by the fact that the Riksdag had voted, to my great dismay, to permanently ban Gustav Adolf's descendants from the throne. (As head of the "Gustavian" party, the faction that wished for a continuation of Gustavus's lineage, I was incensed by that ruling, being in favor of Gustav Adolf's young son, Gustav, being chosen as crown prince.) Shortly after the coronation, Adlersparre proposed that Prince Christian August of Augustenberg, viceroy and governor of Norway, a distant descendant of Swedish royalty, be named crown prince, and the Riksdag acceded to that suggestion. It was hoped that Christian August would enjoin Norway to unite with Sweden, an ambition of Gustavus's that had never been realized. The new crown prince—he would be renamed Karl August to make his name sound less foreign—arrived in Sweden in January of 1809. He was officially welcomed at Göteborg by my brother, Fabian, chairman of the State Banking Commission; I welcomed him to Drottningholm Palace, upon which occasion I addressed him in French, as was habitual in the aristocracy. The prince replied that he knew Swedish and would prefer to speak it, which led to a bad start in our relations.

Crown Prince Karl August would not be popular with the nobility. Small and fat, very ugly, with a short, thick neck and a face heavily marked with smallpox, he habitually locked himself up in his study instead of frequenting salons or theaters. Always modestly, if not frugally, dressed, whenever he went out he visited welfare institutions, homes for the aged, orphanages. Nervous and melancholy, he never gave or attended court dinners, and spent most of his time doing good works. And although he was a heavy drinker—an addiction that would perhaps contribute to his early death—he had a pronounced aversion, much like Gustav Adolf, to most kinds of luxury. However unpopular with aristocrats, many of whom referred to him as "Prince of the Mob," he grew to be greatly beloved by the citizenry, and by King Karl himself: his simple, affable manners led the public to look on him as their protector against the privileged few. It was soon clear to me that Karl August, with his distaste for aristocrats, would have little tolerance for our family, the foremost representatives of the Gustavian nobility; and that like the public at large he would look on our formality and reserve as arrogance and cynicism. In fact Sophie and I would soon hear that Karl August described us, the Fersens, as "a survival from a bygone era, refined on the surface although fundamentally barbaric and unchristian." *Gode Gud,* what a judgment! We indeed came from "a bygone era", but in what sense, my sister and I wondered, could we be considered "barbaric"? It was clear that we were now looked on as outcasts.

Less than eighteen months after his arrival, on May 28, 1810, as he was reviewing troops in the southern province of Scania, Crown Prince Karl August suddenly grew unsteady on his saddle, and fell off his horse, unconscious. Notwithstanding the care offered by his physician, Dr. Rossi, who had been traveling with him, he died a half hour later. Rossi called in professors from the nearest city, Lund, who performed an autopsy, and diagnosed that the prince had died of apoplexy.

Stockholm's citizens were grief-stricken by news of the popular prince's death, and rumors instantly arose that he had been poisoned. "A bleak cloud hung over the capital," as one witness put it; "all faces were desolate and somber. . . . It is as if everyone had lost a close relative, a dear friend."

I was then at Löfstad, and upon hearing the news, I decided to stay there. According to the daily reports I received from friends, the doctors' diagnosis of apoplexy did not appease the crowds, who seemed determined to believe that the crown prince had been poisoned. Mind you, accusations of poisoning all too frequently arose when eminent persons died premature deaths. Whenever a distinguished member of the Riksdag died, an autopsy was habitually ordered to decide whether there had been foul play. Karl XIII himself had feared that Danish officials had intended to poison him. Shortly before the crown prince arrived in Sweden, a member of the Riksdag had suggested that there was a Gustavian plot to poison him before he reached Stockholm. Moreover, Crown Prince Karl August had been in frail health long before he arrived in Sweden, and suffered from vertigo. As soon as he settled in Stockholm his frequent illnesses incited many rumors of attempted poisonings. Such accusations focused on such Gustavian families as the de la Gardies, and on my old friend Armfelt. And upon the crown prince's death they centered all the more onerously on us, the Fersens, because the de la Gardies and Armfelt had not been in Stockholm at the time of Karl August's death.

I WRITE THESE reflections three weeks after the crown prince's demise, on the evening of June 19, the eve of the ritual that will commemorate the reception of the prince's body in Stockholm. In view of the hostility borne to the Fersens by the capital's bourgeoisie, who control the Swedish press, it is inevitable that our own family would be suspected of having poisoned Karl August. My sister Sophie has been particularly singled out as a culprit. As a powerful, highly intelligent woman who is the closest lifelong friend of Queen Charlotte, Karl XIII's wife, and is said to wield great influence over her, she is very unpopular among Stockholm's citizens. As one prominent member of the Riksdag put it, Sophie stands "high on the lists of intrigue," and the king himself recently described her as "a big devil." Moreover, she had earlier been suspected of having plotted the murder of her husband, Count Piper, and of poisoning her lover, Evert Taube (I've already mentioned that absurd charge), because he was leaving her his considerable fortune.

It should also be noted that several of the king's councilors are convinced of the Fersens' guilt. King Karl XIII himself believes that the murderer of his "beloved son" came from the high nobility. Instead of letting Dr. Rossi's diagnosis stand, he has sent two other eminent professors to Scania to inquire further into the cause of the crown prince's death. These doctors, while confirming Rossi's diagnosis of apoplexy, have criticized some of the methods employed by their colleague. The rumors of foul play that are currently spreading through Stockholm have been amplified by the fact that Italians have always been looked on as specialists in poisons. And suspicions of the Fersens are all the more widespread because Dr. Rossi is a protégé of our family, who had procured him his position as court doctor.

Pamphlets, broadside, leaflets, have begun to circulate in the past weeks. "Papers scattered every night in the streets of the city are calling the Swedes to vengeance," the French ambassador recently related; "accusations are being made against the Fersens and their friend the queen; the police are on constant guard." One particular leaflet, addressed to "The People, Karl August's Avengers," calls for a general uprising in which "blood must flow." Referring to our family palace, another pamphlet calls for revenge against "the highly distinguished monstrosities in Blasieholmen." Yet another warns that "certain high and distinguished persons" intended to poison the crown prince, the first among whom was "the haughty Count Fersen" and his "unscrupulous" sister.

So this is the threatening atmosphere of suspicion and intrigue that pervades Stockholm on June 19, even as I write. Tomorrow I shall have to take my place as grand marshal in the ritual cortege that will solemnize the arrival of the dead prince's body in the capital. Warnings of impending trouble have already reached me in Löfstad. I was made all the more aware of Emelie De Geer's affection for me yesterday, when she urged me not to leave for Stockholm for the crown prince's observance. Emphasizing reports of impending violence, she begged me to plead illness, and wept bitterly when I replied that as grand marshal it would be unthinkable for me not to take my place in the cortege. How she clung to me when I left for the city!

Earlier this afternoon, once arrived in Stockholm, I received a visit from my predecessor in the post of grand marshal, Count J. Oxenstierna, a fine poet and splendid man, who also implored me to stay home the following morning, and even offered to go in my place. To him I replied that I could not afford to confirm the suspicions held against me, and that proper measures were surely being taken to protect all officials. Yet a desire to reassure myself on that score incited me to go to the Haga Palace earlier tonight to see the king. Upon arriving and asking a courtier to announce my visit to the monarch I was told that King Karl did not have time to receive me. I asked the courtier to try again, explaining that I needed some more detailed instructions concerning the procedure of the crown prince's funeral cortege. The courtier returned and in an uneasy tone said, "His Majesty has so much to do that it is impossible for him to see Your Excellency." I was shocked—for the king not to have time for his grand marshal! But I bowed to the ladies gathered in the antechamber and conversed pleasantly with them to allay the embarrassment this incident might bring me. I bore in mind a rather offensive statement, repeated to me by a courtier, that the king had made about me in recent days: "It would not hurt if that haughty lord were taught a lesson."

Earlier tonight, after my return from the palace, Sophie and I gave a superb supper at Blasieholmen—"worthy of a king," as one guest told me. In the midst of the meal it occurred to me that the occasion might be ill-chosen: the sight of our brightly lit palace, on the eve of an event dedicated to the dead crown prince, could offend some Stockholmers. Seeing the frugality of the court, and our nation's piteous financial straits, Sophie and I have been as frequently criticized for our lavish ways as for our meticulous avoidance of the ascending bourgeoisie. But do I really care? Entertaining friends is one of my favorite pleasures; it is the surest remedy for my depressions, which in the past few years have become greatly aggravated.

How heavy are my thoughts as I prepare for bed tonight! The following morning, June 20, will be the nineteenth anniversary, to the day, of the flight to Varennes, that ill-fated venture through which I had hoped to save the life of my one great love. I have no fears whatever concerning the alarming predictions for the following day's events. I am only sorrowing for the failure of Varennes, and remembering with longing the only true happiness life has brought me—the love Toinette and I had for each other. Had she not been the one who designated me as *"Le Chevalier Sans Peur et Sans Reproche"*?

CHAPTER 15

Sophie:
JUNE 20, 1810

OH, IF ONLY I'd been at his side that day, if only I'd taken more seriously the threats of violence spreading throughout the city, if only, if only—my beloved Axel might have been safe.

On the morning of the twentieth, as Axel was about to depart from our home, Blasieholmen, to attend the crown prince's cortege, our old coachman—a man who had been with us since our childhood, who like all our domestics adored Axel—implored him to not leave home.

"It's predicted that there's going to be much violence, Your Excellency," I heard the old man say. "Please, please don't leave the palace."

"If you're afraid of driving me, dear Johan, I'll find another coachman," Axel replied. "But I must go."

We parted at 9 a.m. Axel went on to breakfast with General Suremain, an officer of French descent and one of our highest-ranking military leaders. Suremain would relate that Axel was as composed as ever on that occasion, "showing the calm of a man whose conscience is pure and who is disturbed by no fears." Yet I later learned that my brother was carrying, in his jacket, one of those threatening anonymous letters that had been circulating in Stockholm since the crown prince's death.

"To Axel Fersen. Wretch. Read this letter and tremble. Do you and your clique believe that 2 million people will permit some aristocrats to let the horrors they commit go unpunished, that they will allow themselves to be trampled by conspiring traitors; shall this unhappy land eternally remain under the oppression of audacious violent men? . . . The hour of retribution will come! Even though your abominable father the proud aristocrat succeeded in his game . . . even though your long neck . . . escaped the guillotine in France . . . will this ancient realm gradually lose its independent existence among the nations of Europe through the faithlessness, infamy, and treason of its nobles? . . . Despicable creature, when you come into the city in all your presumed greatness and pomp, know that the lowest peasant spits on you and feels himself to be a greater man than you, arrogant wretch! . . . Know that this letter is the voice of the public. . . . Karl August will be avenged."

RIDING OUT INTO the city early that morning to do some errands, I noticed unusual situations: taverns were giving away free beer and schnapps; brewers' carts stood all around the city, supplementing the already large amount of ready liquor; officials were distributing money to some of the poorer and rougher-looking citizens.

The crown prince's hearse had entered the city through its southwestern district, and that is where the cortege began, among hundreds of glum, mournful citizens. The procession set forth at half past noon. Ringing of church bells, firing of many cannons. At the head of the cortege rode General Silfversparre, surrounded by horse guards, followed by the carriages of various officials, among them my brother, Fabian's. Then came Axel's coach, followed by the crown prince's hearse. No member of the royal family was present, the king being at Haga attending a council meeting. The Stockholm civil guard was nowhere to be seen, and police troops were equally absent. General Skjöldebrand, another eminent career officer, wrote the following description of my brother's carriage:

"It was a magnificent old-fashioned state coach drawn by six white horses with morocco harnesses, richly ornamented with gilded bronze. On either side of the coach walked lackeys in opulently trimmed liveries. Fersen himself sat in the coach dressed in mourning clothes, with the grand marshal's staff in his hand, and after him came the hearse covered with a simple black canopy, dusty after the journey and without ornament. . . . The splendor in which the grand marshal rode made an unpleasant contrast to the simplicity of the hearse. . . . He looked like a triumphant conqueror dragging behind him a defeated foe."

Well, yes, sure, how many times have I heard of our taste for luxury and ostentation, our love for pomp and pageantry. Axel was grand marshal; his finery was following prescribed court ritual. But on this particular occasion he may have overdone it, may have been tragically out of touch with the mind-set of Stockholm's people. In the southern area of Stockholm, the crowd is said to have remained sullen, inimical in its silence as his cortege passed by. But as it crossed the bridge into the Old City, on its way to the Royal Palace, the populace grew increasingly menacing and aggressive toward my brother. And at the entrance to Stora Nygatan, a narrow street lined with centuries-old buildings that is the heart of ancient Stockholm, the large, vile mob that had assembled there was armed with rocks and logs. They began to attack Axel's coach as soon as it entered the street. Stora Nygatan is less than a dozen yards wide, so the troops at either end of the cortege had no way of seeing what was happening to my brother. Within a few minutes the coachman and Axel were grievously wounded by the attacks. One witness, a visiting professor from Copenhagen, saw my poor brother in his carriage "pale as death, in the most frightful state of fear and distress." He had knelt down on the floor of his coach, according to this witness, attempting to protect himself from the assaults by covering himself with his cloak. From a narrow side alley a group of men surged toward Axel's horses and unharnessed them.

A Danish officer was standing in front of 1 Stora Nygatan, at the street corner that faces Riddarhus, the House of the Nobility. Axel opened the door of his carriage and cried out to him, "For the love of Christ, save me!" The Dane put his arm around Axel and hurriedly accompanied him to the second floor of the building, which was a popular tavern, thinking he would find safety there. But the customers, more than a hundred of them, mostly of the middle class, instantly recognized Axel; and, urged on by a French-born actor called Lambert, they greeted him with jeers and insults. He was not only accused of being the crown prince's murderer; others denounced him for "conspiring against liberty in Sweden as he had in France"; yet others, absurdly, for being responsible for Gustavus III's death. Axel replied that he was innocent and demanded to be judged in a courtroom. In the street below the tavern the mob had tripled in size and grown equally abusive, shouting, "Death to the grand marquis! Fersen to hell!" Axel attempted to seek refuge in a back room of the tavern but that also was instantly filled with crowds of wretchedly belligerent men. As the tavern's customers grew increasingly hostile Axel was stripped of his coat and his sword, and most of his decorations were thrown out of the window to the populace below.

At this moment General Skjöldebrand was riding toward the Royal Palace to wait for the cortege's arrival. He saw the grand marshal's coach pass by, empty, all its windows broken, its walls and roof in shambles. Having heard that Count von Fersen was being held in a house on Stora Nygatan, he rushed toward that street. In front of the tavern's entrance he saw General Silfversparre surrounded by a group of citizens vociferating attacks against "that bastard Fersen." "Calm yourselves," Silfversparre was saying, "calm yourselves. Criminals must be judged legally." General Suremain urged Silfversparre to summon troops to quell the increasingly hostile mob; but that villainous Silfversparre—I hold him accountable—dismissed Suremain's fears, said all would be safe, and entered the tavern. Suremain jumped on his horse and galloped toward Haga to report the events to the king.

General Skjöldebrand tried to get a nearby battalion to restore order, but its commander replied that he had been given no orders to deal with the crowd, and those troops soon disappeared.

As for the despicable Silfversparre, once in the tavern, he asked the customers what their intentions were toward Fersen. They replied that he should be arrested. Silfversparre offered to take him to the palace. "Oh no, no, he'd be released," the drinkers cried out, led by a Finnish-born seaman, Otto Tandefelt. "Take him to the city hall," Tandefelt and the others shouted, "or a criminal prison." The customers roared their approval of this last suggestion. The general agreed to bring Axel to the city hall if the citizens in the tavern promised not to attack him. Going to the tavern window, Silfversparre then announced that decision to the crowd below, but many of the rabble protested that Axel would never be brought to justice, and requested that he be instantly thrown out of the window.

Silfversparre then accompanied Axel to the back room of the tavern. With what foul riffraff is our city filled! Drinkers in that space also insulted him and our entire family, and, breaking their promise, began to strike him with their canes and umbrellas. "You will die before midnight tonight," several yelled at him. "The Piper woman and two others will die!" "I see that it will soon be my final hour," my brother is heard to have moaned as he followed Silfversparre down the stairs. Oh my darling Axel, why, why were we so hated? The canes and umbrellas were significant—the attacks on Axel had not been initiated by the poor of the city, but by citizens of the burgher class, which so detested us. One witness would later describe the marauders assaulting Axel as "part of that middle class, which, more than the lower class, envies aristocrats and sees them as criminals."

As Silfversparre and my weak, stumbling brother descended the stairs, part of the tavern crowd followed them, tearing out Axel's earrings and tufts of his hair. My poor Axel staggered under the assaults, fell on the stairs, was picked up again, and finally reached the door sill of the tavern, where he was met by a clamorous mob, which had grown far rougher. He who had so loved uniforms and ceremonial dress was now barefoot, his trousers torn, his shirts stripped from him. But the Order of the Seraphim was still suspended, on a ribbon, around his neck. As he reached the ground floor, members of the crowd demanded that he take it off. "The king gave it to me; only the king can take it away," Axel whispered, barely able to speak. The riffraff violently pulled off the decoration and tore it to shreds. Silfversparre was also attacked, struck on his cheek. It was at this crucial moment that Silfversparre went off to the palace to find his horse. In this melee, my cherished Axel found himself alone, covered with blood, wounds all over his head and trunk, still being struck by powerful blows.

A major general, von Vegesad, tried to protect him from the mob by placing him against a wall, behind his horse. "Save me," Axel beseeched him. But the terrified animal, rearing and bucking, pried loose. Two other officers courageously came to his aid, and lifted him up. "Help me, boys," Axel pleaded. The young men led him toward Riddarhus, across the street from the tavern. The square in front of it being filled with a mob, they managed to take my brother to the city hall next door, and placed him in the guardhouse, which they barricaded. Axel fell into a chair and asked for a drink of water, promising large rewards to whoever could bring him to safety. But he barely had time to finish the water, for the door of the guardhouse gave way and a band of men assaulted him. So this is the way my beloved brother met his end: he was dragged out unto the courtyard of city hall, next to Riddarhus, the building where my family had met for generations to discuss the destiny of our country, and there he was kicked and stampeded to death by the barbarous crowd. The final blow was given by the villain Tandefelt, who jumped on his chest and crushed his rib cage.

Even after my brother's death, the mob continued to kick and desecrate his corpse. Only when Silfversparre returned on his horse, aghast at the sight of Axel's body (he had wished to humiliate my brother, but mightn't have wanted to go further), did the crowd begin to disperse. Shreds of Axel's hair and clothing were carried away by hundreds of citizens. Of his tattered garments only one sock and a belt remained intact. A few hours later his body was dumped into a wooden coffin and placed in a police watch room, where crowds queued up for hours to see his mutilated corpse. Fragments of his clothing and strands of his hair, so my witnesses reported, were being sold for astronomical prices in Stockholm's streets.

We were offered one kind gesture. A young man who described himself as a mason brought Axel's gold watch to Silfversparre, saying that he was "not a thief," but simply one of the avengers of Karl August's death. This watch was the very one Marie Antoinette had given my brother in 1792—on its enameled surface were carved their initials, "A and F." Axel had worn it faithfully ever since. Only when I was told this story did I realize that my brother had died on the nineteenth anniversary, to the day, of the flight to Varennes, a venture undertaken to save the life of his great love.

It was ten at night. I, Sophie, was at home in Blasieholmen, in the company of a few friends and of my seven-months-pregnant daughter, when news was brought to me of my adored brother's death.

I don't need to linger much on my sorrow, for my passion for my brother has been amply documented in these pages. I shall only say that I was flooded by memories of our shared childhood, our shared youth: the way we raced home from church to devour the X-shaped saffron buns traditional to that holiday. Painting the sign of the cross on our foreheads and on our cattle's noses on Maundy Thursday. Walking down the streets of Stockholm's Gamla Stan in the full daylight of June midnights, our arms around each other's waist. Standing by Axel as he painted his exquisite watercolors of the lake at our estate in Löfstad.

However, I barely had time to give vent to my grief, or to summon more memories, for those loved ones who surrounded me urged me to seek a safe hiding place. "All Fersens will be persecuted," so the advice went. "Protect yourself!" I first sought asylum at the residence of our foreign minister. Through tornadoes of rain and wind I then fled, disguised as a peasant woman, to Vaxholm Fortress, a prison in which I sought protective custody. I remained there for many weeks. Queen Charlotte herself was suspected by citizens because of her close friendship with our family, and for a long time was prepared to flee from Haga. The crowd continued to be restive until the following month, when the crown prince was finally buried in Riddarholm Church.

I hardly need to say how much grief and shock there was among our friends and acquaintances. "That His Excellency Fersen was innocent, I am convinced, and for several reasons," the chief master of ceremonies at the court, L. von Hausswolff, wrote about Axel. "*Primo*, he was a good and honest man. *Secundo*, he was too proud and haughty to involve himself in any plan against the crown prince, which would disgrace himself and his entire family. *Tertio*, he was too indolent to think of anything that might change his way of life. This man was thus the victim of circumstances that only the future will reveal."

"Our cannibals exceed the Parisian monsters," exclaimed Axel's comrade Gustav Armfelt, who had been abroad at the time of my brother's death, and soon thereafter moved to Russia. "Where were the troops, for heaven's sake? However haughty he was, that Axel von Fersen, so honest, so amicable, was sacrificed to popular furor—this is an enigma that only time will solve."

Yes, where were the troops, as the grieving Armfelt put it? The "enigma" was easily resolved by me, and by anyone who was familiar with the nature of Karl XIII's court. The king's closest advisers had everything to fear from the Gustavian faction led by my brother, which desired Gustav IV Adolf's young son, Gustav, to be crown prince. Adlercreutz and Klingspor themselves had participated in the arrest of Gustav IV Adolf, and Silfversparre himself had led him to prison. The king, sick and aged, was much influenced by these acolytes, and they had easily swayed him against all Gustavians, of whom my brother was the most prominent member.

Queen Charlotte and I lobbied relentlessly for an inquest that would rehabilitate Axel and prove his innocence. Our wishes were finally granted. An inquisition was begun a few weeks after his death. In November of that year our supreme court formally absolved my brother and all the Fersens of any culpability in the death of the crown prince, ruling that Gustav Adolf had died a natural death.

Queen Charlotte and I were still not satisfied. We wished a ceremony to be held at Riddarholm Church, where members of the royal family and high officials had traditionally had their memorial services. At first Karl XIII hesitated to extend this honor to Axel. But by August 1810 the Riksdag, faithful to the tradition of inviting foreign dignitaries into the Swedish royal family, had elected a new crown prince, the forty-seven-year-old French general Bernadotte. The Riksdag had wished the country to be led by an eminent military leader because of the constant threat of a war with Russia, and Bernadotte fitted the bill perfectly. He was an illustrious hero of Napoleon's wars who had led his troops with particular valor at Austerlitz. Bernadotte secured Bonaparte's permission to become crown prince of Sweden. Eager to unify the country, "Karl Johan" Bernadotte—so he was renamed— was all too happy to begin his tenure in the Swedish royal family with a gesture of reconciliation toward a family as distinguished as the

Fersens; and he prevailed upon the king to have Axel's memorial held at Riddarholm.

THE STEWARD OF OUR ESTATE at Steninge had come to claim Axel's body the morning after his death. It had been embalmed and placed in a small garden pavilion, with the plan of burying him later in our family vault. But there again Stockholm citizens, constantly doing all they could to oppose the nobility, had run afoul of our wishes. A few days before the scheduled burial two officials arrived from the capital, forbidding our family to proceed because Stockholm's denizens looked on Axel's corpse as having been "stolen" from them—the mob at Riddarhus Square had condemned it to the gallows hill. So the body continued to remain in the garden pavilion while Fabian and I, wishing to reemphasize Axel's innocence, lobbied King Karl to have him buried at Riddarholm with the full ritual due a grand marshal and Knight of the Seraphim. With the continuing support of Queen Charlotte and of Bernadotte, who allayed the king's fear of further public disturbances, our cause prevailed. And in December Axel was reburied in Riddarholm Church, with the kind of ceremonial pageantry that would have delighted him. In his eulogy at the funeral, Bishop Gustaf Murray spoke of Axel as "the undeserving victim of a misled public's bloodthirsty frenzy."

As for the pavilion in Steninge, it was converted into a little brick chapel of Romanesque Gothic style, sheltered by a great oak, which bore the following inscription:

"Here were kept for four months the mortal remains of Count AXEL VON FERSEN, Grand Marshal of the Kingdom of Sweden, while the powers that ended his days refused to let him rest in the tomb of his ancestors. May Truth recalled by time protect in History his memory and render justice to his virtue. . . ."

I wished to pay further tribute to that remarkable man, my brother. So the year after his death I erected a monument in his memory in the park of our estate in Lövstad. Its inscription reads as follows:

COUNT AXEL VON FERSEN

GRAND MARSHAL OF SWEDEN

CHANCELLOR OF THE UNIVERSITY OF UPPSALA,

GENERAL OF THE CAVALRY

KNIGHT AND COMMANDER OF THE PRINCIPAL ORDERS OF THE KINGDOM

BORN SEPTEMBER 4, 1755

HE WHO WISHED TO COMBAT ANARCHY AND POPULAR FUROR

WAS ITS VICTIM

ON JUNE 20 1810.

LET HIS INNOCENCE BE ACKNOWLEDGED!

LET INNOCENTS BE AVENGED!

HIS MEMORY PRESERVES GLORY AND TRUTH.

Blessed are you when you are reviled and persecuted, and all kinds of evil are said against you. . . . Rejoice and be exceedingly glad, for great is your reward in Heaven.

Matthew, Ch. 5, Verse 11.

AUTHOR'S EPILOGUE

Sweden had long had the reputation of being an orderly, law-abiding society, and Fersen's assassination may have shocked the nation more than any event in nineteenth-century Swedish history. It caused a wave of fear that Sweden stood on the brink of a violent revolution. It occasioned a pronounced swing to the right in the nation's political life—within two years freedom of the press, for instance, grew extremely limited. Among liberals, Karl XIII was much criticized for his callous indifference to Fersen's fate; and Fersen's murder led to a national longing for a monarch who would be far more vigorous and skilled than Karl (such a ruler would readily be found in Bernadotte).

News of Fersen's end also consternated the rest of Europe. It is Napoleon Bonaparte, this time, who may have had the last word. Upon hearing of Axel's demise he declared to the Swedish ambassador: "Count von Fersen's assassination was perpetuated with the acquiescence, might I even say the assent, of your government . . . Be on your guard!"

Sophie Piper survived her brother by six years, dying in Lövstad in 1816.

Axel's brother, Fabian, died in 1818. Fabian's younger son, Gustaf Hans, who died in 1839, would be the last male member of the Fersen clan.

Bernadotte ascended the Swedish throne in 1818, upon the death of

Karl XIII, and took on the name Karl XIV Johan. He proved to be a most popular and effective monarch, and reigned until his death in 1848.

After being exiled, Gustav IV Adolf traveled restlessly throughout Europe for some decades and died in Saint Gallen, Switzerland, in 1837.

The Comte de Provence ruled France as Louis XVIII from 1814 until his death in 1824, except for the interruption of Bonaparte's Hundred Days (1815), during which the former emperor attempted to regain control over the nation.

Provence's younger brother, Comte d' Artois, reigned as Charles X from 1824 to 1830, and became increasingly hated for his ultra reactionary politics. The last Bourbon king of France, he was deposed in 1830, sought exile in London and then in Prague, and died in 1836 during a trip to Italy. He was succeeded by the far more liberal Duc d'Orléans, who ruled as King Louis-Philippe.

Fersen's friend Gustav Armfelt expired in 1814 in Tsarkoye Selo, having moved to Russia and taken on Russian nationality a year after his friend's death.

Fersen's hopes that Marie Antoinette's son Louis-Charles, the last dauphin of France, was his child, came to naught. Recent DNA studies have proved that Louis-Charles was the son of Louis XVI.

MARIE ANTOINETTE'S CORRESPONDENCE with Fersen has its own dramatic history. After Fersen's death, all of his archives were preserved by Sophie's progeny—his nephews and grand-nephews. One of them, Baron Klinckowström, published the whole of his correspondence with the queen in 1877. This edition provoked great consternation among historians, for many passages of these letters had been censored, replaced by rows of dotted lines. Baron Klinckowström refused to publish the originals, pretending that the obliterated passages revealed political secrets that would displease the king of Sweden. This explanation was manifestly disingenuous, for the obliterated passages mostly occurred at the very beginnings and ends of the letters, intimating that they concerned the expression of tender, intimate emotions. Continuing to refuse communicating the original letters, Fersen's grand-nephew, Klinckowström, pretended that he had burned them.

More than a century later, in 1982, Marie Antoinette scholars were surprised and relieved to hear that the letters that had been believed destroyed in fact existed. The Klinckowström family had put them up at auction at Christie's, in London, and they were bought by France's National Archives, where they remain to this day. However, the most sophisticated current techniques of decoding the originals, or bringing to light the phrases written in invisible ink, have failed. One single missive of Marie Antoinette's escaped the prudish Baron Klinckowström's vandalism. It is the one dated June 29, 1791, written shortly after her return from the Varennes venture, which begins with the phrase "I can only tell you that I love you," and ends with the words "Adieu, the most beloved and loving of men. I kiss you with all my heart."

AUTHOR'S NOTE

This is a historical novel. The major events and personages cited in it are authentic. All correspondence between Axel von Fersen and his lovers, relatives, and friends, and all of Fersen's journal entries, are directly quoted from manuscripts—many of them published—that are preserved in French and Swedish institutions.

ACKNOWLEDGMENTS

My foremost debt is to Ann Godoff, my cherished editor and publisher, who has given me invaluable guidance throughout the writing of this book. Gratitude also to my treasured agent, Lynn Nesbit, whose enthusiasm has ever been a source of inspiration and encouragement. And my thanks to Lindsay Whalen of The Penguin Press for her precious help in the manuscript's editing.

I am most grateful to Gary Tinterow for introducing me to the former Swedish Consul General in New York, the Honorable Ulf Hjertonsson; he generously presented me to those friends of his in Stockholm who could help me with my Fersen project. My appreciation to Sigrid and Kai Falkman, to Goran Berg, and to Christina Oldfelt Ekéus and Rolf Ekéus for their warm hospitality. My particular gratitude to Michael Sohlman, who found me the best possible guide to all places and issues relating to Axel von Fersen—the esteemed author Malte Persson, whom I also thank from the bottom of my heart. And my appreciation to the staff of Stockholm's Royal Archives, where Fersen's journals are kept, for their unfailing amiability and thoughtfulness.

I equally want to acknowledge my debt to Caroline Weber, who offered me precious advice concerning all that related to Queen Marie Antoinette; to Jonathan Fasman, who gave the manuscript a dedicated reading; to Stephana Bottom Webb, whose large collection of books on the French Queen—generously loaned to me for over two years—was a treasure trove; to Haley Hogan, for her meticulous research assistance; to Lillian Lovitt, Carol Haxo, Celia Britch, Karen Farrell, and Johanna Snyers for helping me to keep body and soul together, year in and year out; and to my male trinity, my late husband, Cleve Gray, and my sons Thaddeus and Luke, whose love and support have been my life's greatest blessing.

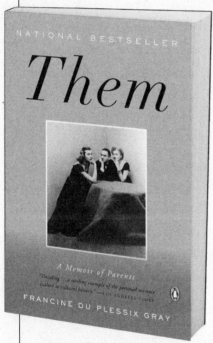